White Lake Road

Volume I – "Bad Hombre"

A Novel by Mike Beardslee

"White Lake Road"

Introduction

Welcome to Volume #1 of the novel, "White Lake Road". There will be a grand total of 10 volumes that will depict how a high school student who transferred to another high school for his senior year, overcame adversity and insecurity to have "the greatest year of his life."

This story is loosely based upon my own senior year of high school which took place during the 1969-70 school year. While I am many ages removed from those days of my life, I still treasure the friends and great moments of that closed period of my existence.

What you are about to read contains many factual moments of my life. The reverse of this is that I have also used some creative writing skills to allow the direction of this novel to read as to how I would have actually liked my life as a 12th grader to really have taken place.

So, if your memory or research skills show that a certain athletic conference does not exist, a result of a High School Band District Festival rating is different than what history shows, then that is when you will find the imagination of Mike Beardslee's running rampant.

The format for this novel will written in the style of a person making daily entries into a journal or log showing what happened on such and such date of the year. Volume I will start with the latter part of August 1969 and run through the end of September 1969.

I hope that you enjoy reading about the ups and downs that this high school student goes through with not only their first month of a new school year and a different educational facility, but in future volumes as well.

Sincerely,

Michael K. Beardslee

"White Lake Road"

A 1968 Detroit Tigers Memory

"There's a line drive to right field!! The Tigers win it!! Here come's Al Kaline to score…."

Ernie Harwell – September 17th, 1968. The night that the Detroit Tigers clinched the American League Pennant for the first time since 1945.

Dedication

This is the completion of Volume I and this work is dedicated to Mr. Edward Eugene Abbott, who made a high school trumpet player, who in his own mind thought he was hot stuff, ultimately into a halfway decent trumpet player for Fenton High School. I thank you for your efforts, kind sir.

"White Lake Road"

Chapter I – "Gallia Est Tres Divisia"

August 1969

After a lengthy summer of attempting to determine where I was going to spend my upcoming senior year of high school, of which, included an ongoing conflict with my mother, I, Mike Beardslee, will be attending a different school system for the first time since I was in fourth grade when entering the halls of State Road Elementary School.

This change in my life came about when at the end of my junior year of high school the rumors that the school millage for the upcoming school year was not going to pass turned into true rumors. The good citizens of Fenton, Michigan soundly defeated the passing of the school millage. That meant that school curriculum activities such as athletics, marching band, cheerleading, choir, etc., would not be making an appearance on any future resumes for the graduating Fenton High School senior class of 1970. This also meant that there was a good possibility that a brand new constructed Fenton High School was going to sit empty till who knows when.

Since marching band, trumpet playing and athletics, specifically basketball and track, are such a big part of my life, and truth be known, probably the only reason that I attend school and am not currently working on the assembly line at General Motors, my senior year of high school has the potential to be very nondescript and unmemorable.

My folks had talked this situation over with me and if push came to shove and the austerity budget went into effect slashing away all extracurricular school activities, then I had their blessing to attend another high school for my senior year. There were, however, two stipulations that my mother placed on me before this new high school thing could take place. First, I had to participate in band, basketball and track. No problem. Secondly, and this might be the deal breaker, I had to find another person to attend this new high school with me. That might be a problem.

I had spent the majority of this past summer away from the comforts of my residence located on White Lake Road, Fenton, Michigan. This included a couple of weeks at the Interlochen National Music Camp in the Allstate Division. (I hope my mother never discovers that I spent more time playing basketball and volleyball there than I did practicing my trumpet). That was followed by a stint as a volunteer member of the Student Conservation Association. (SCA). The SCA allowed high school students the opportunity to work in various national parks of the United States. I was based out of the Olympic National Park located in Port Angeles, Washington. Just a beautiful area that I hope to revisit someday and eventually make it my permanent home. Including travel time that was another four weeks away from White Lake Road.

Before departing for my stay in the Olympic Mountains where I was to eventually spend the bulk of my time making wood shakes for the roof of a cabin that the SCA was building for a national park forest ranger, my mother advised me to give some serious consideration as to

where I might want to spend my senior year of high school. Her thoughts were that the millage had been resoundingly defeated twice so far and with the final vote coming up in the next two weeks, there was no way that the citizens of Fenton would change their minds or votes in this election. I mean let's face it. My future is in the hands of the tax payers of the city of Fenton, many of whom I have never met face to face and they, in turn, have never heard of Mike Beardslee.

Two weeks came and went. The school millage did not pass and judgment day for my future place of education has arrived. I cast my ballot for Swartz Creek High School. To me it made all of the sense in the world. I had spent my first four years of my public-school career there and thought that it would be a nice touch to graduate as a Swartz Creek "Dragon." I still knew some of the Swartz Creek kids from competing against them in athletics. It would border on old home week for me. There was no doubt in my mind that my mother would accept my excellent selection.

While I was mentally envisioning the huge reception that I was going to receive on my first day of school as a student of the Swartz Creek public school system I discovered how wrong I was wrong in my thinking. I was even more wrong than the character that Eli Wallach portrayed in the movie, "The Magnificent Seven." ("I know you won't use those guns against me. Only a crazy man makes the same mistake twice.") My mother's selection for my senior year of high school was Holy Redeemer High School. I about died when I heard those words come out of her mouth. Holy Redeemer?? A parochial school?? Gimme a break!!

At Holy Redeemer, the guys have to wear ties to class every day. I have even heard that the Latin classes are very intense and that my limited Latin terminology of "Gallia est omnes tres divisa" isn't going to cut it at Holy Redeemer. I have not even mentioned the part yet, that all students have to attend mass every Friday. Every Friday!! This is coming from a kid who hates it when Christmas Day falls on a Saturday or Monday. When that takes place, it means I now have to go to church two days in a row. Oh, man, this ain't good.

My mother was born in Europe and to this day is an extremely devout catholic. However, her devoutness to the catholic church was never inherited by her two children. I must have underestimated how disappointing it was to my mother that neither I nor my younger sister, Katie, never really showed any interest in attending a catholic school. I mean zippo interest. At the beginning of every elementary and junior high school year my mother always asked us if we were interested in attending St. John's Catholic School in Fenton, Michigan. (At least I think it was a question.) The answer was always no, not interested, maybe next year. I now wonder if my mother sees this as her last opportunity for at least one of her children to attend a catholic school.

One evening before I was getting ready to call it a day, my mother came to me and said, "Tomorrow you are going to officially decide which high school you will be attending this school year." Okay!!

"White Lake Road"

August 1969 –Chapter #2 – "Decision Made Plus One"

To say the least with this impending decision facing me I did not sleep much at all the entire night. When I woke up the next morning, however, I had my mind made up. While eating a breakfast of oat meal with an estimated six pounds of brown sugar added to the main dish and promptly washed down by a glass of cold milk, I advised my mother that I going to stay at Fenton High School and graduate as a "Fenton Tiger."

I could see the hurt and simultaneous sadness in my mother's eyes but I could just not see myself setting foot inside a parochial school other than for a dire need to use a bathroom or get out of a torrential rain storm. In addition to the wounded look on my mother's face you could also tell that my decision to pass up the opportunity to do the things that I enjoyed most in life, specifically in reference to band and athletics, and then to actually attend a high school that would not allow me to participate in either activity, was to say the least, mystifying to her. I spent the rest of the day lying real low in what is known to many Fenton High School Band members as "Beardslee's Infamous Barn!!"

Things were quite coldish between my mother and me for the next few days until one Saturday evening while the Beardslee family was eating supper; my father suggested as an alternative that Hartland High School would be a good place for me to attend high school this year. It made sense. For years, I had taken private trumpet lessons from the high school band director, Mr. Anderson. I also knew some of the Hartland kids from either Interlochen or past catechism classes. Plus, my mother was a former teacher in the Hartland Consolidated School District, so it wasn't like I would be walking into a brand-new school district with no past history. Also from a pure travel standpoint it wasn't too bad of drive from "White Lake Road."

After hearing my father's proposal, both my mother and I stopped our forks in mid bite and stared at each other. While we both still wanted our own way, our eye contact pretty much cemented the fact that this was an excellent compromise. Mike Beardslee was going to spend his senior year of high school as a "Hartland Eagle."

The official start of the school is getting closer and closer being just one week away. After the decision for me to attend the Hartland Consolidated Schools, further developments started to take place in the Beardslee home. The first event was surprising. I'm not too sure what caused this occurrence to take place but I am glad that it is being set in motion. I was not going to be the only member of the Beardslee family to continue their high school education at Hartland High School.

Shockingly, my younger sister, Katie, "decided" to attend Hartland High School this year as well. Let me take a second to define just how astonishing this decision is. There is no other student in the history of Fenton High School that loves that school more than my sister, Katie. She absolutely could not get enough of that place. I saw the same thing last summer at

Interlochen with the kids that went to Chelsea High School. Chelsea High School was the mecca of their life. All they could ever talk about was Chelsea High School. You mention to them that the world-famous pianist, Van Cliburn, was performing at Interlochen this Saturday and the Chelsea High School kids would instead start talking about the fact that they had the greatest homecoming parade in the state of Michigan. Katie Beardslee would fit in quite well with the Chelsea High School kids.

My sister Katie does not simply enjoy life; she attacks it at the speed of sound!! In just this past school year, she was freshmen class- vice president, an extremely active member of the student council, played tympani in the symphonic band and tenor drum in the marching band. To top it off, with that busy schedule the lowest grade that she got last year was a "B+", and that was from a Geometry teacher who prided herself on giving 75% of her students a grade of "D". Other than my efforts as a trumpet player and extremely active participation in the band, everything else in life, I pale miserably to Katie; at least that is what she has advised me twice a day for at least the past 10 years.

That's what makes the decision for Katie to accompany me to Hartland High School so confusing. My sister is a very goal oriented person and has already planned out her remaining three years at Fenton High School. These goals include being a top 10 graduate in her future senior class; student council president and an officer in the band and choir. In addition to these lofty goals, Katie spent all last school year campaigning with the Michigan High School Athletic Association to make Girl's Cross Country an official school sport in the state of Michigan. And don't count her out from getting that mission completed, either.

The only thing I can think of is that with the austerity issues staring the Fenton Area Schools in the face, much like me, Katie really did not want to go through a school year without the chance to run track, play and march in the band and sing in the choir. Thus, there will be two less Beardslee's attending Fenton High School this school year.

However, from the bits and pieces that I am gathering, the plan is for Katie to only spend her sophomore year at Hartland High School and then, provided that there will be extracurricular activities available, go back to Fenton High School for her junior and senior years.

The Hartland Consolidated Schools won't even know what hit them once she sets foot on their school grounds. I do wonder, however, what my mother promised Katie to give up life as a Fenton High School student. I suspect that this means that Katie will now get her way and attend her dream college of Colorado University in Boulder, Colorado rather than attending a college closer to home per my mother's wishes.

Am I glad that Katie will be attending Hartland High School with me this year? Yes, I am. But make no ifs, ands, or buts about it, no matter what high school the two of us attend together, Katie Beardslee is not Mike Beardslee's little sister. No, I am Katie Beardslee's brother and I have come to the conclusion that that is my official title in life. Katie Beardslee's brother. Katie's friends, and there is a million of them out there, probably don't even realize

that I have a first name of, "Mike". No, whenever Katie's friends see me they shout out "Hey, there's Katie Beardslee's brother!!"

Someday my tombstone will have an engravement that reads, "Here lays Katie Beardslee's brother. First name unknown."

Chapter #3- Howe, Indiana or some place in Canada.

One evening after returning from a short two-mile run, I walked through the garage door of our White Lake Road home and entered through the "breakfast room" where I immediately spotted Mrs. Koop and Mrs. Rodenbo, the mothers of my best band buddies, Jim Koop and Terry Rodenbo, respectively, speaking with my mother. Other than Mrs. Rodenbo coming here to beg Katie to go out on a date with her son, I could think of no really good reason why these two parents would be here at the same time. My first impulse was to ask a typical, Mike Beardslee smart you know what question like, "Were the charges dropped?" Or, "Are you sending your sons to the same military school in Canada that Dave Fabrey's parents banished him?" However, there was a sense of seriousness that was consuming the room and I thought better about asking any flippant questions. I was soon to find out that the purpose of this drop in was more of an official visit verses a social call.

Despite Katie and I being sworn to absolute silence by our mother of the family decision to leave the Fenton Schools and attend the Hartland Consolidated Schools for this upcoming school year, (Just for the record, my mother has never met a secret that she could keep) somehow the word had leaked out, thus prompting this official type visit from Mrs. Koop and Mrs. Rodenbo.

While I was not a party to any of the actual discussion that took place, my mother eventually informed Katie and me for the purpose of this unexpected visit. First of all, Mrs. Koop and Mrs. Rodenbo wanted to verify the rumors that had been floating around the streets of Fenton about Katie and I not attending Fenton High School this year. My mother confirmed that these were not rumors but were indeed fact.

The second question from our guests was simply, "Why'? My mother's response apparently went something like this, "Since the school millage was soundly defeated for the third and final time in yesterday's election, I decided that I wanted what is best for my children. Under normal circumstances it would be best for them to attend Fenton High School. Yesterday's election results showed that these are not normal circumstances, thus, Katie and Mike will instead be attending the Hartland Consolidated Schools system this school year."

Translation: If the Fenton Area School system cannot provide the best educational environment for my children, then I will find a school system that will.

Mrs. Rodenbo shook her head in agreement and said, "I want what's best for my boy Terry as well. I want him participating in band, and be a member of the wrestling and baseball teams this school year." However, Mrs. Rodenbo had also made it very clear that no matter how the millage vote went next year, Terry Rodenbo was going to graduate from Fenton High School as a member of their 1971 Senior Class. Her precise words were, "Terry will only attend Hartland High School for his junior year and only his junior year." This was similar to my mother's decision that Katie was only going to attend Hartland High School for her sophomore year.

Mrs. Koop took an alternative approach to her oldest son's future education. While she knew Jim Koop enjoyed being in the high school band with Terry Rodenbo any myself, she also knew her number one son well enough to know that he enjoyed smoking cigarettes, flirting with girls and giving teachers a tough time even more than getting a quality education. Mrs. Koop felt that James William Koop the II needed a fresh start and this was cheaper than sending him to Howe Military Academy in the state of Indiana, which I suspect is an everyday threat in the life of Jim Koop. (Just for the record, this is the same military academy that my mother has always advised me that I was in danger of attending. Her exact words are, "You will look absolutely handsome in a button-down uniform with a broad stripe running down the side of each pant leg!!") Whenever Katie hears my mother use that uniform line on me, she squeals with laughter and says, "Yeah, Mike. You'll be wearing the same type of pants that Mingo wears on the Daniel Boone show!!"

Man, somewhere in the country of Canada, Dave Fabrey is having a good laugh at my expense.

Thus, it was officially decided that Jim Koop and Terry Rodenbo would join Katie and I as students of the Hartland Consolidated School system for the 1969-70 school year which starts six days from now. I readily admit that I enthusiastically welcome their company as there is safety in numbers.

"White Lake Road"

Chapter #4 – "E-6"

August 1969

Five more days till the start of the school year and the Labor Day weekend is almost upon us. It also means that the start of the Detroit Lions football season is just around the corner, three weeks from this Sunday. But who's counting?? Labor Day weekend also means that my favorite season of the year, fall, is also gets closer by the second. In fact, come to think of it, fall is the only season of the year that I actually like.

However, with all of those things to look forward to, probably the worst thing in the world could have happened to me today. Timeout for a history lesson. During the summer of 1962, I was playing little league baseball as a member of the "VFW Panthers." We were the equivalent of the 1962 New York Mets of little league baseball as we went 1-15 that season. I still have no idea to this day how the Lake Fenton Lakers lost to us.

I've told this story so many times that I have actually come to believe that what I am writing really happened. I was doing my imitation of Chico Fernandez, shortstop for the Detroit Tigers, and pretending that I could really play the short stop position and field a ground ball that was hit directly to me.

In my feeble little mind, I remember the ground ball hitting a rock that created a bad hop, which then caused the baseball to change direction hitting me smack dab in my mouth breaking portions of my two front teeth. In reality, I was such a terrible fielding short stop that I probably whiffed on the ground ball and that's what actually caused a bloody lip and two broken front teeth. Thus, ending my chance to become as poor as fielding short stops in the major leagues as both Chico Fernandez and Don Buddin. (Boston Red Sox Shortstop). I betcha both those guys have vanity license plates on their motor vehicles that read "E-6."

As painful of a physical injury as that was to me as a nine-year-old kid, it also turned out to be the greatest thing that could have ever happened to me in my life. Prior to this incident my two front teeth were what you would politely call "bucked." Those teeth would have guaranteed me a starring role on either TV series, "Green Acres" or "Hee Haw" and my character's name would have been "Buck Beardslee." My two front teeth simply were not aligned with the rest of my front upper teeth.

Through my inability to field a slow ground ball that was hit directly to me, I avoided having to wear braces on my teeth. However, when I reach the age of 15 or 16 years old my current front teeth would now have to be capped.

The breaking of my two front teeth allowed to continue to play trumpet and avoided me having to play another instrument with a bigger mouthpiece like the baritone or trombone. Ain't no way I was ever going to play the sousaphone. If I had to play either of the latter instruments it now meant also having to lug around a bigger instrument and instrument case wherever I went. I hope that this potential loss of upper body strength does not hurt me when I get older.

“White Lake Road”

I can honestly say that the only thing in my life I am half-way decent at is my ability to play the trumpet. Other than a unique skill to grab defensive rebounds, I am an unexceptional basketball player at best. While I enjoy running on the track team I would classify myself as an okay performer when running the 440 Run and the occasional leg on the mile relay team. I do score points in dual meets but I have, however, always fared poorly in the regional and league meets.

What I do best is play the trumpet. There are very few things in life I enjoy more than playing the trumpet. The only other things that come close, and they’re a distant second, are reading the “Sporting News” on Saturday mornings and watching anything on television that features Stephanie Powers. (Please, please, please, NBC, bring back the television show, “Girl from U.N.C.L.E!)

Playing the trumpet is my identity. My one goal in life is to become a professional trumpet player in the Seattle Symphony. (I’m going out on a limb and assuming that the city of Seattle has a symphony). I do not look forward to the day that I set my trumpet back into the trumpet case and close that case for the very last time. In fact, I cannot even fathom that day ever occurring.

I knew that eventually instead of having two little spikes for front teeth that caps were going to be placed over them. I was advised by my mother that for my senior year of high school that I was finally going to have my two front teeth capped. This was mainly so that I could actually smile for my senior picture that will appear in the high school year book.

Well that dreaded moment of actually starting to get my teeth capped was taking place today. I went to our family dentist, Dr. Alfred, this morning for phase one of Mike’s new front teeth. Temporary caps would be placed in my mouth covering up the two little spikes that now pass for my two front teeth. (They’re ugly to look at and do not promote smiling.)

The temporary caps look okay, but they make the front of my mouth feel big and clumsy. This is not good for a trumpet player. Let’s me put it this way, no future Seattle Symphony trumpet player wants to have big and clumsy teeth.

While I eagerly looked forward to having two new front teeth, my gut instinct was that the temporary caps would affect my trumpet playing and not in a positive way. That was all I could think about while driving back from Flint to Fenton. I wonder how many motor vehicle accidents that I caused on southbound U.S. 23 today?

As soon as I reached “White Lake Road” I sprinted into the house, grabbed my trumpet, and then dashed out to our barn. I did not want any witnesses to hear what was going to take place when I placed my lips to the mouthpiece of my trumpet as this could be ugly.

This turned out to be a good decision on my part. My tone, if you could even call it that, was so feeble that it certainly did not meet Webster’s Dictionary, or as they used to say on the television show “Laugh In”, “You can look it up in your Funk & Wagnall’s” dictionary definition of the word “tone.”

When it comes to determining whether a trumpet player s any good or not, a trumpet player must pass a two-prong test. The first prong of the test is the trumpet player's tone. Is the sound of their trumpet tone such that it would cause a person walking by to stop dead in their tracks and think to themselves, "Wow, they're good!!"

The second prong of the test is whether that same person not only likes the trumpet player's tone, but can they clearly hear and distinguish every single note that the trumpet player is playing. Right now, I have no tone or even sound coming out of his trumpet because of these temporary caps. Thus, the second prong of the test is a major, major issue.

I cannot believe that I am washed up as a trumpet player at the age of 16 years!!

I left the barn and went back to the house in shock and incoherent about what had just taken place. I kept mumbling to myself. "I can't play the trumpet anymore. I can't play the trumpet anymore." When I told my mother about this tragedy she had the same sense of helplessness and sadness that was traveling through my entire body.

A few moments later the two of us started to settle down and my mother recommended that I go see Mr. Anderson, the band director at Hartland High School and my private lesson trumpet instructor since I was in sixth grade, to see if he had any miracles up his sleeve. My mother would immediately call Dr. Alfred, himself, to see what short term ideas that he had to get me back to playing the trumpet again. My mother also made Katie go along with me to make sure I would not do anything overly dramatic and stupid to shame the Beardslee name.

"White Lake Road"

Chapter #5- "Three Options"

August 1969

After exiting U.S. 23 onto Clyde Road, my panicked state of mind had me taking an extremely sharp and dangerous curve on a dirt road at 25 MPH instead of the 10 MPH posted speed limit, scaring Katie half to death before finally pulling into the Hartland High School parking lot.

Once stepping out of my mother's car I ran at my 56.9 flat quarter mile pace where I burst through the school's front entrance and continued running down the hallway to the Hartland High School Band Room. Luckily Mr. Anderson was there in his office where it appeared he was on the receiving end of a talking-to from a parent. "Mr. Anderson, I demand that we have a flag corp with the marching band this season, and furthermore, I want my daughter to be the captain of this flag corp group!!"

When Mr. Anderson spotted me my body language must have tipped him off that I was in dire straits as he immediately stopped paying attention to the parent, and whom I believed to be the daughter that was being pushed for being the flag corp leader, and rapidly waved me into his office.

The mother and the young lady then got up and without giving any type of goodbye stomped right out of Mr. Anderson's office. Those two didn't even have the decency to stay and hear the depressing narrative of poor Mike Beardslee's teeth. Their loss.

I gave Mr. Anderson the "Readers Digest" condensed version of what was happening with my teeth. After listening to my frantic tale of despair and how my life was going to end Mr. Anderson said, "Mike, I have seen this take place before at my previous job at Beaverton High School. I had a trumpet player there, John Cummings, who had a similar problem to yours. I'm going to share with you the same three options I provided to him. First, you can play another brass instrument like John Cummings did. He wasn't even half the trumpet player that you are. In fact, he was a mediocre trumpet player at best. His teeth were messed up to the extent that his mouth would not fit a trumpet mouthpiece enough to allow him to get much of a tone at all. Very similar to your current predicament. John Cummings, did however, became a half way decent baritone player"

Also to John Cummings' credit, he became heavily involved into music theory, music arrangements and marching band routines. In fact, when I left Beaverton High School to come to Hartland High School, the school board could not find a band director in time for the start of the school year. John Cummings stepped up and in essence was an acting band director. He prepared the football halftime shows until a new band director was hired. John Cummings then pursued a music career after graduating from Beaverton High School and is currently the low brass instructor at Central Michigan University."

"White Lake Road"

"The second option for you Mike is if you do not want to play a low brass instrument is to switch over to playing in the percussion section. Snare drum, tympani, etc." I about choked to death right on the spot when Mr. Anderson made that suggestion. There ain't no way that I would ever consider playing a percussion instrument. Not even if "April Dancer", the star of the former TV series "Girl from U.N.C.L.E", AKA Stephanie Powers, promised me that she would travel all the way to state of Michigan to watch me play the bass drum in the homecoming parade and then go to the homecoming dance afterwards as my date. No way!!

There are not too many things in my life that are beneath my dignity, but being a percussion player would be one of them. Of all the percussionists, I have been in band with over the past eight years, I betcha 90% of them don't even know how to read music!! Make that closer to 95%!!

However, let me retract a portion of that last statement. There is one reason why I would even consider becoming a percussion player. And that is based upon the good advice that my marching band compadre, Jim Koop, once gave me. Jim Koop's pearl of wisdom went something like this; "No matter what ever happens in life, Beardslee my good friend, always remember this, the really good-looking girls will always go out on dates with drummers before they would go out on a date with trumpet players." Hmm. Maybe I shouldn't be too hasty in disregarding option number two.

The last option that Mr. Anderson provided for me was to simply go back to the dentists' office and have the dentist take the temporary caps off since they were there for nothing more than cosmetic purposes. "Chances will be that the future permanent caps will be more fitted to your mouth and be less cumbersome. You have gone seven years with having two little spikes for front teeth. Another month probably won't hurt you. Then after an adjustment period with the new caps you will be back to your old trumpet playing self." Yes!! That means I can be Mike Beardslee again!!

Option number three it is!! And I'll tell you what, this last choice certainly beats lugging around a baritone case or even worse, carrying a bass drum during marching band season and a Memorial Day Parade when the latter temperature is a non-parade friendly 90 degrees outside.

As Katie and I reached home my mother advised me that if I left now and went back to Dr. Alfred's office, he would take the temporary caps off and let me keep my spiked teeth for another 4-6 weeks when the permanent caps were installed. Gotta admit, that's a big load off of my mind.

It was back to Flint, Michigan and it took two seconds for Dr. Alfred to pop off the temporary caps. It was then off to Patterson's Ice Cream to celebrate the end of a stressful day with the world's best ever butterscotch ice cream cone. I had forgotten how much fun it was to eat a butterscotch ice cream with spiked front teeth.

“White Lake Road”

Later that night while out running on the “back 40” of our White Lake Road property, not that I paid any attention to her, of course, but my mind did wander back to the red headed girl with short hair and emerald green eyes, who could pass for the actress Jill St. Johns younger sister that was in Mr. Anderson’s office with her mother. Maybe you should give this flag corp thing some real serious thought there Mr. Anderson.

A little over 100 hours till the start of what might actually turn into an interesting school year.

"White Lake Road"

Chapter #6 "Two Surprises or Four on the Floor"

August 1969

As the weekend was approaching, despite the fact that I am an officially registered student of the Hartland Consolidated Schools for the upcoming school year, I'm starting to have some doubts that this will even take place and that I will end up being back at Fenton High School for the 1969-70 school year. I'm basing my uncertainties on basic logistics. Hartland High School is 14 miles, one way, from our "White Lake Road" residence. The question now becomes; how are the four newest transfers to Hartland High School even going to get there??

Will my father, who works second shift at General Motors, and is home by midnight at the earliest, get up bright and early in the morning and take us into school? Does this mean that my mother will have to leave right from her job at State Road Elementary School as a 5th grade teacher and drive direct to Hartland to gather the four of us up? That's probably not going to happen as one of the primary reasons why my mother left the Hartland Consolidated Schools as a 6th grade teacher in the first place was that she did not like the drive from Fenton to Hartland.

My biggest fear is that since we do not live that far from where the Hartland Consolidated School district extends, only a couple of miles, (In fact my military school buddy, Dave Fabray, he and his sister Mary Ann, technically live in the Hartland Consolidated School district but still attend Fenton High School, at least Mary Ann does) that my folks will find some subdivision in Hartland where a Hartland School bus picks up school kids, and the four of catch the bus there to get to Hartland High School. However, again somebody is still going to have to pick us up at the end of the school day. And what about nights where there is basketball, wrestling, baseball or track practices?? "Lions, Tigers and Bears, Oh, My!!"

Well, I am very glad that my parents are smart enough to get all of this figured out for him. Despite being home from the Student Conservation Association stay in Port Angeles, Washington, for at least two weeks, my body is still on Pacific Coast Time. I stay up late at night watching movies on Channel Six, WJIM out of Lansing. Last night I watched "Fixed Bayonets", a Korean War movie starring Richard Basehart, better known as "Admiral Nelson" on the TV series, "Voyage to the Bottom of the Sea. These movies are usually over by 1:30 AM and I finally get to sleep 30 minutes later. While I probably miss breakfast, don't worry, I'm always up in time for lunch.

I woke up at my usual late morning time and walked into the "breakfast room" of "White Lake Road" and I was surprised to see my father talking to another gentleman whom apparently works with my father at "Old Buick" or "Plant Seven". This was a strange site because in my 16 years on the face of the Earth I do not ever remember meeting another person that my father worked with or anyone other than a blood relative calling by his first name, George. I didn't even know or think my father had any friends at all since I had never seen him with one before. That was surprise number one.

"White Lake Road"

Surprise number two was that the Beardslee's just became a three-car household. Sitting out in the driveway was a 1965 Jeep CJR. It seats four, and from the looks of it not very comfortably, and is burgundy in color. Just imagine a freshly opened cask of ale from an Errol Flynn movie, that's what color the jeep is. The jeep is a four speed and only has 82 miles on it. I assumed that the odometer had been turned back a couple of times after reaching the 100,000-mile mark but I later discovered that was indeed the actual mileage.

I took the jeep for a test drive around "the block". No, not a city block like the "city kids" of Jim Koop and Terry Rodenbo are used to. This was a country block that consisted of six miles starting off at the White Lake Road residence, south on Hartland Road, hang a left on Foley Road, take another left on Denton Hill Road and down the home stretch for the last mile back on White Lake Road and in the driveway of where the Beardslee family resides.

I had forgotten how much I hated driving a stick shift, four on the floor and was lucky to even get the shifter into reverse gear. Shockingly I was able to complete the test drive with only putting my left foot on the brake instead of the clutch once. Eh, maybe twice.

I must admit the jeep does drive very nice but the shifting of those gears is going to take some getting used to. I haven't driven a four on the floor since taking drivers education during the summer of 1968. Heck, I'm not fully convinced at this point in my young driving career that I have even mastered the art of driving a car with an automatic transmission let alone a manual transmission.

During my six weeks of Driver's Education I learned how to drive a four on the floor in a 1968 Grand Torino. That baby car had some kick to it!! However, this was not the type of motor vehicle to let brand new drivers learn how to drive. I found it to be a little intimidating and apparently, I wasn't the only one. Whenever it was my turn to drive that Grand Torino I could feel the sweat of the previous driver's back on the driver's seat.

In fact, the only good moment that I remember from being in that 1968 Grand Torino was when Jim Koop, Bill Wilhoit, Marva Morrison, who was four months pregnant at the time, and I were out riding with Mr. Hewitt, not exactly the most patient driver's education teacher in the world, for "expressway driving day".

We were northbound on US-23 and Bill Wilhoit was driving. Bill Wilhoit was trying to pass this little tan VW which probably only had a "one" cylinder engine. On Bill Wilhoit's first pass attempt the VW sped up and would not let Bill Wilhoit pass. This set of events took place again and Bill Wilhoit still was unable to pass the VW after three cracks at it. Finally, Bill Wilhoit floored the 1968 Grand Torino and took it up to about 85 MPH, (mind you this is an unlicensed driver operating a Driver's Education car) and just blew the doors off of the VW. I didn't know who was going to have a baby first; Mr. Hewitt or Marva Morrison.

After we got back to Fenton High School the four of us kids were shaking like a leaf as we knew we were going to get the "A responsible driver never drives the way you did today, Wilhoit!!" lecture from Mr. Hewitt. Surprisingly, all Mr. Hewitt said was, "Nice driving, Wilhoit."

"White Lake Road"

I was shocked that my parents actually went out and bought any type of car let alone a 1965 CJR Jeep for me to be the primary driver, especially because I vividly remember my father telling me that in World War II, American jeeps were probably responsible for more deaths to American soldiers than the march to Bataan.

The son of my father's co-worker, a Mr. Ellsworth, had left for the country of Canada to avoid being drafted into the United States Army and most likely to be followed by a guaranteed tour of duty in South Viet Nam. The son has been gone out of the United States now for a couple of years. Mr. Ellsworth bought the jeep for his son and ever since the son's departure the jeep has been sitting in their back yard taking up space doing nothing more than creating a sad memory for Mr. Ellsworth.

I myself do not know a whole lot about jeeps. The only time ever I rode in one was when Bill Nagy gave some of us kids a ride in his dad's jeep one Sunday afternoon on the back property of White Lake Road. One moment we were driving along and all of a sudden Bill Nagy had to make a real sharp turn to miss hitting a "No Trespassing" sign. I still remember all of riders just screaming like wild banshees when Bill Nagy made that swerve to avoid running over that sign. Man, that was great!! I can just imagine what Bill Wilhoit would have done to that sign if he was driving a 1968 Grand Torino.

While I am thrilled about having a set of "wheels" it will be strange to actually be driving to school this year instead of riding a school bus. I've been taking a bus to school since September of 1957. I suspect that I won't miss that.

What also will be interesting will be to see how my riding partners take to the new jeep. Jim Koop will think it's cool. My mother, however, has already given me the "there will be no smoking in the car" speech. Sorry Koop. It gets worst. That radio dial is never going to leave WJR 760. No WTAC or CKLW. I'll be out voted on the latter before we even leave the driveway.

Terry Rodenbo will like the jeep because he is my relief driver. What few times I have ever had to drive in the city of Flint, I always had Terry Rodenbo go with me as I was too scared to drive. Once we hit the city limits of Flint, I simply pulled the car off to the side of the road and Terry Rodenbo took over.

The happiest person about the new jeep?? That's easy, Katie. Katie has already figured out that the jeep of today for her older brother is the jeep of the future for her. One year from now Katie will have completed Driver's Education and she will probably have full control of the jeep. I can guarantee you this. It will not take Katie three attempts to pass a VW with a "one" cylinder engine on an expressway. It won't even take her one attempt to pass a Grand Torino with an eight cylinder on an expressway.

The purchasing of this burgundy colored jeep pretty much removes all doubt as to where I will be attending his senior year of high school.

"White Lake Road"

Chapter #7 – Planet Zectron

August 1969

Labor Day weekend is upon us which means a new school year is just around the corner. The last couple of Labor Day weekends the Beardslee family has trekked up to Mackinac City to specifically walk across the Mackinac Bridge with thousands of other people. Not really my idea of how to spend a Labor Day weekend but my father and I were out voted 2-2.

The only good part of the trip was knowing that once I made it across four miles of an extremely cold, bitter wind in my face and the fear of looking down at the Straits of Mackinac that once I hit Mackinac City I could walk five feet in any direction and find a store that sold Mackinac City fudge. I love vanilla fudge!!

The power brokers in the family, my mother and Katie, however, with the memory fresh in their minds of being stuck in traffic for exactly 50 minutes waiting a for a freighter to go excruciatingly slow while the Zilwaukee Bridge was in the process of being raised and lowered, decided that there will be no Labor Day Mackinac Bridge walk this year. The decision of not going back there doesn't break my heart any, but man, I have to admit, that is really high-quality vanilla fudge.

This year, the decision, and without any input by myself at all for the 16th consecutive Labor Day Weekend, the Beardslee's will be attending the Michigan State Fair in Detroit, Michigan. This doesn't particularly excite me either. The only thing I know about a State Fair was what I had seen in the movie, by sheer coincidence titled, "State Fair." The flick starred Pat Boone, Ann-Margaret and Wally Cox. What I remembered most about that movie was enjoying the singing of Pat Boone, that Ann-Margaret should have been far, far more scenes, and that I hope I do not grow up to look or sound like Wally Cox.

Once we arrived at the state fairgrounds it wasn't so bad walking around the displays and seeing all of the food vendors. I went up to one booth that had a large crowd around it and a gentleman was hawking something by the name of "Super Ball." I listened to his presentation and "Super Ball" turned out to be a ball about the size of a tennis ball, dark purple in color that could bounce all day or bounce higher than any tennis ball or other toy ball previously invented.

The sales person then tossed a "Super Ball" on the cement surface and the whole crowd watched in amazement as the "Super Ball" just bounced and bounced never stopping once. Then the salesman pointed out to the audience the two-story building that was behind us. He then slammed the "Super Ball" down on the cement as hard as he could and the "Super Ball" bounced higher than the two-story building. Hey, maybe this State Fair stuff isn't so bad after all!!

My mind was sort of made up to purchase one of these babies but what clinched the deal was when the proprietor told the horde that something called Zectron is what gave the "Super Ball" the capacity to bounce higher and longer than any other rubber ball that Mattel or

another toy company could or would ever produce. Once I heard that word Zectron it was all over. I just imagined in my child like little mind that Zectron was a Planet where Superman spent his Labor Day weekends. The cost of the "Super Ball" you ask?? $.98. A real bargain!!

I continued to wander around the various displays of the State Fair and despite the fact that I am now a proud owner of a "Super Ball" and the spiked teeth to back it up; the one thing I noticed was that while the State Fair was packed with people, I wasn't seeing any familiar faces at all. You would think that I would stumble across somebody from Fenton High School or someone that I had competed against in sports or met at a band function. But of the 90 some minutes that I have been here at the State Fair, otherwise than blood relatives, I have not seen one person I knew at all. Not a one!!

That all changed in the next 50 yards.

"White Lake Road"

Chapter #8 – Two Woodwind Players

August 1969

As I walked down the causeway, I heard the sound of what was unmistakably the resonance of a high school band performing. I located where the music was coming from and discovered that there was a group named the "Michigan State Fair High School Band." I looked through the group starting with the trumpet players to see if there was any one that I knew. While I did not recognize any trumpet players I did get the pleasant surprise of seeing a couple of my Interlochen buddies. One was Howard Feldman, a cabin mate of the infamous "Cabin #5, a clarinet player, and Allen "Bad Hombre" Rothstein, a bass clarinet player, also an alumnus of Cabin #5 and one strange dude. Make that one really strange dude. Both guys attended nearby Oak Park High School.

Bad Hombre was quite the character. There are two things that come to my mind when I think of Bad Hombre. First was when I was sitting in the All-State Band rehearsals counting the seconds away of our 90-minute practice session, I would look over at Bad Hombre in the Bass Clarinet section and he was just sitting there playing along, wiggling head from side to side with a big silly smile on his face just having the time of his life, while all the real musicians surrounding him had these very solemn, intellectual looks on their faces. Believe me it was not hard to pick out Bad Hombre in a Bass Clarinet section.

What I remember the most though about hanging out with Bad Hombre was how much time we would spend playing basketball instead of practicing our instruments during the allowed recreational/free time that we had during our stay at "Fort Interlochen." That was the best $150.00 my parents had ever spent on me.

Bad Hombre and I would take on all challengers. We would play basketball against anybody. Usually our competition was against two staff members of Pinecrest Hall where our meals were served. These guys were stronger, quicker and simply far better basketball players than me and Bad Hombre. Add to the fact that these two dudes had a career of correction facility employees written all over them made for some formidable competition.

The way our two-man team worked was for me to play down low, play defense and rebound. Bad Hombre would take care of the perimeter defense and outside shooting. Whichever team got to 15 baskets first was the winner. Bad Hombre and I went head to head with the Pinecrest guys for a grand total of 10 games, of which, they that just pounded us in the first nine. I mean those contests weren't even close. At the end of each whipping Bad Hombre would say, "I knew that I should have implemented a mercy rule right after the first time we faced them."

As Jim Koop has always preached to me, "Every dog has their day, even you, Beardslee." In the last Friday before us All-State kids were to go home, Bad Hombre and I actually reached our potential and finally beat the Pinecrest guys, 15-14. Bad Hombre got hot from the outside and hit seven shots in a row. I tipped in an offensive rebound, admittedly a fluke shot on my part, that gave us our 15th basket and we avoided a tenth consecutive thrashing!! This promptly caused Bad Hombre to celebrate this big victory by mooning the Pinecrest guys. Maybe losing those nine games wasn't such a bad thing after all.

As much as I loved teaming up to play basketball with Bad Hombre, his idea of an outside jumper and mine did not exactly jive with one another. Bad Hombre's outside jumpers were not being taken from around the key but rather 35-40 feet away from the basket. Dave Bing and Jimmy Walker, the starting guards of the Detroit Pistons, wouldn't even shoot the rock from that long of distance. Well, maybe Jimmy Walker would.

It was a thing of beauty when Bad Hombre made one of his jump shots. The key operative word being "when", because if that long jumper did not go in, which it did not 80-90% of the time, then those Pinecrest boys would just beat the be-jeebers out of me, even worse than Dave Austin the power forward of the Brighton Bulldogs did when going after a rebound.

The last time I had seen Bad Hombre was when my folks picked me up at Interlochen last July. I made the colossal mistake of introducing Katie to Bad Hombre. Bad Hombre took one look at Katie and said to me, "Hey, Doc Savage (the nickname I was christened with at Interlochen) I'll be attending Fenton High School this fall just to be around your beautiful sister!!"

Bad Hombre, being the ladies' man that he thinks he is, then said to Katie," Hey, Doc Savage's sister, don't accept any dates for your high school prom next Spring because you've got a date already in me!!" Katie's cool and calm response was, "I don't date woodwind players, buddy." A great come back.

While walking back to my parent's car, Katie hissed at me in a venomous tone of voice and said, "Don't ever introduce me to any other bass clarinet players by the name of "Bad Hombre" as long as you live, which not counting tomorrow, will not be that long!!" Thanks, Bad Hombre.

Howard Feldman, much like Bad Hombre, was a woodwind player, clarinet. The difference between these two woodwind players was that everybody, with the exception of Katie, thought Bad Hombre was a great guy but a little on the weird side. I'm not so sure that was the case with Howard Feldman. You have to realize that Howard Feldman wasn't just an ordinary clarinet player; he was an exceptional clarinet player, and man oh man you better be an exceptional clarinet player if you owned a clarinet that had gold keys on it like Howard Feldman did.

I have spent time in both the athletic and music worlds and the one thing that athletes and musicians have in common is there are some large egos. Howard Feldman had a sizeable ego to go along with his very direct personality that could take some getting used to. For whatever reason, though, I had the ability to make him laugh and he took a liking to me. Howard Feldman was the unquestionable leader of our cabin and made it a point to get me involved with any of the shenanigans that Cabin #5 became famous for during our two weeks stay at Fort Interlochen.

"White Lake Road"

Based upon the first week's tryouts Howard Feldman was named the first chair clarinet player for the All-State Band division. That's a pretty impressive achievement considering the number of talented musicians who were gathered at the National Music Camp just outside of Traverse City, Michigan.

Instead of tryouts the second week at Interlochen, a different format to determine what chair a person would have for that week's concert too place. This was "challenge week." I'll use the trumpet section as an example. We started at the very bottom of the trumpet section and worked our way up the ladder from the last chair player to the first chair player. Two trumpet players would play the same passage from a song that was going to be played in our Sunday concert. The rest of the trumpet players had their heads down and listened to the two players complete their playing. Votes were then taken and whichever trumpet player won could keep on challenging until they lost. It was not much fun and very nerve racking.

A person could go up or down depending on the voting. Since I stunk up the joint during my first tryout and initially placed 18th chair out of 24 trumpet players, I was able to battle my way up to 15th chair through the challenge process until I was beaten by my Cabin #5 buddy, Gary "Louie" Levine. (He was right up there with Bad Hombre when it came to serious strangeness).

Should I have done better in tryouts and challenges? You betcha!! That wasn't going to happen as that would have required me to cut down on my basketball playing time with Bad Hombre. And the truth of the matter was that I played far more volleyball than I did basketball during my stay at the All-State Band Division. What part of the "best $150.00 my ever parents spent on me" did you not understand??

While funny things, and I do not mean "ha ha", can happen in these challenges, I don't think Howard Feldman was too amused by what happened to him in the clarinet challenges. All week-long Howard Feldman had been politicking for a couple of clarinet players to get a higher chair, which meant by the laws of gravity that someone else was going to go down a chair or two in the clarinet section.

Well, "The man with the Golden Keys" who considered himself the best clarinet player at Interlochen, regardless of classification, All State Band or Nationals, and had no problem telling everyone that fact, was in for a big shocker. Howard Feldman's continued repetition of this message apparently was not taken to well by the other All State Band clarinet players and Howard Feldman found himself voted out of first chair down to third chair clarinet.

Of course, Howard Feldman took his demotion like a pro. He came back to Cabin #5 all in a rage, bellowing, "I was shafted!! I was shafted!!" A great line that I have used numerous times since my tour of Fort Interlochen was completed.

While talking to Bad Hombre and Howard Feldman today at the Michigan State Fair where the two of them again were again telling me that they truly did have police officers on duty throughout the whole school day at Oak Park High School, of which, I still find shocking, I heard a sound from behind me. The Mike Beardslee two-prong test of a trumpet player, 1)

good tone and 2) can you hear every note, was being demonstrated by a world-famous trumpet player not less than 20 feet from where I stood.

"White Lake Road"

Chapter #9 – "Java"

That world-famous trumpet player was none other than Al Hirt!! Al Hirt was here at the Michigan State Fair!! I could not believe it!! Christmas came early for me!! The question now was whether he was here to perform or did Al Hirt come all the way from New Orleans, Louisiana to purchase a "SuperBall"???

This just shows you my lack of knowledge of how a State Fair works. Apparently, it is a common practice for professional musicians to come to a State Fair, stay for however long, and do their act. My lucky timing today was such that Al Hirt and his band were just minutes from starting their show.

Again, I showed my ignorance as to the workings of a State Fair and asked Howard Feldman what the cost of the Al Hirt performance was. I survived the Howard Feldman, "Even Bad Hombre knows this look" and he replied, "There's no charge. It's included in the cost of the ticket to attend the State Fair."

Okay. Let me get this straight. 1) I don't have to pay an additional amount of money to watch Al Hirt perform in person;2) I am the new proud owner of a "Superball" and; 3) I still do not look and sound like Wally Cox. Wow this is one great day!!

Al Hirt, while he is no Ann-Margaret, he and his band put on a really fantastic show for the crowd. Al Hirt played the song "Java" which is one of my favorites of all of his arrangements. If my teeth ever allow my trumpet playing skills to get back to what they were a few weeks ago, I would love to get brave enough to see if Mr. Anderson would let me play "Java" as a solo with the Hartland Senior Band sometime this year. If Mr. Anderson's answer is yes, then they will have to turn people away from the front door of Hartland High School. I guarantee it.

The group also performed "When the Saints go Marching In" and it was interesting to see how the rest of the members of the band, which consisted of a saxophone player, drummer, piano player, trombone player and clarinet player, each get a chance to display their skills when playing their individuals solos. It was also fun watching Al Hirt and the clarinet player, who bears a striking resemblance to Sonny Elliott, the local weather man on Channel 4 from Detroit, kid around with each other. Overall just a very entertaining performance to watch.

This day was fantastic so far and for one moment I thought it was going to become an absolutely perfect one. After the Al Hirt concert was over, Howard Feldman said to me, "You know, that if you have pass you can walk right back there and meet Al Hirt if you want. All of us kids in the band have talked to him or members of his group this past week." This is great!! Al Hirt is going to get an opportunity to meet Mike Beardslee!!

Howard Feldman was kind enough to loan me his back stage pass to see if I could locate Al Hirt and meet him in person. I wandered around back stage for a few seconds and lo and behold, standing not more than 10 feet in front of me was the one and only, Mr. Al Hirt!!

I started to walk towards him with the intent to introduce myself when suddenly a security guard stopped me and wouldn't let me go one step further. I tried to be nice and charming telling this obstruction that I was a trumpet player as well and would consider it an enormous honor to meet and spend a few seconds with the great Al Hirt. I mean, come on, he's only 10 feet away from me and just standing there. The response from the security guard was in the tone of voice that implied, "Beat it, kid. Come back when you can hit a double high "C" on your trumpet". Considering the current condition of my teeth, I'm light years from hitting a high "C" let alone a double high "C."

It quickly dawned on me that the Beardslee charm had the same effect on this security guard as it did with beautiful women. None. None at all. Needless to say, I did not get the opportunity to meet Mr. Al Hirt today. A huge disappointment for me.

As the award, winning composers Rogers and Hammerstein wrote in their lyrics from the movie "State Fair":

"Our state fair is a great state fair

Don't miss it, don't even be late (boom, boom, boom)

Dollars to doughnuts that our state fair is the best state fair in our state"

Despite the fact that I did not get to introduce myself to Al Hirt, this was still one fantabulous day overall. It was especially terrific to see some of my old Interlochen companions again. I had forgotten how much fun that I had had with the Cabin Five guys last summer. Toss in the hours I will spend watching the "Super Ball" continuously bounce across our basement floor will amuse my little mind to no end. This was one great Labor Day weekend. I gotta admit, though, the only thing missing from today was a couple of slabs of that Mackinac Island vanilla fudge. That would have made a mighty good late-night snack.

Another important reason for today to be such a nice Labor Day is because the dynamics of the Beardslee family will change over the next year. Where will their oldest son be one year from today? In my mother's eyes, I will be preparing and packing for the start of my college years. However, I have no plans to attend college. None at all. If you thought that the Holy Redeemer vs. Swartz Creek issue was tense in the confines of "White Lake Road", then stick around.

It's Sunday night. Tomorrow brings a new month and Tuesday brings a huge change in my 16 year life.

"White Lake Road"

Chapter #10 – "Wall Drug, South Dakota"

September 2nd – I didn't sleep very well last night. I normally don't any way. On a school night, I usually go to sleep around 10:30 PM, wake up around 11:30 PM and then spend the next seven or so hours tossing and turning just never really getting any serious type of slumber at all. At least not the kind of sound snooze I get when I doze off trying to watch episodes of televisions shows like "The Avengers" or "Mannix.". Then I barely make it to the first commercial.

But last night was worse than usual. What was the main contributor of my bout with insomnia? That's easy. It's the first day of school for what is to be my senior year of high school. A milestone in any high school student's life. But this day was a little bit different for Mike Beardslee.

You would think that since this is my thirteenth "first day" of school that I would be an old pro at this and have the drill down:

- ***New school clothes. Check.***
- ***See old friends again. Check.***
- ***Hope that another trumpet player that is better than me has not moved into the Fenton Area School district this past summer. Check. (Make this one a double check).***
- ***Also, hope that a bunch of good, or even mediocre runners for that matter, have not moved into the Fenton Area School district that will bump me off from running on the mile relay team this upcoming Spring.***

With the exception of new school clothes only the future will tell for the last three check list items. However, I have a new orange long sleeve shirt, small brown checked pants and a new pair of black penny loafers to wear this school year. You just know that outfit will cause other kids to come up to me and say, "Wow, Mr. Ricky Nelson, you're one sharp dresser!!" Oh, yeah.

My new school clothes also remind me of one of the many "Kooperism's" that I have received over the last few years from a one Jim Koop. "Always remember, Beardslee. The difference between me and you is this. New clothes make you look good. I make the new clothes look good."

And these encouraging words are coming from the guy who is going to be begging me to smoke in the jeep just three seconds after we pull out of the driveway of "White Lake Road."

As I was staggering up the stairs to the breakfast room it dawned on me that I will now have to re-orientate my whole life. The days of walking down the drive way to wait for Mrs. Wolverton to pick me up with Bus #23 are over. I will now have to drive 28 miles round trip, using a stick shift no less, to attend school.

"White Lake Road"

Another part of the re-orientation of Mike Beardslee's life is that I'll have to get used to is waiting every morning for Terry Rodenbo's mother to drop him and Jim Koop off at "White Lake Road". Then with my luck I will have to wait around further while my mother makes a quick breakfast for Terry Rodenbo so as my mother put it, "That he will have sufficient strength for his first day of school." Gimme a break. The guy probably gets a better breakfast than I do.

Breakfast time is usually very quiet in the Beardslee household. But today breakfast was probably more tense than quiet. My mother had prepared eggs over easy and toast for the first meal of the day. Every time I have eggs for breakfast I put ketchup on them and every time Katie sees me do this she gives me a ton of grief. "Why are you spoiling a good breakfast with ketchup?" This morning the sound of ketchup squirting out of the container was a little noisier and the response of "Why are you spoiling a good breakfast with ketchup?" had a little bit more of a sting to it.

I know what I was uptight about. Today, other than Katie, Jim Koop and Terry Rodenbo, there will be very few people, if anyone at all that will know who Mike Beardslee is. My mother taught 6th grade for two years for the Hartland Consolidated Schools and her former 6th graders are currently seniors and juniors. These kids, if they even exist as students of the Hartland Consolidated Schools anymore, will probably remember my mother but I will be just another new student wondering where the nearest bathroom is located.

My main concern was the "new student" thing. The changing of schools means the leaving of old traditions and learning new ones. To varying degrees, I was worried about the following groups of people: Principal; coaches; teachers and students. How would I be received by them?

I have never had that much interaction with the five school principals that have been in charge of the several school buildings and grade classifications throughout my school career. So, I wasn't particularly worried about whom ever the principal of Hartland High School was. I must admit, though, if former Fenton High School principal, Robert C. Walker, showed up at my doorstep of "White Lake Road," It would take a platoon of Green Berets to find me. For some reason that man always scared me. Still does.

Coaches and teachers? There's a little more trepidation on my part with that group. Of all of the basketball and track coaches I have had throughout junior high and senior high I have never had a particular closeness with any of them. While a couple of the coaches I've had were brilliant from a tactical standpoint, they were not someone that inspired me to run up a hill for them into the face of machine gun fire. This was, however, totally different then my dealings with band directors, of which, I could never be around enough.

What will the teachers be like? Friendly?? Mean?? It was not uncommon for students from St. John Catholic School to transfer to Fenton High School after completion of the 8th grade. There was one teacher on the Fenton High School staff who would always say to one of the former St. Johns kids when they got an answer wrong, "Public school kids would have gotten that answer right." Will I now be on the receiving end of a commentary from a Hartland High

School teacher where they say, "This topic is common knowledge, Beardslee. Even second graders know the answer to this question. Didn't they teach you anything at Fenton High School??"

But of all the above classifications the one that I fear the most is the students. Who will be the bully that wants to take cuts in the lunch line or beat you up for your lunch money? Will I be able to distinguish which group of students are the "liars "and "spies"? The latter of which I have been flat out bad at since my Kindergarten days.

Most important to me is how will I be accepted by the high school band kids? Will I fit in or be treated like an outsider? What happens if I take over the first chair trumpet position from a trumpet player who also happens to be the most popular person in the band? I saw that happen at Fenton High School when Carl Peters came to Fenton High School as a new student and took the first chair trumpet position from Ray Sortman. It took Carl Peters quite some time before he made any friends in the Fenton High School Band. Will that happen to me and I then get to wear the villain tag for my senior year of high school? We'll find out.

While I was thinking this to myself I kept peeking over to my mother with the hope that she would ask Katie and I, "Do you two really want to go through with the transferring of schools? Because if you don't want to attend Hartland High School then I can arrange for the both of you to stay at Fenton High School for this school year." Not a word was spoken by my mother on the subject. Nor did Mrs. Koop or Mrs. Rodenbo act like they were overly concerned with their sons attending a new school system this year. Guess who is driving a stick shift for the next nine months round trip from Fenton, Michigan to Hartland, Michigan? No, it's not Mrs. Wolverton.

Before the four of us piled into the jeep and got the show on the road, the most important decision of the day was going to have to be made. Where was everyone going to sit in the jeep twice a day from September through June? At least I knew where I was going to sit. Terry Rodenbo made it a point that since he was the unofficial "relief driver" he was going to ride "shot gun." That left Jim Koop and Katie to decide who was going to sit where in the back seat. Jim Koop decided to sit directly behind me. Why does that scare me?

It was west on White Lake Road to U.S 23 where a left-hand turn found us traveling south and me never leaving the right-hand lane of traffic until the Clyde Road exit. We were now traveling on a side dirt road with an extremely sharp curve where hanging from one of the trees off to the side of the road was a sign that read, "Wall Drug, South Dakota." That sign has probably been there for at least a couple of thousand years.

" On a family vacation a few summers ago, we traveled to see Mount Rushmore, one afternoon my family and I kept seeing road signs that read; "Wall Drug, South Dakota 50 miles;" Nearing Wall Drug, South Dakota;" Gas up while you are in beautiful Wall Drug, South Dakota;" "You are leaving beautiful down town Wall Drug, South Dakota. Please come back and see us again." I mean we were seeing Wall Drug, South Dakota signs at least every mile.

"White Lake Road"

Later that evening the Beardslee family finally pulled into Wall Drug, South Dakota and it was sure not the metropolis as advertised. It was the proverbial one stop light and a couple of buildings type of town. I overheard one other traveler say, "Man, all those signs on the side of the road and they lead to absolutely nowhere."

When I saw that "Wall Drug, South Dakota" sign on the tree this morning that same traveler's word came back to me. Is my transferring to Hartland High School a road to nowhere and have I led three other people to the state of Michigan's equivalency of "Wall Drug, South Dakota?" I sure hope not.

The drive continued as we passed the Cromine Library, Cromine Elementary School, where my mother started her full-time teaching career. Then past a little grocery store, that would have fit in very well in Wall Drug, South Dakota. This was the store that if I did well during my trumpet private lesson with Mr. Anderson, my mother would buy me an ice cream bar.

We finally turned into the parking lot of Hartland High School. I looked at Terry Rodenbo, Jim Koop and Katie with an expression on my face that probably read, "It's not too late to turn around. Nobody here will ever know the difference if we just pull out of this parking lot and drive back to Fenton."

There were no takers though and somehow four new students of the Hartland Consolidated Schools alighted from the jeep. While not exactly humming, or whistling the theme song from "The Magnificent Seven" to gain confidence, we sluggishly made our way to the doors that would officially start the 1969-70 school year.

"White Lake Road"

Chapter #11- "Crabby Appleton"

September 2nd – I had been in Hartland High School many times before since I had started taking private lessons from Mr. Anderson in 6th grade. Add to it the number of times I had been here for sporting events and I have a pretty good idea of where everything is located in this building. Principal's office is to the right as you enter the school building. The lunch room is to your left. The gymnasium and band room are straight ahead. Piece of cake.

Katie had been in Hartland High School a handful of times before but this was the first occasion that Jim Koop and Terry Rodenbo were setting foot in this educational setting. As we were getting closer to the school's front doors Jim Koop stopped, took a look around the structure and commented, "Geez, Beardslee. This building looks an awful lot like Lake Fenton High School. Are you sure that having to drive a stick shift did not affect your sense of direction?" Noooo, this is our "home" till June of 1970. Man, come to think of it, that's a lot of downshifting between now and then.

I cannot emphasize how nervous I was upon entering the school building. My legs were wobbly causing me to stumble over my own two feet. Any type of loud and sudden explosion would have caused me to jump from the cement sidewalk to the top of the school roof with no need for a running start.

My three traveling partners, who had it much more together than me, went to the principal's office to get their class schedules. I instead practically sprinted to the nearest bathroom to settle down my nerves. I was so anxious about this first day of school that I started to open up the door to the women's bathroom before I caught myself. Man, nobody should be this jittery!! I mean it's only 7:55 AM!! What am I going to be like when the school year officially starts in five minutes??

I finally made my way to the principal's office and got my class schedule. The first thing I do whenever I get a class schedule is to check what hour Band is. I still remember Jim Koop running up to me one year ago with panic in his eyes telling me, "Band is second hour this year!!" Senior Band at Fenton High School had traditionally been fourth hour probably since John Phillip Sousa composed his first march. Second hour is a god-awful time to have Band class mainly because my "chops" aren't even awake by that time of the morning. The only worse hour to have Band class would have been first hour. That was a terrible decision on some administrator's part but was consistent with a lot of other events, which with the exception of the Detroit Tigers winning the World Series, made me enjoy very little about my junior year of high school.

The first look at my class schedule shows that Band is fourth hour. Perfect!! If I ever amount to anything in life I will decree that in the state of Michigan that high school Senior Band class will always be scheduled for fourth hour just before lunch time. No exceptions!!

The class schedule for my senior year looks like this:

First Hour	***American Literature***	***Mrs. Lawrence***

Second Hour	*Study Hall*	*Mr. Appleton*
Third Hour	*Psychology*	*Mrs. Gooden*
Fourth Hour	*Band*	*Mr. Anderson*
Fifth Hour	*Michigan History*	*Mr. Vickers*
Sixth Hour	*Economics*	*Mr. Collins*

Overall not too bad of a schedule for the "greatest year of my life." While a couple of the teacher's names sound familiar, other than Mr. Anderson, I'm not so sure that I can place a name with a face.

Granted, it not's like I have spent a large amount of time so far at my new high school but it was dawning on me that I hadn't even seen some of the kids that were sixth graders from mother's class nor had I spotted any of the Hartland kids that had been in catechism classes with me at St. Johns Church. Gee, maybe I am at Lake Fenton High School.

Today I am walking down the school hallways looking at other kids. Not only do they not say "hi" to me, they don't even give me a second's look. So far, I am nonexistent.

This is the complete opposite of what the first day of school would be like for me if I was back at Fenton High School. There after not seeing friends for the past couple of months I would be shaking hands, smiling away, waving to old pals till my right shoulder ached. On that first day of school I was always glad to be back and thrilled to see my buddies again.

The first day of the school year was a joyous event for me and I was always in high spirits. Day Two?? Now that was an entirely different matter. Thanksgiving vacation couldn't get here fast enough.

While my debut as a Hartland Consolidated Schools student hasn't been anything to write home about, it still beats my first day as a student of the Fenton Area Schools. Now that was a warm welcoming.

I was in fourth grade and standing outside of State Road Elementary School just scared stiff. Even more scared than I am today. The first Fenton kid that came up and talked to me was named Eddie Williams, another fourth grader. Eddie Williams was a small runt of a kid, but nevertheless, a really tough looking runt of a kid. The first words out of Eddie Williams' mouth to me were, "Does your mother where army boots?" I was either speechless or crying, probably both, but I did not respond to Eddie Williams' warm greeting.

That incident took place eight years ago, and I swore to myself that the next person who asked me "Does your mother wear army boots?" my comeback will be, "No, she doesn't. But my younger sister does, and she's going to walk all over your face with those army boots!!"

"White Lake Road"

"Walk All Over Your Face with Those Army Boots!!" Now that sounds like the title of a tune that belongs on the flip side of a record for Nancy Sinatra's smash hit, "These Boots Are Made for Walkin."

It's class time. First hour is American Literature. I selected this course because I absolutely love to read. My whole family is like that. You name it, autobiographies, history books, mysteries, and "The Sporting News Magazine," especially the latter, are my favorite types of reads.

While I was performing my tour of duty with the Student Conservation Association last summer I read a book titled "The Year of the Rat." I found it to be a very intriguing paperback book that discussed the various escape routes that Adolph Hitler was going to use to flee Berlin, Germany in the last days of World War II.

This was a fascinating read and swore that when I got back home to the state of Michigan I was going to seek that book out so I could add it to the "Mike Beardslee Memorial Library." I've tried a couple of local used book stores and even a St. Vincent De Paul thrift store to track down this book but with no luck. (And no, I do not buy my school clothes at the St. Vincent De Paul thrift store).

American Literature will be taught by a Mrs. Lawrence. She looks real young and appeared very nervous while taking attendance. I suspect that she is fresh out of college with this class being her first teaching job. Mrs. Lawrence and I have a lot in common this morning from an anxiety standpoint.

I looked around the classroom and despite my earlier thoughts that I did not know anyone here at Hartland High School; I did see a couple of guys who looked familiar. One particular student was Alex Felton. I remembered him from my cross-country days. He's an excellent harrier and a year ago, Alex Felton took first place in the league meet and there is a good chance of him repeating that accomplishment this fall. However, for whatever reason, Alex Felton has never made that same impact in track season. In fact, I do not ever remember seeing him run in any track meet during the spring. That is rare for an outstanding cross country runner.

Another fella that I recognized is someone who received a big write-up last summer in the "Fenton Independent". It was one of those "stars of the future" type articles and if I remember correctly his name is Steve Gilmore.

I also vaguely remember the name Steve Gilmore from my mother's teaching days at Crouse Elementary School here at the Hartland Consolidated Schools. There were two boys that she just gushed about constantly around the supper table at "White Lake Road" and Steve Gilmore was one of them. My mother taught the highest-level reading group of the sixth graders and as a fifth grader Steve Gilmore was advanced enough that he was placed in this prestigious reading group. A rarity for a fifth grade at Crouse Elementary School.

"White Lake Road"

My mother's favorite story about Steve Gilmore was when there was a basketball game between the sixth and fifth graders of Crouse Elementary School which was apparently a big deal. Steve Gilmore pretty much beat the sixth graders by himself and that was when he started to be tagged as the next "greatest athlete ever" to wear a Hartland Eagle school jersey, regardless of the sport.

I remember Steve Gilmore more for taking fifth place in the pole vault as a freshman in the conference track meet last spring. While that athletic feat pales miserably to being the only fifth grader in the highest sixth grade reading group, I was impressed.

As I left American Literature Class to go to second hour, Mrs. Lawrence pulled me aside and whispered to me, "I'm glad to see that I wasn't the only person in this classroom that was petrified to be here." She must have been referring to the stoic impression on my face along with my complete silence throughout the entire 55 minutes of class time. Yeah, the word petrified is an accurate way of describing how I am feeling so far.

Second Hour is Study Hall. Last year at Fenton High School I spent my Study Hall time working in the band room. I'd practice my trumpet, file music, and basically do whatever was needed for the betterment of the Fenton High School Band. Over this past summer, I decided that once outside of school, other than practicing the trumpet and running, I could never bring myself to do any kind of studying or homework. None!! Thus, the executive decision to use the Study Hall hour this year for its intended purpose. Study!!

While I'm pretty sure I will like my first hour class, I'm not so sure that Study Hall is going to be a barrel of laughs. Mr. Damien Appleton, AKA as Coach Appleton, and as I was soon to discover, AKA as "Crabby Appleton", a take-off of the villainous character from I think the "Captain Kangaroo Show", is the proctor for Study Hall.

It took a few seconds but it finally dawned on me that I've seen Coach Appleton in action before on the sidelines of a basketball court and stalking the infield of track meets. Coach Appleton just doesn't scream at his athletes, he shrieks at them. I remember once during my freshmen year; Hartland High School came to Fenton High School to play a varsity basketball game. I was playing in the pep band that night and watched Coach Appleton just start to go berserk on his players when Fenton starting guard Vance Huff continuously was beating a full court press by the Hartland team all by himself. Vance Huff then would dump the ball inside to Don Madden or Mike Madden all night long for uncontested layups It was text book basketball and great to watch if you were a Fenton Tiger follower.

After being down some 30 points going into the fourth quarter of the contest you would have thought that Coach Appleton would have let up on his tirades. He didn't and was really taking it out on one specific Hartland hoopster. Coach Appleton's rants had gotten so out of line that even the Fenton fans were encouraging and being supportive when this picked on Hartland player made even an average play on the court.

The really fun part of the evening came during a time out when Coach Appleton was just reaming out some poor kid in a big-time way. Jim Koop, who else, stood up from the stage

where the pep band was located and yelled out to Coach Appleton, "Man, I bet you're one mean drunk!!" Oh, my goodness, the Fenton side of the court just erupted in laughter!! They were showing no mercy to Coach Appleton.

The not so fun part of that same evening took place next. Because I was sitting next to Jim Koop when he yelled out that classic line, Coach Appleton looked over at the band and glared at me. I MEAN GLARED!! Apparently, Coach Appleton thought I was the one who had made that reference towards him and he even took a few steps in my direction before an assistant coach blocked Coach Appleton's path, probably saving me from a serious whooping. Man, I hope Coach Appleton doesn't remember that incident. If he does, I'm cooked.

At the start of Study Hall Coach Appleton read my name and then he looked at me for a long second or two. I think he knew that he had seen me before but luckily, he didn't put two and two together and remember who I am.

Before Coach Appleton's memory banks kicked in I caught a break when a kid, probably a freshman, came swaggering into Study Hall and innocently said to Coach Appleton, "How ya doing "Crabby Appleton"?? It's the first day of school, barely a little over one hour into the school year and I got the opportunity to watch some poor teenage adolescent get it with both barrels from "Crabby Appleton." After a couple of minutes of witnessing this dressing down first hand by Coach Appleton I made up my mind to stay as far away from this mean, miserable, and maladjusted human being as I could. At least until track season starts.

Things finally calmed down in Study Hall and I actually recognized another student. I knew him as somebody that I have competed against in sports but have never ever spoken one word to him. This fellow was sitting next to Alex Felton and his name is Max Perry.

Max Perry is an even bigger mystery than Alex Felton. I've played basketball against Max Perry before, specifically during my junior high school days. Max Perry was an outstanding center and if I remember correctly, the "Flint Journal" named Max Perry as one of the top 10 junior high basketball players in the state of Michigan. Not just Livingston County. Not just Genesee County. The entire state of Michigan. And believe me, there's a ton of outstanding basketball players just within a 50-100 miles of the town of Hartland, let alone the whole state of Michigan.

However, similar to Alex Felton's disappearing act during track season, Max Perry's on the floor basketball contributions for the past three years have been pretty much nonexistent. He's become the Harry Houdini of the hardwood court. Max Perry has done a disappearing act. Now when I hear the name of Max Perry, I think of the guy who won the high jump at the conference meet last May, not as one of the top ten junior high basketball players in the entire "Great Lakes" state.

Neither Max Perry nor Alex Felton gave any hint of recognition of myself as they had their noses buried in what looked like a three-foot-thick Physics text book. Those two were plowing through the pages of that schoolbook just like I do when I read my "Sporting News" magazine on Saturday morning. I wanted to stroll over to Alex Felton and Max Perry and say, "Gimme a break, guys, it's the first day of school. You're making the rest of us look bad."

I thought twice about saying anything to them because if they understood the contents of the Physics book they were reading, then Max Perry and Alex Felton were intelligent enough to rig some fancy explosive device that could blow up the jeep. Now that would be a warm welcoming for the first day of school.

An interesting Study Hall session was completed and while heading to my third hour class I was suddenly reminded of a song that Katie used to sing along with from the cartoon show of "Tom Terrific" that went something like this:

"My name is Crabby Appleton, I'm rotten to the core. I do a bad deed every day, and sometimes three or four. I can't stand fun for anyone, I think good deeds are sappy, I laugh with glee, it pleases me, when everyone's unhappy."

Why do I suspect that these words will become the official "fight song" for second hour Study Hall?

"White Lake Road"

Chapter #12- "30-11-22"

Third Hour is Psychology Class. I have no clue as to why I signed up for this course. I've never really had any grandiose interest in the topic of psychology, not unless you count my watching episodes of the television series, "The Twilight Zone." There's some mind-blowing stuff on that show.

I suspect if I had not registered for Psychology Class it would not have interfered with my master plan of enlisting in either the Air Force or Coast Guard when I turn the age of 18, a little over a year from now. The real reason for me taking this class was more so of my way of getting out of taking a terrifying science or math class. I still have nightmares of Algebra I class from my freshman year. That's right, you heard me, Algebra I, not Algebra II.

So far the first few hours of my Hartland Consolidated Schools debut had me recognizing a few people but no one was still even paying attention to me. I mean no one!! Finally, ole Beardslee was acknowledged when a booming voice appeared mysteriously from the sky demanding an answer of the question, "You're Mary Beardslee's son aren't you?"

I looked to the front of the room and timidly shook my head in agreement to the asker of this all- important inquiry. At the same time, I was thinking to myself, "If this woman was a man, she could play the role of Sergeant Friday of the TV show, "Dragnet," better than the star of the series, Jack Webb, himself. In fact, she is probably more qualified than Jack Webb to play the same role that he starred in the movie "The Drill Instructor".

The booming voice belonged to the teacher of the class, Mrs. Gooden, whom I had actually met once in a visit to Crouse Elementary School located smack dab in "downtown" Hartland, Michigan. Mrs. Gooden was once a member of the "Women's Army Corps" (WAC) for 20 some years and after leaving the WAC's earned a teaching degree. Mrs. Gooden, who proudly went by the nickname of "Sarge", started her teaching career as a first-grade teacher at the Hartland Consolidated Schools.

According to my mother, Mrs. Gooden ran her first-grade classes just like a World War II military tactical operation. This was especially noticeable when getting the "troops" ready for outdoor recess during winter time. Her first graders had specific steps and a tight time frame to get on their snow boots and winter pants. My mother once mentioned that she didn't know if Mrs. Gooden's method of getting her first graders ready for recess was to teach them responsibility or for Mrs. Gooden to get them out of the classroom faster so that she could go and sneak a quick smoke in the teacher's lounge.

After receiving a direct order from Mrs. Gooden that as soon as I walked through the door way of "White Lake Road" I was to give my mother a big hug from "Sarge", class then started. While looking around the class room I again saw a few people that I recognized. Not only recognized but remembered one of the guys as specifically being a member of my mother's first of two 6th grade classes at Crouse Elementary School. His name is Steve Weldon.

While Steve Weldon was not one of the students that my mother gushed about like she did Steve Gilmore, she always described Steve Weldon as "Very bright and polite." My mother also added that Steve Weldon was quite typical of many of the students in her class, that his family was extremely poor. More than once my mother stated that she suspected that when Steve Weldon went home from school that there was no guarantee that there was any food on the table for him or his five brothers and sisters.

Any clothes that I had either out grown or books that I was done reading always ended up being given to Steve Weldon. My mother, who for many of the early years of her life was also raised dirt poor, would occasionally pack an extra sandwich for Steve Weldon under the guise of "My eyes are bigger than my stomach." That's how much she cared for Steve Weldon.

Steve Weldon has also turned out to be a halfway decent cross-country runner for Hartland High School so I'll be seeing him a lot during track season. But again, exactly like Alex Felton, where does Steve Weldon disappear to when it came time for dual meets and the league conference meet come track season? Maybe I won't be seeing a lot of him this spring.

I knew Tom Beaver from the Saturday morning catechism classes at St. John's School where he and "Big Jim" Hutchinson would come up from Hartland to join us Fenton, Lake Fenton and Linden attendees from 10:30 AM to 11:30 AM. Just a lousy way to spend a Saturday morning. Tom Beaver looked over in my direction in class this morning, but like Steve Weldon, showed no indication that he even remembered me.

Tom Beaver and I had faced each other many a time early on in our basketball careers. I remember him as an excellent one-on-one player that could foul out the opposing basketball team all by himself. Tom Beaver was constantly at the free throw line during a basketball game. Unlike Max Perry whose basketball career disappearing act started after the eighth grade, Tom Beaver continued to receive his share of playing time during his freshmen and sophomore seasons, but I never ever remember hearing or reading about him during the 1968-69 high school basketball season. I'm not sure if he was even on the Hartland varsity basketball squad last year.

Where Tom Beaver has been successful, however, at least from an athletic standpoint based upon more than a few articles I had read about him in the "Flint Journal", was that he was one of the best golfers in the Genesee-Livingston Conference. In fact, if Tom Beaver makes all-conference this spring, he will be the first golfer to earn that honor for four consecutive years.

After third hour was over I located where my locker is and it's just down from the band room. A couple of new things with the locker situation here at Hartland High School are that this is the first time in three years that I have a new locker combination. I had gotten used to my "30-11-22" locker combination. I could have been in a coma for 200 years and when coming out of that coma if the first question asked to me was, "What's your locker combination? I would have spit out "30-11-22" with no hesitation. This school year I am burdened with a new locker combination of, "0-29-9." However, it just doesn't have the sing songish sound of "30-11-22" to it, though.

Also, this year I get a locker all to my lonesome. I do not have to share a locker with another student like I did at Fenton High School. While buying school books for the beginning of my freshman year I discovered that unlike junior high, at the senior high level you had to share a locker with another member of the freshman class. Locker mate assignments were based upon alphabetical order of your last name.

I went into a panic when I learned this. According to my calculations I was going to have to share a locker with a kid by the name of Scott Berns. That was not good news.

Now just imagine a high school student with the physical build of the mythical character "Paul Bunyan". Now imagine this same high schooler riding a motorcycle through small towns leading a gang of motorcyclists in the terrorizing of these towns people and their homes. You have just met Scott Berns, potential locker mate extraordinaire.

Of all of the male athletes of the Fenton High School class of 1970, Scott Berns was head and shoulders above the rest. Scott Berns should have been the all-state football player, gone undefeated in wrestling, easily hit .500 in baseball and would have been outstanding in all of the field events in track.

Nope. Scott Berns decided to bypass the life of an outstanding Fenton High School athlete and instead traveled in the fast lane of being a juvenile delinquent and just a sharp curve away from leading a life of crime. Scott Berns was the type of kid who would steal tips off of the counter at Herllichs' Drug Store; steal gym clothes out of gym lockers; change grades on his report cards before his parents could see his actual grades; and threaten kids for their lunch money or lunches.

My biggest fear was that if Scott Berns was my locker mate that he or one of his gang would steal something of mine, keep it for themselves or sell it. I could also see Scott Berns and his posse pilfering some other poor kids stuff and blame the theft on me when the stolen item was found in our shared locker.

Christmas came early the first day of school in September of 1966 for old Beardslee. While I was in Homeroom, first hour, locker assignments were being given out. I had been dreading this day for weeks. I looked at the slip of paper with the locker information and saw that my locker number was "A-9" with a locker combination of "30-11-22." The best news in the world, however, was that my locker mate was not the feared hoodlum Scott Berns, but instead a kid by the name of Jay Barker.

Jay Barker had moved to Fenton from I believe Southfield, Michigan, where ever that is, literally at the end of my eighth-grade year. He was very quiet, seemed nice and absolutely loved the Detroit Red Wings. The day that I learned that he was going to be my locker mate I suspect that he was embarrassed about the fuss that I made over it. I was so ecstatic that you would have thought Jay Barker had just saved me from drowning in Byron Lake.

There will be individuals who will benefit from me not attending Fenton High School this school year. Someone else will be first chair trumpet. There will be a new band president.

There will even be a new 14th best player on a 13-person varsity basketball squad, an honor that I held last season. I just hope that Scott Berns does not replace Mike Beardslee as a locker mate for Jay Barker.

Give it a few years or maybe even months, but just imagine walking into a United States Post Office one day and when you look at the "Top Ten Most Wanted Criminals in the United States" posters to see if any of your blood relatives are listed, I guarantee you that Scott Berns' poster will be there for probably the 37th week in a row. When you spot his poster, you be sure and tell him that Mike Beardslee says, "30-11-22."

Up next is fourth hour.

"White Lake Road"

Chapter #13 – "T to the Third Power"

September 2nd – Fourth Hour means Band Class!! My all-time favorite hour of school!! I overheard a Fenton High School student by the name of Roger Klamert once say, "The only reason why I come to school is because of football." Guess what. The only reason why I get up in the morning on a school day is because I know that I will get to be in Band Class in a few hours. It's the very first thing I think about in the early A.M. and sometimes it's the only thing I think about, with the exception of reading a "Sporting News" magazine and hoping that there are reruns of the TV series, "Girl from U.N.C.L.E" on any time of day or night."

Upon officially entering the band room for the first time as a Hartland Consolidated Schools student, despite the numerous times I had been in this band room prior to this moment, I noticed two things that were different from the Fenton High School Band Room. First, the Hartland High School Band Room had a double door entrance whereas my former school's entrance way consisted of two separate and typical class room doors. How did Bill Wilhoit and other sousaphone players ever get themselves and their sousaphones through those doors? The latter would have been fun to watch during a fire or tornado drill.

The second difference between these two rooms was that there were tiers of bleachers for the band to sit and rehearse at Hartland, just as you would have for a concert. At Fenton High School, it again was like a typical class room with all chairs even on the floor. We never sat on bleachers until we played in a concert. Man, oh man, why am I even thinking about the Fenton High School Band Room on my first day as a student of an entirely new school system??

There is one tradition that I continued this morning but with a little variation to the past years for the first day of Band. Fenton High School was not famous for growing their own first chair trumpet players. Carl Peters, Ray Sortman and Guy Thompson are all proof of that. All three of them moved in from other school districts and at one time or another throughout their band careers at Fenton High School were first chair trumpet players. And if Mike Kakuska, who had moved from the state of Illinois to Fenton, Michigan had decided to pursue a band career rather than strictly an athletic career at Fenton High School, he would have been in the running for the first chair trumpet honors as well.

I vividly remember Guy Thompson's words to me just before he graduated from Fenton High School in June of 1968. "You better hope that a great trumpet player moves into the Fenton Area School district over the summer, because if one doesn't, then the trumpet section for next year here is going to be in a lot of trouble!!" Ouch!!

That was always my fear over the summer while walking the 51 acres of "White Lake Road." Everyone associated with the Fenton High School Band thought that Ray Sortman was the greatest trumpet player ever in the history of Fenton High School. But guess what, the next school year Carl Peters moves to the city of Fenton and not only became first chair trumpet of the Fenton Senior Band but was a big factor in seeing Ray Sortman move to play another instrument, the baritone. A sad way for Ray Sortman to finish out his band career at Fenton High School.

"White Lake Road"

First chair trumpet players typically have large egos and when it comes to trumpet playing, I am no different. However, I still cross my fingers every night that when I wake up for a school morning that Guy Thompson's warning does not becomes a reality and I do not suffer the same trumpet playing "death" that Ray Sortman did.

The difference on this school day, however, was that I am the "hunter" rather than the "hunted". For the first three years of my private lesson taking with Mr. Anderson he constantly talked about his students, specifically David Reagan and Mary Ann Timmons. The instruments that those two "greatest musicians ever" played respectively were trumpet and saxophone. Mr. Anderson couldn't shut up about those two soon enough as far as I was concerned, especially when it came to David Reagan.

Mr. Anderson up through my eighth-grade year was always comparing me to David Reagan. "His tone is better than yours." "David Reagan is starting to double tongue and triple tongue just as good as some of my senior high school trumpet players." "The same etudes that you play I can have David Reagan put a sharp or a flat in front of every note and he can transpose those same exercises immaculately."

To say the least, I had had it up to the Moon with David Reagan. But strangely enough over the last few years of private lesson taking I rarely ever heard David Reagan's or even Mary Ann Timmons' names being spoken from the lips of Mr. Anderson. Not that it bothered me any. But once the selection of attending the Hartland Consolidated Schools was made, I started to give a lot of thought about David Reagan and his tone being better than mine; his far superior triple and double-tonguing skills to my own; and David Reagan's talent to transpose music with numerous flats or sharps in front of every note while simultaneously leaping tall buildings in a single bound.

Before my problems with my front teeth slowed me down, every time I practiced the trumpet I was trying to prepare myself for battle with Dave Reagan for the first chair trumpet position of the Hartland Senior Band. The lip slur drills, double and triple tonguing exercises, increasing my ability to play scales with more sharps and flats and trying to increase my range higher than "high C" was done with the intent of now having Dave Reagan cringe every time he had to hear about my trumpet playing ability.

However, when my eyes searched around the band room this morning, I did not see Dave Reagan. I just assumed Dave Reagan heard that Mike Beardslee was in town and that caused him to run home from school crying to his momma. At least that's the rumor I'm thinking about having Jim Koop start spreading around Hartland High School.

I casually asked one of the band kids which person was Dave Reagan. The answer I received was shocking. "He and Mary Ann Timmons got drunk one-night last winter and eventually had to get married. She is staying home with their new born son and Dave Reagan is now working full time in some factory in the city of Pontiac." Wow, maybe that triple tonguing is more lethal than I thought.

My eyes continued to explore the band room and who I did and did not see over the next few seconds was thought provoking.

"White Lake Road"

Chapter #14 – "F.W. Dixon"

September 2nd – I saw Jim Koop sitting in a chair all by his lonesome. As I walked towards him he shot me a look that had, "Beardslee, what did we get ourselves into here?" written all over his face. I'm not so sure.

I then looked over to the other side of the Band Room and there was Terry Rodenbo and Katie sitting with some of the Hartland Band members just talking and laughing it up like they had been students of the Hartland Consolidated Schools since Kindergarten. Those two get along with anybody and were acting as what a first day of school should be like.

I looked to the south end of the band room and saw the red-haired girl with emerald green eyes sitting across from me. There was no recognition on her part of me; no walking across the band room to welcome myself and Jim Koop to the Hartland Senior Band; and no show of concern as to how my teeth were going to affect my trumpet playing ability for marching band season. Nothing!! It's still good to see that my knack to have a crush on a pretty girl and that same pretty girl not even knowing that I even exist, crosses county lines.

My mother's past trips to the Smith-Bridgman's Department store in down town Flint to purchase all of my beloved "Hardy Boy Books" authored by "F.W. Dixon" has finally paid off. I used all of the detective skills that Mr. Fenton Hardy, Frank Hardy, Joe Hardy and Chet Morton used in those novels solving mysteries all over the world to learn the identity of the red-haired girl with emerald green eyes' name. When Mr. Anderson called off the name of Teri Andrews, she raised her hand. Piece of cake. If Chet Morton can solve a whodunit, so can Mike Beardslee.

The person sitting next to Teri Andrews was what caught my attention next. That would be a guy who had the looks of a basketball center/high hurdler and he was dressed to the hilt. The crease in his pants was so sharp that you could cut my mother's Saturday evening meal of pork chops with them. The penny loafers on his feet were so shiny that you didn't need a mirror to make sure that the part in your hair was straight. The yellow shirt the guy was wearing was so brilliant looking that the shirt itself could have passed an Algebra II class with straight A's. That's right, you heard me, Algebra II, not Algebra I. The only thing missing from this fellows clothing ensemble was an ascot tie; a blazer; and a pipe, just like the one Sherlock Holmes would puff on.

From my angle, I could see that the Teri Andrews, and whom my crackerjack investigative skills would later uncover the identity of her companion to be named Greg Sanders, were holding hands and sitting so close to each other that you could not fit a piece of notebook paper between them. Jim Koop saw me gawking at the two of them and said, "I betcha he's a drummer, Beardslee." Ha Ha.

I finally remembered where I had seen the kid that earlier had provided me an update of Dave Reagan and Mary Ann Timmons. My streak of analytical abilities continued as his raised hand corresponded with Mr. Anderson saying the name, Jason Shattuck. Clue #2 showed Jason Shattuck tapping his fingers on a trombone case. That tells me he plays the trombone.

"White Lake Road"

Man, I'm getting so good at this business of diagnosing clues I should change my name to "F.W. Beardslee"

Last year Fenton High School had hosted the Genesee-Livingston County League Freshmen Basketball Tournament. I was "volunteered" to work that three-day tourney. The Brighton High School Freshmen team was picked to easily win the necessary three games to become champions with maybe a slight threat from the Fenton and Swartz Creek teams. The remaining basketball squads, including the Hartland Eagles, were considered non-factors and would probably have no effect on the tourney outcome.

Hartland opened up against Swartz Creek in game number one of the tournament and behind 20 some points and double figure rebounds by Jason Shattuck, Hartland led the whole game and presented some excitement for a tournament that was mainly attended by parents and cheer leaders, by upsetting one of the better teams in the competition. The next game for Hartland was against the host team, Fenton, and despite an extremely quiet first half by Jason Shattuck, his individual strong second half performance carried the Hartland Eagles to a three-point win over Fenton for Hartland's second consecutive upset victory.

Despite another 20 some point performance and numerous blocked shocks by Jason Shattuck, the Brighton Bulldogs blasted the Hartland Eagles 57-34 to win the freshmen tournament for their fourth time in five years. Jason Shattuck for his efforts was named to the all-tournament team. Well, Mr. Jason Shattuck, I just hope you are half as good of trombone player as you are a basketball player.

I continued to look at the band members that were sitting where low brass players traditionally assemble in band rehearsals. In addition to Dave Reagan and Mary Ann Timmons not being current members of the Hartland Senior Band, I did not notice any other Hartland students who were band members of Mr. Anderson's 6th grade band that he and my mother just raved about.

Missing people included Jimmy Young. Not a half band trombone player and whom my mother said someday would become a world-famous scientist. Herman Libbs?? He thought that he was a good trombone player but was mediocre at best. Jim "Big Jim" Hutchinson?? My mother always said that he was one of the nicest and shyest boys that she had ever met and a pretty decent baritone player as well. All three of them nowhere to be seen. Come to think of it I have not seen any of these guys walking in the hall ways of Hartland High School this morning, either. Where did they all disappear to? Planet Zectron??

One of the books in the "Hardy Boys" series is titled "Missing Chums." Did F.W. Dixon write another "Hardy Boy" manuscript titled "The Missing Band Kids" and Smith-Bridgman's was sold out of them when my mother was shopping there one Saturday afternoon?? Hmmmm.

However, the one student that my mother just oozed about, even more than Steve Gilmore, strangely enough, while currently nowhere to be seen in the Hartland High School Band Room, was soon to make his presence known.

"White Lake Road"

Chapter #15 – "Two Lessons Learned"

September 2nd – As Jim Koop and I sat eating our lunches in silence, we saw across the lunch room Terry Rodenbo and Katie once more laughing it up with a crowd of kids. And this bunch of Hartland High School students were a totally different batch than what we saw our traveling companions yakking it up just 10 minutes ago in Band class.

I said to Jim Koop, "You know, all we're going to hear about on the way home tonight from those two is what a great place Hartland High School is and all of the new friends that they made today." Jim Koop's response was, "Not if we leave now and without them." It's tempting, very tempting.

As I was getting ready to bite into my bologna sandwich, a person walked up to me and said, "You probably don't remember me but my name is Mark Nevers." Ah, the infamous Mark Nevers. My mother's all-time favorite student of her six plus years of full time teaching and the son that she never had. My mother just absolutely loved Mark Nevers, another member of her first sixth grade class at Cromine Elementary School.

When I was a sixth grader at State Road Elementary School for whatever reason one day there was no school for students in the Fenton Area School district. And I don't know what got into me as this is something that Katie would do, not me, but I asked my mother if I could go to school with her and be a part of her sixth-grade class. My mother agreed to the suggestion and even sounded thrilled by the idea. Thus, for one school day, I was an honorary sixth grade student of the Hartland Consolidated Schools.

Overall, my visit had been very nice and I even had the opportunity to attend a sixth-grade band practice. As I sat and listened to this bunch of elementary school kids rehearse I was shocked at how much better they were than the State Road Elementary School Band that I was a member. The elementary school band that I belonged to was belting out classics like "Bobby Shafto" and "Hot Cross Buns." The Cromine Elementary School sixth grade band was playing John Phillip Sousa marches. And quite well I might add.

Mark Nevers that day had taken me under his wing to make sure I knew where to go for any class room changes, where the lunch room was, etc. Mark Nevers was a former trumpet player who had made the switch to play the baritone. And in listening to him play at that rehearsal Mark Nevers was far better than any baritone player that we had in the State Road Elementary School Band.

That same night my mother gave Mark Nevers a ride home and once there, Mark Nevers took out his trumpet and started to play a couple of lines of an etude. In looking at the music he was playing I noticed that there were a lot of black notes on that sheet of music and it was rather obvious I was not able to play the trumpet at the same level of Mark Nevers. After finishing the etude Mark Nevers handed me his trumpet and said, "Go ahead. Your turn."

Thank goodness, my mother stepped in and said it was time to go because if I would have had to play that same etude that Mark Nevers had just completed, it would have been embarrassing. I don't know who it would have been more humiliated by my performance, myself or my mother, but I can assure you that it would have been a really, really quiet ride back to "White Lake Road" that evening.

I learned a very valuable lesson from Mark Nevers that day. Up to that point in time even on a good day I was a very mediocre trumpet player and was not taking the playing of the trumpet very serious at all. I was third chair in the trumpet section at State Road Elementary School behind two fifth graders, Kathy Smith and Dennis Scott. One day the State Road Elementary School Band put on a little concert for the rest of the school and when my sixth-grade buddies saw that two "little fifth graders" were better than me, I really heard about it. "Those fifth graders are better than you, Beardslee?? That's embarrassing!!" And they were right.

My mother later arranged for me to take private lessons from Mr. Anderson. That was step one in the right direction for my trumpet playing career. Step number two was that on my own I started to take practicing the trumpet more meaningful. The 30 minutes that my mother usually had to force me into practice in our kitchen at "White Lake Road" was no longer a torture for me to do. It eventually got to the point that my mother did not have to tell me when to practice the trumpet. I was now practicing on my own and actually enjoying it.

I knew that I was making progress of becoming a half way decent trumpet player when one day near the end of my sixth-grade year, there was a band class called "Sectionals", where only the individual sections of the band would meet with Miss Franklin, the elementary school band director. For whatever reason that day I was the only trumpet player to show up for class. I showed Miss Franklin the etude book that Mr. Anderson was having me use and Miss Franklin, an accomplished trombone player, and I started to play duets from that book. I held my own and when I saw other teachers at State Road pop their heads in the school gymnasium and say, "Hey, you guys sound good," that was when I knew that my embarrassment of being a second-rate trumpet player was closer to becoming a thing of the past.

While Mark Nevers was talking to myself and Jim Koop out of nowhere an instant recall popped up in my mind and I suddenly remembered the moment that I learned that Mark Nevers was no longer a member of the Hartland High School Senior Band.

During my freshman year, my mother was carting me back from my trumpet private lesson when she stopped to buy gas. The person who came out to pump the gas was none other than Mark Nevers, himself. My mother was just absolutely thrilled to see Mark Nevers and so proud of him that he was holding down a job. That joy turned to disappointment for my mother when she asked Mark Nevers how did he enjoy being in senior band? Mark Nevers's response was, "I'm not in band any longer. Some of the guys that I hang out with told me that I should cut out from band, so I did."

It was a silent ride home to "White Lake Road" that evening. Even more hushed than the previous ride of three years ago from Mark Nevers's house. This time there were slight tears in my mother's eyes for 13.9 miles of this 14-mile drive. It made no sense to her that a student like Mark Nevers that was so dedicated and talented in band would simply quit with no real logical reason. I must admit that I didn't understand the logic of, "I should cut out from band,

so I did." This was especially surprising coming from the Mark Nevers that I had met and heard so much about.

Kids' dropping out of band was nothing new to me. I saw it every year at Fenton. Rarely do kids who start out in elementary school band last all of the way through their entire high school years. In fact, of all of us fourth graders who started out in band at State Road Elementary School, only Sally Helmboldt and I were still in band as of our junior year at Fenton. And now that I'm gone, Sally Helmboldt is the lone remaining member of the State Road Elementary Beginner's Band from November of 1961.

During my fourth grade through seventh grade band years, the Fenton High School Senior Band was outstanding. They would annually get an "I" rating, the highest rating possible, at District and State Band Festivals. In addition to the talented musicians in the band, there were also, regardless of their individual musical skills, numerous dedicated student leaders. I.E., Bruce Helmboldt, who later a member of the Michigan State University Marching Band, Marlene Becker, Jim Welsh, Don Smith, Jerry Collins, Connie Foley and Carl Peters. The list could go on and on for this exceptional group of Fenton Senior Band members.

The average size of a high school band in the state of Michigan is probably 60 students. Of those 60 students, at least 10 of them are truly devoted to the point where band is the most important thing in their life. Of those 10 students, maybe half at best are truly musicians that are talented enough to go beyond the high school level and pursue a music career.

The wheels started to fall off the Fenton Senior Band program after my seventh-grade year. This was when all of the first and second chair players in all of the sections of the band graduated. Then, for whatever reason, the third and fourth chair players quit band. That now meant that your fifth and sixth chair players, mostly under classman, now had to take over the lead music positions and the student leadership of the band. There are very few sophomores and freshmen that from a performance and leadership standpoint are prepared to take on this responsibility. "The Flying Dutchman" and I bordered on it but as sophomores we were still light years from being the same quality of musicians and leaders as the above-named people.

The departure of these band students sent the Fenton High School Band in such a funk that the band director at the time, Mr. Frank Tambourino, made the bold decision to include selected eighth graders to be in senior band. There was no doubt that Mike Beardslee was going to be one of eighth graders selected as my mother would not have it any other way. So, I and about 10 or other so eighth graders became members of the Fenton High School Senior Band. The best part of that was now we got to have 5th hour lunch!! Only two more classes to go and you were done for the day!!

Due the youth of the band and a large lack of talent, with the exception of my sophomore year, when there was a little blip on the radar showing some improvement, those Fenton Senior Bands I was a member of were bad. I mean really bad!!

I realized today that much like the band kids I started out with at State Road Elementary, the sixth graders of six years ago that were Mr. Anderson's pride and joy, appear to be long gone

from the Hartland band scene. Come to think of it, of the roughly 40 members of the Hartland Senior Band sitting in the band room this morning, I betcha at the most there were 5-10 combined seniors and juniors in attendance. That means that at least 75% of this band will consist of sophomores and freshmen. As I have learned over the past few years, this is not a formula for success.

Unless you have some strong leadership from your seniors and juniors it could allow for band members to become a member of "the walking dead" instead of being a member of a vibrant senior band that was capable of being special. I have witnessed the "walking dead theory" in three of my four years as a member of the Fenton Senior Band. Those were not fun or productive band seasons.

A perfect example of this was last year when the senior band was scheduled to have the band picture taken. We had to be in our band uniforms for the photo shoot and Miss Franklin recommended that due to the time constraints of the picture shoot there was no time allowed for us to change into our band uniforms. Her suggestion was that we wear our band uniforms throughout the entire school day. There was such a back lash from us band kids for this request, myself included, and that Miss Franklin backed off of the idea.

Looking back on that day I wondered what made me be so embarrassed to wear my band uniform to my non-band classes? I should have been proud to wear that band uniform but I was not. The question now was which was worse, Mark Nevers "cutting out from band" entirely or myself, still being a member of the band but "cutting out from band" in a different sort of way.

Speaking with Mark Nevers today made me realize that I had learned two valuable lessons from him even if they were almost six years apart. 1) He helped me realize that I was an embarrassment as a trumpet player and if I was ever going to improve it was going to take more than my mother forcing me to practice every night. At some point, it was going to have to come from me.

The second learned lesson from today's conversation was that I was not running to become a member of the Hartland High School Senior Band, but rather, I was running away from being a member of the Fenton High School Band. At some point during this upcoming school year I will have to decide whether or not I am going to again be embarrassed to be seen in my band uniform for band functions and non-band classes.

It's been a long day already with my fifth hour class only a few minutes away from starting. And I am still not even half way through my bologna sandwich.

Chapter #16 "Charlies Conditioning Camp"

September 2nd - After the completion of my soul-searching lunch hour, my next class is "Michigan History" with a Mr. Vickers as the instructor. I'm actually looking forward to this course. It's unbelievable how little I know about the state of Michigan considering I have lived here for almost 17 years. Oh, I can name all of the Great Lakes, but if you asked me for directions to Lake Erie I would have no clue how to get you there.

Other tidbits about the state of Michigan that I'm also incapable of explaining include: I have no idea how the city of Lansing became the capital of the state of Michigan; there are many major rivers in the state of Michigan but the only two that I'm really aware of are the Flint and Shiawassee Rivers. And the only thing I really know about the Flint River is that the good people of Flint, Michigan used to swim in it years ago. Now, however, I read and hear that the Flint River is so unclean that a person wouldn't even consider sticking their big toe in it.

When I was in third grade my teacher, Mr. Dan Williams, asked me to point out the state of Michigan on a United States map. I had no clue where to find my home state and got laughed at pretty good from the rest of the class. That's when I first learned that the state of Michigan is shaped like a mitten.

I've gotten better since third grade. Not only can I name all of the Great Lakes, but you'll be happy to know that nine years later I am still capable of finding the state of Michigan on a United States map plus; that the city of Mackinac is not spelled with a "w."

Locally, I can find my way around the town of Fenton pretty good. And I think that I could even get to down town Flint on my own pretty easily. But if you asked me for directions to cities like Clarenceville, Dearborn Heights, Garden City or Livonia, there is no way that I could get you there. My directions would cause you to either end up in the Upper Peninsula or the state of Ohio. And depending how much you like to drive, maybe both places in the same day.

Once settled in class I heard a commotion behind me and spotted two guys that were getting razzed big time by other class members. The pair looked like they were poster boys for a United States Marine Corp recruiting office. Their faces were extremely tanned and they had the U.S. Marine type buzz haircut.

Apparently the two guys had just recently attended a football camp by the name of "Charlie's Conditioning Camp" and were entertaining their classmates with accounts of having to run up "Suicide Hill" for conditioning purposes, carrying large logs on their shoulders in team races and doing extended pushups. I have no idea what an extended pushup is and I don't think I ever want to know.

"White Lake Road"

I had previously heard of "Charlie's Conditioning Camp" from my old Study Hall buddy, Steve Anderson, at Fenton High School last year. He and a couple of Fenton footballers went there to get in shape for the start of two a day practices for the beginning of football season. I didn't get a blow by blow description of what took place at "Charlie's Conditioning Camp" from Steve Anderson. All I ever got out of him was that "Charlie's Conditioning Camp" was where "high school football players went to die."

I did recognize the two "celebrities" as Pete Mason and Tom Moran. Both were basketball opponents throughout the past few years but like some of the earlier basketball rivals I have mentioned, I do not remember seeing either one of these two on the basketball court last year at all.

I do remember Tom Moran from the junior high basketball games as having an outstanding jump shot. It seemed like he was always open and never missed a shot. I remembered Pete Mason more for being a half way decent 100-yard dash sprinter from the past few track seasons as he placed in the conference finals of that event. Strangely enough, I don't ever remember him running the 220-yard dash. Usually if you run the 100-yard dash you automatically run the 220-yard event.

I was happy and envious with the reception that those two received from their classmates. It was such a joyous moment, that even myself, a total stranger, also wanted to get in on the action and say, "Wow!! Your hair is shorter than Sergeant Carter's of the Gomer Pyle" TV show!!" And then proceed to rub their buzz cut heads like everyone else in "Michigan History" class was doing. And since I do not know where Pete Mason's and Tom Moran's skulls have been recently, I would then immediately drive straight to the M-59 Truck Stop as fast as I could and drown my hands with gasoline. Premium, not regular.

As I was walking to my sixth hour class I thought to myself that that was what a first day of school should be like. Friends being delighted to see each other after a long summer vacation. Would it have been like that for me if I was a still a student of Fenton High School? I really don't know. But I can dream and I can visualize my buddies saying to me, "Hey, Beardslee!! How was Interlochen?? Glad to see you made it back from the mountains, Beardslee!!" At least that is what my little mind hopes would have taken place.

One more class to go and the last hour of what has been so far, a very disheartening day.

"White Lake Road"

Chapter #17- "30 Seconds"

September 2nd – Sixth Hour and the last session of the day is Civics/Economics Class. These classes will be broken up into two semesters. In my case I will be taking the Economics section this current semester.

This Economics Class actually scares me quite a bit. I have always heard that it is a difficult course and other than "Buy low and sell high", I know nothing about the concepts of economics. I betcha I know more about the subject of Algebra I than I do about economics.

What makes these two courses worse, though, is you have to pass both of them in order to graduate from high school. I mean you have to pass these babies to get your high school diploma no matter how well you do in any of your other your school programs. Plain and simple as that. And I thought that there was pressure to pass Drivers Education and get a driver's license!!

At the beginning of every school year at Fenton High School I would notice a student or two whom you had assumed had already graduated with the previous senior class. But there they were all bright-eyed and bushy-tailed right back at dear old Fenton High School for their first day of "Grade 13". Right, cousin Davey??

When I walked into this classroom I saw that the students already there were in a cheerful mood. They kept shouting to each other the phrase, "30 seconds!! 30 Seconds!!" They were squealing with delight after saying the phrase "30 Seconds" numerous times.

I had no clue what was so funny about the expression "30 Seconds "so I tapped a student on the shoulder and asked why everyone in the class was laughing so hilariously over the term "30 Seconds"?? Well that question brought the level of joviality from just a group of kids laughing to the point that they were now in a whistling, stomping their feet on the floor, and throwing money on the stage frame of mind.

After getting a look that read, "Where have you been? The Moon??" (Yes, as a matter of fact I have. Me, Neil Armstrong and Buzz Aldrin just got back from there a little over six weeks ago) I finally got a response as to why the "30 Seconds" saying was such a big deal.

The class teacher, Mr. Collins, has this thing that if a class gets out of control even slightly, he yells out "30 Seconds!!" That means that a class now has to wait 30 seconds till after the bell has rung before they can finally go to your next class or to leave school. If you get two "30 Seconds" called out on the same class now you have the added pressure of being tardy for your next class; missing the school bus or being late for an after-school event. Why do I get the feeling that those "30 Seconds" are going to feel instead like "30 minutes?"

The pattern of slight detections of people whose paths had crossed with me continued during 6th hour. One guy who I was pretty sure a cross country runner by the name of Al Dowty was sitting a couple of rows across from me. I remembered hearing about Al Dowty being named as the captain of the Hartland Cross Country team as a junior. That's an impressive honor.

"White Lake Road"

Athletic teams just don't give out an accolade like team captain to high school juniors every day.

I also think that a one Mr. Al Dowty placed in the top seven runners in the Genesee-Livingston County Cross Country League Meet last year, which is the equivalent of making first team all-conference. In addition, if I remember correctly, Al Dowty was even a half-way decent sixth man off the bench in basketball as well.

But even if Mr. F.W. Dixon, himself, sat me down in the confines of "White Lake Road," I'm not so sure that even that best-selling mystery writer could explain to me why Al Dowty, who was such a good cross country runner never placed or possibly ever ran in the league meet for track season. That was still a mystery to me. If you place in the top seven runners in the cross-country league meet, there are enough running events in a track meet for a talented runner to excel in and get points.

The other student I recognized while waiting for "30 Seconds" to be yelled out was sitting one seat up and over to my left. I knew his name as well, Ric Adams.

Ric Adams was the starting point guard during his two years at the junior high level for the Hartland Consolidated Schools. Like Max Perry, Ric Adams was considered one of the 10 best junior high players, regardless of position, in the state of Michigan. When Ric Adams had the basketball in his hands, his passing skills were so fantastic that he reminded me of former Boston Celtic great and current Cincinnati Royals head coach, Bob "The Cooz" Cousy. I still vividly remember some of those Ric Adams full court bounce passes that led to uncontested layups for his teammates.

That Hartland Junior High basketball team was superior to any opponent that they faced. Their nickname was, "The UCLA of Junior High Basketball", a takeoff of Coach John Wooden's UCLA basketball squad, of which, I am a huge fan, that had been winning the NCAA basketball championship if my math is correct four of the past five college basketball seasons.

I don't know who tagged the Hartland Junior High Basketball team with this nick name, but it certainly was appropriate. "The UCLA of Junior High Basketball" was definitely as good as their undefeated record of 15-0 over the course of two seasons would suggest.

But there was some unknown about Ric Adams just as there was with some of the Hartland athletes I have commented on earlier. Ric Adams' mystery, however, was different than the others. In his case the question to me was, what was one of the best junior high guards in the state of Michigan upon entering high school doing being a member of the freshmen basketball team rather than being on the junior varsity basketball team? Or even go the route that a former Fenton High School basketball player, Bobby Niles did, and make the varsity squad as a freshman?

That's question number one. The second question is, much like with Max Perry, Tom Moran, Al Dowty, Alex Felton, Tom Beaver and Pete Mason, where has Ric Adams been as an on-

court basketball contributor for the past two years?? I betcha I have gotten more playing time than Ric Adams did for his sophomore and junior years combined.

No way would have any of the varsity basketball coaches in the "GL Conference" have ever predicted that coming out of junior high that all of these members of "The UCLA of Junior High Basketball" team would have become more anonymous than myself from a basketball playing standpoint. Let's face it, you look up in the dictionary the phrase "Anonymous Basketball Player" you would find a picture of me sitting on the bench during a basketball game enjoying the sounds and tunes of the local high school basketball pep band.

I know one thing for sure, if I make the Hartland Consolidated Schools Varsity Basketball team this season and have the privilege of appearing on the basketball court simultaneously with Ric Adams, I'd better be real ready for one of his renowned no-look passes. If not, my father's eye vision insurance through General Motors will be shelling out plenty of money for some new black horn-rimmed spectacles for me.

The sixth hour Economics class must have been the recipient of a "First Day of School Special" as Mr. Collins did not tag us with a "30 Seconds" today.

"White Lake Road"

Chapter #18 - "The University of Fenton"

September 2nd – The end of the first day of school as an official member of the Hartland Consolidated Schools system for me was finally completed. Once it dawned on me that I had driven a car to school and not ridden a school bus I then sprinted to the jeep as fast as my 56.9 flat 440 Run legs would take me. Jim Koop who has never run a day of track or cross country in his life and has smoked more than a few cigarettes over the past few years was right with me every step of the way. In fact, Jim Koop would have gotten to the jeep first if he hadn't hesitated for a second in trying to decide which rear passenger door he was going to use to enter the jeep.

Within the first 15 seconds of stepping inside of Hartland High School this morning, deep down inside I knew that I had made a huge blunder in not attending Fenton High School for my senior year. Man, even Holy Redeemer High School with their mandatory dress code of tuxedos, top hats and tails, learning a couple of thousand lines of Latin a day, plus having to go to church every Friday morning, was looking really good at this very moment.

Terry Rodenbo and Katie, however, were approaching the jeep in a much different manner than mine and Jim Koop. Those two were waving good bye to their new friends and saying that they would see them tomorrow at lunch time. Terry Rodenbo and Katie then entered the jeep jabbering about a thousand words a minute sounding like the two magpie cartoon characters, "Heckle and Jeckle", going on about how much that they had enjoyed their first day of their new high school. How come those two aren't miserable like I am??

My mother arrived home from her first day of school at State Road Elementary School about 30 minutes after Katie and myself. She was very quiet and it was obvious that something was bothering her. It's not like my mother to ever let the two of us kids in on any of her problems or burdens of the world that she carries. Since this was the first day of the school year I wondered if she got stuck with a real trouble making kid in her class room, which would then lead to a long school year, or does she have a new principal that was hired from outside of the Fenton School district and now has she to learn somebody else's ways of doing things.

With the opening of the new Fenton High School the Fenton Area Schools have now gone to a middle school concept rather than having a traditional junior high school. That means that grades 6th-8th will now reside in the old Fenton High School where Katie and I had spent our last few years. My former sixth grade teacher, Mr. Roger O'Berry, will now be at the middle school. Mr. O'Berry had a nice big class room at State Road Elementary and always promised my mother that if he ever left State Road Elementary School she could have his room. That now meant she would have to move all of her school stuff across the hall way. This also means that one-day next week I will be tapped on the shoulder and have to perform some manual labor. Come on, Mr. O'Berry, would it have killed you to have stayed at State Road Elementary School??

That was my first guess about the troubled looks my mother carried throughout supper. Later that evening Katie got the full scoop and advised me that my mother was getting some severe criticism from several of her fellow teachers, who for whatever reason, were not taking too kindly to the fact that an employee of the Fenton Public Area Schools was sending two of her children, both of whom who still reside in the Fenton Area School district, to another public-school system to continue their education.

That was blasphemy in the eyes of these handful of co-workers and I betcha all the money on Planet Zectron that those same teachers wouldn't have blinked an eyelash if Katie and I had ended up at Holy Redeemer High School. It's a common practice in Genesee County for students to leave a public-school system and end up at the Holy Redeemer's, St. Michael's, Flint St. Mary', St. Matthew' and Flint Holy Rosary's of the world. But rarely do you see students transfer from one public school to another public-school system that does not involve a family move or some type of shenanigan concerning athletics.

My mother's situation is also compounded by the fact that the Fenton School Board had an emergency school millage election passed in the last few days after Katie and I had been enrolled in the Hartland Consolidated Schools. This now meant that all the school curriculum activities that had been slashed as part of the austerity budget were now restored at Fenton High School for the 1969-70 school year.

This fact became known to all of us in the confines of "White Lake Road" the next morning after the votes were officially tallied. But even with that major change of events there was no indication that either Katie or I would be leaving the Hartland Consolidated Schools to come back to our old stomping grounds. Furthermore, Mrs. Cooper and Mrs. Rodenbo had shown no interest in having their sons come back to the Fenton Area Schools either.

I strongly suspect that my mother will now be getting a lot of, "Mary, when are your children coming back to Fenton High School to continue their education??" from her fellow co-workers. The last time any issue of where Katie and I were to attend school was when St. John's Church was putting a big push for all of their parishioners with young school age students to attend St. John's School. Shockingly my mother left that decision solely up to Katie and me with the decision being made to stay with the Fenton Area Schools.

However, once the two of us had enrolled into the Hartland Consolidated Schools system there was no getting in the time machine and playing the "Lets guess where Katie and Mike are going to being attending school this year" game all over again. Hint: The selected school is 28 miles away round trip and due south on U.S. 23.

It sounds like my mother had herself one crummy day, even crummier than the one I had. The good news for my mother and I is that there are only 179 more school days left in the school year.

Despite getting a telephone call this evening from my good buddy, Pat "The Flying Dutchman" Goode, it made my day even more depressing. The purpose of the phone call was primarily to see how my first day of school went. However, "The Dutchman" went into great length of what HIS first day of school was like at the new Fenton High School.

"The Dutchman" pointed out the following:

- ***Size of Fenton High School – "The Dutchman's" big concern was the length of Fenton High School and whether students that had to go from one end of the building to the other end could make it in the five minutes allotted between classes. As "The Dutchman" put it, "You'll have to be pushing coals to make it."***

- ***Swimming Pool – The new high school will have a swimming pool and Fenton High School will field a swim team for the first time ever for this school year.***

- ***Auditorium – There will be an auditorium where assemblies and concerts will be held. The seats will be cushioned!! That will certainly beat sitting on those hard bleachers or folding chairs for these same events when held in the gymnasium of the old high school.***

- ***Gymnasium – The new gymnasium, despite not being currently completed will seat 3,000 people, three times as many as the previous school's gymnasium. I'm not even sure that the town of Fenton even has a population of 3,000 people.***

- ***New Football Stadium – Instead of wooden bleachers where the Fenton Tigers faithful had to sit on cold football nights, they will now be sitting on cement seats for these same chilly football evenings.***

- ***All Weather Track – This one really hurts. For years, the Fenton High School track and cross country teams had to do their workouts on a grass field. That is probably why Fenton rarely ever hosted home track meets. This is just great and the story of my life. Fenton High School now has an all-weather track and I am attending another high school that doesn't.***

- ***The band room was huge as was Miss Franklin's office. Now instead of shelves to store instruments, there was an "Instrument Room." My, my. The Dutchman also pointed out that within a week, yard lines were going to be painted on a parking lot at five-yard intervals to be used for marching band practice. Not only am I out of using an all-weather track I'm also out the use of an "all-weather marching band practice field" for my senior year. Am I jealous yet?? As Dick Martin of "Rowan and Martin's Laugh-In" TV series would say, "You bet your sweet bippy I am!!The Dutchman's description of what I am missing out on from strictly a new school point does make the decision to attend Hartland High School much harder to swallow. Based up the portrayal of the new Fenton High School it has a lot of amenities that Hartland High School does not. And to be honest, I'm not even sure Hartland High School is even on par with the old Fenton High School.***

The new high school was supposed to open in the fall of 1968 and the class of 1969 was to be the first to graduate from the new high school. However, money and construction delays postponed the debut of the new high school. Now, my former classmates, the class of 1970, have the honors of being the first graduating class of the new high school. That's a part of history that I am going to miss out on and disappoints me greatly.

"White Lake Road"

The editor of the "Fenton Independent", Robert Sibling, wrote a scathing article that was opposed to the building of a new Fenton High School. He specifically stated that this school structure was so large that with all the additional "bells and whistles" that the building will eventually contain, it should not be called Fenton High School, but rather instead should be hailed as "The University of Fenton."

The new Fenton High School had brought about a lot of heated debate. There was the faction that said, "The old high school was good enough for me, so it's good enough for my kids!!" Others felt that a new high school would be a magnet for families that were looking to move farther away from down town Flint or; a quality town for General Motors executives to raise a family.

The final iota of news shared to me by The Dutchman has no impact on me, but will definitely be demoralizing to my traveling partners. Starting this school year there is no longer a dress code at the "University of Fenton." Dress shirts and pants can be replaced by blue jeans and sweat shirts. Dresses and dress slacks can be replaced by blue jeans and Levi pants.

I never wear blue jeans as I do not like the way they fit on me. You could put a $1,000.00 bill on the floor right in front of me and tell me that if I can bend over and pick it up without bending my knees, that one grand is all mine. If I had a pair of blue jeans on I couldn't even come close to picking up that money. Even if you upped the ante with an incentive that I would be allowed to watch "The Girl from U.N.C.L.E." on TV for 24 hours straight with no commercials included, that piece of paper with Grover Cleveland's picture on it could not be picked up by me. No way.

However, Katie loves her blue jeans and probably owns a couple of thousand pair. Same with Terry Rodenbo. Outside of school he is always wearing blue jeans. But Jim Koop is going to be the one most devastated by this lack of a dress code. He LOVES his blue jeans and matching blue jean jacket. I betcha he was wearing a pair of blue jeans and that same blue jean jacket when he came out of his mother's womb at birth.

Sad news for my traveling companions is that Hartland High School still has a dress code of no blue jeans or sweat shirts. There is no more type of shocking information that my traveling companions can receive than to learn that they are missing out on a "blue jeans year." And I ain't going to be the one to tell them.

It's time to pack it in for this depressing first day of school for myself. The only good thought that I have from today is this; I bet you one dozen doughnuts from "Supremes" that Eddie Williams is still a student of State Road Elementary School; still in Mrs. Wise's fourth grade class; and that he's the only fourth grader in the state of Michigan with a driver's license.

Try them army boots on for size Eddie Williams!!!!!!!!!!!!!!!!!

"White Lake Road"

Chapter #19 – "Hold the Phone, Junior"

September 4th – I gave a lot of thought as to the telephone conversation that I recently had with "The Dutchman" and came to the decision that I was going to cut his losses, leave Hartland High School and head back to where I belong, Fenton High School. I have decided that I am a "Fenton Tiger" at heart and not a "Hartland Eagle." In my mind, I belong back at Fenton High School.

Like the great line from the best western movie ever made, "The Magnificent Seven", "Maybe it's time to turn mother's picture to the wall and get out of here." Maybe before the school year gets too far along it was time for me as well to" turn mother's picture to the wall", put my tail between my legs, show up at the doors of Fenton High School, and hope that the old saying of, "It's easier to seek forgiveness than permission" will apply to me.

Transferring back to Fenton High School will not come easy. The original agreement amongst all of the parents of me and my traveling partners was that if three of us decided to transfer back to Fenton High School, then the fourth person would be obligated to return as well. Thus, I'll have to convince at least two of my traveling partners to come back with me.

After I collect the necessary yes votes my master plan is to finish out this week at Hartland High School and start back up at Fenton High School next Monday, September 8th. That should be early enough in the school year so that my spot on the bench for varsity basketball season won't be given to some other well deserving sole. Also, my planned arrival time shouldn't interfere with my goal to being voted one of the captains of the track team this spring. This is going to work out pretty good from a timing stand point.

However, once I enter through the doors and into the hallowed halls of Fenton High School I strongly suspect that there will not be a big parade in my honor welcoming me back. Oh, there will be friends and students glad to see me. But there will also be a handful of people who thought I was dead and some others who wished I was dead. In addition, my one-week delay of coming back to Fenton High School could very well create some obstacles to the individual honors that I was hoping to obtain during my senior year of high school.

However, where the real troublesome issues that I will be confronted with is going to with Band class. Last year at this time, Steve West, an oboe player, with the talent to become a professional musician and play in a big-time symphony someday, was accepted into the "Interlochen Center of the Arts" as a full-time student for his senior year of high school. This is a prestigious honor. The Interlochen Center of the Arts does not award scholarships of this type to people like "Bad Hombre" and myself. That is unless they are in the need of students who would rather play basketball than practice their instruments or attend rehearsals.

Poor Steve West was just verbally ripped apart by a large majority of the Fenton Senior High Band members when they became aware of his departure. Steve West, admittedly a strange sort of duck, however, was very dedicated to the Fenton Senior Band, especially when it came to the writing and reading of our football halftime show scripts. Suddenly in the eyes of some Fenton Band members Steve West became a traitor, a deserter and somebody who thought he

was too good to be a member of the Fenton High Senior Band. Poor Steve West deserved better than that.

My worry was that upon my return to Fenton High School, is that the same things are going to be said about me. I probably wouldn't get the verbal abuse like Steve West did, but I would get my share of criticisms. I can just hear it now. "Not only did Beardslee think he was too good be out here in the hot sun at marching band camp with us, now he also thinks he is too good to be a member of the Fenton High School Band!! Who needs him!!"

In addition, my decision to run from Fenton High School rather than to Hartland High School will probably end up hurting me for the two personal Band goals that I had set for myself. It was a big ambition for me to become the first ever two-time Fenton Senior Band president. I could just see people like John Perkins and Mary Morrison, two nasty rivals, using my recent departure and possible return against me when it came to the election of Senior Band president. "If you don't get your way, Beardslee, what high school are you going to be attending next week??" Ouch.

However, the biggest carrot on the stick for me was something called the Arion Award. This award is given to the most dedicated senior of the Fenton Senior Band, and I have been fixated on winning this award since I was a sophomore when I first became aware this honor. Now even that goal for me will be pretty much impossible to reach. I can just hear the Mike Beardslee bashers stating to other band members, "Mike Beardslee is no better than Steve West!! He didn't go to marching band camp because he wanted to work in a national park rather than make the effort to help us become a better marching band!! He's more worried about being the center of attention than doing what's best for the band" Always remember, musicians, just like athletes, can be mean. Maybe, even meaner.

The first of my traveling partners that I shared my transferring back to Fenton High School plan was Jim Koop. I don't think it mattered either way to Jim Koop as to which band he was going to march in this fall, Fenton's or Hartland's. So, I'm taking that as a yes vote.

I also advised Jim Koop of the terrors that I thought we would face when we walked through the band room doors of the Fenton High School. Jim Koop, as only as Jim Koop could, simply responded, "Ah, Beardslee, my friend, they probably don't even know were not there anymore." That might be a good thing.

Two yes votes are in and I need at least one more affirmative vote in the ballot box to be even taken seriously from all involved parents to get this transfer thing a done deal. However, getting Katie to agree to come back to Fenton High School with me was not going to be easy. In fact, you can mark her down for a no vote right now and not even bother to read the next two paragraphs.

Even after only two days here at Hartland High School Katie has developed a big following. And not just band kids, but what also seemed to be the entire sophomore class as well. Also, another big incentive for Katie to stay at Hartland, not only for the current school year but her junior and senior years, was that Katie had her eye on the jeep. With her older brother away from the high school scene in nine months, Katie had that jeep earmarked as her "wheels" for at least the 1970-71 school year. I can just see her bopping around Livingston County in "her" jeep and loving every second of it.

But if the four of us go back to Fenton High School then there is no need for the jeep. That baby will be sold and gone as fast as it was purchased. Mrs. Wolverton and Bus #23 will become Katie's set of "wheels" for her junior and senior years of high school. She's not going to like that.

I'm still in need of one more yes vote to get this transfer move on my part to go nice and smooth. The last person to run my quandary past was Terry Rodenbo to get his thoughts and more importantly, an affirmative vote.

After band rehearsal, I proceeded to tell Terry Rodenbo how I was feeling about life in the world of Hartland Consolidated Schools and advised him of my decision that I was going to transfer back to Fenton High School. I spelled out the benefits of the new Fenton High School that "The Dutchman" had shared with me. Also, with it being so early in the school year what could we have possibly missed in just one week? The four of us should be able to pick up right where we left off from last June.

Terry Rodenbo's response caught me off guard. "While you and your mother were fighting over whether Holy Redeemer or Swartz Creek High School was where your senior year was going to be spent; I was doing my research. Just like you, my mother wanted me to make sure that if the school millages kept failing that I was going to be able to attend a high school where I could be on the wrestling team, play baseball and participate in the band. In fact, till you came along with the Hartland Consolidated Schools idea, my mother had me earmarked for attending Lake Fenton High School this school year."

Terry Rodenbo continued, "When the third millage failed this past August, my mother and I contacted the Michigan High School Athletic Association and were advised that when a school district does not pass three consecutive millages, the MHSAA has established a grace period for a student that wants to participate in athletics but has to leave their current high school to do so. The grace period is from one day after the third consecutive school millage has failed to the first day of the state of Michigan public school calendar, which was this past Tuesday, September 2nd."

"The MHSAA advised my mother and I that once a transfer student is enrolled in a school system on the state calendar's first day of school and has officially started attending their new school, this student cannot transfer to another high school to participate in athletics unless until they have sat out a minimum of one school semester. And depending on the MHSAA's findings, a student could even be required to sit out the whole school year from participating in athletics"

Terry Rodenbo didn't come and flat out say it to my face, he's too polite to do that, but he had presented a strong case that if I wanted to transfer back to Fenton High School, that ship may have sailed, as I was in danger of for sure missing at the least the first semester of being eligible for basketball and worst-case scenario, the full seasons of both basketball and track. I hate these moments when Terry Rodenbo is smarter than I am.

Now let's see; Fenton High School – Very good possibility of missing a portion of basketball season, if not all, plus having a track season that may be in jeopardy as well. From a Band standpoint, I will be a member of the Fenton Senior Band as soon as I walk in the school building but will face a few Fenton Senior Band members rounding up votes to get themselves elected Band president that I so kindly vacated and; make the competition for winning the Arion Award much more difficult for myself.

Hartland High School – I am already here so I would be eligible to play varsity basketball, if I make the squad, and, run track at the time when the talent level for track teams will possibly be at an all-time low in the Genesee-Livingston County Conference. There will be less pressure from a trumpet playing standpoint till I get better adjusted to my temporary caps and hope that once the permanent caps are put in next month that will be a smooth adjustment period. Even Jethro Bodine, of the TV series, "The Beverly Hillbillies" with his alleged sixth grade education knows the answer to this predicament.

Why do I feel like the little kid hanging on to a balloon, standing all by his lonesome, while a parade marches farther and farther away from me down the street? Well, at least I know one thing, by deciding to stay here at the Hartland Consolidated Schools and gutting it out for my senior year of high school, it won't be the last blunder I make this decade. As Katie would say, "What a bummer!!" Make that bummer with a capital "B".

"White Lake Road"

Chapter #20 - "Armour Hot Dogs"

September 5th – It's Friday!! Week I is almost done and only 35 more weeks to go before the end of the school year!! It's also time to break out my new school clothes which consists of a light orange shirt, tan checked pants and black penny loafers. I must admit that I am one snappy dresser!! Be sure to add ruggedly handsome to that self-description as well.

These new set of threads remind me of the title of one of the many books written about New York Jets quarterback, Joe "Broadway Joe" Namath. This manuscript is titled, "I Can't Wait Until Tomorrow, Because I Get Better Looking Every Day." I mean let's face it, when you read that book title, who are you going to think of first? Joe Namath or Mike Beardslee?? (I know why I'm laughing, just out of curiosity, why are you??)

Marching band practice has been the focus the last couple of days during fourth hour. The Hartland High School marching band has caught a big break for the beginning of the new school year. The first two football games for the Hartland Eagles are away games. We don't have a half-time show to perform in until two weeks from tonight. That's a lot of time for a marching band to prepare for a pre-game and half-time show. We have no excuses not to be ready to go.

So far, these marching band practices have been a mini-marching band camp in itself. Fundamental city all of the way. You name it, we did it, from eight steps for every five yards; staggered two-steps; spin turns; to the rear march; field sweeps; pin wheels and even a little six steps-to-every five yards.

My first impressions of the Hartland Consolidated Schools Marching Band? Well, I find myself comparing the Hartland High School Marching Band to some of the past Fenton High Marching Bands that I was once a member. There are more differences than similarities. The Fenton Band has at least one-third more marchers than Hartland. Thus, the Fenton Band has more sound power than us. As the crow flies the Fenton Band when performing the right type of song, fast and loud, could probably be heard three miles away. At this point the Hartland High Band couldn't wake up a snoring drunk even if we snuck up behind them and broke out into the song, "Joshua."

From a trumpet playing standpoint, thank goodness that Jim Koop has been carrying the load by blasting up a storm. The problem is however, he is one of the few brass players, Terry Rodenbo and Jason Shattuck being the others, who have a clue of what it takes for a marching band to sound like a MARCHING BAND!! The Hartland Band is too quiet from a marching band sound standpoint. Right now, we sound "pretty". That's like saying a football team plays soft. You don't want a "pretty" sound from a marching band. You want "PRETTY LOUD".

My trumpet playing out on the marching has been okay but it has not been marching band okay, so you have to put me in the "pretty" sounding category as well. The situation with my teeth has prevented me from where I need to be from a marching band sound. I can't "blast"

like I was doing a year ago at this time. Then, I could clear out a high school gymnasium with one good trumpet blast.

It shows you how one's life can change in 12 months. Literally 365 days ago from today, I got a call at home from Jim Koop. He had somehow been hooked into filing sheet music for the Fenton High School band director, Miss Franklin, and said that he had something to show me that night. Not tomorrow during second hour, but tonight. I said sure and then spent the time waiting for his arrival with two questions on my mind; 1) What was so important that Jim Koop had to pedal his bicycle all the way out to "White Lake Road" from down town Fenton on a school night and; 2) What was Jim Koop doing filing sheet music. He never files sheet music. I mean never!!

Jim Koop arrived and he had brought with him the first trumpet part for one of the songs that we were going to play for our first half time show of the season, "Georgie Girl." A terrific song. (Don't ask who wrote or performs this tune. If it's not the "Herb Alpert and the Tijuana Brass", I probably have never have heard of them).

The key here was that the sheet music to "Georgie Girl "had not even been passed out to the rest of the Fenton Band yet. Well by the end of that evening Jim Koop and I had practiced "Georgie Girl" enough times that we had this puppy memorized and all ready for the following Monday's band rehearsal when the rest of the band was to receive the sheet music to this musical arrangement.

At that said marching band rehearsal Jim Koop and I were blasting our little brains out with our trumpets. I can still remember Larry Anderson, a freshman trombone player, turning around and looking at us with a surprise that two trumpet players could produce more sound than the rest of the band combined.

When we broke into the song "Georgie Girl" Jim Koop and I drew even more looks from the Fenton Band members where in addition to our blasting of our trumpets, we were standing and playing this song without any music, strictly from memorization. Miss Franklin looked at both Jim Koop and me with a puzzled look on her face and then remarked to the rest of the Fenton Band members, "If those two can memorize this song so quickly, then I am going to require that for this marching band season that the whole marching band memorize all songs for each and every half-time show." That was followed by some very serious groans and well known international hand signals from the rest of the members of the Fenton High Marching Band.

Jim Koop looked around the band room and saw all of the daggered stares that he and I were getting. Jim Koop then remarked to me, "Gee, Beardslee, where's Steve West when we really need him?"

Later at lunch time, Terry Rodenbo came up to Jim Koop and myself and asked, "How did you two memorize that song so fast?? The sheet music was just passed out at the beginning of rehearsal." He badgered us all the whole time I was downing a baloney sandwich and a carton

of milk. And to this day Terry Rodenbo still has no idea of the "Mystery of the Memorized Music" story written by "F.W". Cooper and "F.W." Beardslee.

While the Hartland High Band has to get away from sounding "pretty", I will say this about these guys, what they lack in marching band volume; they certainly have the dedication, discipline and spirit of a quality marching band. When Mr. Anderson says "Ok, everyone back to the end zone," these guys don't lollygag around. It's a race to see which instrument section can get to the end zone first. From day one out on the marching band field Katie was yelling, "Come on drummers!! Let's be the first ones back to the end zone!!" Now it's a contest to see who can get to the end zone before the drummers.

This brings me to the other comparison that I can make between my former high school and current high school bands. Discipline. During my four years of marching band at Fenton High School I witnessed some devoted and disciplined individuals to marching band practice. The Guy Thompson's, Mike Hick's, Beanie Bretzke's, Jean Vosburgh's and Gayla Woolford's of the world, they realized how important on field discipline and self-control to marching band rehearsals were.

However, they may have been the only ones that grasped that concept. The vast majority of the Fenton Marching Band members, including myself, simply did not get how discipline and self-control went hand-in-hand when preparing for a halftime show. In fact, it was the lack of those two characteristics that always led us to scrambling, even on the day of our last marching band rehearsal, to get it together so that we had our marching band routines down for that night's halftime show. That's cutting it a little close.

I suspect a great majority of high school marching bands in the state of Michigan do not excel at both marching and playing their instruments at the same time. It takes some getting used to and if people think that marching and playing a musical instrument simultaneously is easy, then may I suggest you try doing it sometime in your back yard. The only high school marching band that I have personally seen that could constantly meet these criteria successfully was Flint Northwestern's High School's marching band. Maybe, Linden High School's marching band as well.

Last summer one evening while in the woods of the Olympic National Park as a part of my Student Conversation Association tour, I was just completely bored out of my mind. After I got done hoping that the Detroit Tigers had miraculously taken the lead of the American League East division over the hated Baltimore Orioles, a lesson that I should have learned about marching band discipline last October was starting to sink in.

Paul Romska was a tenor saxophone player who had moved from Saginaw to Fenton at the start of the 1968-69 school year. Miss Franklin had made a big deal about the fact that Paul Romska's former high school band had been selected from 80 some high school bands to tour and perform for six weeks in Europe. Impressive stuff.

During marching band practice that year the Fenton Band was trying to do a formation for a half-time show that was shaped like a hot dog and to be used as we marched down the football

field. Rehearsal wise, it was going badly so my ever-ongoing quest for cheap attention, broke into singing the "Armour Hot Dogs" jingle that originally sounded like:

"Hot dogs, Armour hot dogs;

What kind of kids eat Armour Hot Dogs?

Fat kids, skinny kids, kids who climb on rocks;

Tough kids, sissy kids, even kids with chicken pox love hot dogs,

Armour Hot Dogs The dogs kids love to bite!"

I changed the lyrics on the fly and came up with the following:

"Hot dogs, Armour hot dogs;

What kind of band kids eat Armour Hot Dogs?

Brass kids, drummer kids, drum majors who climb on rocks;

Woodwind kids, majorette kids, even band directors with chicken pox love hot dogs,

Armour Hot Dogs The dogs band kids love to bite!"

Absolutely brilliant!! No, make that Beardslee brilliant!! This medley caused the members of the Fenton Band to laugh so hard that everyone had to stop marching and the whole practice routine came to a complete halt. Luckily it was time for second hour to end and it was back into the high school with the rest of the band singing the words to the theme song of "Armour Hot Dogs.".

Later that same day at lunch time, Paul Romska came up to me and said, "You have probably heard about my former band and our tour of Europe last summer. What you did not hear is how disciplined and efficient our rehearsals were. When the band director raised his arms, we started to play. When we had to stop during a certain passage in a song, we immediately stopped. There was no talking in between and no joking around. We had a goal of being selected as the high school band to go on this European tour and our discipline and efficiency allowed us to reach this goal."

"While the little ditty that you sang today was very funny and I was right there along with everyone else laughing and singing, it caused the rehearsal to be disruptive and lead to a lack of discipline and efficiency on the entire band's part. Ask yourself this Mr. Beardslee, what would happen if this same scenario played out on a Monday rehearsal and it rained so hard that we could not get out to practice our halftime show the rest of the week. Not only did we lose those remaining rehearsals, but Monday's rehearsal was the only practice time that we

could have marched through the entire halftime show and at least become somewhat familiar with the marching routines."

The reprimand was finally coming to an end when Paul Romska concluded, "If the Fenton High School Marching Band ever wants to become a group that wants to put on more than one good halftime show a year, then discipline and efficiency must become part of every rehearsal, not just the morning of when the half-time show is to be performed. And as the unquestioned leader of this marching band, it has to start with you."

I didn't like being lectured to, especially from a new student to Fenton High School. It took 10 months while sitting around a camp fire in the Olympic National Park watching other people play Gin Rummy for Paul Romska's message to sink in, but it finally did. Paul Romska, who later that school year fell back into my princely good graces and became a good buddy of mine, probably does not realize the invaluable lesson that he passed on to yours truly.

As I mentioned earlier, my trumpet playing sounds "pretty" and my on-field sound production is nowhere where it needs to be. And due to my front teeth issues, my sound power may be like that the whole marching band season. However, this might be as good as any time to use the message that was delivered to me from Paul Romska. Maybe my major contribution this marching band season will be as a better on field leader from a discipline and efficiency standpoint rather than a trumpet player who has an obvious puff mark on their upper lip from blasting away on their trumpet.

For this 1969 marching band season, Jim Koop's half of the band will easily exceed mine. However, maybe this will be the marching band season that I can now look the Guy Thompson's, Mike Hick's Beanie Bretzke's, Jean Vosburgh's, Gayla Woolford's of Fenton High Marching Band past in the eye and say to them; "Yeah, I finally got it. I'm sorry that I didn't learn as fast as I should have"

Just before the end of today's marching band practice Mr. Anderson announced, "On Monday we will be electing band officers, so give some thought as to which of your band mates are the most qualified for these positions."

Chapter #21 - "Lunch Room Conversation Hall of Fame"

September 5th – It's day number four of the school year and I have already fallen into a rut. My "lunch crowd" on a daily basis has only been Jim Koop and myself. Then, starting yesterday, Terry Rodenbo must have been demoted to the "second team lunch crowd" because he is no longer dining with Katie's lunch group. The three of us are apparently not good enough to hang out with Katie's lunch buddies. How do we know that? Katie told us that right to our faces. And I have still not received an invitation to sit and eat lunch with Teri Andrews, either. I'm putting the chances of that offer being right up there with General Custer wanting to go the best two out of three with Chief Sitting Bull.

The topic of conversation with the my select lunch crowd is always the same. Band. Not sports. Not girls. Not other classes. Just Band. There is an exception to this rule and that's when Jim Koop and I discuss the all-important subject of how many elementary schools in the state of Michigan that will be named after us some day.

Today, however, for whatever reason, my lunch crowd was a little different which also led to an area being discussed other than Band. I was invited by Tom Moran and Pete Mason to sit with them at lunch today. I initially thought that they wanted to converse about was the "Tigers." I immediately went into my Detroit Tiger spiel that if Dick McAuliffe recovers from his knee surgery and somewhere along the way a solid third starting pitcher is acquired or developed from within the Detroit Tiger farm system, then just maybe the "Tigers" will be fine come the start of the 1970 baseball season. Maybe.

I was mistaken. It was not the Detroit Tigers that Tom Moran and Pete Mason wanted to discuss, but rather it was the "Fenton Tigers" varsity football team, with their questions primarily focusing on the storied tradition of the Fenton High School football program.

During my previous lunch hours, I have probably been positioned about 10 feet from where Tom Moran and Pete Mason sit and eat. Every single lunch period I have heard the same unrelenting, mocking statements that their "buddies" say to those two guys concerning the "Hartland Eagles" varsity football team.

Let's just put it this way, I wouldn't want any one speaking to me about the Hartland Band in that same manner. And to anybody that did talk that way about the Hartland Band to my face I would simply turn Katie loose on those big mouths and sit back and have me a good laugh while they begged for mercy.

While I am sure, at least pretty sure, that these comments to Tom Moran and Pete Mason were made in jest, some of these barbs had some sting to them. Examples being thrown at them included: "There are certain things in life that are guaranteed. Hartland High School losing to Fenton High School in a varsity football game is one of them." Considering the 63-0 thumping that Fenton gave Hartland last year, there might be some truth to that statement.

The other quip that I overheard, and must admit that I thought was absolutely hysterical, "Tom Moran was our leading scorer on the varsity football team last season with four touchdowns. I should also point out that he was our only scorer."

Biting humor kind of stuff that will no doubt go down in the "Lunch Room Conversation Hall of Fame." It makes me wonder what is being said about me in the "University of Fenton" lunch room right this very second.

After the barbs and zingers calmed down, Pete Mason opened the conversation by asking me what varsity football game days were like at Fenton High School. Until Pete Mason had asked that question it suddenly dawned on me what was missing at school today. There was no indication at all that there was a Hartland High School varsity football game tonight. I hadn't seen any paper footballs pasted to the varsity football player's lockers indicating their football jersey number. And sitting across from Pete Mason and Tom Moran I noticed that they were not wearing their football game jerseys today either. Also, there were no cheerleaders walking around the school hallways wearing their cheerleading uniforms. In addition, there was no mention of a pep assembly by Mr. Anderson for this afternoon. All indicators that there was nothing out of the ordinary about this particular school day from any other school day.

There was also nothing to distinguish that Tom Moran and Pete Mason, who had been announced this morning over the PA system as captains of the "Hartland Eagles" Varsity Football team, from just two guys just sitting at a typical high school lunch room table eating tuna fish sandwiches and counting down the minutes before the first week of the school year was over. Being named a captain of the football team is a huge honor at any high school in the United States of America. Maybe not so much here in Hartland, Michigan.

Again, the noticeable lack of excitement that I noticed today was so much a part of the tradition of a "Fenton Football Friday" at Fenton High School. I went into great detail of what a big deal that a "Fenton Football Friday" pep assembly was like. There were speeches from the coaches and team captains and for the first "Fenton Football Friday" of the season all of the players were individually introduced.

That "big barn" named Jennings Memorial Gym at the old Fenton High School served two purposes in life. It could hold heat and noise really well. After a pep assembly of this type it was guaranteed that a ton of students would be deaf for the next two hours and those that didn't have their hearing affected had to drink a couple of thousand gallons of "Gatorade" to replenish their bodies from sweating to death.

After I finished up telling the guys how a "Fenton Football Friday" was a special event, especially for home games, the look on Pete Mason's face showed pure envy. He was sitting there drooling just for the opportunity to live that experience at least once in his high school football career.

I also went into detail as to the great tradition and rich history of the Fenton High School Varsity Football team. This included great players like: Bruce McLenna, Jessie Madden, "Powder Puff" Huff, Jim Czmerak, Bob and Marv Pushman, Bobby Niles, Don and Mike Madden, Steve Barker, Ben Lewis, Bill Hajec and there's a whole lot of more that I'm not even mentioning.

Undefeated football seasons were the norm at Fenton High School. And let me define what I mean by undefeated seasons. These no loss seasons were just not restricted to the varsity squad. It included the junior varsity and freshmen football teams as they annually had undefeated seasons as well. In fact, it was not uncommon for all three football squads to go undefeated in the same football season. Actually, come to think of it, it was more of a rarity when the three squads did not go undefeated in the same season.

The Fenton High School varsity football program has consistently been considered one of the top five football teams in the Class "B" Division ever since I can remember. The "Fenton Tigers" we're typically the biggest game on every opponent's schedule that particular football season. While there is no playoff format for high school football in the "Great Lakes" state, there is no doubt in a lot of people's minds that the Fenton Tigers would have represented themselves well against all competition no matter the playoff format. No doubt at all.

I suspect that the upcoming football season for the Hartland Eagles will be long and ugly. Consistent with a varsity football program that has lost every game for the past two seasons and has a total of four wins in their last six seasons.

It will be interesting to see how the 1969 Fenton Tiger rendition of varsity football will stack up against their predecessors from a historical perspective. While I think that they have the capability of going undefeated, the Swartz Creek and Brighton varsity football teams will be extremely talented. Maybe even more talented than the Fenton Tigers.

I am basing this on a tidbit of information from last spring concerning the Fenton Tiger Varsity Football team shared to me by Bruce Gold while he and I were dying a slow death in Latin I Class. (Worst class ever!!) Bruce Gold said, "We're going to have a great offense next year. We could even score 30 points against the New York Jets. But our defense is going to be like a sieve. Even "The Little Sisters of the Poor" will have no problems moving the chains on us." That will make one Tom "He was our only scorer last season" Moran really happy.

I have always compared my trumpet playing abilities to the great trumpet players of Fenton Senior Band past, specifically Carl Peters and Ray Sortman. And in that evaluation, I always thought the name of Mike Beardslee from a trumpet playing standpoint should never be mentioned in the same sentence with those two greats.

At times, I wonder if my Fenton High School football playing buddies like Jim Vincent, Dennis Osterman, Terry Size, Dan Barkman, Robbie Gilbert and Bruce Gold, all very good

football players, feel the pressure of the high standards set by previous great "Fenton Tigers" football teams. Do my buddies compare themselves to Fenton legends like the above mentioned gridders? That group of Fenton icons' talent and skill levels allowed them to be constantly named to All State football squads or in Don Madden's case, All-American recognition from Parade Magazine. Will their names be mentioned in the same breath as Bruce McLenna, a former Detroit Lion football player? Either way, I hope my buddies are enjoying their "Fenton Football Friday" today.

I really liked my lunch room conversation with Tom Moran and Pete Mason. But what I really appreciated, though, was not only did they enjoy hearing about "Fenton Football Fridays", but they also didn't look down their nose at me for not playing high school football. That happened more than a few times back at Fenton High School. In some football players' minds if you didn't play football there was something wrong with you. I was on the cross-country team for a couple of years so I shared a locker room with the gridders and I always got the "sissy sport" thrown in my face. A lot. I didn't like that one bit. So, to be able to talk with two varsity football players, captains of the team no less, without the "You couldn't even make it through one of our football practices, Beardslee, because you're not tough enough" speech, was a pleasant surprise.

I must admit that going back into the time machine and reminiscing about "Fenton Football Fridays" made me realize what an extraordinary happening it really was. I hope the "Fenton Tigers" go undefeated and maintain their great football tradition. I would also love to see at least once this season where Tom Moran and Pete Mason could experience that magical moment in their high school football careers of what a "Hartland Football Friday" should be like.

"White Lake Road"

Chapter #22 – "The Jack of Diamonds!!!!!"

September 5th – I was walking to the jeep at the end of what was probably going to go down in my life as one of the worst first weeks of school ever. Even my first weeks of Kindergarten at Mary Crapo Elementary School and State Road Elementary School as a fourth grader, while no great shakes, had these past four days beat by 5,280 feet.

Okay, let's do the math. So far, thanks to Tom Moran and Pete Mason, I have had one enjoyable school day out of the first four. If this keeps up 25 % of my school days (45) will be good and the other 75% of the school days (135) I will be kicking myself for leaving the Fenton Area Schools. That's a real swell start to the "the greatest year of my life."

The only person I can think of in life that would be happy with a percentage of 25% would be former Detroit Tiger starting shortstop, Ray Oyler, who was a great fielder and one lousy hitter. Ray Oyler would have sold his soul to Lucifer, himself, if he could have hit .250 on the major-league level. In fact, I would sell my soul to the Beelzebub, (What a great name!!) to have two decent days in a row as a student of the Hartland Consolidated Schools.

Just as I started to enter into the jeep I felt a jagged type pain in my stomach. I betcha the pain was similar to when Errol Flynn jammed a dagger into Basil Rathbone's stomach in a scene from the greatest movie ever made, "The Adventures of Robin Hood". Add the event on the beach from the movie "Captain Blood" when my main man, Errol Flynn, also won a sword duel to the death with Basil Rathbone and that describes perfectly the agony that was so extreme in my gut that it was making me almost double over and taking my breath away. In fact, this was such a tortured feeling that I was going through, I'm quite positive that it would have killed a lesser person.

I didn't think my stomach discomfort was the result of the cheese sandwiches and the six pounds of mayonnaise loaded on them that my mother had made for my lunch today. I love those sandwiches as they have been the highlight of my Friday school day lunches ever since I was a first grader.

I have read that the human body has a memory. That must be true because it suddenly dawned on me what the cause of this intense shockwave to my body was. One year ago, on the first Friday of the 1968-69 school year, I received my walking papers from a one Jane Roberts. Just imagine movie star, Dana Wynter, (yes, that's right, the actress who starred in the movie "The Invasion of the Body Snatchers") with freckles. There's your visual of Jane Roberts.

I have repeatedly tried to forget this day when my heart was ripped out of my body and stomped on with both feet of Jane Roberts. Nevertheless, this moment is eternally etched in stone in my mind. I vividly remember everything that took place to the first shock of the breakup to the following waves of devastation. Here goes:

Pat "The Flying Dutchman" Goode had loaned me a mysterious little oriental style type box. The intent of this secretive oriental designed box was to try to find all of the hidden type entrances plus the nooks and crannies that would allow a person to figure out how to open

and reach the hidden compartment center of this oriental box. Once there, the discoverer could find a prize, usually some type of piece of candy or similar treat.

Trying to get to the secret center of this box amused my little mind for days until I was finally able to get to the box open and reach the final slot. In reaching this final step I discovered inside what must have been a tootsie roll that after trying to bite into it had to must have been at least 500 years old. Thanks, "Dutchman!!"

A fantastic idea suddenly dawned on me!! This oriental mystery box would give me a badly needed reason to stay in contact with Jane Roberts. My master plan was to give the oriental box to Jane Roberts to open where she would find the grape lollipop that I had placed in there. Brilliant!! Oh, and it gets better!! In addition, now Jane Roberts had to return the oriental box to me and that would give me another chance to be with her. This strategy was so magnificent that you could accuse me of just flat out showing off. And you would be right!!

The weather on that disastrous Friday afternoon was warm and sunny with a gentle breeze. Good weather to end the first week of a school year. The last hour of the school day had been completed and I was in the band room with "The Flying Dutchman" and Miss Franklin when Jane Roberts came walking up to me in a hurried manner but with a smile on her face. For the first time in months I thought that Jane Roberts was actually glad to see me or even better, finally invite me to join her family and some of her other friends for the weekend in Clare, Michigan, wherever that is, at the Robert's family owned cottage.

Jane Roberts handed me the oriental box and advised me how easy it was to find the secret panels. Miss Franklin looked at the oriental box with some intrigue and said, "Hey, let me try that". At that point, Jane Roberts practically ripped the oriental box out of Miss Franklin's hands, then thrust it back into my fingers and at the same time hurriedly saying, "There's something in the box for you." Jane Roberts then spun around and hastily exited out of the band room without even a thank you for the grape lollipop.

Miss Franklin and "The Flying Dutchman" suddenly became deathly quiet. They were smart enough to know what was in the secret hiding spot of the oriental box. Me?? The kid who didn't even know how to spell his own last name when he was in second grade, (Yes, I knew how to spell "Mike") had no clue has to what was coming next. I was like the operator of the motor vehicle who saw two lights coming toward him in his lane of traffic one dark evening and thought that he could drive in between the two "motorcycles."

I went into one of the band practice rooms and shut the door for privacy purposes. I then opened the oriental box so quickly that I was quite proud of myself. Good news was just around the corner for you know who!! That is when I discovered that the two "motorcycles" that the driver was going to drive in between was instead a single motor vehicle with both head lights on.

Once inside the oriental box secret passage I discovered that there was a folded-up piece of paper. I started reading that note quicker than I do my "Sporting News" magazine on a Saturday morning. However, this communication wasn't about the Detroit Tigers acquiring

Eddie Mathews or Elroy Face in a trade for future minor league prospects to help the Detroit Tigers down the American League pennant stretch run.

This also was also nowhere near the type of note from last June where Jane Roberts thanked me for such a good time of having butterscotch sundaes afterwards on our first date. No. This message was advising ole Beardslee to take a long walk off of a short pier. We were officially no longer a couple.

After reading that note a couple of more times I now know how the "Cincinnati Kid" character played by my other main man, Steve McQueen, felt when in a high stakes poker game with, "Lancey Howard", a poker playing legend portrayed by the brilliant actor, Edward G. Robinson, slapped down on the table a "Jack of Diamonds" to go with the rest of the diamonds in his hand for a royal flush. Lancey Howard won the poker hand and $5,000.00 that the "Cincinnati Kid" did not have.

I still remember "The Cincinnati Kid" with that shocked look on his face just staring at that "Jack of Diamonds", breathing heavy and drops of sweat rolling down the side of his face. Mike Beardslee doesn't just remember that scene from the "The Cincinnati Kid", I was living it.

Now realizing that my life was coming to an end, despite trying to hide the obvious tears running down my face in front of "The Flying Dutchman" and Miss Franklin, I handed the oriental box bank to "The Flying Dutchman" and proceeded to sprint out of the band room and Fenton High School as fast as my 56.9 440 legs would carry me.

"White Lake Road"

Chapter #23 – "The Boulder Fields"

September 5th – Somehow without causing any motor vehicle accidents while crossing Silver Lake Road, I made it to Jim Koop's house which was located just a few blocks away from Fenton High School. Once down in Jim Koop's basement I shoved the poisoned note into Jim Koop's hands and asked him to read it while I continued to blubber and cry my eyes out.

Jim Koop kept repeating the words of, "You're a free man now, Beardslee. You're a free man now, Beardslee". While I realized that these words were true and very good advice, I could not escape the written words that Jane Roberts had placed on an ordinary piece of note book paper taken from an everyday spiral note book. That's just great; public humiliation and the fact that my feelings were not even good enough to be crushed on personalized stationary paper.

My first thought was that as soon as I got back to "White Lake Road" I would call Jane Roberts and beg like a dog with brown eyes for her to take me back. But even an emotionally drained 15-year old kid, like myself, was able to figure out in my own little mind that that probably wasn't the smartest thing in the world to do.

Thank goodness there wasn't a home football game that night where the Fenton High School Band would have had to perform a pre-game and half-time show. I don't know if I would have had it in me to do those shows. I could just see myself fighting off the tears and trying to play the Fenton High School fight song, "Stand Up and Cheer "at the same time.

To make things worse it also would have been very stressful to sit in the same section of the football bleachers and have the rest of the band members notice that Jane Roberts and I weren't sitting together, let alone not even talking with each other. That whole scene would have made for a tough evening on ole Beardslee.

As if my Friday had not been ruined enough already, now I couldn't even concentrate on the important things in life such as the Detroit Tigers-Minnesota Twins baseball game scheduled that night. Denny McClain was going after his 28th victory of the season and the Detroit Tigers were trying to shrink their magic number in the single digit range so that they could clinch their first American League pennant since 1945.

Oh no, ole Beardslee boy instead felt it was more important for him to lie on my bed and cry his eyes out. Not even the familiar and friendly voices of Detroit Tiger play-by- play announcers, Ernie Harwell and Ray Lane, were going to be the tonic for my ailments. My "Go Get em Tigers" had gone up and left for that mournful night.

The next day I spent moping around all day at "White Lake Road" feeling sorry for myself and fighting off the urges to walk/run over to Jane Robert's house and do a sit-in or maybe even a starve-in until she and her family got back from Clare, Michigan. She would then take pity on me and let me back in her life. But as Jim Koop pointed out while sitting in his basement yesterday afternoon, I should have seen this royal dumping coming my way at least two months ago. And he was right.

"White Lake Road"

The town of Fenton just like any other town in the United States of America has a 4th of July parade. It was my brilliant idea to get as many kids as I could from the Fenton High School Band to march in this parade. That bunch of kids, of course, included Jane Roberts.

Between me, Terry Rodenbo and Katie, we were able to scrounge up about 20 kids to march on my mother's birthday. Not a bad amount considering that school was not in session!! Was this the start of the campaign for me as Vice-President of the Fenton High School Band?? Scouts honor, it never crossed my mind. (You may want to consider the source on that last comment.)

Miss Franklin who was impressed that there were 20 some band kids dedicated enough to give up their time off in summer for possibly the most popular national holiday of the year for state of Michigan residents, suggested that we have at least one rehearsal before the 4th of July parade. Her thinking was that since end of the school year was almost four weeks ago, there were Band kids, unlike myself, of course, who had not touched their instrument since the Fenton Senior Band performed for commencement night.

Despite my happiness of getting that many members of the Fenton Band out for this parade rehearsal, it was rather obvious to me that Jane Roberts had no desire to be there either from a marching band standpoint or for the two of us to be seen to the rest of the Band as a couple.

I'll give you an example. When Jane Roberts would line in the marching band formation I would line up behind her. However, at the last second, she would dart to another row changing her position. That, of course, meant that I would have to dash to another spot in the formation to again be right behind her. It got so ridiculous that Jim Koop said, "Geez Louise, Beardslee. Watching the two of you is right out of the nursery rhyme, "Mary Had a Little Lamb."

I didn't appreciate that "Kooperism" at the time, but looking back on it he was absolutely right. "Mary had a little lamb, little lamb, little lamb. And wherever Mary went the little lamb was sure to go." You hit in right on the head, Jim Koop.

During the summer of 1968 my family and I headed out to Estes Park, Colorado, the gate way to the Rocky Mountain National Park. One hesitant goal that I had during that trip was to climb the mountain, Longs Peak, all 14,229 feet of it. My parents had climbed Longs Peak a few times and prior to this summer I had never ever had any great urge to do this. However, my mother put the carrot in front of the stick for me when she said, "Just think of the wonderful story that you can tell Jane Roberts when you get back to Fenton that you climbed one of the most difficult mountains in the Rocky Mountain National Park." I'm sold!! When do we start??

Well for the first time ever the entire Beardslee family climbed Longs Peak that summer. The total hiking distance to the top of Longs Peak is roughly eight miles. The first five miles was just a typical mountain trail, one foot in front of the other, and I was thinking to myself, "Hey, this ain't so bad." Once that section of the trail ends you have now officially have reached the "Boulder Field".

This is where the fun begins. For just under the distance of an 880 run you have to scramble over boulders. Some are small in nature and some are as big as a house. No mean feat to do in high top tennis shoes. One you have mastered the "Boulder Field", you have now reached the "Key Hole."

The "Key Hole" is place where there is a small hut for people to stop before making the final descent up to the summit of Longs Peak. It was at the "Key Hole" where I made up my mind that I couldn't go one step further as altitude sickness, it's not real air at that altitude, was starting to kick in on me. Katie broke out some oranges for us to eat and that gave us enough strength to tackle the last stretch of the trek.

It took myself and Katie five hours and fifteen minutes to reach the top of Longs Peak. It took us another seven hours to get back down to the parking lot. Nothing in the two years of cross country, three years of basketball and track practices, plus one year of Algebra I, produced a more physical draining effort on my body. Even my three weeks in the Student Conservation Association in the Olympic National Park last summer scrambling across the "Skyline" was a stroll in the park compared to climbing Longs Peak.

Will I ever climb Longs Peak again in my life? Never. Not to impress Jane Roberts, which ultimately it did not one bit, or even Stephanie Powers.

The second goal of the Estes Park, Colorado trip for me was to purchase a nice gift for Jane Roberts so that I could get back into her good graces after the great efforts she made to ignore me at the marching band rehearsal for the 4th of July Parade. In down town Estes Park, I finally found a T-Shirt shop that had two sweatshirts, different colors, with the initials of "CU" for Colorado University embroidered on the left shoulder. I thought that the sweatshirts were groovy (like I know what that word means) and could imagine in my child like mind of how good the two of us would look when we wore these sweatshirts together in public.

Once back to Fenton, Michigan, since I had not seen Jane Roberts for at least three weeks I planned out what my strategy would be when I went to her house to give her the sweatshirt. My master plan included telling her about the "Boulder Fields" and how exhausting and dangerous it was to hike. Once I got done impressing her with that I would break out her gift of the "CU" sweatshirt. This is a classic example of masterful planning. Masterful I tell you!!

However, I knew my plans had the potential to go down the outhouse trail when I first arrived at Jane Robert's house and was greeted at the door by Mrs. Roberts. I was promptly advised that Jane Roberts was not there right this second and no one seemed to know where she was. This is not good. Now I had to be entertained by Jane Roberts mother, who probably had far better things to do, while Jane Roberts younger sister went out looking for her. Have I mentioned yet that this is not good?? Wait to you read the next paragraph.

Ten to fifteen minutes later I heard Jane Roberts sister yell, "I found her and she doesn't want to see him!!" Despite Mrs. Roberts's best efforts to try and drown out the last half of that cutting statement, I heard every single word of it. Maybe I should revise my plan and open with giving her the sweatshirt and save the drama of the "Boulder Fields" for my big finish.

Another 300 long seconds went by and Jane Roberts finally made her unenthusiastic entrance. As happy as I was to see Jane Roberts, it was more than obvious she was not glad to see me let alone have any desire to sit and talk with myself. There was no smile; no sparkling of the eyes, nothing, just Jane Roberts staring at the carpeting of her living room hoping that if and when she looked up I wouldn't be there. I toyed with jokingly asking her if she even knew I had been in the state of Colorado for the past two weeks, but I knew the answer to that question once I was greeted at the door by Jane Robert's mother.

Despite the fact that everything was going wrong for me this evening, Jane Roberts did gladly accept the CU sweatshirt that I had purchased for her. However, the only thing that the beautiful wearing apparel from the land of the Rocky Mountain National Park brought was Jane Roberts making it perfectly clear that we should wait until the start of school to see each other again.

That's just great. That's four weeks, a total of 672 hours, or 40,320 minutes more of table-crumb status for me. I declined a ride home from Mrs. Roberts and walked the entire three miles home to "White Lake Road" in the rain wishing I was smart enough to take the "CU" sweatshirt gift back so that I could at least use it as a covering when the light rainfall turned into a downpour for the last rain soaked mile to the safe confines of "White Lake Road". Even scrambling over the "Boulder Fields" was more enjoyable than this.

What are the chances you ask that Jane Roberts on the first day of the 1968-69 school year would be standing in front of Fenton High School under the big lettering of "Jennings Memorial Gym" waiting to greet me with a smile and a wave? About the same odds as successfully lighting a match from a "say Pepsi please" matchbook on the first try while standing right next to a tornado. Ain't going to happen.

"White Lake Road"

Chapter #24 – "Hey, Lassie!! Have you seen Timmy lately??"

September 5th – The following Sunday after being dumped by Jane Roberts I wasn't feeling any better and was still out of sorts. The Sabbath consisted of more sulking and even worse, a loss of appetite. I couldn't even eat a slice of my mother's world-famous butterscotch pie. It's got a smooth filling and a flakey crust that just melts in your mouth. I could just hear my buddy Terry Rodenbo saying, while anxiously rubbing both of his hands together, "Means more for me!!" Yes, Terry Rodenbo, on this miserable day it does.

While I continued to mope around "White Lake Road", Katie finally cornered me and asked me what I was so uptight about. I confessed my tale of sadness to Katie and between more sniffles on my part I could tell that this breakup had Katie almost as distraught as me.

Jane Roberts and Katie are actually very good friends ever since they met at "Sixth Graders Visit Day." "Sixth Graders Visit Day" is the time that the sixth graders from State Road Elementary school would visit Fenton Junior High School. It's not as glorious as it sounds. It means getting up an hour earlier to catch the high school bus and the dress code in the junior high banishes all sweat shirts, blue jeans, as well as making the wearing of a belt mandatory.

Upon arriving Fenton Junior High School, the sixth graders are teamed up with a seventh grader for the whole day. Katie who had been anxiously waiting this day for at least a minimum of two years had been matched up with Jane Roberts. Since that day between band, the track team, swimming at Jane Roberts house that is located on Silver Lake, a once a summer week end trip to the Roberts cottage in Clare, Michigan, plus the annual tobogganing party at "White Lake Road," the "dynamic duo" had spent more than their share of time joined together at the hip.

Katie despite her longtime friendship with Jane Roberts had not been real excited about me starting to date her. In fact, Katie had numerous times warned me, "Stay away from her as a girlfriend!!" Katie knew that it would be only a matter of time before Jane Roberts would give her brother his walking papers. Katie, as usual, was spot-on. I just didn't anticipate that the "go play on the expressway note" approach would be as soon as September 6th, 1968.

I think what had made Katie so upset about this break up was that Jane Roberts instead of giving me the bad news face-to-face simply handed the oriental mystery box to me so that while I was fumbling around trying to get it open, Jane Roberts now had time to escape from my sight. In Katie's own words, "That lacked class. That action was totally tasteless on Jane Roberts's part."

While tasteless or lack of class is a good way to describe the action of Jane Roberts, if I was back in my "Accelerated English Class" instead of using the word tasteless, I would have used the word "coarse." As in it was "coarse" behavior on Jane Roberts's part by not dumping me face-to-face. Now all I have to do is figure out how to apply the only other word I remember

from "Accelerated English Class", "pince-nez", into the woeful actions that were dealt to me that somber Friday afternoon.

Katie was so worked up about me getting discarded by Jane Roberts that I had to calm her down and promise a "Hollywood Candy Bar" for the rest of the month to Katie for her not to telephone Jane Roberts and ream her out. As deserving as Jane Roberts was of the "Wrath of Katie", I did not want to see their friendship of the past four years go down the drain and into the sewer just because of me.

Katie then asked me if I would be okay for tomorrow at school when I would return to the scene of the breakup, the band room, my all-time favorite location in all of Fenton High School. Silence was my answer. For the first time in a long time, maybe even ever, I was not looking forward to setting foot in the Fenton High School Band Room.

Lastly, Katie, as she typically does, gave me some great advice, almost as good as Jim Koop's pearls of wisdom, "You're a free man, Beardslee." "You know, Jane Roberts is going to go through a lot of boyfriends before she graduates from Fenton High School. You will not be the only guy who is going to get his walking papers from her." Yeah, that's probably right. All of us "dumpees" can then become charter members of the "Jane Roberts Broken Hearts Club" and take turns seeing who gets to be chairman of the board.

Katie had mentioned one word in our conversation that held my attention. That was the word "tomorrow." Tomorrow is Monday. Tomorrow, specifically 9:00 AM, second hour, is Band class. Tomorrow, I'll be sitting on one side of the band room and Jane Roberts will be sitting on the other side. Tomorrow, I will have to do my best to avoid Jane Roberts for the entire 3,300 seconds of that scheduled class. Tomorrow, also brings the end of me carrying Jane Robert's tenor drum to and from the band room for marching band rehearsal for her. I will miss that enjoyable task.

Now I know how Timmy feels when he is sitting at the bottom of the well that he has fallen down into for the third time in the past week. Timmy is just sitting there crying, his shirt torn, clothes all wet, knowing that once Lassie finishes watching an entire episode of "Rin Tin Tin" and finally comes to rescue him, that Timmy knows the future holds another whooping for him. His third, coincidentally, in the past week.

I suspect that tomorrow was going to be one lousy day. Unlike Timmy, though, I just didn't have a clue of the whooping that was going to be coming my way.

"White Lake Road"

Chapter #25 – "Valentine's Day"

September 5th – I still remember waking up that Monday morning and usually unless I get the flu, which I'm good for every other year, I don't ever miss a day of school. I mean ever. But if there was ever a day of school to skip for no other reason than "I just don't want to go," then September 9th, 1968, was the day. Simply put, I was too scared to go and confront the mental torture that was facing me during second hour of Band. That will be the first time that I will have seen Jane Roberts since our infamous last meeting.

My anxiety was now causing me to have the shakes. Just imagine Don Knotts playing his character, "Dr. Jesse W. Haywood", in the movie, "The Shakiest Gun in the West." I was that bad. I had twice dropped my spoon while trying to eat my oatmeal and the two pounds of brown sugar that I had put on it. My original intent was to put three pounds of brown sugar in the bowl but the remaining pound was on either the breakfast table or the breakfast room floor.

The heebie-jeebies were still haunting me when I tried to board School Bus #23 that same morning. I tripped on the second step and practically ended up in the lap of the bus driver, Mrs. Wolverton.

As the morning went on the more nervous I became. In Mr. H.L. Connelly's first hour Speech Class, I was still pretty jumpy. Just imagine a cat in a room full of rocking chairs, that was me. The minutes were ticking away before the start of Second Hour. Jane Roberts's school locker was right next to the band room and our paths were sure to cross even before the start of a class that I never, never dreaded attending.

For the first time in three days I finally did something clever. Instead of walking past the high school office, down the hallway of where the teacher's lounge is located and the corridor that takes me past the cafeteria, I instead went the opposite way through the outside area of Fenton High School to get to the band room. That way I would not have to walk past Jane Roberts's locker and would not have to see her until I was in the band room with about 60 other kids. A brilliant strategy!! You and Lassie could learn from me, Timmy!!

Almost one year later to the day, what I saw next has stayed with me that entire time frame. Despite my superbly planned escape route, walking directly towards me was Jane Roberts and Tom Valentine. And it was rather obvious that they were a couple by the way they were strolling together. Tom Valentine had one gigantic smile, no make that a smirk, on his face as he was walking along with Jane Roberts. That totally unexpected site hit me like a ton of bricks.

Tom Valentine??? Tom Valentine?? Really!!! Really!!! Jane Roberts chose Tom Valentine over charming, witty, reflexes as quick as a cheetah, ruggedly handsome, Mike Beardslee?? The same Mike Beardslee who has able to spell his own last name since the third grade??

"White Lake Road"

Gimme a break!! I had never ever really been a big fan of Tom Valentine and seeing him walking down the halls of Fenton High School with Jane Roberts made me like him even less.

Tom Valentine and I had a history with each other and not a pleasant one as he had pulled some fast ones on me. When Tom Valentine was on the JV football team, I was a member of the cross country team during my freshman year with both teams sharing the same the locker room. Despite the fact that Tom Valentine was a marginal football player at best, it still did not stop him from giving us harriers, especially myself, a constant verbal lashing.

Tom Valentine would say stuff like, "You sissies aren't tough enough to play football". "You guys wouldn't even last through one football practice in full pads". "And if any of us "sissy cross country boys", especially you, Beardslee, ever set foot on a football field I would hit you so hard that you would regret the day you were born!!"

Tom Valentine kept shooting his mouth off until one day, Steve Harris, the captain of the cross-country team, challenged Tom Valentine to come and join the "sissy cross-country boys" in a cross-country workout that consisted of; a six-mile run to be followed up with pace work of six timed 660's. Take my word for it, that's one killer workout. That throwing down of the gauntlet by Steve Harris shut Tom Valentine's big mouth up during the remainder of the cross country and football seasons.

Once both of these sport seasons were completed I thought my troubles with Tom Valentine were over. Unfortunately, Tom Valentine and I were in the same gym class. The only activity that we ever played in P.E. Class was dodgeball. Starting at 8:00 AM, first hour, five days a week, it was dodge ball. One day when a game of dodge ball had been completed I was trotting back to one end of the gym when I was blindsided in the left part of my head by a dodgeball that had been thrown by an up-close Tom Valentine. I went down for the "eight count" and while getting back up I heard the taunting words of Tom Valentine, "How do you like them apples, sssssissy cross country boy??"

I didn't. Even "sissy cross country boys" can get upset and as I slowly arose I started to saunter over to Tom Valentine with the intent of beating him within an inch of his life. Tom Valentine saw that I meant business and started to run away from me.

Now let's analyze this. A JV football player, who based upon his physique, could easily pass for the "Pillsbury Doughboy's" twin brother, trying to run from a "sissy cross country boy" in an enclosed gymnasium. You do the math.

What was I going to do with Tom Valentine when I caught him, you ask?? Well, after watching professional wrestling on many a Saturday morning during my early years of my life, I was finally going to put that gained knowledge to good use.

I was going to use my best "Leaping Larry Chene" moves on Tom Valentine. I would start off with a head lock just to get his attention. Follow that up with a "pile driver" move to let Tom Valentine know that he was messing with no "sissy cross country boy." I would then finish Tom Valentine off with the world famous "flying head scissors" move.

After a 1-2-3 count-out is done and Tom Valentine is officially pinned, I will forever be known as Mike "Leaping Larry Chene" Beardslee!!" The dominator of "Pillsbury Doughboy" clones!!!

At least that's how things would have taken place on "Planet Beardslee." However, that little weasel was smarter than I gave him credit. Tom Valentine ran up to his fellow sophomores, Dale Flore, Robbie Joslyn and Kenny Madden. Three pretty tough dudes, especially Dale Flore. Those three guys saw what the issue was and started walking towards me with the same intent of doing to me as to what I had planned to do to Tom Valentine. I could not take on any of this trio one-on-one, let alone all at the same time. I hadn't watched that much professional wrestling to pull that off. The "Pillsbury Doughboy" stood a few feet hiding behind his protectors the whole time giving me his smirk of a smile that I despised with a passion.

I did get some satisfaction in the following dodge ball game, however, when my "World Culture I Class" buddies, Leroy Lantzy and Mark Taubitz, got some revenge against Tom Valentine. Mark Taubitz "accidentally" ran into Tom Valentine knocking him down hard. Man, it was great to see Tom Valentine's head bounce off the gym floor a couple of times. While Tom Valentine staggered to his feet he then became a recipient of a dodge ball to the face thrown by Leroy Lantzy at close range. And Leroy Lantzy, a southpaw, could throw a dodge ball the way that Sandy Koufax, former pitcher of Los Angeles Dodger fame, could throw a fast ball. FAST!! Those "hits" sustained by Tom Valentine were the chief topic of discussion during next hour's World Culture I class.

By now you have figured out that I am not a big admirer of Tom Valentine. Despite his badgering of me during my cross country days and the dodge ball incident, the primary reason, or at least until I saw him and Jane Roberts walking closely together that Monday morning in the school hallway, the thing that irks me the most about Tom Valentine is that sneer on his face that masquerades as a smile. He's got that down physical characteristic down to a science.

On September 9th, 1968, that big "smile" was again on Tom Valentine's face. This time that "smile" was a combination of: smirk, sneer and an evil all tooth grin. Tom Valentine spotted me and the type of "smile" that you wish you could rub off his face with sand paper got larger and larger the closer the two of them strolled toward my direction.

Tom Valentine stopped in front of me with Jane Roberts snuggled right next to him and said, "Hey, ssssssissy cross country boy. How ya doing??" Before I could respond with witty repartee, Tom Valentine said, "Hey, that's great." With that, arm in arm, Tom Valentine and

Jane Roberts continued to amble past me down the hallway. Man, where's Leroy Lantzy, Mark Taubitz and those dodge balls when I really need them?

Needless to say, the sight of Tom Valentine's wicked smile on his face and the visual of Jane Roberts walking side by side with him in the hall ways of Fenton High School, right outside the Band Room no less, remained with me the rest of the school day, the school year, the following summer while at Interlochen and out in Port Angeles, Washington, and especially today, my one-year anniversary of being kicked to the curb by Jane Roberts. I vividly remember every heartless second of that Friday afternoon continuing through that Monday morning. And I mean every second.

Did anything positive come out of this bleak episode of my life?? Well, according to Jim "Confucius" Koop, there was. His pearl of wisdom was this; "Look on the bright side, Beardslee. That royal dumping by Jane Roberts will prepare you for the next time it happens. And knowing you, Beardslee, it will happen again." That's better advice than what Jim "Confucius" Koop usually gives me, which is, "As long as you are still alive, Beardslee, I will never be the ugliest trumpet player in the world."

Paul Mariat, an outstanding musician, really knew what he was doing when he composed the number one record hit for the year of 1968, "Love is Blue." Yes, indeedy do, it is.

"White Lake Road"

Chapter #26 – "Grilled Tuna Fish Patties"

September 5th – To say the least I was pretty quiet on the ride back to "White Lake Road" from Hartland High School this afternoon. I was so engrossed in my "one-year anniversary" that I completely missed the White Lake Road exit and had to exit off at Owen Road instead. And the only reason I got off there was because Jim Koop said, "Beardslee, my friend, do you have immediate plans to drive to Flint to get some doughnuts from "Supremes'?"

My traveling partners were probably attributing my silence to the fact that I am not enamored one bit with my new status as a student of the Hartland Consolidated Schools. That was partially true, but my quietness was more due to the memories of this same Friday of one year ago. I hope I do not let the lingering stranglehold of that disastrous day continue to haunt me for the "best year of my life." I know myself well enough to know that that could very well be the case.

My inability to still get it through my head that I am no longer a "Fenton Tiger" but a "Hartland Eagle" continued when Katie asked me if I wanted to go to the football game tonight with her and Terry Rodenbo. I automatically assumed that Katie meant the Fenton-Montrose football game. Despite the chance to see my old "All-Star Band" buddy, Bill Cornell, who is an outstanding athlete for the "Montrose Rams", there was no way that I was going to drive to Montrose, Michigan, just to see a high school football game; even if it meant passing up the opportunity to drive past the "Supremes" doughnut store twice in the same night. Then it dawned on me that Katie was actually referring to the Hartland-Holy Redeemer football game. Duh!!

I immediately passed on the chance of a life time to attend this athletic event for a couple of reasons: 1) Unless I am marching in a half time show or playing in a pep band at an away football game, I have no desire to watch a high school football game in person. I mean none. The same goes for attending a college football game. I'm more of a professional football fan, especially when it comes to the Detroit Lions and New York Jets.

Let's just put it this way, I would much rather sit and watch in person an early 1960's Kansas City Athletics-Washington Senators American League baseball game than sit through either a high school or college football game. And let me add that those Athletic-Senators baseball teams were god-awful, usually guaranteed to finish a least a couple of thousand games out of first place behind the New York Yankees.

My second reason for not wanting to attend my new place of education's football game, not counting the lack of confidence in my driving skills in the Flint area, is the fear of once I set foot on the sacred grounds of Holy Redeemer, I will be kidnapped by members of the Holy Redeemer congregation. I will then be interrogated as to what I did with the church envelopes given to us students in catechism classes for the purposes of making contributions to Holy Redeemer Catholic Church, just like our parents. I strongly suspect that Holy Redeemer's

financial records would show that not one of those stinking envelopes of mine were ever used for donation purposes.

Then, after being cross-examined for countless hours I would receive the following punishments; for every breathing second of the rest of my life, Latin would be my only spoken language, not Pig Latin mind you, but Latin. I'd take my chances going through life speaking Pig Latin. The second chastisement placed upon me would be that for the rest of his life I could only eat the meal of grilled tuna fish patties. The all-time worst meal a good catholic family could ever eat for supper on a Friday night.

So, despite the fact that I have no urge to go watch tonight's Hartland-Holy Redeemer high school football game at Holy Redeemer Field, I must concede that the last time I had set foot on the sacred grounds of Holy Redeemer, it turned out to be a very enjoyable evening. I went to see some professional wrestling matches with Ronnie Jones, my Godmother's son. Man, it was great to see the wrestling legends like: "Leaping" Larry Chene, "Dick the Bruiser", "The Sheik", "Haystack Calhoun", and "Bobo Brazil in person." No doubt all men of good character who as part of their appearance fee were required to teach a catechism class, hear confessions and pass the collection plate at 9:00 AM Sunday Mass on behalf of the Holy Redeemer Catholic Church.

While Terry Rodenbo and Katie had to make their own arrangements to go see the "Eagles-Knights" do battle, I will simply stay within the safe confines of "White Lake Road", hunker down for the evening and count the seconds away until the Detroit Lions play their exhibition football game against the Philadelphia Eagles tomorrow night. Now that's a football game worthy of my attention!!

Man, I'm glad that this first week of school is over. And no, the supper in case you decided to ask at "White Lake Road" this evening was not grilled tuna patties.

"White Lake Road"

Chapter #27 - "The Million Dollar Movie"

September 6th – It's the weekend!! Like millions of other people in the state of Michigan, I enjoy being away from school or work for some 60 hours. The funny thing is that my favorite times of the week are Saturday mornings and Thursday nights. The latter evening was because starting at 7:00 PM on Channel 9 out of Windsor, Ontario; I religiously watched a TV show that was titled, "The Million Dollar Movie." It would show movies like "Tarzan of the Apes" and "Bomba, the Jungle Boy", of which, as a youngster, I just couldn't get enough.

And life was really good for me because the "Million Dollar Movie" would be over in time to watch another favorite TV show of mine, "My Three Sons". Whenever I got done watching an episode of that show I just knew deep down in my heart that I was a better trumpet player than son number two, "Robbie Douglas." Make that much better.

Not only was Thursday night just a great TV night but this was also the evening my mother was usually taking evening classes at Flint Junior College to get her Bachelor's degree. That meant Katie and I could eat TV dinners on TV trays in the family room and watch classic movies like, "Tarzan's New York Adventure." While it was a treat to eat supper, and watch television at the same time, normally taboo in the "White Lake Road" household, I must admit that some of those Swanson TV dinners were not a whole lot better than the grilled tuna fish patties we ate for supper on Friday nights.

My typical routine for a Saturday morning in the fall is to wake up and ran a couple of miles on White Lake Road. The first mile a nice easy jog and after turning around at Ben Eisley's house, I try to run at a 7:00 mile pace for the return mile. That's a good pace for marching band season but once I start to train for basketball tryouts I will lower that pace to a 6:30 mile. At a minimum, I will need to be consistently running a sub six flat mile pace when track season comes around so that I can reach my goal of placing in the 440 run at the Genesee-Livingston County league meet next May.

During this run, I perform the weekly ritual of guessing who is going to be on the front cover of the "Sporting News" magazine that is delivered to "White Lake Road" every Saturday morning at or around 10:30 AM. Reading that publication is the highlight of my weekend. Correction, make that the highpoint of my life.

With the regular major league baseball season entering into the last month of competition and preparing for the debut of the divisional baseball playoffs, a concept that I'm still getting used to, my thoughts lead me to believe that either Tom Seaver, the outstanding pitcher of the "Amazing Mets" would grace the cover of the world's greatest periodical, and if not "Tom Terrific", then for sure, Gil Hodges, the manager of the New York Mets. If either one of these gentlemen make the cover of "The Sporting News", then based upon my lunchroom conversation with Tom Moran yesterday, who I discovered is probably the only New York Met fan who resides in the state of Michigan, then he will be one happy puppy.

"White Lake Road"

The change in this weekend as compared to one year ago showed a marked difference in my emotions. The Jane Roberts issues will probably never escape my mind. However, I have done a better job of "making friends" with those matters. And the escape that I used to try to rid myself of these demons, the 1968 Detroit Tigers, have disappeared as well. Detroit Tigers' pitcher, Denny McClain, is not going to win 30 baseball games in consecutive seasons, and the hated "Baltimore Orioles", seem to have had the American League Eastern Division clinched since Memorial Day weekend.

At breakfast, I got the "Readers Digest" condensed version of the Hartland-Holy Redeemer football game from Katie. Holy Redeemer scored a late touchdown and was successful on the two-point conversion to win 8-7. The funniest moment of the game, at least according to Katie, was when a Holy Redeemer running back fumbled the football which led to a scramble for the recovery of the ball. Katie said, "Pete Mason came out of the pile with the football, handed it to the referee, who then proceeded to award the ball to Holy Redeemer!!"

Based upon the information provided to me by Tom Moran and in combination with the math skills that I gained in my "Modern Math" class as a seventh grader, (You would be proud of me Mr. Gordon), this is the 27th consecutive defeat for the Hartland Eagles varsity football team. Ouch!! Maybe the Hartland High School gridders should do whatever it takes to get the Pittsburgh Steelers on their schedule.

Katie also made mention that she had seen a ton of Fenton High School kids and was glad to see her old friends. I waited in between bites of my poached eggs to anxiously await Katie to include in her statement, "And everyone was asking about you and saying how much you are missed." Nary a word about me not being enrolled at the Fenton Area Schools apparently came up in conversation. Do my friends that I went to school with for the past eight years even know I'm gone?? Evidently not.

Katie did have one interesting tidbit of information that she received from "The Flying Dutchman." Due to the fact that that Fenton High School now has two high school bands, a Symphonic and Concert, and are considered two separate classes that meet different class hours; this split-up of bands means that marching band rehearsals have to take place at night during the weeks that a half-time show takes place.

So, if Katie, Jim Koop, Terry Rodenbo and I were back at our old stomping grounds, we would be spending Tuesday and Thursday nights from 7:00 PM to 9:00 PM at marching band rehearsal. This will be interesting from an attendance stand point how these rehearsals work out. Looking at this through the eyes of a high school band director, the logistics of just getting two bands that have rehearsed separately during the school day lined up into one large band only a couple of times a week would be one terrific nightmare. Finally, one positive thing from being a student of the Hartland Consolidated Schools has finally happened to me.

The rest of my Saturday was sitting down in the family room of "White Lake Road", and putting the demo records that Mr. Anderson gave me yesterday on the old record player. It's

common for vendors in the music publication business to send out demos of songs to high school band directors in order to drum up business. I love collecting them and especially enjoy the ones that feature the "Bill Moffitt Sound Power Series." He cranks out some great marching band arrangements including my all- time favorite, "March America."

Today's demo record featured a jazz tune by the name of "Flutes, Flutes, Flutes." I listened to that song a couple of thousand times while reading my September 6th issue of "The Sporting News."

And my apologies to the Hartland Varsity football team for mentioning their 27-game losing streak. My stretch of guessing who will grace the face of the "Sporting News" and being incorrect easily doubles that of the Hartland Eagles three seasons of going winless, as Ron Santo, starting third baseman for the Chicago Cubs, made the front cover of my favorite publication.

Chapter - #28 – "Two Guys with an Asterisk(s)"

September 8th – The ride this morning for the start of week two of "The greatest year of my life", was on the soundless side. There was no talk about the Hartland-Holy Redeemer football game. Since there is no half-time show for the Hartland High School marching band to perform at this upcoming Friday night there was not any conversation concerning the music we would be playing and the types of marching band routines that we would have to learn this week.

I was thankful that the noise level was not too high in the jeep. I was deep in thought concerning the band elections that were going to take place in about four hours from the time my feet hit the ground of the Hartland High School parking lot.

Are high school band elections as riveting as the John F. Kennedy-Richard Nixon presidential election of 1960; the close race for the United States presidency just one year ago between Richard Nixon and Hubert Humphrey; or the Thomas Dewey-Harry Truman presidential election from 1948? No, not even close. But take my word for it, these band elections are a huge deal and in their own way carry a certain amount of strategy and drama.

I have observed enough high school band elections over the past four years to have a pretty good idea how today's band election was going to shake down. My thoughts are: Teri Andrews is a cinch to be elected band president. For this office election, it will probably boil down to a popularity contest and I do not see anyone who will pose a threat to Teri Andrews. She might even run unopposed.

Now in the one short week that I have been a member of the Hartland Senior High Band I have not witnessed any of what I would refer to as "band president characteristics" from Teri Andrews. Other than showing up for band practice every day, I have not observed one single instance where Teri Andrews has done anything extraordinary to promote or make the Hartland Senior Band one ounce better. But who is going to be foolish enough to run against her and get more than a handful of votes? You got it. No one and you can multiply that number by three.

And if the rumors that Terry Rodenbo has been hearing are even remotely true about Teri Andrews' worthless boyfriend, Greg Sanders, running for vice-president, then I have a serious problem with that. For marching band season Mr. Anderson gave all of the Hartland Senior Band students an option of being in marching band or not this fall semester. If you chose not to be in marching band then you were put in study hall or you just sat on the sidelines and watched marching band practice and received an "Incomplete" as your grade for Band for the first none week marking period.

The only Hartland Senior High Band member to take Mr. Anderson up on this offer was Greg Sanders. He plays the trumpet and there isn't a high school marching band in the state of Michigan that will ever turn away another trumpet player. But he still opted out of marching band season. If Teri Andrews wins the presidency then Greg Sanders is a shoo in for the vice-

president position. He's worthless as a band member and he'll be even more worthless as a band vice-president. Worthless!! And you can multiply that word by any number you want!!

The combined secretary-treasurer office race is more-wide open. However, another Teri Andrews connection will extend to her best little buddy here at the Hartland Consolidated Schools, Randi Lynch. She'll probably get some token competition but certainly not enough to overcome a Teri Andrews' endorsement.

I had given some thought this morning as to nominating Terry Rodenbo for the secretary-treasurer slot. Terry Rodenbo is more than ready for a band officer's position based upon the dedication that that he had shown over the last year to the Fenton Senior High Band. He would be a perfect candidate to perform the secretary-treasurer's responsibilities.

However, Terry Rodenbo, just like the rest of us transfers from Fenton High School, while not considered quite as big of an outsider as Jim Koop and myself, he, as well as Katie, are still brand-new members of the Hartland Senior Band. Newer than new in fact and that issue may not translate into votes.

Terry Rodenbo would indeed get a few votes, three for sure, but ultimately, he would have a tough road to hoe to be elected to the secretary-treasurer office mainly because other band kids such as Randi Lynch, Jason Shattuck and Aisha Trudeau, are just as excellent candidates as Terry Rodenbo is, but again, can he overcome the home town advantage they have over him? I'm not so sure.

Terry Rodenbo and I had discussed many times during the past year the private goal that he had; Terry Rodenbo wanted to follow in my footsteps as the next Fenton Senior Band president after I had graduated. Included in these discussions were plans to make sure that he was noticed as a viable candidate for Band president. I.E., section leader, band council representative, member of the brass choir, etc. High profile kind of stuff that Terry Rodenbo did accomplish.

Could Terry Rodenbo have become the president of the Fenton Senior band for the 1970-71 school year under normal conditions? No doubt. Now however, by his transferring to Hartland High School with myself it probably puts that dream of succeeding me as president of anything, let alone a high school band, in the category of "ain't gonna happen".

Mr. Anderson started off the nomination process by advising the Band members as to the importance of selecting the right people to represent the Hartland Senior Band, not just during Band functions but outside of the Band as well. While Mr. Anderson droned on about how important it is to elect fine upstanding citizens who listen to "Radio Free Europe" every night, I reminisced back to some of the previous Band elections that I had and had not been involved in over the past few school years.

When I was in eighth grade, the junior high band director, Mr. Frank Tamburino, AKA "Mr. T.", a great band director, announced during the first few weeks of the school year that the

"White Lake Road"

Fenton Junior High Band was going to elect band officers. Something to the best of his knowledge had never occurred before in the history of the Fenton Junior High Band.

The day of the junior high band elections came and while riding the bus to school that morning I hadn't given the thought of being elected as an officer of the Fenton Junior High Band much consideration. Similar in that I had never given being a member of Student Council or any other school function any type of semi-serious deliberation, either.

There were far more important things in life for me to be concerned with, such as; will "Chip Hilton", the legendary high school star of the book series written by Clair Bee, going to recover from a broken leg that he sustained in a motor vehicle accident and be ready to play in the Valley Falls-Rutledge high school football game? Another hands wringer is whether Chet Morton, the ever-faithful companion of Frank and Joe Hardy, be able to maintain his voracious appetite through the 180 some pages of "The House on the Cliff", only the greatest "Hardy Boys" book ever written!! This kind of stuff is far more important than any junior high band election!! (I see you guys shaking your heads.)

However, once the third hour bell rang commencing the start of Band class it came time for nominations for Band president. I was just sitting there thinking why Clair Bee would have Chip Hilton sustain a broken leg during football season with the two most important games left on the schedule. I thought to myself that if I ever wrote a book I would never; never have the star of the novel suffer any broken bones before the big game of the season. Others yes, but certainly not the star of a Mike Beardslee novel.

Then from the other side of the band room I heard the name "Mike Beardslee". I had just been nominated for junior high band president. I was surprised by this nomination and was even further flabbergasted when I beat my opponent, and future nemesis, John Perkins. I had just been elected as the first time ever president of the Fenton Junior High Band. Excelsior!! (Whatever that means.)

The presidency of Mike Beardslee was to be short-lived, however, as my reign of terror lasted a little over one school week. Along with a handful of other eighth graders from the junior high band, I was promoted to the Fenton High School Senior High Band. I had hit the big time!!

So, similar to former New York Yankee right fielder, Roger Maris, whom when he broke Babe Ruth's home run record of 60 home runs in the 1961 major league baseball season had an asterisk placed next to his name in the record books, so will I.

Roger Maris' asterisk was for breaking Babe Ruth's home run record in a 162-game season, rather than the 154-game season that Babe Ruth played in 1927. But the purpose of that asterisk pales miserably to when the history of the Fenton Junior High Band is documented for posterity. A review of those archives will show that I will have an asterisk next to my name as the first elected president of the Fenton Junior High Band with a footnote that reads: "Elected but did not fulfill his entire term."

For the next two band elections at Fenton High School I was nothing more than a casual observer, much like today is going to be. I saw Bob Spears get elected as band president my freshman year and the following band election saw Guy Thompson, the band member who most deserved to be band president, unselfishly throw all of his support to Mike Hicks, allowing Mike Hicks to be elected as Fenton High School Senior Band president.

The surprising thing about the selection of Mike Hicks as band president was that he was a member of the Junior Class. A junior being elected for the vice-president or secretary-treasurer position was not uncommon. But a junior band president, now that was a rarity, even for the drama filled, life on the razor's edge world of high school band elections.

At Fenton High School the election of senior band officers traditionally took place at the end of the school year. So as the last days of my sophomore year were coming to a close, ole Beardslee was starting to beat the drum for myself to become vice-president of the senior band for my upcoming junior year." Beardslee for Vice-President!!"

Oh, it didn't stop there, my master plan was after winning the senior band vice-presidency position, come my senior year I would just slide myself right into the senior band president spot. A brilliant strategy!! No, make that a flat out brilliant strategy!! There is a difference, you know.

Well for whatever unknown reason, the Fenton Senior Band elections were not held at the end of my sophomore year. Along with Drivers Education and whether the Detroit Tigers could hold on to their first-place position in the American League, I now had something else to be all apprehensive about for the summer of 1968.

Chapter #29 - "Dog and Suds"

September 8th – Four months later Election Day for the Fenton High School band officers finally came about in September of my junior year. Similar to presidential candidates for the United States of America at that time, Richard Nixon and Hubert Humphrey, I was out stumping for votes for an elected office, the vice-presidency of the Fenton High School Band. Hey, this is important stuff!!

I was pretty sure the band election would go something like this: Mike Hicks would be re-elected as band president, probably unopposed. I would win the vice-presidency race hopefully by defeating John Perkins or Tom Douglas. The final officer's spot, secretary-treasurer, would go the Pat "The Flying Dutchman" Goode, who would also beat the two previously mentioned pretenders to the crown.

I had even gotten into the "Mike Beardslee time machine" and given serious thought as to how my senior year band election was going to end up happening. Both me and "The Flying Dutchman" would each move up one slot. I would become band president and "The Flying Dutchman" would now be band vice-president. Add "The Flying Dutchman's" girlfriend, Jan Sears, to the ticket as secretary-treasurer and that's one pretty decent set of senior band officers. "President Beardslee". Aaahh, now that's got a nice ring to it.

I remembered while sitting in the Fenton High School band room just imagining how the title "Vice-President Beardslee" would sound in the languages of Latin and Pig Latin, when I saw my good buddy, Terry Goff, approaching me with an extremely determined look on his face. My first impression at the sight of Terry Goff was that he must have finally eaten some of the hamburgers and hot dogs that he deep-fried up when he used to work as a fry cook at "Dog and Suds."

Terry Goff said to me in a voice that equaled his look and walk, "There are a lot of people in this band that want you as band president and will cast their vote for you. Just say the word and I'll get the votes and then nominate you. Do you have any problem with that??"

Before I could stammer out that the original election plan was for me to nominate Mike Hicks for president and Pat Goode to nominate me for the vice-president slot, (I mean, I did practice all summer so that I could say "Iceva Residentpa Eardsleeba" twice in a row flawlessly), Terry Goff did a to the rear march and started moving around the band room in an effort to gather up votes for Mike Beardslee for the office of band president. NOT vice-president of the band.

I thought to myself, this is not good and started to see my life flash in front of me. There is no way that I was going to defeat an incumbent band president. No way!! And even worse, if I get slaughtered by Mike Hicks in this particular election, and it could very easily happen, then what kind of an affect would this have when it comes time for the vice-presidency voting? I didn't like where this band election was headed for myself as I could easily see that my 1-0 record in band elections was soon going to become 1-1.

"White Lake Road"

The band election process got started and before I could even get my hand up to nominate Mike Hicks for president, Terry Goff nominated me for the same office practically before Miss Franklin even completed asking the question "Are there any nominations for president?"

While I was somewhat embarrassed by Terry Goff's nomination, my gut instincts told me that I was now not the person to nominate Mike Hicks for band president. That could lead to a whooping of me not only for the band presidency election but could possibly cause Mike Hicks to pull any of his support of me and dash my chances for the vice-presidency slot.

A total of 51 acres compile the property of "White Lake Road" and this past summer I walked every inch of that land going over in my mind each possible scenario as to how this election was going to take place. I nominate Mike Hicks for president and he wins. The "Flying Dutchman" nominates me for vice -president and I win. Jan Sears nominates "Flying Dutchman" for secretary-treasurer and he wins. This stuff is not calculus, or in my case Algebra I. However, I did not anticipate a development where a Terry Goff, or anyone else for that matter, would nominate me for band president. This is strictly out of left field kind of stuff.

Mike Hicks was the second and only person nominated for band president. The two of us both headed out into the hall way outside of the band room across from the wood shop and metal shop class rooms. The two of us nominees chatted very cordially as we both knew deep down inside that Mike Hicks was going to win the election. I mean for goodness sake he was an incumbent president!! That was like Adlai Stevenson or Barry Goldwater running for president of the United States against Dwight Eisenhower and Lyndon Johnson in their respective campaigns. Presidents Eisenhower and Johnson, the incumbents, easily won. No contest. Landslide city!! And I didn't see a different result taking place this morning, either.

Miss Franklin called the two of us back into the band room and even though the election results would be listed on the white board in the front of the band room, I never even bothered to take a peek to see what the final tally was. I just went and sat down by Jim Koop and Terry Rodenbo feeling a whole lot less confident about becoming "Iceva Residentpa Eardsleeba" than I did while walking around the 15,000 pine trees located on "White Lake Road" this past summer.

While sitting down I felt that people were staring at me and I finally took a quick peek at the white board where the only name appearing there was Mike Beardslee. Not Mike Hicks' name but Mike Beardslee's. That is when it dawned in me that I had won the election. I was elected band president bringing my record in band presidential elections to a stellar 2-0. Hey, that's Denny McClain kind of numbers!!

While I was thrilled with winning the band presidency one year earlier than my master plan called for, it was also a bittersweet victory for me. I had just defeated a good friend in Mike Hicks. He had taken me under his wing and always made me feel that I was an important part of the Fenton School bands ever since I was in seventh grade. Mike Hicks didn't have to do that, but he did.

"White Lake Road"

Part of my non-trumpet playing success in band was the fact that power brokers such as Don Smith, Bob Spears, Brian "Beany Bretzke", Guy Thompson and Mike Hicks mentored me and treated me like somebody important when I probably really wasn't. I still remember the morning at the end of my freshman school year when Bob Spears, Guy Thompson and Mike Hicks asked me to join them and represent the freshmen class band members when they presented a going away plaque to "Mr. T.", who was leaving Fenton High School after 14 years of service.

Those three valued band members didn't have to include me in that presentation, but they did, and I am forever grateful. That was their way of showing me what quality Band leadership was and subtlety letting me know that when my turn came, like it did in September of 1968 when the torch was now being passed to me, that I would be ready to continue the leadership of those before me and more importantly, show guidance for those that were to follow Mike Beardslee.

There were, however, two downsides of winning that band president election. Number one was that the friendship and mentoring between Mike Hicks and myself that had existed the past four school years, pretty much disintegrated into dust particles that morning when we both were called back into the band room by Miss Franklin. Sad. Very sad.

The second pitfall was that I now probably owed Terry Goff, who no doubt was very instrumental in getting me elected band president, the hamburger or hot dog of his choice at "Dog and Suds." Not only will this meal probably cost me a couple of thousand bucks, it will also mean that I will have to watch Terry Goff eat. Sad. Really, really sad.

"White Lake Road"

Chapter #30 – "Math V vs. Tequila "

September 8th, 1969 – As pleased as I was to be elected band president of the Fenton Senior High Band, I was equally shocked. And as my first duty of my newly elected office I now had to run the elections for the two remaining Band officer positions. I was so nervous that my legs were shaking like the leaves on an elm tree that was being attacked by Mother Nature caused winds of 35 MPH. I was also surprised that my vocal chords were even working when I went to ask for nominations of the vice-presidency slot; the title that I had been hoping to win for the past 120 or so days.

My mind was in no way on the next round of future Band officers. I still could not get over the fact that I had just defeated Mike Hicks for the band presidency. Not only was I still taken aback by this upset victory, but I was flat out mystified by it. How did I pull that off??

When you compared myself and Mike Hicks strictly from a high school band standpoint there were indeed similarities. One likeness being that we both had a strong passion for the Fenton Senior Band. Where the major variance existed was that we had different personalities. Mike Hicks had a more forceful persona than I did. He was far more businesslike. Maybe in his role as drum major his temperament had to be like that.

While I had the same obsession about the band that Mike Hicks did, I was friendlier and more out going to my fellow band members. I liked them and they liked me. Despite being a member of the basketball and track teams, this was my favorite group of people to chum around with. I was a 'band guy." Mike Hicks was more of a "Math V" (I think that subject has something to do with mathematics on the planet Jupiter) and "Physics" type of guy. Mike Hicks would spend his spare time reading the same 40,000-page volume books about math and science that Alex Felton and Max Perry studied, and probably enjoy every word and formula.

There were two specific events that defined the difference in personalities between Mike Hicks and me. They both took place during my freshman year of high school when the two of us were members of the Fenton High School Basketball Pep Band. (Note: I should point out that this pep band was bad. Make that embarrassingly bad. Let's just put it this way, if you were a member of this pep band, your blood relatives would never admit to it).

There were other high schools like; Flint Bendle, Swartz Creek and Brighton that had terrific sounding basketball pep bands, especially Flint Bendle's'. We were so bad that it got to the point where one-day Mr. Joseph Horak, the high school principal, stopped Guy Thompson and me in the school hallway and asked, more to Guy Thompson than myself, "If we had ever heard the Flint Bendle or Swartz Creek basketball pep bands perform?"

I wasn't smart enough to put two and two together to realize that this was a subtle hint by Mr. Horak of "How come the Fenton High School basketball pep band could barely scrounge up 10 kids to perform at basketball games when those two schools easily had 25 band kids just

blasting out their individual gymnasiums?" Thank goodness Guy Thompson knew what Mr. Horak's message was and spelled it out to me.

Guy Thompson and I discussed this matter and with him doing most of the thinking and planning, "we" came up with a speech hoping that it would inspire more Fenton Senior Band kids to play in the basketball pep band. The only kicker was that Guy Thompson put the onus on me to be the presenter of this plan to the rest of the band under the guise of "He thought that he might have a bad cold that day." Yeah, right.

The big day came, Guy Thompson, whom my mother always said that we could pass for twin brothers, and I got up in front of the band. Being "volunteered" as lead speaker I pointed out the other pep bands, especially Flint Bendle and Swartz Creek, were "hot stuff" and could blow out a whole gymnasium by themselves. They were that good and loud. I then pointed that we had the same amount of talent and numbers that those two schools had and we should have no problem getting 25 kids as our basketball pep band for every game. It was our turn to show basketball fans that we could rock Jennings Memorial Gymnasium just as good as any other high school basketball pep band.

Luckily, this meeting increased pep band attendance but we were still mediocre at best. However, whenever Mr. Horak saw either Guy Thompson or me, despite the fact that I could barely understand him through his thick eastern European accent, Mr. Horak always commented on how pleased he was to see that there were more Fenton Band kids being a part of the basketball pep band.

That basketball pep band gathering, mainly through Guy Thompson's backing, was my first step into the world of band leadership. I was finally noticed as someone other than a kid who was the owner, and who had no problem letting everyone know it, of a Bach trumpet that costs $495.00. Now along with Mike Hicks, I was considered a future leader of the band. Both of us knew that it was our destiny to become president of the Fenton Senior Band. It was just a matter of when.

While that basketball pep band meeting led me to the path of band president, a basketball pep band incident with Mike Hicks might have led to his not being re-elected as band president. One Fenton basketball game night, Mike Hicks was conducting the pep band as the designated student conductor and we were performing the song "Tequila", good old "number seven" in our glorious basketball band pep band books, a tune probably played by every high school pep band in the state of Michigan. Maybe even in parts of the Orient as well.

There comes a part in the song where the pep band stops and the band members yell out "Tequila!!", then continue on to finish the song. This specific night when the break in the music came, before us kids in the pep band could make the song required yell, Jim Koop let out a whistle that was so loud and earsplitting that you could not only use that whistle to cut through a cement block, you could also hear it all the way from Fenton, Michigan to Fruitport, Michigan!! Wherever that is.

This impromptu whistle broke up 99.9% of the pep band. Because we were laughing so hard at Jim Koop's hysterical whistle we never even finished the song. Jim Koop and I were cracking up so much that we were practically in tears. That piercing whistle was magnificent!!

However, the other .1% of the pep band, which consisted solely of Mike Hicks, who did not have the same jovial outlook on life as Jim Koop. Mike Hicks promptly threw Jim Koop out of the pep band right that second. Jim Koop packed up his trumpet and left the stage area where the pep band was housed in a matter of seconds. Despite being begged by Mr. Tamburino and his successor, Miss Franklin, Jim Koop refused to ever play again in the Fenton High School basketball pep band. And that group needed Jim Koop far more than he needed them.

A great many of the Fenton Senior Band members thought that Mike Hicks had overstepped his bounds when he kicked Jim Koop out of the basketball pep band that night and became leery about Mike Hicks.

That little incident died down and did not become an issue until it came time for senior band elections when all of us band members assumed that Guy Thompson was going to be elected as band president, as well as he should have been, with Mike Hicks was a year away from running for senior band president. Little did any of us band kids expect Guy Thompson to throw all of us support behind Mike Hicks for band president when band election time came. Mike Hicks won because Guy Thompson settled for the band vice-presidency position.

When I became the newly elected president of the Fenton Senior Band my first duty was to open up nominations for the band vice-presidency position. I was extremely relieved when Mike Hick's name was called out. If he wins maybe he'll fill the same mentoring role as Guy Thompson did when he was vice-president. While Mike Hicks was the president of the band, Guy Thompson was the unquestioned leader of the Fenton Senior Band, allowing Mike Hicks time to grow into his role.

The next name tossed out for nomination of this office was Pat "The Flying Dutchman" Goode. No offense "Dutchman," I thought to myself, but there ain't no way you are going to defeat Mike Hicks for vice-president.

Out into the hallways these candidates went. I asked for the raising of hands and I was shocked to only see some 20 votes being tallied for Mike Hicks. Even as poor as Algebra I student that Mike Beardslee was, I could figure this one out on my own. "The Flying Dutchman" was going to get the remaining 40 some other votes. Mike Hicks was defeated for the second straight election.

With one more election to go for the secretary-treasurer position I was now praying very hard that Mike Hicks would not be nominated. I didn't want to see my mentor and good friend go 0-3 in band elections on the same day. No person deserved that cruel fate. You guessed it; Jan

Sears was nominated and won just as easily as "The Flying Dutchman" did by getting at least double the number of votes as Mike Hicks.

As pleased as I was to become the Fenton Senior High Band president one year before my own personal time table, I felt bad for Mike Hicks. I felt like Mike Beardslee had failed him. When it came time for nominating speeches that day, unlike Guy Thompson, not one person spoke on Mike Hicks' behalf. He was simply nominated. Whereas, Terry Goff, gave me a rousing speech that if one existed, would have easily placed Mike Beardslee in the Fenton High School Hall of Fame. Maybe even have my own wing.

Should Mike Beardslee have been the one to speak the accolades of Mike Hicks? Yes, I should have been the" Guy Thompson" of that band election, declining the nomination for president and opening the way for Mike Hicks to be re-elected to the office that he deserved far more than Mike Beardslee. It would not have killed me to wait one year for this position. However, I didn't even utter one word of praise for Mike Hicks. Never even came close to doing so in fact.

One of my last memories of Mike Hicks for that dark day was him just sitting in the back of the band room with his head in his hands just staring at the floor probably feeling totally humiliated. I don't know if he shed a tear that day or night but he would have had every right to do so.

After that Band election, Mike Hicks somewhat disappeared from band after marching band season. I suspect that Miss Franklin let him have study hall second hour instead of coming to band rehearsal. The only time you ever saw Mike Hicks during second hour band was one week before a concert that we had scheduled. Other than that, I suspect Mike Hicks spent "band time" studying to get ready for his entrance examinations so that he could attend General Motors Institute.

Guy Thompson at the time of the Mike Hicks debacle was a freshman at Western Michigan University. He later came back to visit "White Lake Road" and after my mother was done gushing over the "college man" and treated him like the son she never had, Guy Thompson proceeded to give me some great advice to being a successful band president; "You are no longer a trumpet player who can only worry about what it will take to become and stay the first chair trumpet player. Now every single person in that band regardless of class or instrument is your primary concern."

Those exact words came to my mind some nine months later as I was sitting in the Hartland High School band room. Suddenly, just like everyone else in the band room, I about fell out of my chair when I heard the first person's name being nominated for the office of Hartland Senior Band president.

"White Lake Road"

Chapter #31 – "Pretty Boy"

September 8th – The first nomination of the Hartland Senior Band election was a real bombshell. Teri Andrews stood up and I immediately thought that she was going to nominate herself for president of the band. That was pretty gutsy. Even I would not have been daring enough to nominate myself for band president if I was back at Fenton High School.

But when the words came out of Teri Andrews' mouth with unmistaken conviction, "I am proud to nominate one Greg Sanders for band president!!" myself along with every other human being in that band room could not believe it. You just knew everyone, including Mr. Anderson, was fighting the urge to scream out at the top of their lungs to Teri Andrews, "ARE YOU STUPID??" Maybe, maybe not.

This is just a gut hunch on my part, but my theory is that in Teri Andrew's mind, that by her nominating Greg Sanders this is the only way that he was ever going to get elected to any senior band officer position. Teri Andrews had enough clout in this band that a ringing endorsement of Greg Sanders by her for the band presidency pretty much guaranteed the weasel a victory. But again, the question arose; why was Teri Andrews foolish enough to nominate Greg Sanders, of all people, for band president? My first impression was this nomination bordered on being laughable. Make that belly laughable.

This nomination, as strange as it is, makes me think that there is a pre-arranged nomination for the vice-presidency spot, of which, that will most likely be Terri Andrews herself. Nobody will probably run against her as there is not one person seated in this band room that could run against Teri Andrews and win any band officer title. Her opponent, if one even existed, probably wouldn't even get many votes. Once elected vice-president Teri Andrews will now have two other officers on her executive board letting her become the "Guy Thompson" of the Hartland Senior Band. She won't be president but I guarantee this, she'll still be calling all of the shots.

Mr. Anderson after getting over the shock of Greg Sanders even being nominated for any band officer slot let alone band president finally stammered out, "Are there were any other nominations for this office?" Mr. Anderson let about 10 seconds pass by before he was getting ready to close down the any other submissions and name Greg Sanders as band president for the 1969-70 school year when a voice off to my right said, "I nominate Mike Beardslee for band president."

The nomination of Mike Beardslee for Hartland Senior Band president caused a noticeable buzz from the other members of the Hartland Senior Band. And you could tell by the shocked look on Greg Sanders' face that the planned script for his nomination and election of band president had just taken the proverbial unexpected turn.

The person who nominated Mike Beardslee was none other than my younger sister. Katie walked down from the percussion section to where Mr. Anderson standing on the podium and promptly gave him a look that said, "I am going to stand on the podium, so move aside, buster; "then declared, "My brother as an eighth grader was voted the first ever band president in the history of Fenton Junior High Bands." (Thank goodness Katie did not mention that I was junior high band president for only a week.) "Last year as a junior he was elected president of the Fenton Senior Band defeating an incumbent president. He was also the chief officer of the Band Council which sole purpose was to allow a student voice in all band functions."

Katie continued, "You've heard his trumpet playing out on the marching band field last week so his trumpet playing ability speaks for itself. That same skill had him selected to an All-Star Band and he also attended the prestigious National Music Camp at Interlochen last summer."

Katie's mentioning of the All-Star Band selection was nice but when she mentioned that I had attended the Interlochen National Music Camp last summer that raised a few eyebrows among the members of the Hartland Senior Band. There is something magical about the name "Interlochen" when spoken and people find it very impressive when they discover that you were a student there. Thank goodness Katie didn't reveal that I had spent more time on the basketball court with "Bad Hombre" than I did practicing my trumpet during my two weeks as a member of the All-State Boys Division.

Katie continued, "But what you have to realize is that the most important thing in life to my brother is Band. Nothing else in life comes before Band. His dedication to the Fenton Senior Band was undeniable. That same devotion will be carried over to the Hartland Senior Band. No question about it."

"You saw his commitment last week went he was out there in the hot sun just like the rest of you. My brother was not taking it easy sitting here in the band room like some people did. No, just like you and I he was preparing for a first-rate half time show as members of the Hartland High School Marching Band."

I could see that Katie's remarks were hitting home. Just looking around the band room people were shaking their heads in agreement with what Katie had just articulated. These kids knew whom she was referring to and that was one Greg Sanders who had never even come out of the confines of the band room and watch us rehearse, let alone show any interest of being an active member of the Hartland Senior High Marching Band. Jim Koop probably put it best when he said, "That Greg Sanders just probably doesn't want to get out on the marching band field and get a speck of dust on his $3.00 pair of socks."

Whether it was Greg Sanders' idea or not to run for band president, and I highly suspect it probably wasn't, not being a current member of the marching band was not the best way to run a campaign to win the band presidency.

"White Lake Road"

I had known Greg Sanders for almost one week now and with the exception of the way he dressed, there was nothing about him that had impressed me. In fact, I'm not sure if I had ever heard him say one word to anyone since the start of the school year. I just remember the bright yellow shirt and sharply creased pants that he wore the first day of school. I just assumed that it was a "first day of school" type of thing, but no, come to find out, Greg Sanders dressed like that every day.

Today for Election Day Greg Sanders was wearing a dazzling pink shirt. I mean it was overpowering!! You could have lit up the whole town of Hartland on a month of January night with that shirt. His light brown dress pants had a crease in them that was so sharp that you could have cut down a sequoia tree with them and not break into a sweat. I'll give it to him, he sure could dress. Greg Sanders wardrobe would never be found on the front cover of "Boys Life Magazine."

Just before Mr. Anderson was going to send the two of us out of the band room and start the voting process, Jim Koop, who else, yelled out, "Hey you!! Pretty Boy!! Yeah, you in the glaring pink shirt!! Good luck "Pretty Boy!!" The whole band room exploded into laughter. I didn't turn around to look but I betcha even Mr. Anderson had a little smile on his face after hearing that Jim Koop line.

It was finally out into the hallway to await the final outcome of the election. This was a walk I made twice before. Once when I wasn't so sure that I was going to be victorious. The second time knowing that I had no chance of winning the position of band president. Today for my third walk of this type, there was no doubt in my mind that I was going to be elected president of the Hartland Senior Band. None.

Once out in the hallway where it was just the two of us, I saw Greg Sanders hang his head in either shame or disappointment. He knew he wasn't going to win this election as soon as the band room doors shut behind him. That Jim Koop comment had put the final nail in the coffin for any chances that Greg Sanders had of being elected president of the Hartland Senior Band.

A few minutes later as we both re-entered the band room Greg Sanders walked directly to the empty chair right next to Teri Andrews and slumped, not sat, into that empty seat. I also noticed that he never glanced at the white board where the final results were posted. "Pretty Boy" knew.

I took a quick peek at the board and the final tally was "Beardslee 35 and "Pretty Boy" 2. Those results were almost as satisfying as the final score of game seven for the 1968 World Series when the Detroit Tigers defeated the St. Louis Cardinals 4-1, making them world champions.

Jim Koop, again, who else, responded when he saw the final counting of the votes and said, "Two votes for "Pretty Boy??" What is this?? Hey, Andrews, did you vote for him twice??" That comment was followed by even louder laughter from the rest of the Hartland Senior Band members. It was clear from the first day that I became a member of this organization that the band members liked Teri Andrews, and some probably even worshiped the ground she walked on. But it was becoming really clear that they had no use for her boyfriend, Greg "Pretty Boy" Sanders.

I looked directly at Teri Andrews half expecting some type of acknowledgment of my newly elected position. Nothing. No nod of the head. No wave. Nothing. Instead I saw a crushed Teri Andrews slouched down in her chair, right next to Greg "Pretty Boy" Sanders, her right hand resting on her forehead with a look of devastation on her face that read, "What did I just do?? What did I just do??"

I didn't want to be the one to tell her but she blew it in a big-time way. Teri Andrews should have run for president herself instead of nominating "Pretty Boy". She would have won easily, probably even run unopposed. Now Teri Andrews could have nominated "Pretty Boy" for vice-president. And despite the fact that the band kids have more than their share of contempt for him, out of respect and loyalty to Teri Andrews, "Pretty Boy" would have been elected band vice-president, also probably running unopposed.

By taking the above steps, the remainder of the election falls into place for Teri Andrews. It also pretty much guarantees whoever the pre-determined nominee is for the secretary-treasurer will be a shoo-in for the victory as well. Mayor Richard Daly of the city of Chicago could not have run this election machine any better himself.

Does Mike Beardslee feel sorry for Greg "Pretty Boy" Sanders? Not one bit. Greg Sanders, I suspect, is one of those types of guys in life that you will never feel sorry for. However, one year later almost to the day, Mike Beardslee still feels bad for Mike Hicks and his final experience with high school band elections.

"White Lake Road"

Chapter #32 – "The Guns of Will Sonnett"

September 8th – While I walked over to the podium to start my first duty as Hartland Senior Band president, two thoughts came to me. First, I noticed I wasn't nervous. No badly shaking of legs and my mouth wasn't drying up which would in turn make my voice sound like "Froggy" of the "Little Rascals."

The second thought took place when I asked myself if I was still a member of the Fenton High School Band would I have been re-elected Band president and bringing my record of Band presidential elections to 3-0, the same record that Detroit Tiger pitcher, Mickey Lolich, had during the 1968 World Series. In Mike Beardslee's feeble little mind I would like to think so, but I would not bet the entire 51 acres of "White Lake Road" on the final results.

Being re-elected the president of the Fenton High School Senior Band would not have been a gimme. Mike Beardslee, with the tremendous assistance of Terry Goff, had shown that there was no guarantee that an incumbent band president would automatically be re-elected. Just ask Mike Hicks about that the next time you see him on the General Motors Institute campus.

For a couple of years there had been talk about the Fenton High School marching band attending a one-week marching band camp during the summer. Us band kids didn't seem to fired up for something like this as it would have meant a school activity that would be cutting into our summer vacation. When band parents discovered that the Fenton Area Schools were not going to pick up the entire tab for the cost of sending their kids away to some marching band camp, they didn't jump on the band wagon, either. (No pun intended.)

So, in the fall of 1968, Mike Beardslee felt pretty confident that when I applied and eventually became a member of the Student Conservation Association (SCA) there was not going to be a marching band camp for the Fenton High School Marching Band on the horizon for the upcoming summer.

I was finally accepted into the SCA in March of 1969. Then as the Mike Beardslee luck would have it, I miscalculated that a Fenton High School Band would ever attend a marching band camp. One week later after I had made my decision to be a part of the SCA, it was officially determined that the Fenton Senior Band was going to be heading off to somewhere around Lapeer, Michigan for a one-week marching band camp during one of the weeks I was scheduled to be out in the Olympic National Park.

With the marching band camp and SCA assignment dates conflicting with each other my mother suggested that I ask the SCA if I could leave one week early and fly back in time for the one week in Lapeer. The only problem with that after being away from my trumpet for two whole weeks, showing up for morning, afternoon and evening rehearsals with out of shape "chops "wasn't my idea of a fun five days. Thus, Mike Beardslee did not make an appearance for the first-time marching band camp ever attended by a Fenton Senior High Band.

The funny thing was that after my parents had dropped me off in Port Angeles, Washington, they now had to bust it back to the state of Michigan so that Katie could attend this same marching band camp. And believe me; Mike Beardslee would have never heard the end of it if Katie had missed even one second of band camp.

While I was busy in the Olympic National Park making wood shakes for a forest ranger's cabin, in my frantic little mind I could see people like John Perkins and Tom Douglas, drum major and assistant drum major respectively, working on the Fenton Band members to gain votes for them to become band president and vice-president while ole Beardslee was out of site and out of mind. This was their big chance to start the ground work to unseat not only Mike Beardslee, but Pat "The Flying Dutchman" Goode and Jan Sears as band officers.

The planets of the universe must have been aligned in such a manner for John Perkins and Tom Douglas to start their senior band officer campaign. Along with me, "The Flying Dutchman" and Jan Sears were also not attendees of marching band camp. "Dutchman" was at "Boys Town". No, not the "Boys Town" that Spencer Tracey and Mickey Rooney put on the map. This Boys Town" convention was being held in Lansing, Michigan, where government issues were discussed with other attendees and state government officials. Jan Sears was away at the Fenton Choir Camp that was being held in Ann Arbor, Michigan.

As was reported back to me by Terry Rodenbo and Katie once I arrived home from the great northwest, more than once it was said to band members by John Perkins and Tom Douglas, "That if Mike Beardslee was truly dedicated to the Fenton High School Marching Band, then he would be out here sweating and getting sunburned just like you guys!! Therefore, he's not worthy of being re-elected as band president." By coincidence, this was the exact same tactic that Katie used in her speech against Greg Sanders just a few minutes ago to get me elected Hartland Senior Band president this morning.

The best story that was relayed to me about John Perkins and Tom Douglas was from Terry Rodenbo. As mentioned earlier, marching band camp week had turned out to be a campaign week for John Perkins and Tom Douglas. Every evening at supper they would go around to the individual eating tables and make their pitches for band president and vice-president.

Thursday night, the last overnight stay for band camp, the two office seekers finally made their way to the table that a group of band kids sat including Terry Rodenbo and Katie. The first words out of John Perkins' mouth was directed to Katie when he asked, "How would you like to be on the same ticket with me and Tom Douglas? That guarantees you an elected position as Band secretary-treasurer during your sophomore year."

Terry Rodenbo immediately spoke up and said, "Hey, about me running on your ticket?? I'm a good candidate!!" The response from John Perkins was, "You may be a viable candidate, Rodenbo, but Katie Beardslee will bring far more votes to our ticket than you."

"White Lake Road"

The second story out of Katie's mouth when I got home to "White Lake Road" from my tour of duty at the SCA was, "You should have heard Terry Rodenbo put down John Perkins and Tom Douglas!! It was great!!

The version I received was the following; Terry Rodenbo's response to being shoved aside by John Perkins went something like this, "You two should consider yourselves lucky that Beardslee, Goode and Sears aren't here this week. Because if they were, then you two would revert back to the nobodies you have always been in Fenton Senior High Band. And if you have any problems with that statement then let me remind you that I have two varsity letters from the wrestling team if you want to take this outside and discuss this issue further."

Everyone at that dining table went, "Wheeeeeeew" Good put down Rodenbo!!" That put a temporary halt to the campaign smearing of the three incumbent officers of the Fenton High School Senior Band. But I don't doubt for one second that John Perkins and Tom Douglas continued to go underground to get the necessary votes that they were going to need to unseat us three present officeholders.

I would have liked to have thought that if I remained a Fenton High School for my senior year that I would have defeated John Perkins for senior band president. However, I actually spent more time walking around the "back 40" of "White Lake Road" thinking what I would have done if Mike Beardslee went the route of Mike Hicks band election wise. I came up with a list of three items.

First of all, I would have given Pat "The Flying Dutchman" a Katie Beardslee/Terry Goff nomination speech for the vice-presidency position. I guarantee that would have led to "Flying Dutchman" crushing Tom Douglas.

I doubt that Katie would have run for the secretary-treasurer positions against Jan Sears, therefore allowing Mike Beardslee to give the same kind of nominating speech for her that I did for "The Flying Dutchman." Other than Katie, there was no one else in the band that would be any type of threat to unseat Jan Sears.

The last item of the list? Here's where it gets tricky. If defeated for band president by John Perkins I would not have gone the same route of Mike Hicks by running and losing all three band officer elections. I would have immediately cut my losses. And at the end of band class I would have walked right down to a counselor's office and dropped out of band. None of this "Oh, don't worry, I'll show up one week before a concert" stuff that Mike Hicks was pulling last year. As the movie character, Chris Adams, played by Yul Brenner told the villain, "Calvera", played by Eli Wallach, in a scene from the movie, "Magnificent Seven", "Ride on!!" That's what Mike Beardslee would have said to himself, "Ride on!!"

I don't know if the Fenton High School Band officer elections have taken place yet, but Mike Beardslee would truly hope that "The Flying Dutchman" just smashes John Perkins in the

election for band president; that Jan Sears runs for vice-president of the band and annihilates Tom Douglas; then finish off Election Day with either Kevin Kenworthy or Paul Romska being elected as secretary-treasurer. That's a pretty solid group of band officers.

All I know is 50 years from now Mike Beardslee can look back and see that he entered three band elections for band president and won all three of them. And as movie actor Walter Brennan, who plays the character of "Will Sonnett" of the TV western series, "The Guns of Will Sonnett" would say, "No brag. Just fact."

Once both of my feet were planted firmly on the band podium, Mike Beardslee started the process of seeing who else was going to join him as an officer of the Hartland Senior Band. This eventually included one individual whose nomination and election I found to be quite surprising. No brag. Just fact.

"White Lake Road"

Chapter #33 – "19-18"

September 8th – Next up for the Hartland Senior Band election was the vice-presidential office. Teri Andrews was immediately nominated. No surprise there. The band room was silent for the next few seconds and Mr. Anderson was getting ready to shut down any further nominations, Jim Koop raised his hand and I thought for a second that he was going to nominate Terry Rodenbo. He would be an excellent band vice-president; however, defeating Teri Andrews would be next to impossible. There was no way I would run against her for any band officer position and even have a remote chance of winning.

Instead Jim Koop, who had that you know what kind of eating grin on his face, boldly stated, "I nominate the best dressed high school band student in the state of Michigan, Greg "Pretty Boy" Sanders, for vice-president of the Hartland High School Band!!"

Man, I thought that the kids in my sixth hour Economics Class knew something about loud laughter and whooping it up. I then came to realize that they're amateurs compared to the sound produced by these band kids when hearing Jim Koop nominate Greg "Pretty Boy" Sanders for band vice-president to run against Teri Andrews. That verbal nomination instantaneously caused one serious groundswell of belly laughs.

The really pitiful part of it was that upon his being nominated for band vice-president, Greg Sanders dutifully stood up and headed out into the hallway just like he did when he was nominated for band president. And, yes, his head was still facing down looking straight at those wing tip Florsheim style shoes he was wearing that were polished to such a high gloss that you could see your own facial reflection in them, even on a day that there was enough snow outside that you had to shovel your driveway.

Suddenly I heard a significant hissing sound from my left that was loud enough to travel the entire band room. It dawned on me that it was Teri Andrews making that serpent like sound and the words that she hissed at Greg Sanders were something to the effect," What do you think you're doing, mister??? Get back there and sit down!!!"

Oh, my goodness, I almost cried when I heard what Teri Andrews jut said, or rather hissed when giving Greg Sanders his orders!! It was hilarious!! I mean it was Jim Koop hysterical, that's how funny it was.

The rest of the band picked up on what was happening to Greg Sanders and started to sing quite sarcastically, "Pretty Boooyyyyyy!!" Pretty Boooyyyyyy!!" It got to the point that Mr. Anderson had to mercifully put a stop to the serenading. I also at the same time made a mental note to myself that my fellow band mates had no problem turning on one of their own. Hopefully Mike Beardslee will not make the "Pretty Boooyyyyyy" serenade list.

Teri Andrews ran unopposed for the band vice-president slot. No surprise there. However, the big mystery still remains, even bigger than what ever happened to Amelia Earhart, why in God's name did Teri Andrews not run for band president? I'm still stumped over that decision.

The final Band office position up for election is the secretary-treasurer slot. From a political standpoint, this was an important selection. It's like the old joke that Jim Koop once told me." Beardslee, "Do you know why there always seems to be three people on a committee? I didn't think so. That's so if two of the committee members have a fight then the third member can break it up." A funny line but it hits home specific to this next election race.

Right this very second you have Mike Beardslee as band president and Teri Andrews as band vice-president. That's one vote per officer on any band issues. I strongly suspect that our votes will consistently cancel each other's out. My other suspicion is that even though on paper Teri Andrews is not officially band president, in all actuality, Teri Andrews will consider herself band president, cast Mike Beardslee aside, and the rest of the band will follow her wishes like they always have.

If Teri Andrews get her pre-planned nominee for secretary-treasurer elected, and that's how you do it in high school band elections, then Teri Andrews will be in a great position to ignore any ideas that Mike Beardslee might have concerning the betterment of the Hartland Consolidated School Senior High Band. Going back to Jim Koop's joke about the third committee member breaking up the fight between the other two committee member's, if the Teri Andrew's nominee for secretary-treasurer gets chosen, I can see a lot of 2-1 votes going against Mike Beardslee on any issue that Teri Andrew's wants.

Mr. Anderson opened up the floor for nominations of the secretary-treasurer position. Candidate names that I have heard being bandied about included Jason Shattuck. He would be an excellent selection. The Hartland band kids like him a lot and he has a "Pied Piper" type leadership style. What could hurt Jason Shattuck, however, is that he is very heavily involved in athletics and until he gets his first varsity letter, athletics will always come before band. Believe me I know that from personal experience.

Aisha Trudeau is a freshman flute player. Aisha Trudeau showed exceptional leadership for any grade band person let alone a freshman, when she went to Mr. Anderson and requested that she play the piccolo for marching band season which would allow more sound for a marching band that is still lacking very badly in sounding like a marching band.

What will hurt Aisha Tredeau is that she is a freshman. This is my fourth senior band election and I cannot ever remember a freshman getting nominated for a band officer let alone getting any votes. With the Hartland Senior Band being made up of so many sophomores and freshman, Aisha Trudeau will be a major factor in future Hartland Senior Band elections. But probably not today.

The front runner for the secretary-treasurer position is Randi Lynch, a sophomore clarinet player, who also is one of the Hartland marching band kids who takes great pride in being one of the first ones getting back to the end zone during Mr. Anderson's "Back to the end zone" order. She is great friends with Teri Andrews. I do not doubt for one second that this will work greatly to Randi Lynch's advantage.

By the look on Randi Lynch's face you could see that she was not surprised by being nominated for this office. But that's how you work it in the world of band officer nominations. Everything is pre-planned. All the way to last May when I was still at Fenton High School with Pat "The Flying Dutchman" Goode and Jan Sears. The three sat down together one evening and strategized who was going to nominate who and for what band officer position. We were going to leave nothing for chance.

The Hartland Band Room was now quiet giving all the impression very similar to Teri Andrew's nomination for vice-president, that the secretary-treasurer position was a done deal with Randi Lynch running unopposed. Then, out of nowhere, an unfamiliar voice said, "I nominate Katie Beardslee for secretary-treasurer."

Much like when I was nominated for the band presidency office, there was that same buzz around the band room caused by Katie's nomination. Her submission was an unexpected occurrence and by the stir it caused you could tell that there was a ground swell of support for Katie. The secretary-treasurer election was indeedy-doody not going to be the wipe outs the previous two office elections had been.

Randi Lynch and Katie proceeded to make the same walk out of the band room and into the school hallway that the Greg Sanders and I had made earlier that fourth hour. Mr. Anderson, himself, then proceeded to take charge of this election. In fact, he made a point of saying, "Teri Andrews and Beardslee, neither one of you will have a vote in the secretary-treasurer election so as to prevent any partiality on either of your part." Good move.

Mr. Anderson then said to the remainder of the band members, "Okay. People voting for Katie Beardslee will line up on the right side of the band room. Those people who are going to vote for Randi Lynch will line up on the left side of the band room. Please remain there while I count the votes."

My first impression? Just doing a quick scan of both sides of the band room, I could see that the final tally was going to be close. Make that really close. Game seven of the World Series close.

Mr. Anderson did the counting all by himself and I could see that Randi Lynch's side of the band room had 18 people standing there. Based upon my fourth-grade math skills, you would be proud of me Mrs. Snoozy, told me that since there were a total of 41 kids in the Hartland Senior Band, minus Teri Andrews, Katie, myself and Randi Lynch's votes, that makes a grand

sum of 37 possible votes. Katie wins the secretary-treasurer position by a tally of 19-18. That's a big victory, not just for Katie individually, but for the Hartland Senior Band as well.

The first thing that Katie did as soon as she realized that she had won the secretary-treasurer position was to walk, no make that stomp, over to where Jim Koop and Terry Rodenbo were sitting, just minding their own business, and promptly smacked both of them upside their heads while saying to each of them, "Thanks for nominating guys!!" That was almost as funny as the serenading that "Pretty Boy" had received earlier. I said almost.

"White Lake Road"

Chapter #34 – "Apple Crisp Ala Mode"

September 8th – By Katie winning the secretary-treasurer position today, her personal goals of becoming a band officer were moved up a couple of years. Katie had always wanted to be an officer in the senior band probably since from birth. Would this momentous event have taken place if she had still been back at Fenton High School? I suspect not.

Katie's best bet to become a senior band officer would have come during the 1970-71 school year when she became a junior; most likely she could have been elected as vice-president of the Fenton Senior Band. And by the time Katie became a senior at Fenton High School she probably could have moved the Beardslee family record for band president elections to a "Ripley's Believe it or Not" record of 4-0.

Today's victory sets Katie up really well for the future Hartland Senior Band elections, that is, if my mother lets Katie come back to the Hartland Consolidated Schools next year. A subject that has not come up yet this early in the school year in the "White Lake" residence. Let's put it this way, Katie's return to Hartland High School is not that rock-solid guarantee to happen.

If Katie is allowed to come back to Hartland High School next year she will be the only returning band officer as Teri Andrews and I will have graduated and departed from the sacred halls of Hartland High School. That will probably guarantee Katie any elected position that her little heart desires. And I can guarantee you that Katie will be gunning for the band presidency position. I wouldn't bet against her, either.

You can probably add Terry Rodenbo to winning a spot as a Hartland Senior Band Officer as well for next year. But again, this will only take place if his mother allows him to come back to Hartland High School. That's probably a longshot at best from what I can tell.

I worry that my transferring to Hartland High school will hurt Terry Rodenbo and Katie if the plug is pulled on them for them attending Hartland High School next year specific to senior band elections. If it was only Mike Beardslee making this journey by himself, then the two of them being elected as band officers of the Fenton Senior Band was practically guaranteed.

Now I am not so sure. Other band members of the Fenton Senior Band will have stepped up to the plate and become future leaders to fill the voids of Mike Beardslee, Katie Beardslee Jim Koop and Terry Rodenbo. Our departures created opportunities for others. Make those tremendous opportunities.

I looked over towards Mr. Anderson and could tell that he was very happy with the results of today's election. Mr. Anderson knew that he could work together with Katie and me, far better than if Teri Andrews had been elected band president.

"White Lake Road"

Years ago, at one of my trumpet private lessons with Mr. Anderson, he explained to Mike Beardslee his teaching philosophy when it came to his band director duties. His approach to teaching was, "We have a job to do and as a group we are going to have to work towards doing that job as best we can." Mr. Anderson is not much of a disciplinarian. And from what I can tell so far with the large lion's share of the Hartland Senior Band members, discipline is not an issue at all. The majority. Not all.

Mr. Anderson and I have developed a good relationship since the start of my private lesson days that started in my sixth-grade year. I have also noticed that he has the same type of relationship with; Randi Lynch, Jason Shattuck and Aisha Trudeau. Likewise, I feel that Terry Rodenbo and Katie have entered into Mr. Anderson's inner circle of trust as well. What about Jim Koop, you ask?? I think that Mr. Anderson is still a little leery of Jim Koop. We all are so why should Mr. Anderson be the exception.

It is, however, interesting to see the relationship that Mr. Anderson has with Teri Andrews. You never see Mr. Anderson going up to Terri Andrews and asking her opinion on the selection of marching band music or how rehearsal went like he does with the inner circle members. Mr. Anderson, I suspect, is polite enough to Teri Andrews only to the extent that it keeps her mother from stomping into Hartland High School and kicking in the door of Mr. Anderson's office to complain how shabbily he has treated her daughters.

Oh, yes, I said daughters. There is a freshman oboe player in the Hartland Senior Band who is just flat out mean!! She yells at everyone and I see very few people yelling back at her. She seems like a really good person to stay away from.

One day at lunch time Terry Rodenbo advised me that the oboe player was Trecha Andrews, Teri's younger sister. When Terry Rodenbo mentioned that tidbit of information I knew immediately who the oboe player reminded me of. It conjured up memories of the woman who was reaming out Mr. Anderson about having a flag corps for band season the same day I was advising him about my teeth issues.

I'll provide you of an example of Trecha Andrews in action. At an earlier marching band rehearsal, she was yelling at some poor freshman alto saxophone player about something, which I suspect, was of no importance. I mean that poor kid was being ripped apart from head to toe.

Jim Koop, who was just standing there minding his own business, strolled slowly up to Trecha Andrews and asked, "Hey, are you related to Coach "Crabby "Appleton??" The rest of the marching band got a good chuckle out of that line temporarily shutting Trecha Andrews up and guaranteeing that the one freshman alto saxophone player now has a slight chance to live to become a sophomore alto saxophone player.

Nasty and snotty are perfect adjectives to describe Mrs. Andrews and Trecha Andrews. And let's take it one step further, when Mrs. Andrews and Trecha Andrews leave the face of the Earth to go to the hereafter, for their destination they will need to be sure and pack an electric fan with them.

The moral of the story is that Teri Andrews will probably never become a part of Mr. Anderson's inner circle. What will be interesting, however, is to see what Teri Andrews will bring to the table as vice-president of the Hartland Senior Band. If it's her mother and sister, then this will be the equivalent of the "Wicked Witch of the East" knocking back a few to many Colt 45 Malt Liquors and shutting down the "Lollipop Guild" for the winter in the "Land of Oz".

While Mr. Anderson, Katie and I were happy with the election results, I could tell by looking at Teri Andrews that she was still none too pleased. She was now over the shock of Greg "Pretty Boy" Sanders not being elected as band president. Shock, however, had turned into outrage. What was my first clue?? When I spotted the smoke that was coming out of her nose, ears plus the top of her head.

The second clue was when I started walking over to Teri Andrews to advise her that I was looking forward to working with her this band season. Instead I was on the receiving end of a, "Get out of my way!!" from Teri Andrews as she brusquely moved right past me. I took that as an, "I'm not looking forward to working with you this year at all, Beardslee!! And, oh by the way, thanks for defeating my boyfriend for band president by 33 votes!!" Don't mention it; I couldn't have done it without him.

Later that afternoon as soon as my mother walked through the doors of "White Lake Road," Katie bombarded her with the news that she had been elected the secretary-treasurer of the Hartland High Senior Band!! As a sophomore, no less!! Somewhere in this spectacular announcement was an, "Oh, yeah. Mike was also elected as band president. "At least I think that I was mentioned in Katie's news bulletin.

Riches came to the victors!! For being elected band officers today my mother gave Katie and me a choice of what we could have for supper tomorrow night and a special dessert for our Sunday afternoon meal. Katie chose spaghetti for tomorrow night. Ah, excellent selection. My mother makes great spaghetti and meatballs, not broken up hamburger spread throughout the noodles, but actual size meatballs. A meal that is fit for senior band officers!!

Mike Beardslee's selection for a special dessert of the weekend didn't take too much time to decide either. I can fire up for a big slab of warm apple crisp with a scoop of vanilla ice cream on the side. And no, Terry Rodenbo, you are not invited to have any of "Mr. President's" apple crisp ala mode.

I know, I know, Terry Rodenbo will have my mother cook up a special batch of apple crisp and homemade ice cream just for him. I can just hear my mother's words now to my father and myself while at the dinner table, "This apple crisp is for Terry Rodenbo, so "please" don't eat any." Gimme a break. He's not even a blood relative and he gets his own batch of apple crisp.

How does it feel for Mike Beardslee to be elected president of the Hartland High School Senior Band?? Good. Good enough for Mike Beardslee to jump up in the air and click his heels together like Ron Santo, third baseman for the Chicago Cubs, does after a Chicago Cubs victory? You'll never know.

I went to sleep tonight feeling pretty decent about myself and life for the first time in I don't know how long. Maybe existence in the world of the Hartland Consolidated Schools won't be so bad after all.

"White Lake Road"

Chapter #35 – "Music Stands Cost Money"

September 9th – That good feeling Mike Beardslee had from the time I fell asleep listening to WJR 760 on the dial and letting Captain Jay Roberts fly us listeners on a flight to San Francisco, California, to the time I woke up this morning at "White Lake Road", came to a screeching halt when I entered the double doors of the Hartland High School band room fourth hour. The first thing I noticed was that Mr. Anderson had company as there was another person in his office with him.

Mr. Anderson said, "Beardslee, round up Teri Andrews and your sister. We need to talk." When the three of us entered into Mr. Anderson' office the above-mentioned company was Mr. Thompson, the Hartland High School principal.

Mr. Thompson stated, "Last night I received a protest telephone call from a band parent stating that she was very upset with the fact that two "Fenton High School" students were elected as band officers because two of the elections were rigged. This parent demanded that there be a new election of officers and the two "Fenton High School students be banned from not only from running for a band officer position, but sent back to Fenton High School where they belong and I quote, stay there till you know where freezes over!!"

Mr. Thompson continued, "The purpose of my visit this morning is to determine if this was a fair election. If I discover it not to be, then I will throw out the election results from yesterday. I will then run the new election myself to pacify this parent." From the tone of Mr. Thompson's voice, you definitely got the impression of, "I've got better things to do than this."

Mr. Anderson then proceeded to describe each election in detail right from the very beginning with the election of the band president. When Mr. Anderson mentioned that Teri Andrews had nominated Greg Sanders for president, Mr. Thompson immediately raised his eyebrows, and then looked at Teri Andrews with a rather obvious "How could you do something as stupid as that" expression on his face.

When Mr. Anderson mentioned that the final vote was 36-3 in my favor and on three separate occasions you could tell Mr. Thompson was doing his best not to break two ribs laughing. Mr. Thompson's response was, "With a score like that there is no need for another presidential election." Mike Beardslee is still in and my presidential streak of band elections remains intact. Hey, Mickey Lolich, we're still tied at 3-0!!

The vice-presidential election result was also not even questioned by Mr. Thompson as Teri Andrews ran unopposed. Mr. Thompson, however, appeared to give the impression that he wanted to ask Teri Andrews a question that would be something like, "Are we going to have a problem with that outcome your highness?"

However, since the election between Randi Lynch and Katie was decided by one vote, this result was going to be scrutinized very closely by Mr. Thompson. Now Mike Beardslee is concerned because if the secretary-treasurer election has to be a do over and Randi Lynch wins, that will cause problems. It's pretty much guarantees that she will always side with Teri Andrews on any band matter. This could lead to me consistently being out voted 2-1. That could make life miserable for "President Beardslee" when my opinion on band matters does not jive with Terri Andrews and "Randi Lynch's thoughts.

Mr. Anderson proceeded to advise Mr. Thompson of what took place for the secretary-treasurer election. "When I called for the raising of hands I could see that the election was going to be close. So, I had the Katie Beardslee voters go to one side of the band room and the Randi Lynch voters go to the opposite side. I then tallied up the votes. I even counted twice to make sure of the final total and Katie Beardslee won 19-18."

Mr. Thompson, after a slight pause, then said, "Ed, I think you did everything by the book and that this election was run impartially and fairly. I see no reason to have another vote on any of the officer positions." Then Mr. Thompson turned facing Teri Andrews and said, "Teri, I will call your mother back today and advise her that the band election results will stay as is." Good call!!

However, Mr. Thompson's statement of, "I will call your mother back today, Teri… ", brought some flabbergasted looks from Katie and I as it was now blatantly obvious that it was Teri Andrews' mother that had called and complained to Mr. Thompson about the senior band elections. Therefore, common sense dictates that Mrs. Andrews heard from her one of her daughters, probably both, that the senior band election was run unfairly.

Once that information was registered in our minds, Katie now put on her "Bobby Kennedy" hat and let Teri Andrews just have it with both barrels. "You tell your mother that the all elected band officers are all registered students of the Hartland Consolidated Schools and not the Fenton Area Public Schools!! Also, just because you were dumb enough not to run for president and nominate your worthless boyfriend for the position instead, does not mean that the band election was run improperly or unfairly!! If you have a problem with what I am saying then is let's go over to your house right now and I will say the same exact words to your mother's face!! These accusations stop here and right now. Comprende??"

Oh, man, that was some tongue lashing!! And it was rather obvious by the expression on Teri Andrews' face, that was turning the same color as her red hair, that she was not used to being talked to like that by anyone, especially from another band member. However, Teri Andrews had made the mistake of making an accusation that there was something not quite right with how the band election was run and was caught. Any person, band member, parent, teacher, administrator, whomever, that makes an unjust criticism of the senior band that Katie was a member of took the chance of being on the receiving end of the "Wrath of Katie Beardslee." Take my word for it; you don't want the "Wrath of Katie Beardslee" upon you. I would think that being shunned would be less excruciating.

The funny thing was that neither Mr. Thompson nor Mr. Anderson made any attempt to stop the verbal pounding that Katie gave Teri Andrews. In fact, for one quick second I thought that I could see slight smiles on both of Mr. Thompson and Mr. Anderson's faces, sort of like they were actually enjoying the on goings. Usually a person in authority would break out a traditional line like, "Okay, show time is over, everyone go to their next class." Nothing like that was said. The scolding stopped only because Teri Andrews stomped out of Mr. Anderson's office and proceeding to knock down three or four music stands along the way.

This action brought the following comment from Mr. Thompson, "Doesn't that girl realize that music stands cost money?" That remark was then followed by laughter from Mr. Anderson and Mr. Thompson. The same kind of hilarity that would come from Jim Koop and me, which on a good day our behavior rivals two typical junior high boys. The only difference is that the majority, not all mind you, of junior high boys are far more sophisticated than Jim Koop and myself.

On the way to "White Lake Road" from school that afternoon, Katie regaled the three of us with what happened at our meeting with Mr. Anderson, Mr. Thompson and Teri Andrews. Jim Koop and Terry Rodenbo were practically crying as they envisioned Teri Andrews stomping out of Mr. Anderson's office and the knocking over of the music stands. The phrase of the day once we hit the Clyde Road was, "Hey, did you guys know that music stands cost money??" I'm sure they do.

Between Jim Koop serenading the three of us with his version of the song "Shaving Cream", it dawned on me that this was the first time that I can ever remember where a band parent has actually complained about how a band director treated their child or had any other complaint with the band director. If something like that were to occur it would probably be over a challenge for a first chair position where a band kid lost their first chair spot. A big deal in the world of high school senior bands. But never an issue concerning a band director's selection of music, marching band routines, or a rating received at a District Festival.

I have seen parents ream out coaches, especially when it came to why a student was cut from the team, why they didn't receive a varsity letter, or why this same child never got off of the bench. My Aunt Betty Beardslee was always fighting with Robert C. Walker, the high school principal at Fenton High School, as she claimed that he was always picking on my cousin Davey. No, Aunt Betty, it was probably because your son and my first cousin, was dumber than a bag of rocks. But again, I could never remember a specific incident when a band parent went head-to-head with a band director. At least not until I arrived at the Hartland Consolidated Schools.

I realize that Katie and I dodged a bullet this morning. I suspect, however, that this is not the last that time Mrs. Andrews and her daughter's paths will cross with ours as Mrs. Andrews continues her quest to demand what is best for her offspring and their specific interests when it comes to the Hartland High School Senior Band.

Can Mr. Anderson continue to hold off these ultimatums from Mrs. Andrews? Man, I sure hope so. To date there has no mention of a flag corps for this marching band season and Katie and I, despite being "Fenton High School students", still remain officers of the Hartland Senior High Band. It will be interesting to see what the next Mrs. Andrews' issue will be. You can bet dollars to doughnuts that she will back on the war path at some point.

"White Lake Road"

Chapter #36 – "Striving for Mediocrity!!"

September 11th – It finally dawned on me this morning what the one major difference to my entering a new school system at the Hartland Consolidated School was verses my starting anew at the Fenton Area Schools. When the Beardslee family moved from Swartz Creek, MI to Fenton, MI, upon entering the sacred halls of State Road Elementary School, while I didn't realize it at the time, I actually knew another student that was already enrolled there by the name of Dennis Barnes.

Dennis Barnes and I were in Kindergarten and first grade together at Mary Crapo Elementary School. For those two years it was well established that Dennis Barnes could run faster, jump higher, was taller than all of us other kids that were his classmates. Dennis Barnes was the obvious leader of all of us future "Swartz Creek Dragons." There was also no doubt that Dennis Barnes was destined to become senior class president of Swartz Creek High School, president of the student council, captain of the football team, etc. His leadership skills and talent was that obvious.

When I first arrived at State Road Elementary School as a fourth grader, just prior to the start of the school day all of us students stood outside the building in what I learned to be the recess area. After receiving my warm welcome from Eddie "Army Boots" Williams, I saw a familiar face in Dennis Barnes and immediately remembered him from my Swartz Creek school days.

While Dennis Barnes and I were not in the same fourth grade classroom at State Road Elementary School, he went out of his way to show me where the lunchroom was, where to line up for the buses, etc. It made a difficult adjustment to new school system slightly easier for Mike Beardslee.

This was the problem that Mike Beardslee had faced all of last week and even into my second week of school here at Hartland High School. In the past, I had my Fenton buddies of whom I could depend upon. But I still did not have that Hartland pal that could show me the ropes like Dennis Barnes had been kind enough to do so eight years ago.

That "friend" here at Hartland High School should have been Mark Nevers. But he paid no attention to Mike Beardslee at all even though we were in the same lunch hour. In fact, Mark Nevers, who usually sat by himself when eating the packed lunch he brought from home, made it rather obvious of going out of his way to dodge me when I had started to walk over in his direction with the purpose of seeing if he wanted to "break bread" together. Mark Nevers moved away so fast that he did more damage to the cafeteria chairs than Teri Andrews does to music stands.

What caused Mark Nevers to grab his pint of milk, stuff the remainder of his sandwich, potato chips and one mean looking vanilla frosted brownie into a paper bag, then immediately stand up and walk hurriedly in the opposite direction of Mike Beardslee? Not a clue.

But it was rather obvious that Mark Nevers wanted nothing to do with Mike Beardslee. I suspect that it was guilt on his part from quitting, or rather "cutting out" of the Hartland Senior Band. What Mark Nevers does not realize is that the Hartland Senior Band needs him far more than what he realizes. He was a halfway decent trumpet player and an excellent baritone player. A general rule of thumb is that if you were a brass player that could stand up straight, knew your left foot from your right, and breathe, there was always room for you in a high school marching band.

I would love to have the opportunity to talk Mark Nevers back into becoming a member of the Hartland High School marching band. However, the odds of doing that are the same as the Detroit Tigers overcoming the 17 ½ game lead the hated Baltimore Orioles maintain in the American League East Division with less than two weeks in the major league baseball season to go. Ain't gonna happen.

The remainder of the Hartland High School teaching staff and student body must have heard about Mike Beardslee winning the band presidency election earlier this week. After being somewhat ignored by groups outside of my world of the Hartland Senior Band, five different individuals at various times throughout the school day came up to Mike Beardslee and actually acknowledged that I am alive and somewhat well as a student of the Hartland Consolidated Schools.

Four out of the five persons I talked with were actually quite pleasant to me. However, the fifth party reminded me of another "Jim Koopism". "Always remember, Beardslee, you can't put lipstick on a pig." My last visit gave credence to that "Koopism" as Mike Beardslee left that "tete a tete" with some serious misgivings about participating in something that I have really enjoyed doing for the past four years.

The first guest into the world of Mike Beardslee this morning was a gentleman by the name of Mr. Stanley Decker. AKA "Coach Decker." I think he teaches American History here at Hartland High School but he is more famous for being the coach of one of the greatest junior high basketball teams ever in the history of the state of Michigan. Coach Decker's seventh and eighth grade basketball teams here at the Hartland Consolidated Schools were so good that they were dubbed "The UCLA of Junior High Basketball". That's quite a handle.

As a member of the Fenton Junior High basketball team I had the misfortune of going up against the "The UCLA of Junior High Basketball" squad twice. That group of Hartland cagers was far superior to any other junior high team that I have ever seen or faced. In fact, I'm not so sure that even as seventh graders those guys couldn't have competed in the freshmen basketball league of the "Genesee-Livingston "and easily gone undefeated. Their talent was that extraordinary.

Coach Decker said to me, "I know that you played varsity basketball for Fenton High School last season. With some of the plans that I have for the Hartland varsity basketball squad I could use a player with your rebounding skills and capability to run the court. Tryouts won't

be for a couple of months but I encourage you to come out for the team. So, between now and November auditions be sure that you are in basketball shape."

Wow!! Mike Beardslee is actually getting an invitation to try out for the Hartland High school varsity basketball team!! Who does this guy have me mixed up with?? There is no way that any basketball coach in the "GL Conference" would mistake Mike Beardslee for elite basketball forwards such as: Steve Blake of Lake Fenton High School; Ron Wiggins of Ainsworth High School; Rick Pertler, Gene Leach, Steve Leach and Barry Johnson of the Swartz Creek Dragons, my two old Fenton High School buddies, Leroy Lantzy and Dennis Baler or Dave Devers, probably the best overall athlete in the "GL Conference", of Brighton High School. No way!!

Those guys are talented basketball players with potential to continue to play at some type of college basketball level. Mike Beardslee is still striving for mediocrity on the basketball court. And, truth be known, I am light years from achieving that.

I wonder what kind of plans that Coach Decker has that he took the time from his busy teaching schedule to meet and speak with Mike Beardslee?? At least I have been given some type of indication that there might be a spot for Mike Beardslee on the Hartland Varsity Basketball team this season. There was no guarantee of that if I had remained at Fenton High School.

However, my next visitor made two guarantees to Mike Beardslee: 1) There was a place on his team with my name on it and; 2) I didn't have to wait until the month of March to purchase a Hartland High School varsity jacket.

"White Lake Road"

Chapter #37 – "Pace Work vs. Long Distance Running"

September 11th – The next visitor was another varsity coach. This visit was initiated by Coach Campbell, the Hartland High School Cross Country coach. The interesting thing about Coach Campbell is that he is not an actual teacher in the Hartland Consolidated Schools. Coach Campbell is instead a substitute teacher who coaches the cross country team. I had never seen that type of arrangement back at Fenton High School and wonder if the Fenton School Board even allowed a person not under contract as a teacher to coach athletics.

After some pleasantries were exchanged, Mr. Campbell got down to business stating, "I have a pretty good cross country team this season, especially my first five runners. Alex Felton consistently runs in the 10:20 and under range for the two-mile run. Hopefully he'll break his own school record again this year. Al Dowty runs a consistent 10:30 flat pace. Then I have Max Perry and Jason Shattuck who float around 11:00 to 11:05. My fifth man is Tom Beaver who is always good for a solid 11:15 to 11:20 pace."

While listening to Coach Campbell, a thought crossed my mind. It just never ceases to amaze me how cross country coaches can rattle off at the top of their head individual runner's times to other people and not have the slightest clue that a great majority of these people on the receiving end of this "sterling" information do not share the same fascination about a cross country runner's mile splits or the age-old riveting argument of; "What's the better workout for the high school cross country runner; pace work or long-distance running? "

On some college campus in the United States of America I betcha there is a Psychology major writing their Master Degree Thesis on this very topic. In fact, I can practically guarantee it.

Coach Campbell continued, "The problem that I have with my team, and this is where you come in, is that my sixth and seventh runners are very inexperienced and can barely break the 14:00 barrier for a two-mile run. Those kinds of times aren't going to get a team qualified for the state meet or win a conference championship."

"If one of my top five runners goes down with an injury then I'm really hurting. I overheard that you had run a couple of years of cross country at Fenton High School and I would love to have you become an immediate member of the Hartland Cross Country team. You would be a shoo-in to be a varsity runner and get a varsity letter. Wouldn't that be a great feeling to wear a varsity jacket while attending basketball games this winter? What do you think??"

Before I could even get a response in, Coach Campbell's next question was, "What's your best time on the two-mile run?" My response was, "I ran an 11:46 with a 5:42 first mile split and a 6:04 second mile split during my sophomore year of cross country." Oh, man, now I'm just as bad as every other cross country coach in the state of Michigan by spouting out my best overall time and mile splits.

What I didn't include in my answer to Coach Campbell was that this personal record for Mike Beardslee was set on the Durand High School cross country course, and while very scenic, the course was flat as a pancake. You couldn't help but not run a good time on that cross country course.

You could just see Coach Campbell's eyes light up when I mentioned my "PR" cross country time. That was a lot better than what his sixth and seventh runners were now doing and would probably ever do this season. Coach Campbell then proceeded to advise me of his plan of action, "Good, that's a great time and you're now two years stronger and your legs are fresh. This is perfect!!"

Coach Campbell then added, "Here's the plan. The regional meet is seven weeks from this Saturday and the conference championship meet is the following Wednesday after the Regionals. "Starting with today's practice I'll have you work out with the team and keep you out of the dual meets for the next couple of weeks. You will still have the chance to get a couple of races under your belt and you should be ready to go for the big races by the end of the season. So, what do you think? Can I count on you for the remainder of the season??"

Mike Beardslee already knew what the answer to this $64,000 question was but showed enough respect to Coach Campbell to not immediately blurt out, "Ain't no way, man!!" I politely declined his invitation to join the Hartland Cross Country team and felt like a heel doing it as Coach Campbell seemed like a nice guy who was very passionate about his role as the cross country coach of Hartland High School.

Cross Country is a tough sport and from my two years of being a member of the Fenton High School Cross Country team, I know how hard it is to get kids to first of all to actually come out for the team and secondly, then keep them for the whole season. It's not uncommon where a kid will show up for one cross country practice and not come back for a workout the next day. cross country is not a sport for everyone. Mike Beardslee is a perfect example of this.

During my freshman and sophomore years of high school, I ran cross county in the fall, played basketball in the winter and ran track in the spring. That's a lot of sports and didn't leave as much time for what I enjoyed the most in life, practicing and playing my trumpet. Homework??What's that??

Mike Beardslee made an executive decision that once I received my first varsity letter in one of the above-mentioned sports, I would then "retire" from one of the two sports that I had not lettered in. During my sophomore year of high school that big day came when I received a varsity letter in Track.

Now the big question was which sport was I going to eliminate for the rest of my high school career? Believe it or not this was a huge dilemma for Mike Beardslee. I loved playing basketball, but admittedly, was run-of-the-mill at best. I was okay in cross country but not

anything great. Of the two sports, I had a pretty good chance for my junior year of being one of the top seven runners on the Fenton High School Cross Country team making me a varsity runner and be eligible for a varsity letter. There was no guarantee that I would ever make the varsity basketball team. To steal a line from Jim Koop, "Beardslee, your chances of making the varsity basketball team are always going to be slim and none. And "Slim" is currently checking his bags in at Bishop Airport."

The decision I reached was to eliminate the sport of cross country from Mike Beardslee's life. My reasoning was this; Band was starting to become a major part of my existence. I had goals in band that I wanted to accomplish. I.E. 1) become a band officer; 2) establish myself as the first chair trumpet player for my two remaining years of high school; 3) win the Arion Award as the most outstanding senior member of the band.

I'm not so sure that I could have reached those goals if I had to choose between how I spent my "White Lake Road" evenings by either practicing the trumpet or taking a nap on the couch in the family room because of being totally exhausted from cross country practice.

To Mike Beardslee, this was an easy decision and proceeded to make this monumental choice during the summer of 1968, between my sophomore and junior year of high school. Not a big deal for me. I didn't bother to put any advertisements in the "Flint Journal" or "Fenton Independent" periodicals; and even if I had placed any announcements in these tabloids, I would have most certainly turned down any requests from "WJRT – Channel 12" to appear and make this declaration on their 6:00 PM news.

However, if WJRT provides limousine service to and from "White Lake Road;" and the chance for an additional announcement on their 11:00 PM news show under the category of "Breaking News", I would have undoubtedly honored that request. Film at 11:00!! Alright!! I could get into that!!

When the month of August came and cross country practice started, Mike Beardslee was not out there running in "Jefferson Hills" or the infamous six mile run that started at Fenton High; down Leroy Street; west on Silver Lake Road; cut across Jennings Road; hit the downhill section of Owen Road; run about a half-mile run on Shiawassee Street and back to Fenton High School for some more pace work. That kind of cross country workout will make you sleep well at night.

While I didn't think that my absence from the Fenton High School Cross Country team was a huge deal, I received a lot of flak about not going out for the season from various parties. My mother was appalled and how in the world was she going to explain this decision to the rest of the State Road Elementary teachers?? Oh, my!!

"White Lake Road"

Jane Roberts was extremely disappointed with my decision despite my saying to her, "This will allow us to spend more time together." (Yeah, you guys read how well that worked out for Mike Beardslee.)

A couple of my cross country buddies were also disappointed and upset with me with my decision to not pursue my cross country career. Jon Ackerman, the biggest Detroit Tiger fan in the world, and I in June of 1968 had made a pact that we were going to get together once a week and go out on cross country training runs. Jon Ackerman called me one evening after cross country practices had started and wondered if I was okay and reminded me that cross country practice was underway. Much like today when I advised Coach Campbell that I had no desire to run cross country, it was tough to give that same news to Jon Ackerman. Luckily it did not put a strain on our friendship.

Mike Evans, a good buddy of mine from the State Road Elementary School days and candidate for school valedictorian, took a different approach as to my not coming out for the cross country team. When he saw at a Monday night Catechism class at St. Johns School, he yelled at me in an attacking type of voice, "HEY, BEARDSLEE!! WHEN ARE YOU GOING TO GET YOUR LAZY BUTT OUT FOR CROSS COUNTRY!!"

I was hurt by Mike Evan's verbal abuse. I simply replied, "Mike, "I'll be out for cross country as soon as you become a member of the Fenton Band again." Mike Evans, an excellent clarinet player, had dropped out of Band upon entering junior high school. Guess who did didn't run cross country for Fenton High School or rejoin the Fenton Senior Band that same fall. You're absolutely right.

I really didn't understand the big brouhaha as to why it was such a big deal that Mike Beardslee didn't come out for cross country his junior year of high school. I wasn't that good of runner and I enjoyed track season much, much more. There were, however, two future moments when Mike Beardslee gave serious thought as to rejoining the Fenton High School cross country team.

"White Lake Road"

Chapter #38 – "I'm fine. Thanks for asking"

September 11th –The first passing moment came after I had made my monumental decision not to run cross country. I was out walking on White Lake Road one morning, in bare feet no less, when I saw a yellow corvair driving towards me. I knew who the owner of the yellow corvair was and was pretty certain that it wasn't Ralph Nader, political activist, who had written many papers about how unsafe it was for the American public to drive a motor vehicle of this type. The owner and operator of this yellow car was none other than Mr. Ray Lane, the cross country coach at Fenton High School. He was absolutely the last person in the world that I wanted to see.

Coach Lane stopped his yellow corvair, rolled down the passenger side window and said to me, "I'll see you at practice tomorrow morning, Beardslee." Then he simply drove off.

This conversation was from the same teacher who if you saw him walking towards you in the hallways of Fenton High School and you were the only two people in that hallway, Coach Lane would not even acknowledge your presence. He would just walk past you. And now he brings that banana colored corvair to a complete stop and actually talks to me about cross country?? I don't get it. Oh, and by the way, Coach Lane, I'm fine. Thanks for asking.

I walked back to "White Lake Road" with my heart going at the rate of a 10:00 flat 100-yard dash. My first thought was to scrounge up a pair of running shoes and go out for a run tonight to see just how bad of shape Mike Beardslee really was in before showing up for cross country practice the next morning.

But from the time of Coach Lane's departure and my walking up the driveway of "White Lake Road", Mike Beardslee had come to his senses. Despite a restless night of sleep, two thoughts came to my mind. Mike Beardslee decided not to return to the world of Fenton High School Cross Country and; if Coach Lane ever receives a letter from Ralph Nader, then I hope he never reads the contents of that correspondence.

The second fleeting moment came this past June of 1969. I was sitting on the couch in the family room of "White Lake Road" doing what I do best in life, reading a "Sporting News Magazine" and watching TV. No particular order. A sudden impulse hit and Mike Beardslee decided that he was going to get in shape and run on the cross country team at Fenton High School for my senior year. That would get me another varsity letter, add another gold bar to the ole varsity jacket, allow me to get in shape for basketball season and have a good senior year of running track. At that time, this idea sounded brilliant to old Beardslee. Beardslee Brilliant!

But by the time I sat down and refocused on reading about the Detroit Tigers doing a slow fade in the American League East Division and trying for about the ninth year in a row to guess the name of a song for a cash prize that movie hostess, Rita Bell, would play during one of the segments of this movie, much like 10 months earlier, Mike Beardslee came to his senses and decided not to rejoin the Fenton High School Cross Country team. This decision was based upon the fact that with two upcoming weeks of Interlochen, to be shortly followed up

with another four weeks with the Student Conservation Association ahead of me for the summer of 1969, getting enough training miles in would be difficult.

Just for the record, I never did win that cash prize for getting the right title of the mystery song probably because Rita Bell has never played any of Bill Moffit's "Sound Power" music arrangements that I absolutely loved playing during marching band season. If Rita Bell had played any of those "Sound Power" hits, however, Mike Beardslee would have won so much money that I would have had my own morning television show on Channel 7. I would have named the show, "Wake up to Beardslee!!" I mean we are talking about seriously big ratings here!!

Was the decision to give up my cross country career a great verdict by Mike Beardslee?? Yes and no. By not going out for cross country, despite my best intentions of "I can run on my own to get in shape for basketball season ", I didn't work out very much, if at all. That led to Mike Beardslee not reporting in shape for basketball tryouts and barely making the squad that season. And by barely, I mean by the hairs on my chinny chin- chin.

Factor in some really super bad eating habits and heading to the couch to sleep instead of the "Back 40" of "White Lake Road" for some hill runs; I just never got into the type of shape that I needed to earn some playing time during varsity basketball season.

What was my first clue as to recognizing that Mike Beardslee just was not in basketball playing shape? While I wasn't the greatest high school basketball player that ever wore a varsity uniform for a Fenton High School basketball team, I always prided myself in winning the majority of line drills that we ran in practice. Some day when a "Line Drill Hall of Fame" opens up, there will be a wing named after Mike Beardslee. I guarantee it. But now I was rarely winning these line drills and was being beaten regularly by guys with no foot speed at all. I mean none!! Sorry, Dave Farmer and Gary Teachout.

That poor conditioning on my part followed me into track season as well. My junior year of track should have been a breakout season for Mike Beardslee. However, again my poor eating habits as well as not working as hard as I had always done in previous track seasons revealed that my 440 time only improved 1.3 seconds from beginning of track season to the end of the track season. By the time the regional and league meets arrived in the latter part of the month of May, I was not even running in the 440 run or a leg on the mile relay team. Mike Beardslee had been replaced by younger, less experienced and hungrier runners.

I still remember one freshman quarter miler saying to me one day during a track practice "See ya on the way down the depth chart, Beardslee." That statement hurt then and to this very day five months later it still upsets me because there was more than a trace of truth to that statement being said to Mike Beardslee's face.

The lesson learned for Mike Beardslee is that once I got back from Port Angeles, Washington and the Student Conservation Association adventure, a workout schedule was developed. Every other day I would be running long distance, minimum two miles. Added to that was doing pushups, shooting free throws, hill sprints and jumping rope. I wanted to get in shape for basketball tryouts, especially after being invited to try out by Coach Decker, and then be ready for track season.

I especially wanted to have a good track season so that I wouldn't have to hear after every track meet the words of, "We would have won this dual meet if we had gotten any points from our quarter milers." I had also wanted to redeem myself from being replaced last year in my most favorite track and field event; a member of the mile relay team.

There were truly some good things that came out of my not running cross country that fall of 1968. With the Band Float being built at "White Lake Road" starting my sophomore year, I was rarely there to help work on that project. Now, with no cross country practice on my daily schedule, I could get home from school and be right there to be in charge of this project.

Also by not running cross country it allowed me to spend more time on other band functions. I replaced Guy Thompson as the person in charge of building the band float. I could practice the trumpet more which helped me solidify my goal of being the first chair trumpet player of the Fenton Senior Band and; hopefully carry on the tradition of outstanding first chair trumpet players set by my predecessors of Ray Sortman and Carl Peters. It also meant the end of going straight from cross country practice to "White Lake Road" for supper and then bust it back into town with the hope that I wouldn't be late to march in the home coming parade or tardy for a pre-game show rehearsal.

If I had remained at Fenton High School this current school year and run on the cross country team, under the current marching band set up with rehearsals on certain evenings, I would have left "White Lake Road" at 7:30 A.M. and not gotten home until 9:30 P.M. That's a long time to go without supper.

One other benefit that I received from being a former cross country runner occurred when one day my Speech Class teacher, Mr. H.L. Connelly, who was also in charge of the high school play, approached me in class one morning and advised me that a person who had auditioned for the role of "Bert Jefferson" in the play, "Guess Who's Coming to Dinner? ", was not working out and asked me read for the part.

I read for the role, eventually got the part and thoroughly enjoyed being a member of the cast. What I didn't enjoy was being physically threatened on a daily basis by Don Simmons, the guy whom Mr. H.L. Connelly took the part away from. Fortunately, the threats of violence never came about. But believe me; Don Simmons, who had some serious "Gold Gloves" background, could have, if he felt the desire to do so, beaten Mike Beardslee to a pulp.

Would Mike Beardslee make the same decision of not running cross country again? In a jiffy. Maybe even faster. While I was criticized and looked down upon by many friends, it wasn't like I was at home sitting on the couch watching the 4:30 movie on WNEM Channel Five. Mike Beardslee became a better trumpet player; a better student; and had a major part in the school play. Life from that standpoint was good.

"White Lake Road"

So as much as Mike Beardslee didn't want to say no to Coach Campbell today, I went ahead and declined his offer to join the Hartland Cross Country team. There were two reasons for this Mike Beardslee decision. One, you don't just one day show up out of nowhere and start running cross country. Oh, your legs will be fresh for the first practice or two and then reality sets in. Your legs then feel like you are running in sand. This could lead to the development of shin splints and that really slows you down for a while. Now your conditioning falls even farther behind the other runners.

A cross country runner eventually gets through these issues and life from a running standpoint gets better. But I showed up once for a cross country season out of shape and Mike Beardslee is not going to make that mistake again.

The second reason why I didn't want to become a member of the Hartland Cross Country team was based upon two past specific events. Despite the fact that I made some great friends from my two years as a cross country runner at Fenton High School, guys like: Steve Harris, Homer Stout, Dave Koester, Doug Arnold, Mike Evans, Paul Evans and Gordie Smith, all great fellas. There were, however, two incidents, one minor, and the other occurrence that even three years later to this day still rankles me.

At the end of my eighth-grade school year there was a cross country team meeting and sign-up. You gave your name, address and telephone number and were given the orders to run at least two miles a day throughout the summer until the start of practices at some undetermined date in August.

During that summer, I spent the majority of my time trying to become a member of the Flint-Hamilton CANUSA games, where track athletes from Genesee County would perform in a track meet with athletes from Hamilton, Ontario. It was a big deal. I made the Flint team for my age group and even ended up getting a bronze medal, my first one ever in a track and field event, for placing third in the long jump. Add a couple of ribbon awards and my name in the "Flint Journal" a couple of times and life was good for Mike Beardslee.

Based upon my success in the CANUSA games Mike Beardslee didn't even give being a member of the Fenton High School Cross Country team to much thought that summer, let alone running the "recommended "two miles a day. Then one August Monday evening the telephone rang at the residence of "White Lake Road". On the other end of the line was Mr. Lane, the Fenton High School Cross Country coach, asking me, "Who did I think I was missing the first day of cross country practice??"

My reply of that I had no idea of when the first day of Cross Country practice was getting me nowhere when Mike Beardslee took a page out of the Jim Koop book of "How to Get Along with Teachers and Coaches", really got brave and said to Coach Lane, "Shouldn't it be the coach's responsibility to let the team members know when and where the first cross country practice is to take place? I mean wasn't that was the purpose of the signup sheet last June??" Oh yeah, that went over real well. Real well.

"White Lake Road"

My plea of "Nobody ever told me when practice was going to be" didn't get me anywhere as Coach Lane wasn't buying into it and my mother, who automatically sides with any teacher that her son is in a jam with, also let me know in no uncertain terms of how embarrassing it was that her irresponsible son couldn't even remember when the first day of when Cross Country practice was.

That was my initial experience with Fenton High School Cross Country and as you can probably tell it didn't go so hot. Things didn't improve much from that evening telephone conversation with Coach Lane, either. I showed up to cross country practice the next morning and what I remember most about that day was the three-mile run and the six 220's that we ran in practice. I had never run three miles or a single 220 before in my life let alone in a single morning. That's when it dawned on me that Mike Beardslee's name was never going to be mentioned in the same breath as Fenton High School Cross Country greats such as; Jerry Stiles, Ron Wardie or Dan Humboldt. Never.

Also for that first day of practice the rest of the Fenton Cross Country team was wearing the "uniform" of the day, sweat tops and sweat bottoms. These sweats had "Fenton High School Cross Country" and a team number on both tops and pants. For the first week of practice guess who was not issued a pair of sweats? Yeah, you got it, yours truly.

I got tired of everyone else looking like they were a part of the cross country team and Mike Beardslee didn't. I finally scrounged up enough courage to ask Coach Lane if I could have a set of sweats as well. There is an old saying of, "Be careful of what you wish for." Mike Beardslee was finally given his "treasured" sweat pants with the anticipation that I now would at least look like a member of the Fenton High School Cross Country team.

However, my highly anticipated sweats had no markings on them at all. None. There was no identification of what cross country team Mike Beardslee was affiliated with at all. It looked like I had walked into my favorite sporting goods store, "All Sports" in down town, Flint, Michigan, and bought a pair of sweats right off of the rack.

It really became embarrassing for me when Fenton High School ran a cross country meet against Atherton High School. After the meet was over, the Atherton Cross Country coach said to me, "Hey, that's nice that Coach Lane lets his team manager run in the meet." That made life in the world of cross country even more excruciating for Mike Beardslee.

When it came time for the end of the season team picture that year there was still no indication or acknowledgement from Coach Lane that my sweat pants were different than the rest of my teammates. Mike Evans, who was on the varsity squad and was entitled to wear "dress sweats" featuring the orange and black school colors of Fenton High School, was kind enough to let me wear his workout sweatshirt top for the photo. At least I looked like I was a member of the Fenton High School Cross Country team rather than a team manager or a cross country "wanna be."

It was nice meeting Coach Campbell today. He came across as a good guy that probably under a different set of circumstances I would have enjoyed running for him. Much like the

invitation I received from Coach Decker to try out for the varsity basketball squad, I also considered the invite to join the Hartland High School Cross Country team an honor. But for Mike Beardslee the answers were; basketball tryouts, yes. cross country season, no.

Chapter #39 – "I Guarantee It!!"

September 11th – The Genesee-Livingston "GL" Athletic Conference consists of 10 high schools. Five school districts are from Genesee County and the same number of schools represent Livingston County. Thus, the name "GL". Despite the fact that every spring Brighton and Swartz Creek High Schools threaten to vamoose from what they consider in their own words, "This Mickey Mouse conference", the "GL" has remained intact with all of the original charter members since its inception in the 1960-61 school year.

The interesting thing about the "GL" is that throughout the years each individual competing sport has been dominated by one high school. In fact, five teams have won the league championship each season of the league's existence.

The breakdown of the conference power brokers looks like this:

- ***Football – Fenton High School***
- ***Cross Country – Howell High School***
- ***Men's Basketball – Brighton High School***
- ***Women's Basketball – Ainsworth High School***
- ***Wrestling – Swartz Creek High School***
- ***Men's Track – Swartz Creek High School***
- ***Women's Track – Pinckney High School***
- ***Baseball – Fowlerville High School***
- ***Softball – Fenton High School***
- ***Golf – Lake Fenton High School***
- ***Tennis – Swartz Creek High School.***

The Howell Highlander's Cross Country team was one of the five above teams to have won the conference championship every year of the "GL" existence with the other four remaining teams being, Brighton for men's basketball; Swartz Creek for men's track; Fenton for varsity football and Ainsworth for women's basketball.

The Howell High School Cross Country team during the first eight years of "GL" existence just dominated the league competition and, in fact, a couple of those years their runners took the first five places in the league meet obtaining a score of "15". That is the best score that a

cross country team can achieve in any meet, dual or invitational. When that type of scoring takes place it's commonly referred to as Howell "skunked" the rest of the competition.

When the "Highlander's" Cross Country teams' accomplishments are mentioned they include the following: nine straight conference titles; numerous regional titles; plus, a couple of state championships. Now you're talking the Boston Celtics/New York Yankees type dynasties when it comes to the "GL Conference" cross country programs.

After the 1967 cross country season, the last season where the Howell Cross Country team could be tabbed as a "super power", it was rather obvious that for the future they just didn't have the "horses" to keep that streak of championships going. This is when Coach Campbell, Hartland's Cross Country coach, made a quote that was right out of "Broadway" Joe Namath's mouth. It was reported in the newspapers that Coach Campbell was cited as saying, "My cross country team will end that Howell High School championship run next year!! I guarantee it!!"

That drew Coach Campbell a lot of unwanted attention for a couple of reasons. First of all, the Hartland Cross Country team had never been a factor in any "GL Conference" championship meet with their best finish ever being seventh place. And that was only because Alex Felton and Al Dowty finished in the top 10 runners at the league conference meet. The remainder of the Hartland High harriers on race day finished in an entirely different county.

I knew some of the 1968 Howell Cross Country runners and they were nice guys. However, you would probably classify them as support runners. None of them were ever going to win a cross country race as an individual. But man-oh-man, could they would run in a pack, which is exactly what you want from your cross country team. And the Howell harriers ran consistent times. Not good one meet and then two minutes slower the next meet. The "Highlander" runners were always going to give a full out effort.

The Howell High School Cross Country coach was a true gentleman by the name of Coach Fitzpatrick. He was the type of coach that if you could not run for him, you could not run for anybody. In fact, one-year Fenton High School was competing against Howell in a dual track meet at Howell High School. I was a freshman and running in a second heat of the 440 for non-varsity runners.

In this heat were myself and my running buddies, Tom Rhodes and Mike Terry. Wearing my school issued Fenton Physical Education gym shorts and my "Broadway" Joe Namath, #12 sweatshirt, Mike Beardslee blasted out a 61.7 440 time which was the fastest that I had ever run in that event. A great time no, but a good result for Mike Beardslee.

After the race, Coach Fitzpatrick, totally on his own choosing, came up to me and said, "You know, if you use starting blocks that will give you faster start and you'll be down under 60 flat 440 before you know it. Now you are edging closer to varsity letter territory." That was awful nice of Coach Fitzpatrick as he didn't have to say that to me at all. But since Coach Lane made no mention of my efforts, then I'll take these words of encouragement, even if they were from an opposing coach.

"White Lake Road"

The Howell Cross Country teams, while not the most talented group of runners, but you just simply could not out work them. They were so dedicated to keeping that conference streak intact that once a week they would travel to Shore Acres, a golf course in Fenton, Michigan, where the "GL" Cross Country league meet was held, to hold their workouts there. As Coach Fitzpatrick was quoted in the "Flint Journal" after winning his ninth consecutive league championship, "My runners knew every inch of that course. They knew how to run down the hills that led to the crossing over a couple of bridges and how to kick in that last quarter mile stretch. I'm just so proud of them."

The Hartland High Cross Country team of 1968, based upon their returning two top ten finishers from the previous year league meet, was the pre-season pick to win the "GL" Cross Country league championship. Since the Hartland High Cross Country team had never been much of a factor in the "GL" final standings, this projected championship did not make any sense to me. In fact, I felt safe in betting all 51 acres of "White Lake Road" and the accompanying 15,000 pine trees that came with this property, that the Hartland High School Cross Country team was not going to win any league championship.

What cross country team would Mike Beardslee have bet the above property to end Howell High School's dominance of consecutive cross country championships? My fearless prediction was the Swartz Creek Dragon's. That was based solely on the fact that they had finished runner-up to Howell Cross Country teams for each of the previous conference championship meets.

It's a good thing that I did not place that bet, because man, I was so wrong. Despite Alex Felton taking individual honors by being the first runner across the finish line, and Al Dowty's sixth place finish, the Howell High Cross Country team, which had a team motto of, "Eight Championships going on Nine", lived up to that motto as they ran in a pack like they had done all season long and kept their "GL Conference" championship streak intact.

The next day at school I heard the Fenton Cross Country runners talk about some of the cracks that people were making concerning Coach Campbell. Stuff like people probably used to say about the Brooklyn Dodgers after they had just lost another world series to the New York Yankees, "Wait till next year!!" Or, "Hey Coach Campbell!! Let's hear your prediction for next year's league championship winner!!" "Chump!!!"

Coach Campbell was shown no mercy, and he, as well as the members of the Hartland High School Cross Country team had become laughing stocks of the "GL Conference" because of his "I guarantee it" statement.

Probably the strangest thing I ever heard mentioned specifically about Coach Campbell's infamous statement was when I caught Coach Lane saying, "A school district should never hire a non- fulltime teacher to coach an athletic team." An interesting statement from a person that I had heard was the teacher's union representative of Fenton High School.

The Hartland harriers took a respectable fourth place last season in the 1968 league championship meet. It was their best finish that they had ever accomplished in "GL

Conference" history. With three pretty good returning runners in Alex Felton, Al Dowty and Max Perry, plus strong pre-season showings by Jason Shattuck and Tom Beaver, the immediate future didn't look to bad for this season's Hartland Cross Country team, despite Coach Campbell's self-admitted lack of quality sixth and seventh runners.

"White Lake Road"

Chapter #40 – "The Master Plan!!"

September 11th - After I got done talking with Coach Campbell, the next person that approached me, visitor number three, was Al Dowty. You have to realize that all I ever hear during 6th Hour Economics Class is Al Dowty constantly talking about the Hartland High School Cross Country team. Interestingly enough, Al Dowty never mentions one word about his basketball playing days as a charter member of "The UCLA of Junior High Basketball."

The one thing you will immediately learn about Al Dowty after you have spent a few seconds around him is that he lives and breathes running. No make that Al Dowty is passionate about running. Al Dowty is one of these guys who at the age of 84 years of age, regardless of the weather conditions, will still be out there pounding five miles a day. And don't be surprised if Al Dowty is still running a sub six-minute mile pace on those runs.

Al Dowty was disappointed to hear that I was not going to join the Hartland Cross Country team for the remainder of their season. Then Mike Beardslee made the mistake of asking Al Dowty how the Hartland Cross Country team was going to do this season. Al Dowty's response was interesting, "Actually we'll be okay. If we get three runners in the top ten at the league meet, we might be able to place higher than last year's fourth place finish." All of us have improved from last year. Alex Felton should again win the overall race and Max Perry is running strong. Plus, Jason Shattuck and Tom Beaver are turning out to be excellent fourth and fifth runners."

Now Mike Beardslee got real bold and asked Al Dowty about Coach Campbell's prediction and predicament that he seemed to have placed on the Hartland harrier's a year ago. Al Dowty's reply was, "None of the other coaches said anything to us Hartland guys about Coach Campbell guaranteeing that Howell would not win the conference meet in 1968. But the other team's runners really let us have it. We got flak like: "Hey, Dowty, where's your fourth-place trophy?? What place did you guys finish end today?? Is your stupid coach going to shoot off his big mouth and make another prediction this year that will make him look like even a bigger fool??"

"The sad part of it is", as Al Dowty continued, "was that we ran a very good race in the conference meet. Some historic events for the Hartland Cross Country took place that day. The fourth-place finish was the highest a Hartland High School Cross Country team had ever placed in the "GL Conference" league meet. Also, Alex Felton was the first runner from Hartland High School to ever to be an individual winner in a conference championship meet. Another unhappy thing about that day was Alex Felton never received the credit that he should have for placing first over all. He ran a great race and beat some fantastic runners."

Al Dowty concluded by saying, "Like I said, there were some shining moments for us that day. The miserable thing is all that was being focused on in reference to the Hartland Cross Country team were the comments that Coach Campbell had made one year earlier. There were a lot of people, especially opposing runners, who just couldn't let go of that."

"Coach Campbell had a lot of hurtful remarks aimed at him that day. While everything appears to have died down for now, the closer we get to the conference meet this season those quips will start to resurface. I felt bad for Coach Campbell for all the grief he took. He took those unkind wisecracks pretty hard. In fact, I was surprised that he even came back to coach cross country this season."

Al Dowty then shifted sports on me real fast by now starting to talk about track season. "You're still going to go out for track, right??" he asked. "Because I've got it all figured out as to how Hartland High School is going to win the "GL Conference" meet. No, make that dominate the conference meet."

Ah, Mike Beardslee thought to myself, this is the infamous "Al Dowty Master Plan for Track Season" that I had heard bits and pieces about since I started attending the Hartland Consolidated Schools. Al Dowty pulled out a spiral note book, opened it up and showed me a couple of pages that had listed every single track and field event to be run in the conference meet with corresponding names of Hartland High runners.

I took a peek at Al Dowty's scribblings and saw my name plugged in for the following events; 440 Run; long jump; mile relay; and 880 relay. I didn't want to be the one to break it to Al Dowty, but I hadn't long jumped in a track meet since I was a freshman, nor had I been a member of an 880-relay team since my sophomore year of track. That's a long time ago, especially for the long jump.

Then it dawned on me the reasoning behind Al Dowty's "Master Plan." In a rule change that came down from the MHSAA last summer, it was now possible for a state of Michigan track runner to be eligible to participate in four events in a track meet. From what I could remember from reading about this in the "Flint Journal" was that other Midwest states had started doing this supposedly because of the lack of kids turning out for the sport of track. This was one way to make sure that a team could field at least one runner in every event.

I didn't know if this was the specific reason for the increase of track and field events that a runner could partake in or not, but I do know for a fact that Coach Lane at Fenton High School had said to me once that he had to scale back the intensity of track work outs because he couldn't get kids to come out for the team. With the exception of the Howell and Swartz Creek track programs, it seemed to Mike Beardslee that the rest of the numbers of the "GL Conference" track squads had diminished greatly over the years. Fowlerville and Hartland High Schools were perfect examples of track teams that never had a history of a large team membership come every spring for track season.

With the "GL Conference" talent, not just numbers, down for this track season, Al Dowty's "Master Plan" is perfect. If everyone on Al Dowty's list scores their projected points in the conference meet, then Hartland wins the championship by 50 some points. Piece of cake.

The questions I did not ask Al Dowty, however, mainly because I wasn't brave enough, would have been something like, did he really believe that the Hartland track participants have the

talent to place in these events and score his estimated points? Is the coaching staff talented enough to win a league championship? Those were the $64,000 questions.

The thing you have to remember is that every team in the "GL Conference" loved to run in a track meet against Hartland High School. It was a guaranteed victory. No, make that a surefire thumping. And runners, who typically did not score points in a dual track meet by placing in the top three finishers, would salivate at the chance to run against the Hartland harriers. It was guaranteed points and with luck, your name would appear with your time in a rack box score that was published the next day in the "Flint Journal" sports section.

Historically, a Hartland High School track team rarely ever scored double figures in a dual meet. Don Madden, one of the greatest athletes ever in the 98 years of Fenton High School existence, could get double figures in a dual track meet all by himself. He would simply win the pole vault, win the 440 run and run a leg on the winning mile relay team. Just winning those events alone netted Don Madden 11 ¼ points, usually enough points to beat a Hartland High School track team. Quite frankly, the rest of us Fenton track guys didn't even need to show up to get a victory over Hartland High School in track. Don Madden could handle that all by his lonesome.

I agree whole heartedly with Al Dowty's "Master Plan", at least on paper. But will the Hartland track team have the proverbial "enough bullets in the gun" to pull this off? I don't want to burst Al Dowty's bubble, but based upon the previous history of Hartland's track team, ain't no way.

I will say this, though, after conversing with Al Dowty and seeing the "Master Plan" on paper, it does make Mike Beardslee anxious for the start of track season.

"White Lake Road"

Chapter #41 – "I Admire Your Notion of Fair Odds, Mister"

September 11th – The visiting hour lamp for Mike Beardslee must have still been on because as soon as Al Dowty departed I had another visitor, Ric Adams, who was representing a different sport based upon our conversation, basketball. Ric Adams asked me if I had talked to Coach Decker earlier this morning. I answered in the affirmative and was then advised of the reasoning behind this contact.

"Coach Decker has been making sure that a lot of the track guys who have played basketball in the past will be trying out for the varsity basketball team in November," Ric Adams advised. "The primary reason is because he wants to run the fast break and a full court press this year".

"Coach Decker figures that since no other team in the "GL Conference" likes to run the court and only a couple of teams have point guards that could possibly break a full court press by themselves, our ability to run and press could be a big step towards us winning the "GL Conference "championship this season. Because of your basketball/track background Coach Decker specifically contacted you and recommended that you be in shape for basketball tryouts in November."

After Ric Adams left a couple of immediate thoughts ran through my head. Again, Coach Decker and now Ric Adams, must have Mike Beardslee mixed up with some other high school basketball player. I am not the type of cager where two months before basketball tryouts a head coach of a varsity basketball team, as well as its probable captain, approaches Mike Beardslee and emphasizes that I be in good basketball shape come time for tryouts because they think you might be a benefit the varsity basketball team. No, I'm more of the type of player where a varsity basketball coach might say to Mike Beardslee on the first day of tryouts, "Oh, so you're out for the team again, huh, Beardslee?"

I do take it as a huge compliment that two former major representatives of "The UCLA of Junior High Basketball" fame approached Mike Beardslee about being ready for basketball tryouts. I can understand Coach Campbell asking me to come out for the cross country team, but being asked to try out for the varsity basketball team still has me somewhat confused.

Now, worthy opponents such as Dave Devers, Wally Franks, Steve Braun, and Rick Pertler are the types of basketball players that a coach wants to make sure that they are going to be there on the first day of basketball practice. Be it wake-up calls, hiring a limousine service, or whatever, but you make darn sure that these types of talented basketball players are there in time for the start of basketball season. But not a Mike Beardslee.

My second thought after speaking with Ric Adams is what the heck is in the water here in Hartland, Michigan that makes Hartland Consolidated School athletes so confident about winning league championships? I mean Al Dowty has his "Master Plan" to win the track conference meet with runners from a track program who in the past three conference championship meets have combined for a grand total of 12 points. If that many. Yeah, the conference is weaker this year in track talent, but it ain't that weak for any reasonable person

to think that the Hartland track team can just waltz in and win the league championship. No way!!

As diluted as the track talent is in the "GL" this year, you have the exact opposite issue in basketball. Teams like Brighton, Fenton, Swartz Creek, and maybe with the transfer of Steve Brown to Lake Fenton from Flint Southwestern High School, will be extremely gifted teams, especially the Brighton "Bull Dogs." They're head and shoulders skill wise above the rest of the "GL" basketball squads.

Much like Al Dowty, Ric Adams was also mentioning the phrase "conference championship" for the Hartland High School Varsity Basketball team more than once in our recently completed conversation. There are certain words in life that people simply do not use in a complete sentence simultaneously, "conference championship" and "Hartland High School Varsity Basketball."

If Mike Beardslee can reach down deep enough into my brain cells and remember correctly from the five words a day that I was required to memorize daily to improve our vocabulary in "Accelerated English" class my junior- year, this is what I think would qualify as an "oxymoron". The word "Oxymoron" translated on "Planet Beardslee" means "Ain't no way."

Despite the glory days of "The UCLA of Junior Basketball" era and I must admit, those basketball squads were outstanding, the Hartland Eagle Varsity Basketball program has recently fallen on hard times. If those squads had won a combined total of 10 games in the past three varsity basketball seasons, and I'm talking actual basketball games against other competition, not inter-squad scrimmages, I would be shocked. And that's putting it politely.

I must admit that the idea of running the fast break and playing a scrambling type 32-minute full court press this basketball season is intriguing. The "GL Conference", much like the "Big 10" college basketball conference, has traditionally been what you would refer to as a "power conference." AKA a "big man's league." The "GL" has for years had exceptionally talented football players also to play a pretty fair game of roundball.

I grew up with this at Fenton High School where Jim Cmerzek, Jim Goodrich, Bill Hajec, Bruce McLenna, Don and Mike Madden, Mike Kakuska, Vance Huff, Steve Barker, and the list goes on and on of "Fenton Tigers" whose talent translated from the football field to the basketball court by still playing with the toughness that was needed to be successful on the gridiron.

Under normal basketball playing conditions when a basketball player drives in for a layup, two things can take place. The player will either score or get fouled. Now when you play in the "GL Conference" and on cold Winter nights face basketball teams like Fenton, Ainsworth, Swartz Creek and Brighton, especially Brighton, who has two monstrosities named Reed Williams and Dave Austin on their squad, now that same basketball player driving to the basket should be sure that mom and dad have a good medical insurance or dental plan,

because when you got close to the basket against a Reed Williams or Dave Austin, you were going to get pounded to what will seem like a one way trip to the center of the Earth.

You have to realize that Reed Williams and Dave Austin from a physicality standpoint were men playing against little children!! You might as well have been going up against former Big 10 musclemen like Walt Bellamy, Bill Buntin, Oliver Darden and Jerry Lucas. The latter four would cause any basketball player to think twice about driving to the basket for a layup.

As I headed to the Band Room I still thought it was interesting to hear the phrase "league championship and Hartland High School" for the track and basketball teams being tossed around by Ric Adams and Al Dowty. But as Charles Bronson (O'Reilly) said to Yul Brynner (Chris), in what has to be one of the 100 greatest movies ever made, "The Magnificent Seven":

Chris: There's a job for six men, watching over a village, south of the border.

O'Reilly: How big's the opposition?

Chris: Thirty guns.

O'Reilly: I admire your notion of fair odds, mister.

Based upon their recent history, specifically the last three years, I just personally do not see the Hartland High School Basketball or Track teams bringing home any championship trophies during the 1969-70 school year. Maybe not even in my lifetime. But I admit, Mike Beardslee does admire Ric Adams' and Al Dowty's notion of fair odds.

"White Lake Road"

Chapter #42 – "The Smiling Cobra"

September 11th – I was chatting with Jim Koop in the school hallway when he said to me in a hush, hush tone of voice, "Be careful, Beardslee. There is a person with the look of a hungry dog in a butcher shop coming our way." I couldn't think of whom he was even talking about and then I heard a booming voice coming at me from over my right shoulder.

I turned around there was Coach "Crabby "Appleton strutting up to me like he was the "Big Man on Campus." Coach Appleton must have taken a page out of Coach Lane's book of etiquette, because the first thing that he blurted out of his mouth was, "YOU'RE GOING TO RUN THE 880 FOR ME IN TRACK THIS SPRING!!"

My first thought was to say, "Hey, Coach Appleton, my transition to the Hartland Consolidated Schools is starting to come around pretty good. So, thanks for your concern." But I kept that thought to myself.

Let me provide you a visual of and a character analysis of Coach Appleton. He is 5'8", weighs about 150 pounds, early 30's and looks more like a Cross Country Coach than a varsity football coach. He also has facial features that are a combination of the cartoon character, "Alley OOP", and movie star, "Victor Jory". The latter being the same actor that played "Injun Joe" in an early "Tom Sawyer Movie" and also played a character of just one really despicable guy in the movie classic, "Gone with the Wind".

Now you know what Coach Appleton looks like, and to put it politely, Coach Appleton has the type of looks that only a mother could love. Mike Beardslee is discovering that Coach Appleton's physical appearance also matches his personality. Intense!!

Add a reptile type smile to his face and this has earned Coach Appleton the nickname that Jim Koop has officially dubbed him with, "The Smiling Cobra." And let me take this time to officially apologize to all of the cobras on the face of the Earth.

Between Coach Appleton's booming voice and using the phrase "RUN THE 880" I immediately went into panic mode. My experience of running the 880 was not a whole lot better than my cross country experiences. First of all, the 880 run has to be one of the toughest races to run in the sport of track and field as you've got two back- to- back 440 laps. Take my word for it; those are two killer trips around a quarter mile track.

I once got stuck participating in the 880 run in the second heat against Grand Blanc High School during my freshman year of track season. I was just a smoking that first 440 and came through at a 63 second split. As the old saying goes, "The bear jumped on my back" for the second quarter mile and Mike Beardslee was passed by all of the other 880 competitors and took dead last in this event with a time of 2:21. This meant my second 440 split was a "non-smoking" 78 seconds.

There are retired assembly line workers from General Motors who probably smoked three packs of Camel double filtered cigarettes during their eight-hour shift for 30 years that once

they doused out the cigarette they were smoking; set down the cup of coffee they were drinking; finished the cream filled doughnut they were scarfing down that they had purchased from "Supreme Doughnuts"; could then walk outside the door of their house and in church shoes, church shoes, mind you, run a 440 faster than 78 seconds. That's how pathetic I ran the 880 race that May afternoon against the Grand Blanc "Bobcats".

I discovered two things about Mike Beardslee during that track meet. First of all, I was never going to become the next Ron Wardie, only the greatest 880 runner in the history of Fenton High School track teams.

Secondly, Mike Beardslee was never going to run an 880-yard race again as long as I lived. My sides still ache from the race that took place almost 2 ½ years ago. You could promise me a varsity letter; guarantee that I would be automatically elected as captain of the track team; have my own wing named after me in the Fenton High School Athletic Hall of Fame; assure me a spot on the 1972 United States Olympic team and a provide me a TV channel that only showed episodes of "The Girl from U.N.C.L.E" every day and night of the week; and Mike Beardslee would still refuse to run the 880 race!!

So, with Coach Appleton's statement of, "YOU'RE GOING TO RUN THE 880 FOR ME IN TRACK THIS SPRING!!", still ringing in my ears, Mike Beardslee still vowed to myself that even if it meant sitting out my last ever season of high school track, I was in no way going to run the 880 race for "Crabby" Appleton. Ain't gonna happen, "Crabs."

Before I started my explanation of why I didn't want to run the 880, Jim Koop started to nudge me away from Coach Appleton down the school hallway. While doing so Jim Koop whispered to me out of the side of his mouth, "Witnesses, Beardslee. Witnesses."

It finally dawned on me what Jim Koop meant by the word "witnesses." By prodding me down the hallway the conversation between Coach Appleton and Mike Beardslee was now going to take place in front of some innocent by standing students. Smart move, especially since none of these students were varsity football players who are in need of Coach Appleton giving them enough snaps during a football game in order to receive a varsity letter

I attempted to explain to Coach Appleton that I was not much of an 880 runner but that I could probably score points for him in a dual meet by running the 440 race. I could also run a halfway decent leg on the mile relay team. He was having nothing to do with Mike Beardslee's reasoning.

Coach Appleton's response was the equivalent of a wild banshee screaming at the top of their lungs, *"IF YOU DON'T RUN THE 880 RACE FOR ME THIS TRACK SEASON THEN YOU'RE NOT GOOD ENOUGH TO RUN ON A COACH APPLETON COACHED TRACK TEAM!!!"*

Oh, yes, you're correct; this conversation was going just swell. With cheese on top.

Mike Beardslee has been yelled at many times in my life and in all honesty, I have never handled verbal abuse very well. But this was now the time to practice another Jim "Koopism" of, "You always stand up to a bully, Beardslee. Always." That "Koopism" applied perfectly to this situation.

After seeing Coach Appleton in action for the past eight school days I have developed a theory about the "Smiling Cobra." My hypothesis is that Coach Appleton started out early in life as a bully, and eventually graduated into becoming a thug.

Getting into a screaming match with Coach Appleton would be like getting into a biting match with a cobra. I wouldn't stand a chance. So, Mike Beardslee stepped in real close to Coach Appleton. Close enough that I could see smudges that indicated that his glasses needed cleaning, and in a polite and steady voice, just loud enough for the half dozen or so people around us could also listen in on our conversation, Mike Beardslee said the following to Coach Appleton;

"Seriously? I mean seriously?? Do you really think that it will break Mike Beardslee's little heart to not be coached by the infamous Coach Appleton?? The coach whose track teams have barely scored a little over a combined total of 10 points in the past three conference meets. There are individual runners in the "GL Conference" that have scored more points than that in the championship meet by themselves. Plus, your distance runners are always so injured that you don't even have any of them compete in races from the 880 on up come league championship time, let alone score points."

"That is what comes to Mike Beardslee's mind when I think of a Coach Appleton high school track program. So, if I do not run track season for you this season then I'll try out for the golf team instead. And just for the record, I would not run the 880 run if Jim Ryun, himself, begged me to do so. And you're no Jim Ryun when it comes to coaching distance runners."

I was quite proud of the line, "I'll try out for the golf team instead". Coach Decker coaches the golf squad and apparently there is no love lost between these two gentlemen. This is going good. First down!! Mike Beardslee!! No make that; Hole in one!! Mike Beardslee!!

I might have spoken to quick as out of the bottom of my eyes I could see Coach Appleton clinching his right fist. That line about joining the golf team must have struck a nerve with him. Coach Appleton didn't use that fist on me but if it wasn't for the fact that this "debate" had not taken place in front of other high school students, it would not have surprised me if Coach Appleton taken a swing at Mike Beardslee with the intent to maim.

Instead, Coach Appleton started to back away from me and at the same time punctuating his next words by animatedly pointing his right index finger towards me in a threatening manner, spelled out, "YOUJUST MADE THE LIST, BEARDSLEE!!" I again looked Coach Appleton in the eye and coolly said, "I've been threatened by better teachers than you." Oh, my goodness I'm turning into Jim Koop even before I reach the age of 17!!

Coach Appleton then glared at Jim Koop and said, pointing in my direction, "YOU KEEP HANGING AROUND WITH BEARDSLEE AND YOU'LL BECOME AS BIG AS LOSER AS HE IS." Jim Koop said nothing and just sort of had that "Jim Koop" grin on his face. After a few seconds of an unnerving silence, Coach Appleton said to Jim Koop, "WHAT'S THE MATTER PUNK, CAT GOT YOUR TONGUE?"

I was hoping that Jim Koop would remain silent and just let Coach Appleton stomp away. However, Jim Koop, in his best Eddie Haskell voice, said, "Coach Appleton, I wish you could just feel the cold chills running down my back right this second. That's how scared I get whenever you talk to me."

It was such an unexpected answer that the original crowd of students, which had now expanded to a larger gathering, just started laughing uncontrollably. And I'm not talking about a "ha ha" type of laugh, but one where a group of people enjoy seeing someone who they don't like or respect, get what they have coming to them kind of laughter.

As I started to walk away from this entanglement with Coach Appleton, Tom Beaver, who had witnessed the whole scene, pulled me aside and said, "Just so you know, you have just made an enemy for life." Yes, I did realize this. However, the one commonality that I have noticed with the bullies that have crossed paths with Mike Beardslee before, my theory is that it does not matter who the bullies torment, they're not a real selective group, but their need for a "whipping person" is constant.

What Mike Beardslee has to hope for is that my belief holds true with Coach Appleton. This means with track season some 5-6 months away he will have another teenager in his sights to flog, probably before he even walks out to his car in the parking lot tonight. If that's the case, Coach Appleton will have forgotten what took place between the two us this afternoon. At least that is what I am is wishing for.

Will I run the 880 this spring for Coach "Crabby Appleton"? Not at all. It's not even an option. Could this mean that I will not run track for my senior year and miss out for the first time in my track career a strong opportunity to earn points and more importantly, take home a couple of medals in the conference meet? Nothing to say what Mike Beardslee's absence will mean to Al Dowty's master plan. Yeah, it might.

"White Lake Road"

Chapter #43 – "Hands Down!!"

September 11th – Word had gotten around Hartland High School pretty fast that Mike Beardslee and Coach Appleton had exchanged words resulting with Mike Beardslee "Crushing Crabby Appleton like the bug that he is!!" During my last couple of classes I tried to explain to everyone that it didn't quite happen that way, but my explanations were falling on deaf ears.

It started off with me having to listen to Jason Shattuck's dramatic reenactment of my line to Coach Appleton, "And you're no Jim Ryun when it comes to coaching distance runners". That got some great laughs.

But the best replication of this confrontation of Mike Beardslee and "Crabby Appleton" came from Jim Koop performing as Edward G. Robinson, the famous portrayer of 1930ish gangsters on the movie screen, of me saying to Coach Appleton while holding an imaginary cigar, "Yeah!! I've been threatened by better teachers than you, Appleton! You got that "tough guy"!!! Yeah!!"

I was tickled pink that I could bring so much enjoyment to the student body of the Hartland Consolidated Schools on a Thursday afternoon. But man-oh-man, the rest of the day I was shaking like a leaf. I kept waiting for Coach Appleton to jump me out of nowhere and do more than just raise his balled-up fist at me. I thought to myself pleadingly, "Strike any part of my body, Coach Appleton, but please don't hit me in the lips."

Then after Coach Appleton had gotten a few punches in on me, he would whisper in my ear, 'TELL JIM RYUN I SAID HELLO, LOSER." Thank goodness, this incident was restricted to my insecure imagination.

But what had me even more worried was that for the second time this week I have noticed an interesting pattern of behavior by the masses here at Hartland High School. I first noticed it when Greg "Pretty Boy" Sanders was being serenaded so sarcastically in band class just three days ago. And today, how the students were so delighted to see Coach Appleton get his comeuppance. I just hope the day does not come when I mess up so bad that I give my fellow classmates the chance to squeal with delight when Mike Beardslee is getting my just desserts.

While there was indeed some personal satisfaction that I received from "standing up to a bully," the fact of it is, I didn't enjoy this particular experience. Even if it involved someone with big time character disorders like Coach Appleton.

I have always enjoyed being around a large majority of teachers that I have had in my school career. Mr. Anderson is a good example of this. There was at one time, not so much now, that I thought I would want to become a sixth-grade teacher, just like Mr. Roger O'Berry, my teacher of that same grade just some six short years ago at State Road Elementary School. That is till I saw my mother spending every evening grading school papers while listening to Ernie Harwell broadcast the Detroit Tiger baseball games.

The other reason that I'm Don Knotts "jumpy" after today's encounter with Coach Appleton is that I still have vivid memories of my General Math Class that was taught by a one Silas A. Smithers. Silas A. Smithers was so old that he made Methuselah look the same age as the children on the TV series, "Family Affair", Buffy and Jodie.

The eighth-grade mathematics curriculum at Fenton Junior High School was divided in three sections. Algebra I for the kids who were smart enough that they were going to take over the world someday; Modern Math II for the kids who were college bound; and General Mathematics was for kids who were either going to spend the rest of their lives in the United States Military or living with their parents.

I, along with Bill Wilhoit, both teachers' sons I might add, were washouts from Modern Math I. I remember sitting down in the General Mathematics class on the first day of eighth grade and being tapped from behind on my shoulder by Bill Wilhoit, who whispered to me, "We're in the "dumb math" class." Bill Wilhoit was right and the huge ugly green covered text book should have been my first clue.

I suspect that Mr. Silas A. Smithers was a pretty fair math teacher when he graduated from college right after the completion of the "Spanish American War." However, for the 1965-66 school year, he could not control a classroom full of eighth graders. He spent the majority of his time disciplining the class. What few minutes remained of the 55-minute class period he used by refusing to answer any questions us students had on mathematics. A pupil would raise a hand in class and Silas A. Smithers' immediate response was "Hands down!! Hands down!!"

That, of course, led to all of us kids constantly raising our hands throughout the entire class period. We could not get enough of that angry look on old Silas A. Smithers' face when he would take his right hand, thrust it in a downward motion and yell, "Hands down!! Hands down!!

Things had really gotten out of hand in that General Mathematics class to the point that one evening my mother received a telephone call from a parent of another student in the class. The purpose of the call was for my mother to sign a petition to have Mr. Silas A. Smithers fired

My mother knew how hard it was to make a living as a teacher and she was not the type of person to get on the band wagon to get another teacher fired. However, Mr. Silas A. Smithers one evening walked out to his car in the teacher's parking lot and was never seen again. His employment with the Fenton Area Schools had ceased.

Us kids in that General Math class took a lot of flak from the junior high principal and assistant principal, Mr. Snow and Mr. Press, respectively, as well as the other Fenton Junior High teachers. In their minds, we were the sole cause for getting old Silas A. Smithers fired. In addition to the mean glares we received from the teaching staff we were also the receipt of additional aggravation by this same group.

If there were a bunch of junior high kids doing typical "junior high shenanigans", the Silas A. Smithers' students were the ones that were sent to the principal's office while other trouble makers received a verbal warning. And while Mike Beardslee could never prove it, I always suspected that if a member of the "I ran Silas A. Smithers out of Fenton Junior High Club", was ever on the fence of grade wise between a "C" and a "B", or more likely a "C" and a "D", it seemed like we never received the benefit of the doubt and always got the lower grade

What I find scary is the similarities between Silas A. Smithers and Coach Appleton. Silas A. Smithers had probably reached a point in his teaching career where his best days as an educator had come and gone. He was no longer suited to be placed in any class room, let alone a classroom full of General Math Class eighth graders.

Coach Appleton comes across as a nasty and miserable human being; he simply is not at the stage in his teaching/coaching career where he should realize that he is an educator; not an authority figure placed on the face of the Earth with the sole purpose in life to bully school kids and get the summers off; in that order. Coach Appleton probably has no more right to be in a classroom than Silas A. Smithers did. Just for different reasons.

It will be interesting to see if the long arm of the Hartland Consolidated Schools extends to the confines of "White Lake Road" based upon my showdown with Coach Appleton this afternoon. If this becomes a major issue rather than just a flurry of words between a student and teacher, then this will not look good for Mike Beardslee. Now I will be the only student with a bullseye on my back. At least during the Silas A. Smithers era, there were 25 other kids that were sharing the blame for getting the old guy canned.

Even after sixth hour I was still unnerved from the results of my visit with Coach Appleton. Enough so, that as soon as Jim Koop, Katie and I reached the jeep, I immediately handed the car keys to Terry Rodenbo so that he could drive us four back to what I am hoping tonight will be the safe confines of "White Lake Road." Hands down.

"White Lake Road"

Chapter #44 – "Touchdown Pass"

September 12th – There was no telephone call last night or even a tap on the shoulder from Mr. Thompson this morning with a short message of, "Mike Beardslee. Do you have a couple of seconds??" I appear to have been spared any fallout from what took place between Coach Appleton and myself yesterday afternoon. Whew!!

While I appeared to be out of danger from trying to explain to Mr. Thompson that I was only following Jim Koop's advice of, "You always stand up to a bully," when Coach Appleton and I confronted each other, Mike Beardslee wasn't totally home free just yet from a different type of "a fate worse than death". Something called manual labor. Ugh!!

This afternoon after school was completed Katie and I had to make a trip to State Road Elementary School for the purpose of bringing boxes of teaching materials too my mother's 5th grade classroom from" White Lake Road". This task consisted of taking way too many boxes from the trunk of my mother's car into her classroom, "Point A to Point B" kind of stuff. By sheer coincidence my mother's classroom was the same schoolroom that I had been stationed at when I was a fifth grader here in the hallowed halls of State Road Elementary School.

Unlike Katie, I feel somewhat uncomfortable when setting foot in the building that I spent my fourth grade through sixth grade years. There are still some teachers here who taught me during those three years who I still feel awkward around. And the one teacher who I always made a point of stopping in to say hello on my few and far in between visits to State Road Elementary School, Mr. Roger O'Berry, is now teaching science at the Fenton Middle School, the former Fenton High School, where the sixth, seventh and eighth graders are now housed.

I always enjoyed seeing and talking with Mr. O'Berry. I don't know who got a bigger kick out me showing up to see him one afternoon with me wearing a brand-new varsity jacket for having lettered in Track, myself or Mr. O'Berry. Probably Mike Beardslee. I do suspect, however, that Mr. O'Berry was also very proud of me for having earned a varsity letter.

That was, however, perhaps the only enjoyable part of the State Road Elementary School jaunts for Mike Beardslee. I was always on the receiving end of questions from teachers that I never seemed to be able to respond with satisfactory answers. And with the fact that I am now a student of another school district, a public-school district no less, I was now opening myself up to being asked a whole new category of embarrassing questions.

Awkward question #1 is always asked by Mrs. Wise, a fourth-grade teacher whose classroom is right next to my mothers'. "How come we see your sister here at school all of the time but we never see you, Mike???

Katie loves coming to State Road Elementary School. If my mother needs help with bulletin boards, the grading of papers or just having Katie come in and play the piano for my mother's classroom, she is there. No questions asked. Katie just enjoys doing this kind of stuff.

In fact, there is a standing joke between Katie and my mother, that when my mother retires from the teaching profession, Katie will be waiting at the front doors of State Road Elementary School ready to replace her as the next member of the Beardslee family to take up residence in that same fifth grade class room. The Beardslee 5th grade teaching dynasty would continue!!

Me?? I'm the complete opposite. What few times I have ever set foot in my mother's classroom I have shown no interest in speaking with her students, what the bulletin boards looked like or even play my trumpet. And Mike Beardslee, since finally figuring out what the three valves on a trumpet are used for in the last few years, has never turned down the opportunity to play the trumpet for anybody, any place, any time. But nary a command performance for my mother's fifth graders.

My typical response to Mrs. Wise's question was, "Well, Band, Basketball and Track keep me pretty busy." Then I would hurriedly duck into Mr. O'Berry's classroom and start to read the same "Chip Hilton" book, the classic, "Touchdown Pass", authored by Clair Bee. I betcha this hard cover back book, which looks like it has been run over by 30,000,000 cars, has not been read by any other State Road Elementary School student since I stumbled across it one rainy," recess is inside today", afternoon in the Spring of 1964.

Those infrequent visits to Mr. O'Berry's room after my departure as a student from State Road Elementary school were always enjoyable for me. I would pour through the book, "Touchdown Pass" and revisit my old friends. This is where I would imagine that Mike Beardslee was as great as athlete as Chip Hilton; could run as fast as Speed Morris; be as big and strong as Biggie Cohen; as funny, but an extremely clutch athlete, as Soapy Smith; to be coached by a person with the great leadership qualities of Coach Hank "Rock" Rockwell and never, never have as dreadful of enemy like the rich kid, "Fats Ohlsen." I betcha when Coach Appleton read this same book series as a youth, he immediately made Fats Ohlsen his idol. I guarantee it.

The funny thing is, however, as much as I loved reading the prose of Clair Bee, every time I read through "Touchdown Pass," I wanted to scream at Chip Hilton, "How could you be so stupid to get into a car with Piggy Thomas when you knew that he has had few to many pints of beer in him??" Piggy Thomas then proceeds to take a curve to fast with his car and rolls same. Chip Hilton sustains a broken leg which causes him to miss his whole Junior season of high school basketball.

I mean it happens every single time I read this first book in the "Chip Hilton" series!! My goodness, what is in those banana splits you guys eat every night at the "Sugar Bowl" that turns an honor student's brain into saw dust?? Even Soapy Smith has enough brain cells in him not to get into a motor vehicle being operated by a drunken Piggy Thomas!! Gimme a break!!

I should have seen awkward question #2 coming my way. But when asked by Mrs. Weigant, my former fifth grade teacher, it still catches me off guard. "Now that you're a senior in high school, where do you plan to attend college, Mike Beardslee??"

"White Lake Road"

Chapter #45 – "Maaak Beardslee"

September 12th – My younger over achieving sister, already has her college destination of Colorado University selected. And I bet you she also has the dormitory, floor and dorm room that she's going to reside in picked out as well. Mike Beardslee likewise has his future planned out. But my plans do not include attending a four-year college, junior college or trade school.

There are a couple of reasons for my lack of interest in attending college. After nearly 13 years of attending various levels of school, I'm not fully convinced that I have actually enjoyed school life. Oh, I like Band and participating in athletics, but the daily grind of getting up every morning, going to and from school, attending classes, doing homework, etc., is just not my thing.

The second reason, and probably the biggest one, is that Mike Beardslee has no desire to attend college because I am deathly afraid of taking the required college entrance examinations. I just have a pronounced fear of taking those required tests. In my mind, I just do not see myself passing them. And even if I did manage to eke out some type of qualifying scores, no self-respecting four-year university would be welcoming the likes of Mike Beardslee with open arms.

However, just like Al Dowty, Mike Beardslee also has a master plan!! A male student similar to myself once they have graduated from high school, who doesn't have any plans to go to college, and has just turned the age of 18 years old, has a high probability of being drafted into the United States Army.

Then following basic training that same male teenager would probably be shipped to South Viet Nam for 365 days. Mike Beardslee knows himself well enough to realize that I wouldn't last in South Viet Nam for 15 minutes. No, make that 10 minutes. Just the name of the country, South Viet Nam, itself, scares the bejeebers out of me.

Instead, Mike Beardslee has decided that I will enlist in the United States Air Force and play my trumpet in the Air Force Military Band. I will do that for the next 30 years, retire before the age of 50 and spend my Saturday mornings running down to the mail box to fetch my "Sporting News" magazine. The remainder of my days will be spent reminiscing about how Mickey Lolich picked Lou Brock off of first base in game seven of the 1968 World Series; taking long walks on the 51 acres of "White Lake Road;" and watching reruns of "The Girl from U.N.C.L.E." Man, I can get into that life style.

What made Mike Beardslee come up with this particular plan in life?? Right after graduating from high school in June of 1968, a fellow Fenton High School trumpet player, Dick Wilcox, enlisted in the United States Marine Corps. His intent was to ultimately become a member of the United States Marine Corps Band.

I would correspond with Dick Wilcox when he was at Camp Pendleton where he had his basic training and see him on his few trips back home to Fenton, Michigan. He and I would talk

about what boot camp was like and more importantly, discuss what his trumpet tryout consisted of for the Unites States Marine Corps Band.

Dick Wilcox advised me, "You have to realize that there are a different number of United Marine Corps Bands with the most famous being the "President's Own Band." There's also a chamber orchestra, chamber ensemble, a drum and bugle corps and some field bands." Dick Wilcox, I believe, was a member of the drum and bugle corps and seemed to enjoy it. As Dick Wilcox said, "I was a better trumpet player than a soldier."

It was those dialogues with Dick Wilcox that led me to reach my decision to join the Air Force rather than attend college. Since I had defeated Dick Wilcox a couple of times in challenges for the first chair trumpet position during my sophomore year of high school, I knew that I was at least as good a trumpet player as him. In the world of Mike Beardslee, if Dick Wilcox could audition and make a United States Marine Corp Band, then so could Mike Beardslee.

Have I informed my parents of my monumental decision to bypass college entirely and enlist in the Air Force? Oh, no, no, no, no, no, no, no. There is a time to lay that news on them and now is not the moment. In fact, I never even told my folks about the occasion on my way home from the Student Conservation Association last August that I made a side trip to a Coast Guard recruiting office in Seattle, Washington. The Coast Guard recruiter was ready to sign me up right on the spot till I made the mistake of telling him that I was 16 years old and still in high school. I was sent packing quickly with orders to come back after I graduated from high school.

I don't think my father will have to big a problem with me enlisting in the Air Force. I think he would rather see me there instead of sitting in a cold rice paddy in South East Asia. My mother?? That' a different story. She will not take this news well at all. Mary Beardslee's son enlisting in the military instead of attending college will be an extreme embarrassment to her. Even any talk of me enlisting into a branch of the military will mean that my apple crisp days with a large scoop of vanilla ice cream on the side will be coming to a speedy end.

Before I could honestly advise Mrs. Weigant that I had not heard from any colleges at this time, I caught a break as she seemed to have a nicotine fit and headed quickly off to the teacher's lounge. However, I won't be able to keep my enlistment plans quiet forever.

This is the month of September and seniors in high school will be receiving college acceptance letters pretty soon. Guys like Alex Felton and Max Perry probably sprint to their mail boxes at home every evening with the eager anticipation of getting a college acceptance letter. Just the same way Mike Beardslee does when I sprint to the "White Lake Road" mail box on Saturday mornings to fetch my "Sporting News" magazine.

Once that college acceptance letter is received then the next step will be for this lucky student to announce their big news to the rest of the world. I can just picture myself walking into second hour Study Hall one morning and seeing Alex Felton or Max Perry telling the rest of us the identity of the university they have been accepted to.

Then at some point the same question that Mrs. Weigant asked me today, "Where are you going to attend college, Mike Beardslee?" will be coming my way. How do I answer that innocent question when I am not ready to announce to the same audience as Alex Felton and Max Perry, that no, Mike Beardslee is going to enlist in the Air Force and not go to college? Hey, I'm open for suggestions.

As somewhat prepared as Mike Beardslee was for the first two awkward State Road Elementary School questions, I was totally caught off guard for the straightforward, uncomfortable question #3. Maybe I was just hoping that this issue would not come up. Man, I was way off base with that wish.

Mrs. Akins was my sixth-grade history teacher and a real taskmaster. Mrs. Akins will never, never, make Mike Beardslee's all-time list of favorite teachers. In fact, she doesn't even rate a "mercy" honorable mention.

Mrs. Akins had decided to stay at State Road Elementary School as a fourth-grade teacher, you poor kids you do not know what you are in for, instead of going with Mr. O'Berry to the Fenton Middle School. She started walking towards me and Mike Beardslee had that same feeling of fear when Mrs. Akins would call on me in history class during the 1963-64 school year. No, make that intense fright instead of fear.

Mrs. Akins was from the state of Virginia and had a southern twang rather than a southern accent when she spoke. It wasn't "Mike Beardslee" when my name came out her mouth, but rather "Maaak Beardslee." So sometimes I didn't initially understand what she was saying to me. Sad to say, today I heard and understood every word Mrs. Akins said. Nice and clear.

Mrs. Akins mentioned "Now that the city of Fenton voters has passed the school millage and restored all sports and other curricular activities, I assume that you and Katie will be returning to Fenton High School to complete the school year. "I was very honest with Mrs. Akins when I responded, "The current plan is for the two of us to complete the entire school year at Hartland High School." I hoped that would be enough for her to drop the subject and mind her own business.

But after what came out of Mrs. Akins mouth next, I just stood there and mentally started to kick myself. I knew that I should have just shrugged my shoulders and gone with my run-of-the-mill line of, "Oh, band, basketball and track keep me pretty busy" and hoped for the best.

Instead, I was on the receiving end of, "You mean to tell me that the two of you that are both residents of the Fenton Area School District, of which, I might add, your mother is gainfully employed; with all athletics, band, choir and other curriculum activities being reinstated for this school year, and the two of are still not going to come back to Fenton High School to complete your education!!"

Mrs. Akins' unrelenting lecture included a really biting remark, "That decision makes absolutely no sense to me at all. My understanding is that the Hartland Consolidated School system is the equivalent of where elephants go to die. It's beyond me, "Maaak Beardslee" why

your mother would pick the Hartland Schools over the Fenton Schools and let them have the responsibility of educating her children."

There was no verbal response back from "Maaak Beardslee" to Mrs. Akins' point of view on my mother's parental skills or my life. I remained silent but my first instinct was to blurt out to her, "And you're no Jim Ryun when it comes to coaching distance runners!!" That would show her!!

However, if "Maaak" Beardslee would have had an ounce of guts, my actual response would have been something like this:

"Mrs. Akins, you may want to further discuss Katie's and my school selection with my parents, but to quote actor Steve McQueen's character, Vin Tanner, from the movie, "The Magnificent Seven", "Fella I once knew in El Paso, one day he took all his clothes off and jumped in a mess of cactus. I asked him the same question, why? He said it seemed to be a good idea at the time."

Well, guess what, Mrs. Akins, some two or so weeks ago when my father recommended the Hartland Consolidated Schools as a compromise for Katie and me to continue our education, it seemed to be a good idea at the time. I wonder how Mrs. Akins would have taken the news if Katie and I would have ended up attending Holy Redeemer High School, a non-public school, which if you remember, was my mother's first selection of schools for her offspring. "Maaak Beardslee" would have enjoyed the look on Mrs. Akins face when that news flash hit the State Road Elementary School teacher's lounge.

The real answer for Katie and I not coming back to the Fenton Area Schools is simple. We now have two full school weeks in the books as students of the Hartland Consolidated School system. While the initial transition has seen more than a few potholes in the road for Mike Beardslee, this second week was better than the first week. Hopefully week number three will be better than week number two and so on and so on. At least that's what I'm wishing for.

Also by coming back to the Fenton Area Schools I suspect that I would be ineligible to participate in sports since I was transferring back to another school district during an already started school semester. That would be tough to swallow, especially to lose out on Track season.

I would likewise have had to give up my Hartland Senior Band president position and that would truly hurt. While that would no doubt please Teri Andrews to no end because this is the only way that her boyfriend, Greg "Pretty Boy" Sanders, is ever going to be elected as Senior Band president. And make no doubt about it, Teri Andrews would get him nominated and voted into that prestigious position the moment I drove the jeep onto Hibner Road after exiting from the Hartland High School parking lot.

The thought of preventing "Pretty Boy" from becoming band president by itself is enough to keep Mike Beardslee at Hartland High School for the remaining 34 weeks of the school year.

"White Lake Road"

It seemed to be a good idea at the time when the four of us kids left the Fenton Area Schools for the 1969-70 year when there was no hope of the school millage passing. Now it seems like a good idea at the time to finish out the school year at Hartland High School for the above stated reasons. I would have liked to have explained my logic to Mrs. Akins, but since her mind was already made up about how it was best for Katie and me to return to Fenton High School, to make it easier for both Mrs. Akins and myself, "Maaak Beardslee" could have agreed with her, but then that meant we would have both been wrong.

Before I left State Road Elementary School, for what I hope will be for some lengthy period of time, I made a quick stop at Mrs. Wise's fourth grade classroom, peeked in the door and saw a big smile break out on Mrs. Wise's face. She knew the exact purpose of my visit. With that big booming voice of hers she said, "You know just as well as I do, Mike Beardslee, that Eddie Williams is no longer in my fourth-grade class!!" Mrs. Wise then shooed Mike Beardslee out of the doorway by pretending to throw an eraser loaded with a couple of pounds of chalk dust on it in my direction.

"White Lake Road"

Chapter #46 – "I Know What's Best for My Daughters!!"

September 12th – Friday nights in the "White Lake Road" household are going to start becoming very busy as football halftime shows are just around the corner. Those evenings are pretty rush-rush. Time will become even more of an issue as instead of a six-mile round trip to Fenton High School, this upcoming marching band season will feature a 28-mile round trip for the opportunity to perform in front of a football crowd. That's on top of an already traveled 28-mile trip for the start and end of a school day. That's a lot of time in a jeep that I am discovering does not ride as smooth as a car, or even a school bus.

Supper this evening consisted of your typical and basic Catholic family Friday night meal: toast cheese sandwiches, tomato soup and a couple of thousand Nabisco crackers. The tomato soup was so thick that the lead character on the former TV series, "Sea Hunt", "Mike Nelson", portrayed by actor Lloyd Bridges, if he had to make a dive into this broth, even with using the best skin diving equipment available, "Mike Nelson" would not have been able to see his hands in front of his face.

Later this evening while reading the "Flint Journal" I noticed that my television watching schedule is discombobulated for this school year's Friday nights that will not involve football halftime shows or hopefully varsity basketball games.

"Get Smart", my second favorite TV show after "Bonanza", is going to be on Friday nights, Channel Six, no less, after for years being on Saturday evenings. This is not good. "The High Chaparral", not that I am super into this show, but I love the theme song and wish we would play it for a halftime show, continues to change their viewing night for what seems like every new TV season and will be on Friday nights for the 1969-70 term.

One TV show that I would like to watch this year but again will miss the majority of episodes because of my Friday night conflicts is: "Here Come the Brides." Katie watched this show last year and seemed to like it quite a bit, especially the theme song. What created my sudden interest about "Here Come the Brides" is that the show is based in Seattle, Washington. After having traveled to the state of Washington last summer, I really took a liking to the cities of Seattle and Port Angeles. Two beautiful cities with the snow covered Olympic Mountain range staring down at you. I would be interested in watching "Here Come the Brides" just to see glimpses of the Olympic Mountains and Puget Sound.

Later that evening while sitting in the family room of "White Lake Road", I was recapping the events of week two of the "greatest year of my life." No doubt it was a big thrill for Mike Beardslee to be elected Senior Band president. That honor falls into the category of "Christmas came early." But there are still some things that bother and puzzle me about this school year so far.

Puzzler number one; why does Mark Nevers continue to avoid me like I am a leper? That's an ongoing mystery to me. I would love to try and convince him to rejoin the Hartland High School marching band. Granted Mark Nevers probably hasn't played the trumpet or baritone for quite some time, maybe even a couple of years. But if you are a brass player who can stand

up straight, can differentiate your right foot from your left foot, and breathe, then there are not too many high school marching band directors in the state of Michigan that will turn you away.

Concern #2 is the attempted overthrow of Katie and myself as Hartland Senior Band executive board members by the Andrews family. That is still very bothersome to me. Mama Andrews and even the younger Andrews sister, Trecha, have the same mentality that Coach Appleton has of, "As long as I can yell louder than you, then I'm right!!"

I have personally witnessed Mr. Anderson being on the receiving end of Mrs. Andrews "I know what's best for my daughter!!" lecture. Now Mr. Anderson is a big boy and can take care of himself. But I wonder if Mr. Anderson is the only teacher that is "privileged" to have this special relationship with Mrs. Andrews or, do the remaining staff members at Hartland High School have this pleasure as well? An interesting question.

Deep down in my stomach, I just know that Jim Koop, Terry Rodenbo, Katie and I have not heard the last of Mrs. Andrews' favorite saying, "I know what's best for my daughters!!" Mrs. Andrews has probably said these words to so many teachers and people in her life that as a parent she takes these utterances as gospel. Mrs. Andrews may know "what's best for her daughters", but she has no clue what is best for the Hartland Senior High Band. None.

But the biggest mystery of the past fortnight, even more unknown than whatever happened to Amelia Earhart, the missing aviator for the past thirty some years; is that you just cannot tell Mike Beardslee that somewhere in the vast state of Michigan that Eddie Williams is still not in the fourth grade. Also, I would bet a dozen of "Supremes" finest date square doughnuts, that Eddie Williams is still the only fourth grader in the "Wolverine State" that has a driver's license. I'll take that bet all day long!!

"White Lake Road"

Chapter #47 – "Whose Half of the Marching Band is Better??"

September 14th – In just under three weeks Mike Beardslee will be getting permanent caps on my two front teeth. Am I excited about this upcoming event?? Maybe, yes. Maybe, no.

From a positive standpoint, I will now be able to actually show off that dazzling Mike Beardslee smile that supplements my ruggedly handsome looks. Currently I have had to limit any smiles on my part because I do not want other people too see the two barely covered spiked teeth that pass for my two front choppers.

And the scary part of it is, when these current temporary coverings start to crack, and I'm surprised that they haven't done so by now, the first thing that people will see when I open my mouth are two spiked teeth that resemble dirty old fangs that even actor, Bela Lugosi, of "Count Dracula" fame, would cause him to dramatically lift his cape up in front of his face to hide these hideous looking spiked teeth.

Maybe this stuff is all in Mike Beardslee's head. But I am truly psyched out over my teeth issue. Has this concern affected my trumpet playing ability?? I know for absolute certain that it has. Oh, I am starting to regain my range and I am getting closer to be able to hit a "high C" in the last week or so.

However, "the getting closer to hitting a "high C" should not be a goal for a first chair trumpet player. When it comes to hitting a "high C" Mike Beardslee should be able to stumble out of bed any day of the week, stagger over to my trumpet case, attach the trumpet mouthpiece to the trumpet, belt out a "high C" and wake up my father who has only been asleep for a couple of hours after finishing the second shift at General Motors. That's what first chair trumpet players do!!

In fact, if the Hartland footballers ever score any touchdowns this season, and strictly from a trumpet playing stand point, the less touchdowns the better, I have been working on a tag on ending for any of the trumpet charges that Jim Koop and I will play. It sounds like something the famous trumpet player and band leader, Harry James, himself, would belt out when he plays a song by the name of "Ciribiribin", specifically the last few measures. Just a great trumpet lick.

It's a great way to end a trumpet charge. But until I can hit a "high C" or Harry James attends a Hartland High School varsity football game and brings his trumpet along with him, that tag on will remain in my head and fingers.

Jim Koop and I had a standing joke that started during our junior year of marching band season at Fenton High School. Every day before marching band practice we would ask ourselves, "Whose half of the marching band is better?? Mike Beardslee's or Jim Koop's??" The answer always made in unison was, of course, "MINE!!

I have avoided the "Whose half of the band question "so far this marching band season. Last year at this time I was asked by my old Mary Crapo Elementary School buddy, Dennis Barnes,

"White Lake Road"

"Hey, Beardslee. While I'm sitting in American History Class you guys are out on the football field rehearsing. And there is this one trumpet player that I can hear above the rest of the marching band. Is that you??"

Since Dennis Barnes asked this question directly to Mike Beardslee instead of Jim Koop my response was, "Yes, of course, it's me." Now if Dennis Barnes had asked this same question of Jim Koop, do you think his response would have been, "Yeah, it's Beardslee that is blasting every ones' ear drums into oblivion." I don't think so. Jim Koop's response would have been a modest, "Yessiree Bob, that's me!!"

But this marching band season the trumpet player that you can hear all the way south on US-23 from Hartland, Michigan to the city of Brighton, Michigan, is Jim Koop. It's certainly not Mike Beardslee. Oh, I'm meeting all of the rules of good trumpet playing; good tone and you can hear every note. But I sound pretty instead of pretty loud. This certainly does not allow me to stake a claim in the worldly question of "Whose half of the band is better?"

I'm sort of relieved that the "who's half of the band is better" type of banter between the two of us in the month of September 1969 hasn't resurfaced. If there was an actual vote for this important topic the result would be similar to the presidential race voting between myself and Greg" Pretty Boy" Sanders. No contest at all. Jim Koop's half of the band is far better than mine. In fact, from the way I am sounding out on the marching band field this season there is no "Mike Beardslee's half of the band."

The Hartland High School Marching Band will have five halftime shows to perform in this football season. I might be able to get back to my old marching band blasting capabilities before I get my permanent caps on. Might, but I'm not holding my breath. If so, that will leave me with three more half-time shows to be of some real help with the rest of the "big blasters"; Jim Koop, Terry Rodenbo and Jason Shattuck.

At least I am being a little smarter concerning my "chops" this marching band season as compared to one year ago when I was suffering from "dead lip disease". The root of this ailment was caused by an even higher degree of foolhardiness then Mike Beardslee normally displays.

"White Lake Road"

Chapter #48 – "Jonny Quest"!!!

September 14th – I currently own two trumpets, which is probably one more than the majority of high school trumpet players in the state of Michigan own. One trumpet is a Holton model that I started out on as a beginning trumpet player in the Fourth Grade. As an eighth grader Mr. Anderson recommended to Mike Beardslee that I move up from a beginner's trumpet to a "Big Boy's" trumpet, of which, I became the proud owner just prior to the start of my freshman year of high school.

Prior to the actual receipt of my new musical instrument I just loved going around telling my fellow band members that Mike Beardslee was getting a new Bach Trumpet and that it cost a staggering $495.00. I was acting like I was the cats' meoooooow!!

My new Bach trumpet came with a Bach 7C mouthpiece that I always used for both marching and concert band seasons. During marching band season last year, I decided to become efficient. Instead of lugging a trumpet case to school with me every day on good old "Bus #23", I would leave one trumpet at school in the band room and the other trumpet at home. I would simply put the Bach 7C mouthpiece into my pants pocket and carry it with me where ever I went. Brilliant!! I mean we are talking Mike Beardslee type brilliancy here!!

Well, you knew this was going to happen, Mike Beardslee outsmarted himself. A couple of times I would accidentally put the Bach 7C mouthpiece in the trumpet case I was to leave at school as most trumpet players do. By doing that when I would arrive home to "White Lake Road" later that evening I would go to practice my trumpet, you got it; Mike Beardslee quickly discovered that I had a trumpet with no trumpet mouthpiece. There was no practicing of the trumpet that night for me, which was the equivalent of the world coming to the end.

Jim Koop always had a great line about me when I would go into panic mode because I had not gotten around to practicing my trumpet yet on any particular day. I would always be saying, "I have to go practice my trumpet. Now!!" Jim Koop's response was, "No, Beardslee. You don't HAVE to practice your trumpet. You WANT to practice your trumpet." He was right. I wanted to practice my trumpet. Other than Saturday morning runs down to mail box to fetch my "Sporting News" magazine from the mail box, it was my favorite way to spend a portion of a morning, afternoon or evening.

This is what probably differentiates Mike Beardslee from a large percentage of my fellow band mates. For these band kids "practicing" their instrument consists of the 55 minutes of Band class. And depending upon the arrangement of a musical composition or the time that Mr. Anderson has to rehearse with a specific section of the band, for example, the clarinet section, factor in time to put together and away instruments at the beginning and the end of the class hour, then realistically, a band student may only actually play their instrument no more than 50% of the entire Band class. A whopping 27 and one-half minutes.

For a good many of my Band classmates, having to practice or even consider practicing their individual musical instrument outside of school time was like a fate worse than death. However, as Jim Koop has pointed out, a day of not practicing the trumpet was the highway to

"Panic City "for Mike Beardslee. I mean I could not even sleep at night knowing that I missed a scheduled day of practicing my glorious trumpet.

I then made the executive decision that since I had two trumpets with their individual mouthpieces, then for marching band season I would again just leave one trumpet at school and the other one at home. I suspect that an employee of the General Motors' engineering department could have figured this out quicker than I did, but again I thought I was being "Ernie Efficient" by not having to lug a trumpet case with me every day on a Fenton Area Schools' yellow and black painted school bus.

Despite Jim Koop's forewarnings that I should not be switching totally different brands of mouthpieces on a daily basis, I continued to do so until I could not even produce one note when I went to play the trumpet. Finally, Miss Franklin, after a severe scolding that included an analogy to my I.Q and a bag of rocks, finally arrived at a solution. She ordered Mike Beardslee another Bach 7C mouthpiece so that I would have one for each individual trumpet case. "Dead Lip Disease" issue officially resolved.

So, considering all of the paranoia that Mike Beardslee has gone through from no caps, to temporary caps and lastly, ugly looking spikes for front teeth; compared to this same time last year I can at least actually play and produce some kind of tone when pressing the mouthpiece against my lips and making a sound like a motor boat.

Luckily since my last visit to Dr. Alfred's office my trumpet range has improved immensely, but I'm still not ready to pull the trumpet mouthpiece firmly against my lips; push down real hard on the second valve of my trumpet, pull my elbows as tight as I can to my sides and pretend that I am playing the last few measures of the "Jonny Quest" theme song. When playing that little ditty, a trumpet player has to use a ladder to hit those high notes. And I betcha those guys playing their trumpets for the "Jonny Quest" theme song don't have capped front teeth issues to worry about, either.

Lastly, today I read in the "Flint Journal" that the Hartland varsity football team lost for the second week in a row, 12-7 to Whitmore Lake High School, bringing their season record to 0-2. The real kicker of this is that Whitmore Lake High School, other than an outstanding women's softball program, is really not known for having much success in any of their remaining sports teams, especially the men's programs. So, for the Hartland Eagles to lose this one, it had to hurt really bad. Really bad.

This especially had to cause some extreme discomfort for Pete Mason. According to this sports article, while playing free safety, Pete Mason made a big play by intercepting a Whitmore Lake pass early in the fourth quarter. However, as quarterback, Pete Mason was leading the Hartland offense down the field, when, and I now quote from the "Flint Journal" article, "Pete Mason while running a quarterback draw play had gained sufficient yardage for an important first down for the Hartland Eagles. However, Pete Mason while carrying the football like a loaf of bread, then had the football knocked out of his right hand by a Whitmore Lake defender, who then recovered the ensuing fumble allowing the "Whitmore Lake Trojans" to hold on for their first victory of the 1969 football season."

"White Lake Road"

That's one lousy way to lose a football game. Pete Mason, Tom Moran and Steve Gilmore are really going to be hearing it from the "lunch crowd" tomorrow.

Week three of the "greatest year of my life" starts in less than 12 hours. And more importantly, there is only one more week till the start of the National Football League season. Thank goodness for that!! A six-exhibition football game season is a tad too many even for a diehard Detroit Lion fan like myself.

At least I'm not some poor Detroit Lions season ticket holder. Joe Falls, a columnist for the "Sporting News", you can see him on page two every Saturday morning, just constantly beats up the Detroit Lions organization for their new ticket policy of charging season ticket holders the same ticket price for an exhibition home game as they do for a regular season home game.

Considering the fact that the Detroit Lions have not made the NFL playoffs since 1957, and are nowhere close to putting a football team on the field that is talent wise capable of making post season play for the 1969 season, either; then if I were a Detroit Lions season ticket holder, the implementation of new season ticket plan just might upset me.

Keep after them Joe Falls!! See you again on page two this next Saturday.

"White Lake Road"

Chapter #49 – "600 on your AM Dial!!"

September 15th – The ride into school this morning was a little more quiet than usual, even for a Monday morning. The Hartland High School Marching Band starting this week is officially off "scholarship." Over the course of the next 30 days we have the following events scheduled:

- ***Three pre-game and half-time shows;***
- ***Two High School Band Days;***
- ***One parade.***

And the above doesn't include any unscheduled pep assemblies that might crop up either.

What little discussion that the jeep contained was focused on what were the music selections going to be for the half-time show this week? The four of us each have our own varying thoughts on this important matter.

Me? I'm not choosy at all. Hey, its marching band music. 99.9% of the pieces that we play are going to have good trumpet parts.

Jim Koop prefers a musical arrangement where the band is in a concert formation and we play a song that will allow the trumpet section to just "blast" away. Let's just put it this way, if Jim Koop was told that the only song that the marching band he was a member of would be performing for each and every halftime show of the football season was "Joshua ", he'd be ecstatic. In fact, Jim Koop would be so happy that he might finally give me a break for one day and not beg me to let him smoke in the jeep.

Katie pretty much takes the same approach that Jim Koop does. She would love to have the percussion section be highlighted in a "drum feature." When a drum feature is done properly it really gets the crowd to a whooping it up and hollering. The problem is that from what I have seen so far in marching band practice, the Hartland Marching Band percussion section as a whole, while high on spirit and marching ability, might not have the talent to pull off the type of drum feature that would cause people to talk about it throughout the whole week end and into Monday morning when school started back up again.

Come to think of it, I have never been in a marching band that had a percussion section as a whole, individuals, yes, to write home about. Granted, anyone that knows one lick about marching band knows that the drum section is not as important as a trumpet section, at least in my trumpet playing opinion, but the percussion section always seems to be the one group of musicians of any marching band that a crowd shows the most interest and following.

Terry Rodenbo takes a different approach to the type of music that he wants to perform for a half-time show. He is more interested in the quality of music that we play. Last year Terry Rodenbo was always picky and critical about the songs that were selected for our half-time shows. And I mean ETREMELY PICKY and ETREMELY CRITICAL.

"White Lake Road"

At Fenton High School Terry Rodenbo would incessantly complain to Miss Franklin, "How come we aren't playing songs like "Aquarius/Let the Sunshine In", "2525" or "Spinning Wheel???" His argument was, "This is what high school kids like!! This is what they listen to on "WTAC!! (600 on your AM dial). Not "Mountain Greenery", "I'll Never Walk Alone" or "Goody-Goody!!"

Terry Rodenbo had a legitimate point. I can only ever remember one song that we performed at a half-time show during my Fenton High School marching band days where the football crowd was really into it. That was during my freshmen year when we played the theme song from the television show, "Batman." The crowd went absolutely nuts!! If both football teams hadn't been all set to come back onto the football field for the second half we could have belted out "Batman" two or three more times and the Fenton fans would have just lapped it up.

Terry Rodenbo and I have had this "caliber of music" discussion many times in the past and it is being carried over into this school year as well when riding in the jeep to and from Hartland High School. I counter his argument with two points. One Terry Rodenbo agrees with and the other he thinks is total hogwash.

Point one and this is the opinion that we disagree upon the most: I have tried to point out to Terry Rodenbo, very unsuccessfully I might add, that it is not just students that attend high school football games. There are parents; alumni; town's folks; who just like to follow the local team. Not everyone that goes to these games listens to rock stations like WTAC (still 600 on your AM dial) or CKLW. And these are the people that are pulling the lever in the election booth when it comes time to determine whether a high school millage is going to be passed or defeated.

For many, the only time these attendees may ever set foot on a public school's property is to see a high school football game. If the team gets blown out and the band is playing songs that this same of group of people do not like or" wasn't played when I was in high school," then my theory is that this could translate into "no votes" when it comes time for a millage election.

In the world of public schools, everything translates to the passing of the school millage. I mean this is the primary reason why Mike Beardslee and Terry Rodenbo are students of the Hartland Consolidated Schools and not attending classes as pupils of the Fenton Area School for the 1969-70 school year.

The response from Terry Rodenbo is always the same when I try to stress my argument: "You're selling and I'm not buying!!"

The second opinion is one that Terry Rodenbo and I actually do agree upon. It's a view, however, that we only share with Jim Koop and Katie. It's a belief that the four of us discussed during our Fenton High marching days and applies equally to our new marching band outfit.

"White Lake Road"

Maybe the reason why we have been affiliated with marching bands that didn't play better music selections was because we simply weren't talented enough. As harsh as a thought as that is, all four of us agree that there is some validity to this belief.

I always wondered how high school marching bands like Flint Northwestern, probably the best marching band in Genesee County, or Oak Park, the home of "Bad Hombre", consistently had the capability of playing music arrangements like: "Aquarius/Let the Sunshine In", "2525" or "Spinning Wheel?" I mean these groups could probably belt this kind of award winning high school halftime music for every show performance of their marching band season.

Then how is it that the marching bands that Mike Beardslee has been a member of for the last four marching band seasons might only be able to put on one great halftime show a season? And the key word being might.

The answer eventually came to the four of us and it was simple: dedication. That was the difference between high school marching bands like Flint Northwestern and Oak Park High Schools of the world and some of the below average marching bands that Mike Beardslee has been associated with since the fall of 1965.

What you could teach the Flint Northwestern and Oak Park marching bands in one rehearsal, it will probably take two rehearsals, at a minimum, for a lot of other state of Michigan high school bands to get the music selections and marching band routines down. When a marching band has a short marching band rehearsal week like the one Hartland is up against for this upcoming Friday night's half time show, every rehearsal second is precious.

With maybe the exception of my sophomore year of marching band season, the Guy Thompson led one, I'm still not fully convinced we could have pulled off playing the above-mentioned arrangements with only one weeks' rehearsal time.

Could the Fenton High School marching bands of years past with super stars like Marlene Becker, Carl Peters, Ray Sortman and Don Smith have nailed these songs down in one rehearsal? That group was so talented that they would not only have had these music selections perfected, but also memorized before their first marching band rehearsal of the week was even half completed. They were that good.

It will be very interesting come fourth hour to learn what music selections that we will be playing for this week's half-time show. Good marching band music usually translates into better individual efforts, improved marching band routines and really good half-time shows.

"White Lake Road"

Chapter # 50 – "Mr. Touchdown!!"

September 15th – There has been good news and bad news for the first two weeks of marching band rehearsals. The good news is that the pre-game show is pretty much down pat. We start off from the north end of the end zone in block formation marching down the field playing the Hartland High School fight song by the name of "Varsity!!" I am also proud of myself for the fact that Mike Beardslee has only broken into "Stand Up and Cheer", the Fenton High School fight song, by mistake only once. Now that got me some "what was that, Beardslee" interesting looks from the rest of the Hartland High School Marching Band members.

From there we break off into a marching band routine to the strains of "Mr. Touchdown." I just love this song. There is only one other marching band song that I like better than "Mr. Touchdown". That's "March America", a great tune for Memorial Day and Fourth of July parades. Honorable mention goes to "Gridiron Heroes!!" The "Detroit Lions'" theme song. I defy anyone in the free world to stare Mike Beardslee in the eye and say that they do not appreciate a Graham T. Overgard musical arrangement. Don't even try it. Can't be done.

After "Mr. Touchdown" we end up in concert band formation and play the "Star Spangled Banner". Once the national anthem is completed, we then split off into two long lines that represent a tunnel for the Hartland Eagle football players to run through while we play "Varsity." Then we do the appropriate right or left spin turns to take us off of the field and voila! Pre-game is done.

I must admit that this is a fast pace, go-go-go type of pre-game show. By the time you get to the concert formation and prepare to play the national anthem of the United States, you can be in a serious huffin and puffin mode.

The bad news is that while we have received the sheet music for the two songs that we are to perform at the University of Michigan Band Day this upcoming Saturday, the University of Michigan fight song, "The Victors" and "St. Louis Blues", the music for our half-time show of this week as of last Friday's rehearsal had not arrived yet. That's not good.

This now means that we'll have to use rehearsal time this week for the practicing of the Band Day music arrangements which will cut into our preparation time for the marching routines that we'll have to learn for this Friday nights' halftime show. From what Mike Beardslee has observed over the past two weeks with the Hartland High School Marching Band is this, there is no doubt in my mind that as a unit we can get the marching band routines down pretty quick.

The musical performance aspect I am not as confident. I'll betcha there are only five to seven, maybe eight tops, performers in the Hartland Senior Band that can sit down and sight read these songs that we are going to perform in five days and have them down pretty good today with no problem. That leaves almost 80% of the rest of the marching band that may not get be

able to play these songs with some proficiency until Wednesday's rehearsal. That's cutting it a little too close for a Friday night halftime show.

Then you have to factor in, and this following statement is solely based upon Mike Beardslee's own marching band experiences, that up to as many as 5% of the marching band members that I have been associated with are simply not able to play any of the sheet music that is handed out to them even if they are given 365 days between half-time shows to rehearse it. The primary reason for that is usually, despite being in high school and having had played a musical instrument for a minimum of three years, those individuals, who shall remain nameless, still do not know how to read music.

This is Mike Beardslee's fifth year of being a member of a high school marching band and I guarantee you that every half-time show there will be one, maybe as many as two, members of the marching band just holding their instrument to their mouths. There is no pushing of the valves or moving of the keys. They can march and do all of the routines/drills okay. But they might as well be carrying a flower pot during the halftime performance because that's the exact same sound they're producing out of their instruments. None!!

Thank goodness come fourth hour upon entering the Band Room there was some sheet music sitting on our music stands. The two featured songs for this week's half-time show are: "Going Out of My Head" and "Up Up and Away." Maybe not in the same high-class category as "Joshua" or my personal all-time favorite of "Georgy Girl", but this is good stuff. I feel real decent about how this week's half-time show is going to go.

The other good thing about this first day of the school week is that the weather is suitable enough so that we can get out and march on the football field. Mr. Anderson told me once that everyone thinks the most important day of the marching band week is the actual game day. "Well, they are wrong, Beardslee. Monday is. It's imperative on Monday that the band has a rehearsal that allows them to get through the entire half-time at least once. The theory being that you have no idea how "Mother Nature" will affect a marching band's practice schedule for the remainder of the week." Makes sense.

We got through the entire half time show during band rehearsal today. Its march down the field in block formation to "Varsity;" break into a marching routine that includes four-person squads doing pin-wheels and reverse pinwheels while playing "Up Up and Away." I'm really starting to like this song. From there we scramble into concert formation and then perform "Going Out of My Head." Play the Hartland High School "Alma Mater" and then march off of the field to "Varsity."

Despite some rough spots, particularly when it came to playing the two highlighted songs, if "Mother Nature" cooperates for the next few days, the Hartland Senior High Band is going to put on quite the half-time show this Friday evening. I'm really looking forward to it.

"White Lake Road"

I'm not the only one feeling good about our first half-time show of the marching band season. The ride home to "White Lake Road" tonight was a festive one. Even Terry Rodenbo set aside his unexplainable fascination with the song, "Spinning Wheel", to give his official approval that the songs selected for this week's football game against Stockbridge High School, where ever that is, and I quote, "aren't half bad."

I suspect, however, that Terry Rodenbo is still reserving judgment to see if the music selections for the remaining four half time shows of this marching band season achieve his high standards. I hope they do. At least in one person's humble opinion, we're off to a good start.

"White Lake Road"

Blog #51 – "Buck Up"

September 16th – My mother came home from work today and had a forlorn look on her face as well as an envelope in her right hand. This envelope looked like a business type one and I wondered if there were layoffs imposed by the Fenton Area Schools or; was there the same certification issue that caused Mark Edward's mother to sweat out whether she was going to be allowed to continue to be employed on a full-time basis at Eastern Elementary School. Either way, my mother's facial expression indicated that she was bordering on tears.

Two questions immediately came to my mind; 1) Where was Katie when I needed her? This is her department, not mine. 2) And why does my mother have to interrupt me when I am watching one of my favorite science fiction movies of all time, "This Island Earth?" That flick is right up there with the "Mole People" that featured Hugh Beaumont of "Leave it To Beaver" fame.

My mother handed me the letter and I saw that it had Gaylord High School letterhead on it. I instantly felt a bit of panic run down my back. Was this letter going to advise me that my old Fenton Senior High and Cabin #5 Interlochen buddy, Eric Donald, was seriously injured or had suffered an even worse fate?

Despite a little bit of trembling in my hands I speed read through the pages of the letter and was relieved to know that there was nothing wrong with Eric Donald health wise. In fact, the letter had nothing to do with Eric Donald as this correspondence was authored by a one Robert C. Walker, the former principal of Fenton High School and current high school principal of Gaylord High School.

Just imagine in your mind actor Clint Eastwood's steely eyed look with the personality of Gunnery Sgt. Jim Moore, the character played by Jack Webb in the movie, "The Drill Instructor." You have just met Mr. Robert C. Walker.

The intent and message of this letter by Robert C. Walker could be placed in the category of "Buck Up", as the content of this dispatch was directly addressing the Beardslee family situation where my mother was an employee of the Fenton Area Schools; resident of the town of Fenton; and whose two offspring were students of an entirely different public, not private, school system.

There was one very poignant passage from Robert C. Walker in this communication that read, "Don't worry about what your fellow teachers think or even what the town of Fenton thinks. Do what is best for yourself and your family. That's what Mrs. Walker chose for our family a few years ago. And the Walker family has not once regretted leaving Fenton, Michigan and moving 175 some miles north to Gaylord, Michigan."

"White Lake Road"

I re-read this letter twice and still could not believe that it was written by Robert C. Walker, himself. If my Aunt Betty Beardslee ever read this same letter she would not have believed for one second that the person who put pen to this correspondence was one Robert C. Walker. Not in a million years.

You could have charged admission for the battles those two had had over my cousin Davey's stunts that he was always pulling off during his Fenton High School days. I mean when Aunt Betty and Robert C. Walker got together, you couldn't tell who was doing the better imitation of Gunnery Sgt. Jim Moore.

Their meetings were, shall we say, slightly confrontational. As my Uncle Don used to say when Aunt Betty was out of hearing range, "When you get two contrarians in the same room, sparks fly."

My Uncle Don and Aunt Betty owned one of the first color television sets that were ever produced. My Aunt Betty would occasionally invite the "White Lake Road" Beardslee's over on a Sunday night so that Katie and I could watch "Walt Disney" and "Bonanza" in color TV. It was great seeing beautiful snowcapped mountains in color while Ben, Adam, Hoss and Little Joe Cartwright rode their horses across the range of the Ponderosa.

Every once in while in the background on these visits Katie and I would over hear Aunt Betty say to my folks, "Well, I have to go into the high school tomorrow morning and straighten out old man Walker again." Katie and I would just laugh and laugh when we heard Aunt Betty make that statement. And believe me, Aunt Betty was not joking!!

Mr. Robert C. Walker and his family had had a similar incident in their lives that the content of the letter to my mother was specifically addressing. While both families experienced a son moving away from Fenton High School to attend another high school for his senior year, this is where the similarities ended. The Walker family situation came under far more scrutiny than what the Beardslee family, as well as the Koop and Rodenbo families, will probably ever have to endure.

"White Lake Road"

Blog #52 – "If my husband is not good enough for this community…."

September 16th – One warm Thursday, summer afternoon between my seventh and eighth grade school years, I was sitting inside the screened in porch of "White Lake Road" reading the local paper, "The Fenton Independent." That is when I noticed an article announcing that Mr. Robert C. Walker was leaving Fenton High School to take over the principalship of Gaylord High School, wherever that is.

This was surprising news from the fact that what few times that I had ever seen or heard of any high school principals leaving that position was when they ascended to the rank of superintendent in the same school district. So, Robert C. Walker's departure to another school district for the same job was earth shattering type of news.

As a junior high student, I never really had any direct contact with Mr. Robert C. Walker. What few times that I had ever seen him wandering around the junior high building area made me want to find the next open locker, jump in, slam the locker door shut and hide until he was gone or until I could figure a way to get out of the locker. That is how much in fear Mike Beardslee was of Robert C. Walker.

However, I also got the distinct impression that Robert C. Walker was not very popular with the Fenton High School students or people in the local community. The only time I remembered ever seeing the Fenton High School student body give Mr. Walker a cheer was for something he did was during a high school basketball pep rally. Other than that one specific event I suspect, just like myself, that the rest of the students of Fenton High School sustained a high feeling of anxiety whenever they saw Mr. Walker coming their way.

This "Hey, maybe Mr. Walker's not such a bad guy after all moment" took place the day of the Class B State Championship basketball quarter final game where Fenton High School was to face the hated River Rouge Panthers. Mr. Robert C. Walker was making some key note comments at the pep assembly when all of a sudden in front of the entire Fenton High student body, and while fully decked out in a coat and tie, Mr. Robert C. Walker performed a head over shoulder rollover type movement on the Phillips Memorial Gymnasium floor. Once back on his feet Mr. Robert C. Walker yelled out to us pep rally attendees, "That if we beat Rouge tonight I will roll across the entire length of the basketball court!!"

Mr. Robert C. Walker brought the house down with his graceful movement and passionate declaration for a Fenton Tiger victory over the River Rouge Panthers!! You cannot tell me that any other high school principal in the state of Michigan has ever received more earsplitting applause from a student body than Robert C. Walker did that very moment.

And that was the only time that I ever witnessed Mr. Robert C. Walker acting like a good guy rather than similar to ramrod Rowdy Yates, portrayed by Clint Eastwood, of the TV series,

"Rawhide" while trying to move cattle from the state of Texas to Dodge City, Kansas and finding dried up water holes at every stop of the way.

So, I'm not totally positive that when the announcement of Robert C. Walker leaving Fenton High School to become a high school principal elsewhere was made public, that too many families in the Fenton community were sitting down at the supper table that night and having themselves a good cry over his departure.

However, it shortly afterward dawned on the good people of Fenton that if Robert C. Walker was moving to Gaylord, Michigan, then so was the rest of his family. This included his son, Terry Walker, who as a high school junior was voted to the Class B Allstate Basketball squad. And in my humble opinion, Terry Walker is probably the greatest basketball player in the history of Fenton High School. My sincere apologies to Fenton Tigers greats: Bob Bruder, Tim Dode, Jim Goodrich and Don Madden.

The Fenton community could probably have cared less that Mr. Robert C. Walker was hitting the road. You can always find another high school principal. Returning 6' 4" all-state basketball players, however, don't fall into high school basketball coach's laps every day. The exception, of course, is the Gaylord High School basketball coach.

All sorts of stories and rumors were starting to float around the town of Fenton that Terry Walker would stay and simply live with another Fenton family and spend his senior year of high school as a "Fenton Tiger." But there was a quote in the "Fenton Independent" from Mrs. Walker that pretty much quashed the rumors that Terry Walker would remain at Fenton High School. Her exact words were, "If my husband is not good enough for this community, then neither is my son." Terry Walker went on to graduate from Gaylord High School in June of 1966.

Despite the fact that Terry Walker was not physically running up and down the basketball court as a member of the Fenton High School Varsity Basketball team any longer, his legacy continued. The "Fenton Independent" would run as many stories and print every box score that they could about Terry Walker's basketball experience at Gaylord High School. In fact, you heard more about Terry Walker as a Gaylord High School basketball player than when he played basketball for Fenton High School.

It didn't help matters much when the Gaylord High School basketball squad made it all the way to the Class B Quarter Finals while the Fenton roundballers were upset by an average at best Holly High School squad in the District Tournament semi-final game. I still vividly remember a Holly Bronco guard by the name of Mark Phalen deciding to beat the Fenton Tigers all by himself. That was one ugly basketball game.

The Holly Bronco surprise victory not only shut down the Fenton High School Basketball for the 1965-66 season, it also allowed for almost two extra weeks and four more basketball games

of newspaper articles in the "Fenton Independent" totally dedicated to Terry Walker and his basketball teammates while Gaylord High School continued their quest for a basketball state championship.

Every time I read an article about Terry Walker and the Gaylord Basketball team in the Fenton Independent, I thought back to another article in this same tabloid from seven months earlier where Mrs. Walker was quoted as saying:

"If my husband is not good enough for this community, then neither is my son."

"White Lake Road"

Chapter #53 – "Senior Weasel and Junior Weasel"

September 16th – You really cannot compare the Mike Beardslee departure from Fenton High School for his senior year in the same vein as Terry Walker's. His exodus impacted the entire high school and community far more than mine. But the difference was that while physically Terry Walker was some 175 miles away and no longer a part of the Fenton population, Jim Koop, Terry Rodenbo, Katie and myself still reside in Fenton, Michigan.

Katie and I live three miles from down town Fenton and I have pretty much been a recluse at "White Lake Road" since the day I had started this new school year. Luckily, I hadn't been on the receiving end of anyone calling me a "traitor" to my face.

That could, however, change this upcoming weekend at the University of Michigan Band Day. There is a high probability that I will run into some members of the Fenton High School Marching Band this Saturday. The big question now is will I receive the same treatment that Steve West received from this identical group of people when he left Fenton High School to spend his senior year as a fulltime student at the Interlochen Arts Academy? I must admit that I can see myself being on the receiving end of this type of conduct. And it has me more than a little on edge.

But the primary recipient of any flak about Katie and me still residing in Fenton but attending another public school will be geared towards my mother. No one at Plant Seven, where ever that is, who works with my father at General Motors probably even knows that George C. Beardslee even has any offspring, let alone what school system they attend. So, he's off the hook.

The fact that this issue was brought up when I was at State Road Elementary School last Friday makes me think that this was the tip of the ice berg for other snide comments towards my mother. Maybe not from all of the 20 some teachers at my former stomping grounds, but a few well pointed arrows will cause the occasional tearful two-mile drive home for my mother.

And that does not even take into account any asides that may come her way while she is buying groceries at Comber & Fox or standing in the checkout line at Hamady Brothers; nor even when she is leaving St. Johns Church after Sunday morning mass while walking back to our car.

My mother is probably not around enough Fenton Area School administrators to get any aggravation from them. Potential flak from the powers above her could come my mother's way only if a parent of one of the students in her classroom has an issue with their child and how my mother is treating this youngster. And I know of one specific parent of a former student who was in my mother's 5th grade class that would have made the fact that Katie and I were attending another public school a major issue instead of focusing on the topic of the student's misbehavior.

"White Lake Road"

My mother has rarely ever had a problem with a parent of a child in her seven years of full time teaching. In fact, it's the complete opposite. Parents WANT their children to be in "Mrs. Beardslee's fifth grade class room."

I can only remember two separate occasions where there was a combative situation between a parent and my mother. My mother did not handle either circumstance very well as both incidents made my mother a nervous wreck, which, of course, caused a considerable amount of stress in the "White Lake Road" household.

My mother's first full-time teaching job for the Hartland Consolidated Schools happened when she took over at mid-year mark for a sixth-grade teacher. Her first experience with an upset parent followed shortly when my mother had to explain to a parent why a straight "A" student, and I'm talking about straight "A's "since the day this particular student had been in Kindergarten, received a "B+" from my mother on her report card. End of the world kind of stuff.

The principal of Cromine Elementary School had my mother change the grade to an "A- "to appease the parent. And let me tell you that that executive decision did not sit well with my mother one bit. All through the remainder of that condensed school year, my mother repeatedly, and I mean night after night, said at the supper table of "White Lake Road, "The student did not earn that "A-. "

The second issue, and far, far more serious of the two, took place about four years ago when a student in her 5th grade class, good old Robert Edmore, a real weasel of a kid, brought a "Playboy" magazine to school when my mother was teaching at Eastern Elementary School in Fenton, Michigan. Robert Edmore was stupid enough to show my mother this magazine so she took it away from him. Robert Edmore was then given leave of Eastern Elementary School for three days "to ponder over what he had done."

Mr. Edmore, Robert Sr., if at all possible, was even a bigger weasel than his namesake, had a conniption fit that is son was suspended from elementary school. I mean, let's face it; a kid really has to mess up to get suspended for three days from an elementary school. Mr. Edmore's outburst led him on a crusade to get my mother fired from her teaching position.

I accidentally once added ammunition for Mr. Edmore's' cause when he called "White Lake Road", of which, he would do continually do to "straighten out" my mother. My mother was not home on one of the evenings so I answered the telephone and had the tremendous honor of speaking with Mr. Edmore.

Looking back on this exact moment, I could swear that Mr. Edmore must be related to Coach Appleton. They both had the tone of voice that demanded you drop everything to tend to their commands. Not wishes; not whims, but commands. Mr. Edmore said, "I'm calling every night to talk to your mother and each time I talk to you or whoever else answers the phone, I am

advised that she is not at home. Is this a regular occurrence for her to be gone away from home this many evenings on a work night?"

My reply was, "Yes, this was normal for her to not be home so many nights per week." And that was the gospel truth as my mother was going to school three nights a week, either at Flint Junior College or Eastern Michigan University, to earn hours towards the completion of her Master's Degree. The problem was that Mr. Edmore ended the telephone conversation before I could explain the purpose of why my mother was gone from home on such a regular basis.

The big meeting finally took place between my mother, Mr. Edmore, Mr. Tomek, the principal of Eastern Elementary School, and Mr. Kaulitz, the superintendent of the Fenton Area Schools. The purpose of this meeting in Mr. Edmore's mind was to get my mother terminated from her teaching position as she had "stifled" his son's constitutional rights of bringing in a "Playboy" magazine to school to show to his friends and keep safely in his school desk.

I only got bits and pieces of what actually took place in this meeting and that was only because of the flak I got from my mother about advising Mr. Edmore that she was gone regularly from home three nights a week and not WHY she was away from her household for this much time on a repeated basis. Man, I got an earful about that.

Apparently, Mr. Edmore raised that as an issue in the conference as a cause to have my mother fired and was promptly shot down by Mr. Tomek's response of, "Mary Beardslee is gone from her home three nights a week so that she can earn her Master's Degree in Elementary Education. She is already one of the most outstanding teachers in the Fenton School District and she is constantly improving on her already exceptional teaching skills."

Yeah, put that in your pipe and smoke it, Mr. Edmore!! You weasel!!

Mr. Tomek's comments were apparently enough to take the wind of Mr. Edmore's sails as once he and his worthless son both apologized to my mother, in writing I might add, the crisis was over. Thank goodness.

While Mr. Edmore was smart enough to know when to put his tail between his legs and slink back to his home, Robert Edmore the II, wasn't. As I mentioned earlier he rode the same school bus that Katie and I did. My mother was smart enough to know that young Mr. Edmore was dumber than a wall that holds up an outhouse, and would continue to shoot his big mouth off about this incident.

My mother said to Katie and me, "I don't want either one of you to retaliate against Robert Edmore. You don't yell at him, nor do you physically strike him. If he says something specifically about me, then let me know. I'll take of that through Mr. Tomek." Well, guess what….

"White Lake Road"

Chapter #54 – "A Specific Event"

September 16th – The next few days after the big meeting, Robert Edmore Jr. was pretty quiet on the way to his drop off point at Eastern Elementary School. Oh, don't worry, Robert Edmore remained the little weasel that he was, and two days later blurted out loud enough for the whole school bus to hear, "Hey, Beardslee. My father and I are still going to get your old lady fired before the end of the school year!!"

Katie, ever the dutiful daughter, relayed that information to my mother and a few days later while traveling to school one morning it dawned on me that there wasn't the usual loud yapping noise coming from the passenger seat immediately behind the bus driver. Robert Edmore hadn't been riding the school bus for the last couple of days. The next time I saw Robert Edmore was when he was getting out of his father's car to start another glorious school day at Eastern Elementary School.

Using my first-rate detective skills from what I had learned from in reading "The Missing Chums", number four in the "The Hardy Boys" series, that scene of Robert Edmore slowly getting out of his dad's car probably meant that ole Robert Edmore was not going to be a guest passenger of a Fenton Area School Bus for a while. That hunch turned out to be a true premonition as Robert Edmore the II, did not ride a school bus that the Fenton Area Schools owned for the last seven months of the school year. And he wasn't missed one bit.

While everything turned out okay for my mother in her predicament with the Edmore family, it did affect her immensely from an emotional standpoint. More than once she had spent an evening sitting in the "Breakfast Room" of "White Lake Road" writing out her resignation. It never got to where she actually offered her notice of leaving to Mr. Tomek, but it was to say the least a very stressful time in the Beardslee household.

I suspect that my mother will continue to get some pointed jabs from her State Road Elementary School co-workers like, "When are Katie and Mike coming back to Fenton High School?" The real kicker is that there is no longer a Roger O'Berry around to tell the other teachers to mind their own business and, "To go back to their class rooms and work on their "glorious" bulletin boards."

My mother can probably handle any of her fellow teacher's snide comments but they still hurt her feelings. Where things could get tense is if "groups of Mr. Edmore" types appear and cause some havoc with the school board claiming that it is illegal and unethical for a teacher who resides in the school district that they teach in to let their children attend another public-school system. I'm not saying that this would ever take place, but it could cause a school board member or school administrator to ask the question of, "Mrs. Beardslee. Is there a specific reason why you have not re-enrolled your children back into the Fenton Area Schools since the school millage successfully passed and all cuts to positions and activities were completely restored?"

That's a great question. And there is no good answer for this inquiry. In all honesty, there is probably no explainable reason for Katie and I, plus Jim Koop and Terry Rodenbo to still be attending Hartland High School. Everything that Hartland High School has to offer so does Fenton High School. The only difference is that Fenton High School students are doing it in a brand spanking new high school building.

Will the pressure become so great that my mother will break out the resignation letters that she had prepared for the Senior Weasel and Junior Weasel conflict, but this time actually sign her name to it, slap a six-cent stamp on this envelope and mail it to Mr. Telgenoff, the current superintendent of the Fenton Area Schools? Maybe yes, maybe no, for a couple of reasons.

Unless there is some specific event that causes my mother to just totally cave in to the pressure and have her pull the trigger of dragging her two kids back into the Fenton school system, then I think the two of us will remain Hartland Eagles for the time being also allowing my mother to keep her job and hopefully keep people off of her back.

Do I think that there is a specific event that is looming out there that will cause Katie and I to have a reversal of schools that we attend? Yes, I do. I just don't know what that specific event is, but I can feel it in my bones that one is out there. And when does this specific event take place? Over Thanksgiving?? Christmas?? Semester break??

The second reason why my mother would pull us kids back to the Fenton Schools and avoid succumbing to colleague pressure is money. My parents are under the assumption that they have between Katie and I, at least six consecutive years of college tuition(s) staring them in the face. My mother came to realization years ago that if she and my father wanted to put us two kids through school, my fathers' single paycheck was not sufficient; no matter how much overtime he could get from General Motors.

This is especially true since Katie has not backed down from her plans of attending Colorado University in Boulder, Colorado. Translation: outstate college tuition. Maybe this is how I could break the news to my parents of my plans to enlist in the United States Air Force. It could go something like this, "Hey, guys, look at the amount of money that I am saving you by not attending college!!" If that doesn't get Mike Beardslee back in the Beardslee Will, I don't know what else would.

Based upon Katie's anticipated college expenses alone, that is what triggered my mother to become a full-time teacher. My mother had the foresight to realize that her paycheck was sorely needed to supplement the Beardslee household piggy bank.

I really don't see my mother resigning from her teaching position any time soon. But, if there were sufficient enough forces such as co-workers, parents, administrative pressure, or that mysterious specific event Mike Beardslee worries about so much, then, yes, I could see her packing it in at the Fenton Area Schools and leave for another school district. The Hartland

Consolidated Schools possibly?? While my mother has never come right out and admitted it, there are times that I think she misses her days at Cromine Elementary School.

After reading the Robert C. Walker letter and having flash backs of Robert Edmore Sr. and Robert Edmore Jr.; in my feeble little mind, I still wonder if the Hartland Eagle's Blue and Gold school colors will revert back into the Orange and Black school colors of the Fenton Tigers before too long.

And if this switch back to the Fenton Area Schools does actually come true, I see two ways of how Mike Beardslee discovers that I am advised of this return for the remainder of "the greatest year of my life:"

1) My mother awakens me one early school morning and tells me to get a move on or I will be late for the school bus. Not to warm up the jeep or that I need to go into Fenton and pick up Jim Koop and Terry Rodenbo, but to hurry up and catch the bus, or;

2) While eating supper one evening at "White Lake Road", a visitor comes to the door. Some papers are exchanged between my mother and the stranger. She then hands both sets of keys to the jeep to this unknown, unfamiliar type person, who then proceeds to drive "Mike Beardslee's jeep" down the "White Lake Road" driveway and heads west when turning onto the road.

In my mind, I can actually see both of these events taking place and that is how on "Planet Beardslee" Mike Beardslee will discover that he is no longer a student of the Hartland Consolidated Schools. It will be interesting to see how, and if, this specific event thing shakes out in real life. You can probably tell that I am still not fully convinced that there isn't a reserved seat on Bus #23 with my name written all over it before the 1969-70 school year comes to a close.

Chapter #55 – "A Self-Proclaimed Magnificent Seven"

September 18th – Busy day today. There's some band business to be taken of; I got to hear about a big cross country meet from last night; and, the coup de grace of today, I had the pleasure of meeting and talking with four other Hartland Consolidated School students, of which, I quickly figured out that they probably don't like a one Mike Beardslee a whole lot. What this quartet doesn't realize is that the five of us now have something in common.

Alex Felton and Max Perry took a few seconds away from reading their 1000-page volume, Physics Class text books to update me about a triangular cross country meet last night between Hartland, Howell and Whitmore Lake High Schools. (Guys, please, please, do not tell me your individual times and mile splits!!) While I was getting the scoop on the cross country meet from these two, back in my mind I wondered if this was a plot on their part to get me real excited about this big meet and then get me to come out and run on the Hartland High School Cross Country team. News flash: Ain't going to happen, fellas.

The final score of this contest was 23-23, a rare cross country meet tie. The big news was, and I had heard rumblings about this last Spring during track season, was that the self-proclaimed, "Magnificent Seven", an all freshmen top seven runners of the Howell High School Varsity Cross Country team, and self-projected to be the most dominant high school cross country team in the state of Michigan this season, was maybe not as good as advertised. I got the distinct impression from this conversation that the Howell Cross Country "Magnificent Seven" were more like the recently released George Kennedy and Monte Markham movie, "Guns of the Magnificent Seven" version as opposed to the Yul Brenner and Steve McQueen classic, "The Magnificent Seven."

Alex Felton advised, "We would have beaten them if it been a dual meet since one of the Whitmore Lake harriers placed extremely high among the finishers. Also, the Howell Cross Country course is flat as a pancake. I look forward to getting those Howell runners on a course with some hills on it."

Max Perry then added something that was a real shocker; at least it was to Mike Beardslee. "Coach Fitzpatrick is no longer the cross country coach of Howell High School. Apparently, there were some parents who had run cross country at some level in their lives and thought that running long distance workouts were what was best for this particular Howell High School Cross Country squad. This group of parents pretty much ridiculed the mix of pace work and long distant running workouts, a coaching style that Coach Fitzpatrick had used only to win nine consecutive "Genesee-Livingston Conference" Cross Country championships with, was not in the best interest of their son's future running careers."

Max Perry stated, "I talked with a couple of the older Howell guys that I knew and they advised me that the parents of the first seven varsity runners demanded that Coach Fitzpatrick be fired or they would immediately pull their kids off of the cross country team."

Whoa!! That's pretty serious stuff. I mean this kind of stuff happens to varsity football and basketball coaches every school. But, rarely, and I mean rarely does this kind of thing happen to cross country coaches.

Two thoughts came to my mind. This would weaken the Howell Cross Country team, or any cross country team for that matter, enough that Howell's chances of winning their 10th consecutive "GL Conference" title goes out the window. In fact, they might not even have enough talent on their squad to place 11th out of the 10 teams participating in the league meet.

Max Perry continued, "Apparently Coach Fitzpatrick didn't want to see the Howell Cross Country team lose out on a shot at winning the league championship meet this year for the 10th consecutive season. He stepped down voluntarily from not only coaching cross country but track & field as well."

I suddenly had a brilliant idea!! Oh, yes, we're talking Mike Beardslee brilliant!! But man, wouldn't it be great if Coach Appleton took a page out Coach Fitzpatrick's book and stepped down as head track coach here at Hartland High School so Coach Fitzpatrick could take over for him this Spring for track season? The chances of that happening? Any number you want multiplied by zero.

But I must admit, that if Coach Fitzpatrick came up to me, put his hand on my shoulders and said it was best for the Hartland Eagles Track team that I run the 880 race, then I would do it. No questions asked. Would I enjoy doing those tortuous two laps around a high school track? Nah!! But I would do it.

One of the first things that I noticed when I originally became a student of the Hartland Consolidated Schools took place during one of my initial lunch hours in the Hartland High School cafeteria. I was walking past these four guys sitting at a lunch table and overheard them talking some serious sports stuff. Over the past few weeks some of the topics that Mike Beardslee eavesdropped on included…

"White Lake Road"

Chapter #56 – "Vince Lombardi or Ted Williams??"

- *Who was the best center fielder in the history of major league baseball: Willie Mays or Tris Speaker?*
- *Who was the better major league baseball manager: John McGraw or Casey Stengel?*
- *What college player should the Detroit Lions have spent their first-round draft pick on for the 1966 NFL Draft instead of running back Nick Eddy?*
- *Who was going to have the greater impact in their new coaching/managing positions in the nations' capital of Washington D.C.; Vince Lombardi for the Washington Redskins or; Ted Williams for the Washington Senators?*

I was impressed!! This quartet really knew their sports!! This means that one of these days when Jim Koop or Terry Rodenbo were not around or they had banished Mike Beardslee from the "Band" lunch table some afternoon, that I could hang out with these "sports guys" and get their opinion on whether they thought Lou Brock was out or safe at home plate in game five of the 1968 World Series. Hey!! This is important stuff!!

But since that first day of my passerby strolls of these four, I have learned their names and also observed some disturbing behavior on their part. Enough so that I should seriously heed the warnings of both Tom Beaver and Pete Mason that it was best for me to stay clear of this crew. Way clear.

The individual names of the group are: Craig Annis, Mark Bernard, Jeff Donzilla and Gordon Simon. All four of these guys are members of the class of 1972, the same as Steve Gilmore and Jason Shattuck.

I've also noticed that the above four mentioned have rather high opinions of themselves. And that they have no problem whatsoever in letting other lunch room students know about what great athletes they are and that when they go home at night their mail boxes are jammed packed with letters containing scholarship offers from every single university in the Big-10 Conference. Yeah, right.

In addition to being quite boisterous I have also observed that this pack of four do not exactly consist of the nicest people on the face of the Earth. I wouldn't quite put them into the "juvenile delinquent" category since I do not see them wearing any black leather jackets or black pointy shoes that people associate with the type of clothing that "hoods" wear.

But these four fellas have the potential to appear and star in the types of movies where motorcycle gangs are terrorizing the town's people of some small fishing village in the state of California. And as the character "Maxwell Smart" of the great TV comedy show, "Get Smart", would say, "And, loving it."

A daily example of their misconduct includes; the throwing of empty milk cartons at unsuspecting students. Plus, the throwing of these same milk cartons at the garbage bins and leaving their missed attempts on the floor for someone else to pick up and toss into the plastic garbage containers.

The worst lack of manners being displayed, however, by this entire group was the tripping of other students and seeing their lunches fall off of their lunch tray onto the floor. From stories that my mother had told me from her time here at the Hartland Consolidated Schools as a teacher, I knew that some of these kids' parents probably had a tough time of scraping up the $.35 daily lunch money fee. To see that food go to waste was bothersome especially since that might be that unlucky student's only hearty meal of the whole day.

The dastardly quartet seemed to always get a big laugh out of this mean stunt. Especially on the day where rolls were part of the hot lunch meal. And man, do those rolls smell great!!

The other type of juvenile behavior on these four parts' that I have witnessed was the yelling at other students across the lunch room like: "Hey Four Eyes!!"" Hey Stupid!!" Or even worse yet, the student who had a pair of shoes that was probably worn by a family relative in Burma during World War II, was promptly nick named, "Shoes," bringing attention to not only how bad of shape their foot wear was in, but the financial straits that this poor kid's family was undoubtedly in as well.

As I learned more about, Craig Annis, Mark Bernard, Jeff Donzilla, and Gordie Simon, it dawned on me that based upon the visitors of one week ago that I had received, Ric Adams and Al Dowty, these four cats were a different breed. And my path is going to cross with this group at some point more than a couple of times during the school year based on the athletic teams that the five of us have in common.

This is what Mike Beardslee learned further about these particular four individuals in recent and various conversations with others….

"White Lake Road"

Chapter #57 – "Big Craig and Little Craig"

September 18th – The one constant item that these four sophomores were persistent in with their daily braggadocio conversations was actually something that Mike Beardslee has some knowledge about. They were all members of the 880 Relay team for the Hartland High School Track squad. And according to them that this upcoming track season they were going to break and set the following meet/league/state records for the 880 relays:

- ***Genesee-Livingston Conference;***
- ***Michigan High School Athletic Association Record for Class "B" Classification;***
- ***Mott Relays;***
- ***Huron Relays;***
- ***Livingston County Relays.***

Those are some pretty impressive goals and an even more of an extraordinary feat if actually accomplished. I know a little something about setting lofty goals when it comes to wanting to see your name listed on a wood slat in a high school gymnasium for a school record set during a track season. From an athletic standpoint, in my humble opinion, there is no higher honor.

I once told Coach Lane when I was a sophomore at Fenton High School that I going to break Don Madden's school record of 50.9 seconds in the 440 Run. That's some serious feet moving. Just for the record when I left Fenton High School I was still 5.9 seconds away from breaking Don Madden's school record.

To put that in statement in perspective, if Don Madden and Mike Beardslee raced against each other in the same 440 event; if I was lucky, at the conclusion of this race I would only be 60 yards behind Don Madden when he crossed the finish line. Could Mike Beardslee ever beat Don Madden, mano e mano, in a 440 Run? Never. Not even on his worse day and me on my best day. No contest.

The above comparison also applies to the Hartland 880 Relay team that I saw in action at last year's GL Conference meet. Granted these four guys were freshmen, but they were still "smoked" by the Swartz Creek 880 Relay team headed up by my good buddy, Rick Pertler. So, if any of those majestic goals are to be reached by this year's version of the Hartland High School 880 Relay team, they should take into consideration that Kearsley and Swartz Creek High Schools have some speed burners returning on their 880 relay teams as well for this upcoming track season.

I admit that Hartland's 1970 version of the 880-relay team will be bigger and stronger. But for them to beat the Swartz Creek 880 relay team, someone is going to have to tell the "Dragons" the wrong date and location of the conference meet. The top five teams score points in the league meet. The Hartland 880 relay team didn't score points in last year's league competition and I'm not fully convinced that they will even place in the top five teams this time around, either.

In fact, Mike Beardslee will make a prediction right now; a whole eight months before the first shot from a starter's pistol goes off in the GL Conference League meet, that an 880-relay team consisting of Craig Annis, Mark Bernard, Jeff Donzilla and Gordie Simon WILL NOT score points in the 880 Relay. Take it to the bank!!

Here is the low down that I have heard on Craig Annis. One, he was probably one of the eight best basketball players regardless of grade classification here at Hartland High School. Al Dowty added, "He's a greedy basketball player, however. Craig Annis will never pass the ball to another teammate even if that teammate is standing all by their lonesome under the basket, the opposing team has already showered; gotten on their team bus and been asleep on their living room couches for at least a half hour."

"Craig Annis also runs the anchor leg of the 880-relay team and has repeatedly bragged about for this upcoming track season of them breaking all sorts of school and conference records in addition to winning the Class B State Championship in this event."

Al Dowty also added, "The problem with Craig Annis is that he is a nasty person with quick fists. It also doesn't help that his father, "Big Craig" is a huge deal in Hartland High School Athletic Boosters. That seems to give "Big Craig and Little Craig" the idea that they both have some power over the various Hartland High School coaching staffs."

Al Dowty summed it up best when he said, "Craig Annis is the type of kid that will knock your books out of your hands in a crowded hall way or trip you when your hands are full. He's trouble from the time that he wakes up for breakfast."

These were some very candid thoughts from a one Mr. Al Dowty. And this is from a guy who prides himself on the fact that he gets along with everybody.

Note to self: Craig Annis sounds like a really good person to stay away from. But that might be a little tricky if we're both going to be members of the track team this Spring.

And an even potential bigger problem is if Craig Annis is truly, truly one of the top eight basketball players here at Hartland High School and "does not make the varsity basketball team and the "new guy", Mike Beardslee does, then I will become the "somebody" being tripped in the school hallway or having my books bashed out of my hands when I least suspect it by a one ticked off Craig Annis. Just don't hit me in the mouth, "Little Craig", after all, I still have "my half of a marching band" to hold up.

Jason Shattuck on a walk back to band room one day after marching band rehearsal filled me in on Mark Bernard and some further general background information on the members of the 880 Relay team. "The one thing I do not understand about those guys," Jason Shattuck stated, "is that we're all members of the class of the 1972 graduating class. There are not that many of us numbers wise in this class so all of us kids have known each other since our Cromine Elementary School days."

"But I'm not convinced that other than their own little clique, that those four like anyone else in the entire sophomore class. Steve Gilmore and I used to hang out with those guys all the time in junior high. But once Steve Gilmore became a freshman he went right to the junior varsity football and basketball teams. That put him on the outs with those four who were on the freshmen football and basketball squads.

"The outs turned to flat out hatred when Steve Gilmore earned a varsity letter as a freshman for his efforts in the pole vault last track season. None of those four guys have their varsity letters yet and it drives them crazy when Steve Gilmore walks through the front doors of Hartland High School every morning wearing his varsity jacket."

I now know why these four do not like Steve Gilmore. It was a matter of pure jealousy. And reading between the lines, when it comes time to select the Hartland High School Varsity Basketball team this upcoming November with six sophomore candidates for this squad, Steve Gilmore's name is going to be the one sophomore that will be on that final list of varsity roundball players. That's an even better pledge then the one I made about the four chaps' chances of getting points in the 880 Relay at the "GL" Conference Meet.

But what I could not figure out was why that quartet of "meanness" didn't like Jason Shattuck, especially since he did not have a varsity letter right this second, either. Jason Shattuck's reply was, "There are a couple of reasons why those four want nothing to do with me. Just like them, I do not have my varsity letter, yet. But unless I really mess up in the next month or so, I will be getting a varsity letter for cross country."

Jason Shattuck added, "From the way I see it, those four at the earliest will not letter until track season is over. Maybe Craig Annis gets one sooner if he makes the varsity basketball team. So, what it boils down to is that those guys are infuriated by the fact that Steve Gilmore and I will have gotten varsity letters before they did."

"The second reason why I am not very popular with Messrs. Annis, Bernard, Simon and Donzilla, is what happened when we were all members of the freshmen basketball team. I was selected captain of that team and Craig Annis and Mark Bernard, as well as "Big Craig," all thought that I was not worthy of that honor. That's when I started to get the cold shoulder and dagger type stares from those two teammates. Man, did they hate me for being named captain. And did I ever see the basketball come my way during an actual game?? No!!"

Jason Shattuck continued, "And to make things even worse, both Craig Annis and I will be trying out for the varsity basketball team this November for the exact same position. Coach Decker is not going to keep more than two sophomores on the varsity squad. I'm smart enough to know that Steve Gilmore is a lock to make varsity. Therefore, it's going to come down to me and Craig Annis. And we both know it."

I then asked Jason Shattuck about Mark Bernard. Jason Shattuck said, "Be careful of him. While Craig Annis is one of the nastiest kids here at Hartland High School, Mark Bernard is one of the most devious. He is a master politician just like his father who is some type of state representative. Mark Bernard has a very selective memory and his favorite phrase is, "I didn't say that. Do you have a recording of what I just said so that I verify that I spoke those utterances and make sure that you are not putting words in my mouth? I'm sure that he has heard his dad use that phrase a million times."

"What's even worse is that not only does he pull this slop on his fellow students, he also does it with teachers as well. And he gets away with it. Measure your words carefully if you ever get into a conversation with him. Mark Bernard is as dangerous as Craig Annis, just in a different way."

Just before Jason Shattuck and I left the Band Room for the cafeteria, I asked him about Mark Bernard's athletic ability, specifically if this guy was going to be a threat to me making the varsity basketball team. Jason Shattuck answer was interesting, "Mark Bernard thinks he is a point guard; the player that is supposed to create offensive opportunities and get the basketball to his teammates. The problem with that is Mark Bernard is just as greedy a basketball player as Craig Annis. Once Mark Bernard gets the basketball in his hands he will not pass it to another teammate. He simply will not pass the ball. The rest of us Hartland guys that are on the basketball floor with Mark Bernard just end up standing around watching four opponents defend him while Mark Bernard gets trapped in a corner. And he still doesn't pass the basketball!!"

"For track season, he is a member of the 880-relay team. Mark Bernard runs the first leg. He's not that fast of sprinter but what makes him and the rest of that relay team so potentially good is that they can make a blind baton pass better than any other 880 relay team in the "GL Conference." If they even spend one second working on their conditioning this spring, which I can guarantee you that they won't, they're capable of getting points in the conference meet come May."

What Jason Shattuck had initially said about Mark Bernard being devious scared me. I have seen kids like this at Fenton High School and most recently during my tour with the Student Conservation Association. Not only are these "Mark Bernard" types underhanded but I have found them to be extremely intelligent as well. A combination of characteristics in people that Mike Beardslee does not fare so well against. In fact, to be brutally candid, I'm usually putty in this type of person's hands. And man, they instinctively seem to know it when I come walking in their direction.

"White Lake Road"

Chapter #58 – "Algebra II"

September 18th – The next person of this foursome that I learned about was Gordie Simon. Just visualize Gordie Simon as an overweight kid who looks exactly like the "Pillsbury Doughboy." Except the "Pillsbury Doughboy "is a much better dresser.

Gordie Simon did not look like an athlete at all. But like the first two members of the Hartland High School 880 relay team previously written about, Gordie Simon would forever be shooting off his big mouth that he was going to be a starter on the Hartland Varsity Basketball team this season and, that the 880-relay team that he runs the second leg on, was going to be conference champs and Class B state champions. In addition, the 880-relay team was not just going to break the Hartland High School record in this event; they were going to disintegrate it!!

It will be interesting to see whose prediction turns out to be more accurate for the final results of the 880 relays in the league meet, Mike Beardslee's or Gordie Simon's. Let's just put it this way, I feel real comfortable with my forecast.

I do, however, hope that Gordie Simon is totally wrong with his prognostication that he and his three relay buddies are going to make up 80% of the starting lineup for this upcoming varsity basketball season. Based off the information that Al Dowty and Jason Shattuck have previously advised me, common sense dictates that Gordie Simon is way off base about this important issue.

One lunch time session last week I saw Tom Moran just casually walk past Gordie Simon and Gordie Simon automatically acted very startled. Sort of like he was half expecting Tom Moran to give him the "two for flinching" type punch in the upper arm area. I later asked Tom Moran about the slight recoiling action by Gordie Simon. That brought a big smile from Tom Moran's face and an interesting explanation of what triggered Gordie Simon's panic like reflexes.

Tom Moran explained, "First of all stay away from all four of those guys. They're dangerous. Each of them in their own way is extremely treacherous. Gordie Simon is the mischievous type. But it's an evil kind of mischievous. Just imagine a really cruel Eddie Haskell. That's Gordie Simon."

"Some of the unkind stuff I have seen him do is throw another kid's packed lunch away when they weren't looking. Not hide, mind you, but actually throw it in the garbage bin. If a student left their seat for some reason during lunch Gordie Simon would pour milk over their hot lunch so that it was totally ruined. And by the time you discover this mean trick, Gordie Simon is nowhere to be found. Lastly, he will trip a person when they walk by him and when the stumbled person turns around to see who tripped them, Gordie Simon, with that fat, chubby face of his, breaks into this all innocent look and asks if that kid is okay."

"The flinching issue you're asking about came about last year. Gordie Simon and I were in the same First Hour Study Hall session. I had this huge Algebra II homework assignment that

had to be done for third hour. Gordie Simon asked me if he could borrow my pencil. I reluctantly said okay, but explained to him that I needed that pencil back real fast."

"A few minutes went by and I again told Gordie Simon that I needed my pencil back. His response was that he loaned it to "so and so". I went to "so and so" and they said they gave it to somebody else. I was smart enough to know that this was a typical Gordie Simon prank. The intent was for me to go around to each kid in the whole study hall to see who had my pencil. Time was my biggest enemy to get this schoolwork completed so I was not too happy with this little hoax of his."

"Now my dad is a principal at a junior high school in the Howell School district. He has always advised me, my brothers and sisters that if another kid pulls a fast one on you, to immediately involve a teacher, no matter how uncool that it may seem."

"I took my father's advice for this particular situation. I went up to Mr. Kraft, the Study Hall teacher, told him of my homework circumstance and lack of cooperation from Gordie Simon concerning my loaned-out pencil. Mr. Kraft called Gordie Simon over to him and the three of us went out into the school hallway. Gordie Simon denied ever borrowing my pencil. Mr. Kraft got nothing out of Gordie Simon to substantiate my story but said, "Don't worry Mr. Moran; I'll track down a pencil for you so that you can finish your Algebra II homework assignment."

"Mr. Kraft went back into the Study Hall whereas I then turned to Gordie Simon and said to him, "I'm going to count to 10 real slow. If I don't have a pencil in my hand by that time I reach that number, you're going to be coming down with one serious stomach ache."

"By the time Mr. Kraft returned with a pencil for me, Gordie Simon had thrown up on the school hall way floor. Mr. Kraft asked me what happened to Gordie Simon. Being the son of a junior high principal, I could not tell a lie. I looked Mr. Kraft straight in his eyes and said, "Something he ate for breakfast must not have agreed with him."

"End of sentence and end of paragraph. I have not had one issue with Gordie Simon since. He still pulls his pranks and tomfooleries on other kids all the time, though. But he always knows that he's always seconds from suddenly coming down with another stomach ache whenever I come near him."

I did ask Tom Moran about the "Big Man on Campus" statements that Gordie Simon was making concerning him being one of the starters on the varsity basketball team for the 1969-70 school year. Tom Moran answered, "If "Crabby" Appleton was coaching the varsity basketball team this season that could very well be the case. For whatever reason, "Crabby" Appleton and those four guys get along really well."

"Craig Annis might make the varsity squad. He is a talented enough basketball player from the neck down. However, Gordie Simon barely made the freshmen basketball team and even then, he never got off of the bench. He probably won't even make the JV basketball team this November without Crabby Appleton calling the shots any longer."

"The only thing that I know about Gordie Simon and his participation on the track team is what Pete Mason tells me. Apparently Gordie Simon runs the second leg on the 880-relay team. But that is the only event that he participates in. Pete Mason also told me that if Gordie Simon ever lost that beer gut of his then he could be running sub 11 flat 100-yard dashes on a consistent basis. That's pretty fast."

Tom Moran ended up by saying, "Be careful of Gordie Simon. I told you about my pencil incident with him. But you have to realize that his evil mischievousness is two layers deep. That's where the real threat is with him. Not only did I have to take time tracking down my pencil that he borrowed, but I never did get my Algebra II assignment done. And that's a tough class for me even when I do have my homework completed."

After Tom Moran departed I came to the conclusion that there were two common themes so far from what have I learned about 75% of the 880 relay team members. First thing learned is that they're dangerous in their own individual way. Second thing learned is that Mike Beardslee should make it a point to stay as far away from them as possible.

However, the remaining member of the 880-relay team, as I was soon to learn about from Ric Adams, made the previous three guys seem like card carrying members of the Vienna Boys Choir.

Chapter 59 – "Dick the Bruiser of Junior High Basketball"

The last representative of the 880-relay team was Jeff Donzilla. However, I have never have once heard him referred to by his given first name. Come to think of it, I've never heard him called by his last name, either. Jeff Donzilla is always called "CE".

I asked Ric Adams one day what was up with the nick name of "CE" and what those initials actually stood for. The answer was more startling than interesting.

"The initials "CE" stand for "Crazy Eyes" was Ric Adams' response to my question. "He was given that moniker from some students who claim that he has an insane type of look on him and the eyes of a crazy person. I don't know so much about the crazy eyes look, but what I do know for a fact is that "CE" has a violent streak in him a mile long."

Oh, this sounds good. Hang on for a second everyone while I run right home and watch the Alfred Hitchcock movie, "Psycho."

Ric Adams continued, "A lot of people think that by the time Steve Gilmore's high school career at Hartland High School is completed, that he will be the most decorated and greatest athlete ever in school history. The funny thing is that "CE" is just as good as athlete, maybe even better, then Steve Gilmore."

"The difference between the two of them is that "CE" has a malicious streak in him that is longer than the Mackinac Bridge. He really likes to rough it up. In football, he just loves to hit. The problem is that it does not matter who "CE" collides into, teammates included. The story that I once heard was that during one freshmen football practice last season, the squad was practicing with no pads doing walk through plays in a no contact drill situation."

"CE" must not have had the phrase "no contact" in his vocabulary, because he just blasted two different Hartland players on consecutive plays. One kid broke his collarbone and the other player broke his right arm. Now that's two team members out for the entire season of football where a lack of players that can suit up for a game is at times a bigger issue than wins or losses"

"The parents of the two injured players went to the Hartland School Board, of which, my father is a member, and what he leaked out to me was that both parents were talked out of suing the school district. Ultimately some financial settlement was reached between the school system and the two families."

"However, and I found this really strange when my dad told me this, was that the settlement agreement included language that as long as "CE" was a student of the Hartland Consolidated School system, he was not allowed to participate in any level of football competition that was representing the Hartland Consolidated Schools. So that is why "CE" is not playing varsity football as a sophomore right along with Steve Gilmore this season."

Ric Adams resumed speaking about Jeff Donzilla." CE's" brutality in athletics was not solely restricted to the sport of football. Coach Decker was coaching the 9th grade basketball team that I was on and one day asked me to tag along to watch a seventh-grade basketball game with him." CE" was a member of that particular basketball team. I was actually impressed watching him play. "CE" was an excellent rebounder, could run the floor well, and played solid defense. From the neck down, "CE" would have fit right in with our "UCLA of Junior High Basketball" team.

"The problem was that when out on the basketball floor, just like the football field, "CE" liked to hit. He believed in "hard fouls." When "CE" went to foul an opposing player, he did it with the intent to maim the poor kid. When he grabbed a rebound, he would wildly swing out with his elbows and pretty much didn't care who he hit with them. At least once a game another basketball player, opponent and teammate, had to leave the game because they were on the receiving end of a "CE" well placed elbow to the skull or facial area that had drawn blood. And that doesn't even count the number of fights he would get try to pick with players on the other team during a stoppage in play."

"Coach Decker did not have the desire to coach the JV basketball team so the future plan was for him to go back down to the junior high level and coach the 7th and 8th grade teams the next school year. However, Coach Decker had seen the problems that "CE" was to not only the opposition but to his own teammates and admitted to my father, "This kid is a walking time bomb. He's going to get the school and me, personally, sued someday. I'm not going to let him cost the Hartland Consolidated Schools all sorts of money, legal bills, and tarnish my reputation just because he thinks he's the "Dick the Bruiser" of junior high basketball."

I thought to myself that the easy way to solve this problem was to not have "CE" play junior high basketball. Right?? Even Jethro Bodine of the TV show, "The Beverly Hillbillies" between chores, his sixth-grade education and his double 00 spy duties could figure that out by himself.

Ric Adams agreed with my thought process but added this choice nugget, "Coach Appleton absolutely loved "CE" and told Coach Decker in no uncertain terms, that "CE" was not only going to be a starter on the eighth-grade basketball team, but he was also going to be named captain of the team as well."

"Since "CE" was going to get preferential treatment over more deserving players like Steve Gilmore and Jason Shattuck, Coach Decker flat out refused to coach the junior high basketball squads of the Hartland Consolidated Schools."

Ric Adams concluded, "That was a huge loss not having Coach Decker coaching at that level. As long as you had Coach Decker teaching those junior high basketball kids, drilling them on fundamentals over and over again until they got it right, then any future basketball coach knew that regardless of a player's talent level, they were getting an Stanley Decker coached basketball player who was automatically a fundamentally sound basketball player."

Ric Adams did not have much to say about "CE" when it came to track season. Again, basing it on what he had been told from Max Perry, Ric Adams added, "From what I gather, "CE" from the 880 races down, including all field events and both hurdle races, could have scored points in any of those events He was that talented. The problem was that "CE" didn't want to participate in any other events. All he wanted to do was run a leg on the 880-relay team. Complete one leg in the 880-relay and he was done for the day. That must have given him plenty of time to work on his tan."

"Where "CE" got it all wrong was when it came time for earning points towards a varsity letter during track season. All he had to do was look at what Steve Gilmore was doing. Steve Gilmore worked hard on the pole vault event and his efforts earned him a varsity letter. "CE" in my opinion is stronger and equally as fast as Steve Gilmore. All "CE" had to do was pick one of the field events, let his athletic ability take over and he would be strutting around the hall ways of Hartland High School with a varsity jacket just like Steve Gilmore."

"Instead, "CE" restricted himself and his talents to running on the 880-relay team with his buddies. And let the record book show that no member of that 880 Relay team currently has a varsity letter."

It was interesting getting a breakdown on these four guys. And the information was consistent with my own thoughts after observing them in action for the past couple of weeks during lunch hour. I easily came to the conclusion that I should avoid these guys at all cost at least until basketball tryouts.

This also means that my name might need to be crossed off of the Al Dowty "Master Plan" list for Mike Beardslee to run on the 880-relay team. These four gents definitely do not give off the type of vibes that they will welcome any new comers with open arms to be a part of that relay unit, even at the cost of making the relay team place higher in the league meet and score more points, which ultimately translates into varsity letters and varsity jackets.

While I think it's a good idea on my part to tread carefully around these four guys, I was, however, disappointed with that decision as I have a good sports topic that I wanted to get their thoughts on; is the "Curse of Bobby Layne" for real or just a myth?? An issue I betcha those 880 relay guys would have just eaten up. Such is life in the Hartland Consolidated Schools.

My plan of avoiding the members of the 880-relay team was short lived, however. As I was walking to trash bin area to throw my emptied lunch bag away, I heard a loud-mouthed voice from behind me yell, "Hey, Four-Eyes!! Yeah, you!! Come here!! Now!!"

"White Lake Road"

Chapter #60 – "As H.L. Connelly used to ask…."

September 18th – I walked, no make that shuffled, ever so slowly over to where the 880 Relay guys were seated. Craig Annis was the one who had ordered me over to him in his best King George style voice, and "Little Craig" did not seem to be in too pleasant of a mood by the way the smoke was coming off of the top of his head.

The first words out of his mouth were, "What were you and old man Decker talking about last week when I saw the two of you in the school hall way?? And don't lie to me about it "Four-Eyes" I saw the both of you gabbing with my own eyeballs!!" I thought to myself, now who could find it in their heart to lie to a kid with the nickname of "Little Craig??" I know, I know. A person by the name of "Big Craig."

To the day that I die, Mike Beardslee will take to my grave the advice that Jim Koop once gave me of, "You always stand up to a bully, Beardslee. Always." It's the best suggestion that he has ever given me. Even better than, "Always remember, Beardslee, the really good-looking girls will always go out with drummers before trumpet players." And that latter line is a true classic.

Both tidbits have passed the test of time and are excellent pearls of wisdom. However, Jim Koop's guidance did not include what does Mike Beardslee do when I have four bullies simultaneously staring me down?? Because that's what I had facing me, four intimidators who were enjoying every second of watching me trying to maintain my best tough guy image.

The problem was that I think I was coming across more as Maxwell Smart or Ernie Douglas rather than what I was really trying to portray; the coolness of Steve McQueen; the tough mobster guy role played by Edward G. Robinson. "Yeah. You got that Rocco?? Yeah." Maybe now is the time I spew out that I have seen the movie, "A Fistful of Dollars", twice. That alone should have this foursome shaking in their boots.

I sensed that the 880 Relay guys were not buying my act of false bravado. The first clue must have been the lack of eye contact on my part. Secondly, there was a definite hesitation and dryness in my voice because it seemed to be forever before I could finally scrounge up enough bravery at an attempt to answer Craig Annis' question.

I decided to go with the flat-out truth and said, "Coach Decker asked me to try out for the varsity basketball team this November. He also emphasized to me that I should be in excellent shape for these tryouts as there was going to be a lot of competition for spots on the team." What followed next was silence with four confused and not to happy looks on the faces sitting on their "thrones" that were disguised as cafeteria chairs. It was more than obvious that my response to them was totally unexpected.

And I knew exactly what the 880 Relay guys were thinking to themselves as I had been in their shoes many a time in my high school basketball playing "career." All five of us varsity basketball candidates knew deep down inside that there were only a certain number of players

that were going to make the varsity basketball squad. A roster usually ranges anywhere from 10-13 players.

The fact that I had personally been asked to audition for the varsity basketball team and "to be sure that I was in shape for tryouts", of which, I ain't even close to being, didn't bode well for this quartet. A distinct possibility now exists of there being one less position on the varsity basketball team for them. Also, since these guys are all sophomores, then at least one 880 Relay member has a year of junior varsity basketball staring them in the face. That also translates into another three to four months wait for that valued varsity letter.

I readily admit that these four members of the human race are not exactly the type of guys that you show any sympathy towards. But Mike Beardslee knew exactly what angst that they were going through right this very moment. I had mentioned in an earlier writing that one of the first things that I do at the beginning of every school year was to look frantically around the Band Room and hope that no trumpet players had moved into the Fenton Area School district since the end of the previous school year.

My insecurities, however, did not stop there with newly enrolled trumpet players. It was the same emotional roller coaster for basketball season. Had another student moved in from another school district like Steve Browning did from Flint Southwestern High School to become a Lake Fenton Blue Devil this past summer? Or closer to home where a one Mike Kakuska moved across from the state of Illinois border into the "Great Lake States" to become a Fenton Tiger.

But my real paranoia was at an all-time high when Track season came around. Any time a new student entered the halls of Fenton High School and I discovered that he had been on the track team from their previous institute of learning, whoa!!; did the Mike Beardslee interrogation ever begin!! "What event did you run? What was your best time? Do you plan on going out for Track this season?"

Oh sure, I encountered the Walter Richards types of the world who met the above criteria as a former member of the Bendle Tiger's track squad but never ended up running a step for the Fenton High School track team. But the reverse of my good fortune with Walter Richards were guys like the above mentioned, Mike Kakuska, and another new student who made Fenton High School his new home by the name of Dick Cardinal.

Both of these guys moved to Fenton High School at the same time, the start of my sophomore year. And it was rather obvious that once track season started that Mike Kakuska and Dick Cardinal were both stronger and faster than Mike Beardslee. Oh, and hang on, it gets better. They both ran the same events that I wanted to run; the 100 and 220 dashes.

Let's just put it this way, upon the enrollment of these two gentlemen into the Fenton Area Schools and also pursuing a career in track, Mike Beardslee never saw the starting blocks or heard the sound of a starter's pistol while occupying a race lane of a 100 and 220 dash again for the next two years of my track regime.

"White Lake Road"

I still remember that Monday afternoon track practice when Coach Lane advised me that I was going to become a quarter miler. Once around the track. A race at that time I might add that I had no strong desire to run and to this day have not entirely made friends with this event. The only good thing about running the 440 Run was that it was not the 880 Run.

So yeah, despite the strong bluster that the 880 Relay guys were showing me this very moment, I thought back to what my former Speech I Class teacher, Mr. H.L. Connelly, used to constantly address to us kids to ask when doing a self-assessment of ourselves; "Are you making an action or decision based on the fact that you are feeling inferior?" And in my case the answer was always a resounding, "Yes!! Yes!! I am inferior!! And are there additional classes, including correspondence ones, that I can take to become even more inferior???"

So, based upon what I had learned from Mr. H.L. Connelly in my first hour class of my Junior year at Fenton High School, I could cut these four clowns some slack as they were inferior with a capital "I". In fact, they had probably been inferior for so long they had it down to a science. The problem was that there was nobody around in their lives like a H.L. Connelly to introduce the word "inferior" into their daily vocabulary.

However, I immediately changed my mind of being so forgiving when Gordie Simon's fat cheeks started to move simultaneously with his vocal chords and blurted out….

"White Lake Road"

Chapter #61 – "Santa Fe Trail"

September 18th – "Hey, Four-Eyes!!" By now I have figured out on my own that when one of these guys yells out that phrase they are referring to Mike Beardslee.

Gordie Simon then piped up and said, "Now let me get this straight, Beardslee. You were a member of the Fenton High School Varsity Basketball team last year. Correct??" I nodded my head in agreement thinking to myself, this isn't too bad so far. I'm okay. I'm good. But as Elmer Fudd would say, "Silly Wabbit!!

Gordie Simon continued, "Just out of curiosity, "Four-Eyes", what was so great about the 20 seconds of actual playing time that you probably received for the entire basketball season that made old man Decker personally invite you to try out for the Hartland High School Varsity Basketball team? I'd really like to know the answer to that."

After Gordie Simon finished with his question the 880 Relay guys just broke into laughter. Just imagine the sounds of pigs squealing at the top of their lungs. That was the resonance of noise coming towards me. But as disgusting of racket that these four persons were generating, it was the expression on the face of "CE" that sent artic chills from the top of my head to the toes on my feet.

There is a movie by the name of "Santa Fe Trail" that stars my "twin", Errol Flynn. I am fortunate enough to watch this film on the rare occasion it is televised by Channel 50 on the "Bill Kennedy Show". That is, if the wind outside "White Lake Road" is not blowing too hard and our UHF antenna decides to work properly on the day of this showing.

In this movie, actor Raymond Massey, plays the character of "John Brown" the abolitionist during pre- American Civil War Days. The thing I remember the most about how Raymond Massey portrayed John Brown was the makeup of his eyes. In this flick, the John Brown character had the eyes of a mad man. When I looked at "CE" he had the exact same look in his eyes that made me think back to the movie, "Santa Fe" with the similar mad man type of eye balls that I remember staring right at me from our television set as I was laying on the davenport in the family room of "White Lake Road."

So, whenever I have the rare privilege of watching the movie, "Santa Fe", in the future, I will now automatically think of "CE" when I see the mad man eyes of John Brown. Thanks for ruining a good Errol Flynn movie, "CE"!!

After getting the fright of my life from "CE's" eyes, I was immediately brought out of this spell when Craig Annis said in a self-centered tone of voice, "Hurry up with an answer "Four Eyes!! Supper is getting cold!!", bringing more screeches of delight from the members of the half-mile relay team.

I have always prided myself on the ability to think fast on my feet. But that Gordie Simon question was a great inquiry. Was it as good as the question that luckily no one from the Fenton School Board ever got around to asking my mother: "Mrs. Beardslee. Is there a

specific reason why you have not re-enrolled your children back into the Fenton Area Schools since the school millage successfully passed and all cuts to positions and activities were completely restored?"

Now that was a potentially outstanding question and Gordie Simon's attempt to interrogate me was right up there with that query. Man, I was now down for the eight count and while I was staggering to get back on my feet I wasn't even certain that a good response even existed to a guy who could have been a stunt double for the television character of "Pugsley Addams" from the TV series, "The Addams Family."

In fact, the one-third of the minute of on court playing time that Gordie Simon had alluded to might have even been generous on his part. Simply put, I had no good response on the behalf of my defense. I had no worthy explanation has to why Coach Decker came to me out of the clear blue sky and asked me to try out for the varsity basketball team. And since I save all of these to use on my mother, I don't even have any really, really good lies for this occasion, either.

The only thing I could think of as to what triggered this school hallway chat was what Ric Adams had mentioned to me shortly after my conversation with Coach Decker had concluded, that the head varsity basketball coach wanted as many track guys on his squad for this season as he could get so that we could be a fast-breaking type of squad this year. But if my thinking was correct about that, then why didn't Coach Decker personally invite the four "track guys" that have been toying with me for the last few minutes to try out for the varsity hoops team as well?? Don't know.

While I was running all of this information through my head and at the same time stalling for an answer to get me out of this jam, I came up with two different retorts. One reply would be about a different topic and just make these guys even more irate with me. But I guarantee you that it would cause them to entirely forget about the varsity basketball issue. Topic number two would shut them up enough that I could use my 56.9 quarter mile speed to go run and hide somewhere else in Livingston County.

Option number one was to mention Al Dowty's "Master Plan" for the upcoming track season. I would simply point out that on this projected roster for the league meet I would be running a leg as a member of the 880 Relay team. Even a former "General Mathematics Class" flunky like myself could figure out on my own that if I was a member of this sacred foursome, then one of them wasn't.

Also, by mentioning the "Master Plan" I would now have the privilege of witnessing the initial smoke that was coming out of Craig Annis' head now turn into Mt. Vesuvius and "CE's" eyes rival and surpass the mad man look of John Brown from scenes in the movie "Santa Fe." There probably isn't a student in Hartland High School that wouldn't pay good money to see these two separate events take place.

And I guarantee you that the mentioning of the "Master Plan" for track season would have gotten the subject of the conversation that took place between myself and Coach Decker deep sixed and forgotten. I wouldn't have been home free, however, because I would then immediately, if not sooner, start to get some serious flak like; "Who do you think you are, Four-Eyes?? What makes you believe that you are good enough to step in and be a member of a world class 880 Relay team???????"

I decided against going the route of the "Master Plan". I took off my "Al Dowty hat" and instead replaced it my "Jim Koop hat." And the following result was much better than I could have ever hoped.

I finally got around to responding to the Gordie Simon enquiry by asking the entire group a question. "Hey, guys. I received my first of four varsity letters when I was a sophomore as a result of my efforts in track season. I then promptly traveled to down town Flint to a sporting goods store by the name of "All Sports" and purchased my varsity jacket."

I now had their rapt attention and by still making good use of my "Jim Koop hat", I now went for the jugular. "When you guys got your varsity letters, where did you purchase your varsity jackets from??"

BLAMMO!! Elvis has left the building; "Here comes Al Kaline to score and the Tigers win the pennant!!"; and "Good night Mrs. Calabash wherever you are." Type in any other phrase or cliché that you want but those four varsity jacketless boys were speechless!! They were dumbstruck enough that it allowed me to escape from the cafeteria to the safety of the school hallway.

As I was making my getaway the first thing that came to my mind, however, was where was Mark "Harry Houdini" Nevers when I actually needed him? That guy knows all the decent escape routes around here at Hartland High School.

Chapter #62 – "What do the "Sporting News", Topps Baseball Cards and Satan all have in common??"

September 18th – Despite my Mark Nevers type of escape from the 880 Relay guys, I was still quite nervous from my confrontation with them for the last two class hours of today. This is the third school district that I have been a student of and while there has been a low percentage of them, nasty kids have existed in all three of my educational stops.

Based upon my extensive research on this topic, I have come to the conclusion that there are three types of time lines for meanness when it comes to school kids. And after my lunch hour session with the above-mentioned foursome, I have hit the big trifecta of meanness, which consists of; elementary school meanness; junior high school meanness and high school meanness.

And as of September 18th, 1969, after reaching my last plateau of meanness, I now have a fulfilled life. That is, with the exception, of course, of marrying "April Dancer", the star of the former TV series, "The Girl from U.N.C.L.E.".

The elementary school meanness that I personally witnessed happening to me, while traumatic at the time, now looking back, it wasn't so bad. Interestingly enough, there were two specific events of nastiness that I would put into the magical world of elementary school meanness, and both took place on the school grounds of Mary Crapo Elementary School during my Swartz Creek Dragon era.

One afternoon recess I slipped on some ice while out on the massive "thousand acres" playground of this elementary school property. I hit my knee on the hard ground and did what all first graders are programmed to do; cried like there was no tomorrow.

If falling down and hurting my knee, plus tearing a minor part of my trousers wasn't bad enough, all of this took place in front of a third grader by the name of Larry Bushnell. He started calling me "Cry Baby!!" that winter day and kept it up for the rest of the 1958-59 school year.

Nine long years later I can still hear the phrase of "Cry Baby!!" being yelled at me by Larry Bushnell as I ran away in shame while looking over my left shoulder to see if I was distancing myself from him as well as trying to out run that terrible expression of "Cry Baby!!" that stuck in my ears for the rest of my life spent as a first grader.

The funny thing is that for my second-grade school year all of the Swartz Creek second graders were housed three to four miles away from Mary Crapo Elementary School in two separate school buildings. By the time all of us second graders rejoined the remainder of the Swartz Creek elementary school kids back as third graders, whenever I saw Larry Bushnell, who surprise, surprise, surprise, was now a fourth grader instead of a fifth grader, to my delight he had forgotten all about Mike Beardslee and me being a "Cry Baby."

This differs from Stevie Leach, of whom I beat in in a race while running one lap around the gymnasium at Mary Crapo Elementary School one rainy afternoon. Stevie Leach and our paths have crossed quite a few times over the past few years between basketball and track events, and based solely upon that one race, Stevie Leach, to this very second, still hates my guts with a passion.

Junior High meanness?? Aaahh, now you're talking about the Mount Everest type of meanness. That age group has malice down to a science as I quickly learned when entering into what was to become two of the lousiest years of my life.

What I did not realize was that the same individual who introduced me to the wonderful world of "The Sporting News" and "Topps Baseball Cards", of which, my mother thinks both of these items are the work of Satan, himself, would also make known to me the world of junior high meanness. When I was a fourth grader at State Road Elementary School I met a fifth grader, by the name of Ricky Loveland, who was a member of what turned out to be Mr. O'Berry's last fifth grade class that he ever taught as a faculty member of this prestigious elementary school.

While riding the school bus home one evening I saw that Ricky Loveland was looking at stacks and stacks of baseball cards. He ultimately let me look at some of his brown, backgrounded 1962 Topps baseball cards where I would devour over the statistics of Detroit Tiger players such as; Norm Cash, Jake Wood, Flint Northern High School alumnus, Steve Boros, "The Yankee Killer" Frank Lary, Al Kaline, Billy Bruton and Rocky Colavito. Great stuff!!

To make our friendship even better was that Ricky Loveland as soon as he finished his "Sporting News" magazine would immediately give it to me, a ritual that took place until I started getting my own "Sporting News" subscription, against my mothers' wishes, of my own as a seventh grader.

I spent a lonely school year as a sixth grader when Ricky Loveland was a seventh grader in the Fenton Junior High School building. Not only was his physical location different but so was his school and bus schedule.

While I enjoyed hanging out with Chuck Miller and Tom Rhodes during my sixth-grade school term, those two did not have the same level of interest that I did in baseball cards or the Detroit Tigers. Nor had they ever heard of the most sacred publication of them all, "The Sporting News." In addition, Mike Beardslee did not share the same fascination of the magazine, "Boy's Life" that my two sixth grade buddies did.

As a seventh grader, at least friendship wise, things got better for Mike Beardslee. Not only was I in the same school building and on the same bus schedule as Ricky Loveland, we were both in my favorite class, and I might add the only one that I enjoyed as a seventh grader, Junior High Band. Life was good!!

However, something that my mother had warned me about during my time I spent as a member of the sixth-grade class taught by Mr. O'Berry, came true. When Ricky Loveland entered the seventh grade my mother advised me that he was going to change as a person." He will become more mature and expand his circle of friends." My mother in essence was saying that Ricky Loveland was going to outgrow Mike Beardslee and the two of us would just simply part ways.

My mother was partially right on her pearls of wisdom that she had imparted to me about Ricky Loveland. He did change. Not in a way that I would have anticipated, or for the better, but yes, he certainly did change.

During my time as a seventh grader and Ricky Loveland's tour as an eighth grader, we both had lunch period during Fourth Hour. And let me tell you, there were some real tough kids in this same time frame with us. Most of them were eighth graders with a few ninth graders, who should have remained scholastically as eight graders, sprinkled in there as well. I suspect their presence was to keep the lunch crowd IQ average below 50.

Oh, man!! Did those guys ever look tough. They acted tough. Dressed tough. They even smelled tough. And Ricky Loveland was drawn to this type of crowd. Not in a way that he wanted to become a member of their group, to hang out with them or even dress like them. That I could probably understand.

No, Ricky Loveland's attraction to this group was the fact that he would let them punch him in his arms. Steal his lunch money. Shove him against the hard brick walls of the school way for no apparent reason. When playing the game of "matching money" Ricky Loveland would win and these guys would just simply take Ricky Loveland's winnings from him and walk away laughing with almost the same swine type of screeches that the 880 Relay guys made earlier today. Ricky Loveland would just simply shrug his shoulders and walk away in an opposite direction of the people who had made him at least $.25 poorer.

The scary part about all of this was that Ricky Loveland seemed to enjoy the abuse that he was receiving from this bunch of ruffians. These guys were never located in the same place on a day to day basis during lunch hour. Probably to hide from any wandering faculty members. But no matter how long it took, Ricky Loveland every day searched this same group down and went through his daily ritual of being smacked around or having his lunch money taken away from him.

Initially out loyalty I would follow Ricky Loveland wherever he went during lunch hour. These tough guys didn't pay a whole lot of attention to me. I did get an occasional shove by them but that was about it. No big deal.

One late morning as Ricky Loveland was getting punched in his arms, one of the punchers looked over at me and I could see a light bulb go on in his head. "Fresh Meat!!" Even an immature seventh grader like myself knew what was going to happen next. Mike Beardslee was going to become a full-fledged member of the "I love to wail on Ricky Loveland Club."

Instinct told me to close my eyes and hope that they did not hit me in the lips or break my glasses. Especially my lips. I then felt a large hand clamp down of my left shoulder and I about jumped through the ceiling. The fist belonged to a ninth grader by the name of Paul Sampson.

Now just imagine a poster child for a "Juvie". You got it. That's Paul Sampson. Paul Sampson was a freshman but physically he had the looks of a 12th grader. He was as tall as Don Madden, who is 6'4" and as big a Brad Lamb, a solid 240 pounder. Both had been starters on some outstanding Fenton Tiger Varsity Football teams.

Paul Saxon pulled me real close to him. Near enough that his cigarette breath started to make me gag. I had never ever heard Paul Saxon say one word to anyone. All he ever did was stand in the hallway during lunch hour and look tough.

Well, this date on the calendar was my lucky day. I not only heard Paul Saxon speak and despite my whole body shaking in fear, I could have sworn that he even used a complete sentence at least once.

"Let me give you some advice, seventh grader. Don't become like your buddy and become a punching bag for these guys. Because once they figure out that you're always going to be hanging out with Loveland, then you will get the same treatment as him. And these guy's arms do not get tired of punching wimpy kids who want to think that they are tough guys by hanging out with us "hoods."

"I'll tell these guys who enjoy punching out Loveland every day during lunch hour to stay away from you while in the school building. But if you're hanging out with Loveland while riding a bus or anywhere else on a school property, then you'll become as big as punching bag as him. Plus, these guys aren't too choosy about whose lunch money or bag lunch they take."

Paul Saxon then gave me a hard-two-handed shove in the chest, leaving me gasping for oxygen, and then he strolled over to Ricky Loveland and proceeded to deliver a one-handed slap upside Ricky Loveland's head that was so hard that even both my right hand and head were hurting.

Paul Saxon's advice proved to be prophetic as the next day Ricky Loveland introduced me to an entirely different foursome that made the members of the Hartland High School 880 relay team look like they were clones of Theodore Cleaver and Lumpy Rutherford.

"White Lake Road"

Blog #63 – "The Cruel Cruisers"

September 18th – While heading to the Band Room after the completion of Mr. Collins' Economic Class, I was getting some serious flak from Jim Koop and Terry Rodenbo about the paranoia I was having with the 880 Relay team. Terry Rodenbo stated, "Hey, they're just punks. Just like the guys who used to slap your old buddy, Ricky Loveland, around."

Jim Koop wasn't much help, either. He would chime in on this topic by saying, "Yeah, and we haven't heard the story about Larry Bushnell in the last five minutes or so where he called you a "Cry Baby" and emotionally scarred you for your entire life. Hey, what grade is old Larry Bushnell in now, second?"

Ha, Ha, Ha, Jim Koop. And just think, with my seventeenth birthday only 264 hours away, in a moment of weakness on my part, I was going to let you light up a cigarette in the jeep.

Jim Koop, along the lines of Terry Rodenbo's comments, then added, "Don't worry about those track guys, Beardslee, my friend. Until they develop their own strut or stomp to walk down the school hallway to let everybody in the whole school building know who they are, they're nobodies. Nobodies!!" And this is coming from a guy who thinks that a "right spin turn" that we use in marching band drills is his and my strut or stomp. Okay.

As much as Jim Koop and Terry Rodenbo would bust my chops about the 880 Relay team guys and my ex-friend Ricky Loveland, the one faction that they never, never, ever mentioned in my presence is the infamous, charter members of "The Cruel Cruisers."

This above-named unit consisted of four guys that we're always menacing and threatening to us innocent types. How daunting are they you ask? They were so daunting, no make that dangerous, that they would make Paul "Juvie" Sampson shake like he was a stunt man for Don Knotts in the movie, "The Ghost and Mr. Chicken." That makes for a tough group!!

As a seventh grader, I had two options as to which bus I could take home from Fenton Junior High School to "White Lake Road." One route was very quick but it did not travel past my home driveway at all. Instead, Mrs. Miller, the bus driver, would drop me off at the four corners of Hartland Road and White Lake Road. I would then proceed to walk the final two-tenths of the mile home. No big deal.

The other bus route would take me right to my driveway. However, I was on the bus for at a minimum of 45 minutes before I eventually reached my final destination. But again, because my bestest buddy in the world, Ricky Loveland, asked me to ride on this same bus with him, I could not turn down the request of the person who had introduced me to the glorious world of the "Sporting News."

But, oh my goodness, this bus ride just turned out to be so extremely long!! I mean let's face it; I am on a school bus for 2700 seconds and I only live three miles from school. Gimme a break!! 2700 seconds, that's a lifetime for a seventh grader to be stationed in one place.

"White Lake Road"

There were four kids on this bus ride that I had referenced earlier, and were self-proclaimed as the "Cruel Cruisers". Meet Dave Churchman, Ray Stackhouse, Bobby Thomas and Eugene Wolfson. Between the four of them they had a combined IQ of 14 and they made this bus trip home to "White Lake Road" insufferable.

But this foursome was canny enough to know that they could run rough shod over every student who rode this bus. You could only be seated where they wanted you to sit on this ride. If they didn't want a rider to be in a certain three-person green covered seat, then they would not allow them to sit there. Instead they would make you stand in the aisle way without being able to hold on to anything to balance yourself all the way to your home. And it didn't help the cause that the bus driver, Mr. Stack, who was totally worthless as well as a lousy driver, never made an effort to control this quartet. None.

Paul Sampson's earlier advice to me had been one-hundred percent correct. Ricky Loveland was not the only one that was being pushed around and getting punched on a consistent basis while sharing a bus trip with the "Cruel Cruisers." I was now included in this daily ritual as well.

On what was to be the last time I was ever a traveler on the "Cruel Cruise Bus", Eugene Wolfson came up to me that day and started to be exceptionally nice to me. I mean this moron was actually using compound words and what bordered on complete sentences while talking to me. And while Eugene Wolfson was telling me that he had heard that I was a very good trumpet player, (I think you mean great trumpet player, Eugene Wolfson) Bobby Thomas came up out of nowhere and sucker punched me with his right fist right into my stomach.

I went down on that grungy and dirty bus floor like a ton of bricks to the sounds of, "You sure got him with a good one, Bobby!! Way to sucker the seventh grader into paying attention to you so that Bobby could sneak up on him and belt him a good one in the old breadbasket, Eugene!!"

And all during this gala affair there I was just laying down on my back, rolling around in whatever the rest of the bus kids had stuck to the bottom of their shoes, rubbing my hands over where my stomach used to be. I was hurting so badly that I did not even have the strength to sit up and vomit all over Bobby Thomas' high-topped converse tennis shoes with my last living breath. Something to this very day that I deeply regret.

That was the last time that I ever rode the "Cruel Cruiser Bus." I walked away from the adolescents who caused the thuggery on this school bus. I also walked away from Ricky Loveland and his passion to be bullied and punched by other kids and never spoke to him again during our time together as students of the Fenton Area Schools.

Instead I went back to alighting off of the school bus driven by Mrs. Miller at the corners of Hartland Road and White Lake Road. Oh, sure, there were some bitter winter and showery walks to be made for the remainder of that school year, but at least now the only way I was going to be the recipient of black and blue marks was when I tripped over my own two own feet while getting off of the bus or slipping on an unseen patch of ice on White Lake Road.

My mother eventually noticed that there were no more visits or telephone calls between myself and Ricky Loveland. The funny thing is for about the past year or so my mother had been on my case that I should expand my circle of friends and not spend so much time only with one friend, specifically referring to Ricky Loveland.

However, after not seeing Ricky Loveland or talking to him any longer, my mother then started to hint that I should be inviting Ricky Loveland over some more to play pool in our basement or shoot baskets out in "Beardslee's Barn." Never happened.

Which of the two groups, "The Cruel Cruisers" or the 880 Relay team were the more dangerous? Good question. The former group consisted of four guys that were physically tough and would fight you at the drop of a hat. Intelligence wise, collectively, they were all dumber than a bag of rocks. And we are not talking about top of the line rocks, either.

The 880 Relay guys are not as tough, even though, "CE", would have loved to have been part of the "Cruel Cruiser" crowd. He could easily have been eventually elected as the "Sergeant at Arms" for them. But the 880 guys as a group were smarter. Way smarter. You knew when and what you were going to get from "The Cruel Cruisers." That was a flat out physical beating. But you never knew when and where the 880 crew was going to strike.

At the end of the day I would think that the results from the Electoral College would show that my future potential basketball and track teammates were going to be the more lethal group to cross paths with and to avoid them at all costs.

I was proud of himself for walking away from the "Cruel Cruisers." Very proud. I never had one ounce of trouble from them after deciding to not share a Fenton Area Schools' form of transportation with them ever again.

However, will I be able to walk away from the 880 Relay team just as easily as I did with "The Cruel Cruisers?" Yes, and no. I can avoid the former group pretty easily at lunch time. Push comes to shove I just eat at the opposite end of the cafeteria of where they are located and to be smart enough to just ignore their demands of "Four Eyes" to be at their beck and call. I can guarantee you this, Mike Beardslee is not going to become the Ricky Loveland of Hartland High School.

Contrary to Al Dowty's master plan of having me run on the 880 Relay team this spring, I suspect that won't take place. As long as I am not a threat to becoming a member of this illustrious unit, then they probably won't be threatened by me, either. At least that's what I'm hoping.

Basketball tryouts?? Now, that's where there will be problems. Make that big-time problems. Those guys could make it tough for me. Like any basketball tryout that I have ever gone through during the past five years, at some point there will be live scrimmaging. That's where the 880 guys can and will conspire to make me look bad.

I fully expect that I will never receive a basketball pass from any of them so that I can score points during the competition for a spot on the varsity basketball squad. That's okay, I am scared of shooting the basketball anyway. But it will be the rocket like type pass from one of them when I am just two feet away that will cause me to not only catch the pass but could lead to a bad sprain or worst-case scenario, a broken finger.

I also have a fear that while running the fast break of being "accidentally" tripped and causing the loss of a basketball possession in addition to looking like an uncoordinated kid while falling flat on my face on a gymnasium floor. Add a push in the back or a well-placed elbow to the ribs or face and those actions could cause an injury to me and lessen the opportunity for me to prove why I should be one of the lucky ones chosen to represent the Hartland High School Varsity Basketball team this upcoming winter.

My old Speech Class teacher, Mr. H.L. Connelly, would classify as Mike Beardslee simply being "insecure." Yeah, you could probably chalk up these fears on my part as being insecure. But I had seen these kinds of shenanigans before at last year's Fenton High School varsity basketball tryouts executed by a one Dennis Runsell.

Luckily, I was not the target of Dennis Runsell while he was pulling this kind of slop on the other guards trying out for the varsity squad. But Dennis Runsells' antics caused some good basketball candidates to be banished to a year of playing junior varsity basketball or even worse, intramural basketball. I don't want to see that same thing happening to me in the basketball tryouts that are roughly just six weeks away. And just for the record, in addition to Dennis Runsell being one of the guards being selected to make the 1968-69 Fenton High School Basketball team, he also started at that position in every game last season and will probably be a starter this year as well.

My future path did indeed cross with the 880 Relay team members. And it happened far sooner than I had anticipated and surprisingly, had nothing to do with varsity basketball tryouts or being in competition with them for a leg on the 880 Relay team.

Chapter #64 – "#19; #22; #40; #98 – Hut, Hut!!"

September 18th – Finally. Finally, Mike I get to do something that I have been looking forward to on what has so far been a less than pleasant day. After school Jim Koop, Terry Rodenbo, Katie and I get to pick up our band uniforms for tomorrow night's first halftime show of the school year!!

I must admit that I'm pretty sure that I have never, ever seen a person actually wearing a Hartland Consolidated School's marching band uniform before in my life. I know that the school colors are of blue and gold but that's about it. But what bells and whistles go with the uniform? I.E., Are their plumes for the hat? What is on the front of the overlay? Do we get to wear the latest rage for marching bands, white spats that are worn over a marcher's shoes when marching? The four of us are going to soon find out.

It takes Katie forever to pick out a band uniform. It has to be the perfect fit. The hat can't be sliding down on her face. The sleeves can't come to her fingers and trousers can't be so long that it would cause her to trip and fall.

I wish I could have been that choosey the very first time I went to pick out a band uniform when I was an eighth grader at Fenton High School. By the time it was my turn to get my band uniform all of the upper classmen had gotten the pick of the litter.

In fact, I didn't even get the opportunity to hand-pick my own band uniform. Beany Bretzke, the drum major of the Fenton High School Marching Band, just tossed me one and said, "Here's your band uniform, eighth grader." Thank you very much.

The band uniform provided to me compliments of the Fenton Area Schools, had a number attached to it, "#40." These band uniforms were making their debut for the 1965 marching band season and I must admit that they were sharp looking. They had black pants with a crease that looked so razor-sharp that you could cut a frozen pound of hamburger right down the middle with it. Add a dark orange stripe down the sides of the trousers and you could see us Band kids in the pitch-dark miles and miles away.

Other standouts of this Fenton band uniform included a snazzy looking orange, feathered type plume for the hat and lastly, a ferocious looking tiger on the front of the overlay that would have even scared off the likes of Johnny Weissmuller, himself.

Compared to what my predecessors had worn to perform in at Fenton High School football games, the new uniforms put those babies to shame.

The problem with the new Fenton marching band uniforms, however, were that they almost had to many "bells and whistles" to them. I.E, did you have to wear suspenders to keep your trousers up? Did the black straps on your shoulders have to be tucked in under the uniform or above so that they were visible on both shoulders? I'm still waiting for an answer on that latter question.

"White Lake Road"

When I originally received #40 it was just way too big on me. The pants were too long. The jacket portion of the uniform just hung way, way too loose on me. #40 became a real pain to put on let alone perform in a pre-game and half-time show. I was not really happy with this outfit to say the least.

As I entered my freshmen season of marching band I vowed that I was going to get me a band uniform that actually would fit me. No such luck. Again, by the time the upper classmen got through with their selections of marching garb, I spared Beany Bretzke the trouble of saying to me, "Here's your band uniform, ninth grader", I simply sought out #40 for another band season and there it was, seemingly just waiting for me.

Either I had finally physically matured or the trips to the dry cleaners that my mother made on behalf of #40 caused a change in the size of this band uniform, but #40 fit me pretty good for the last couple of marching band seasons. I readily admit that the #40 does not immediately strike up the memories that "#98" does, the football jersey that Tom Harmon, the former University of Michigan football all-American, Heisman trophy winner and World War II hero, wore during his time in Ann Arbor, Michigan.

But this number and band uniform were special to Mike Beardslee. The two of us had been through 14 pre-game and half-time shows; eight parades; a combination of 19 concerts; District Festivals; All-Star Band; Band Days and graduation commencements together. And not all of these events were joyous moments for #40 and I, either.

Little did I realize that when I took #40 off after the graduating class of 1969 commencement exercises were completed last June, that that would be the last time that the two of us would ever perform in public together. I thought that we would have one more year of Band together, which would have hopefully included a successful marching band season, a I rating at District Festival, and a trip back to All-Star Band. Apparently, it was not meant to be.

Since to the best of my knowledge there are no immediate plans by the Fenton Area Schools to retire #40, then I hope the band person who inherits "Mike Beardslee's band uniform" and gets the speech of "Here's your uniform, ninth grader", has the same thrill that I had when they are performing in it.

I came back to reality when I heard Jim Koop mutter under his breath, "Oh, my goodness." I looked in the direction of where his muttering was directed and I now understood his utterance. Jim Koop had just gotten his first sight of the Hartland High School Marching Band uniforms. And shall we politely say that he was not impressed.

These uniforms were certainly not the sharp looking band uniforms that we were used to from our Fenton days. My first impression was that the blue color of this attire should have been much darker; the gold color should have been a much brighter gold; the letter "H" on the front of the overlay, should have been bigger or at least bolder. The back of the uniform looked okay but again needed to be a darker blue with a snappy gold trim.

"White Lake Road"

I looked over at Terry Rodenbo and Katie and I could tell by the looks on their faces that neither one of them was dazzled by our new set of marching band threads, either. Especially, Katie.

Last March Miss Franklin advised us Fenton Band kids that it was time for the annual photograph for the school year book of the Fenton Senior Band. As the time for the photo shoot got closer, Miss Franklin announced to us band members, "Due to a serious time crunch with the photographer, instead of taking the time to change into our band uniforms just prior to having the picture taken, you will have to wear your band uniforms for the whole school day."

The back lash from Miss Franklin's recommendation, including myself as the president of the Band, was brutal!! Comments such as: "No way am I going to be seen in that uniform by all of my friends!!" "We'll be made fun of and ridiculed!!" "The ascots are too warm to wear for a concert let alone for a whole school day!!" Man, it was vicious!!

But my favorite comment of all on this potential ruination of all of us band kids, and I don't even have to tell you the identity of the person who claimed ownership to this remark was; "Do the Choir Class students have to wear their robes all day at school when they have their picture taken?? If they don't have to wear their choir robes for each stinking class, then neither do we!!"

If you guessed that the commentator was either Terry Rodenbo, Katie Beardslee or Mike Beardslee, then you would be mistaken.

I thought that statement would put a stop to any further comments on "Uniform Wars", but Katie then stood up and chimed in, "I am proud to be a member of the Fenton High School Senior Band!! And I am equally honored to wear my band uniform to every one of my classes tomorrow!!"

Katie lived up to her testimonial that day and was the only Fenton High School Senior Band member to wear her band uniform from the time she set foot on Bus #23 in the morning and the moment her shoes started walking up the driveway of "White Lake Road" some nine hours later. But in looking at the initial expression on her face when she saw the Hartland Band uniforms up close, I'm not so sure that under the same set of circumstances that Katie would wear this blue and gold uniform from "soup to nuts."

I walked over where the band uniforms were stored on a clothing rack. I spent a few moments looking for a uniform with the #40 sewed into it, but alas, there was none. With my luck Mark Nevers is wearing it while he is pumping gas at the M-59 truck stop.

I did locate, however, two band uniforms that I tried on and both were perfect fits. Now for the final decision. The first uniform was listed as #19. That's former Detroit Piston player, Reggie Harding's uniform number. That's a good number to stay away from. Far away.

“White Lake Road”

My second choice has a #22 listing in the back of the over lay jacket. That number belonged to my favorite Detroit Lion player of all time: Bobby Layne. Uniform #22 it is!!

I was impervious to the discussion my three traveling partners were having in the jeep on our trek home as to the comparison of the Fenton High School verses the Hartland High School Band uniforms, with the latter set of garbs not receiving many compliments at all. As silly and as childish as this sounds, my focus, other than avoiding every one of the 2,000,000 bumps on Runyan Lake Road, was that I hoped that uniform #40 is not upset with Mike Beardslee for not going through “the greatest year of my life” together.

In the next 48 hours, there will be two big marching band events coming up that the four of us will be participating. The first shindig all of us are super excited about. As to the second item on the checklist, Jim Koop, Terry Rodenbo and Katie are all fired up for it but I do not share the same sense of thrill they do. In fact, I can think of numerous other and better ways to spend a whole Saturday than being stuck with my second marching band obligation of the week.

"White Lake Road"

Chapter #65 – Please See Below for Title

September 19th – A big day today!! The Hartland High School Marching Band will make our official debut tonight when the Stockbridge Panthers come to town this evening for the third contest of the Hartland Eagles' varsity football season.

Is the band ready?? I think so, at least based upon our rehearsal that we had fourth hour. We were looking good, especially when it comes to the marching portion of the show. But still, other than Jim Koop, Terry Rodenbo, Jason Shattuck, and an occasion blip on the radar by myself, we are still not a marching unit that produces any kind of worthwhile sound.

Mr. Anderson gave us some reminders about tonight at the end of our practice. What time to be here. Don't be late. Remember your marching hat. That kind of stuff. Then he added a couple of interesting tidbits. "I will be grading tonight's performance and will advise you of the grade after the halftime show. In addition, I will be selecting a "best marcher" and "best section" of the Band based on this evening's efforts. These selectees will be the recipients of ice cream treats."

Hey!! Free ice cream!! Maybe even being seen wearing these band uniforms in public won't be so bad after all!!

The second announcement of Mr. Anderson's caught me off guard, however. "Since high school marching bands attending the "Central Michigan University Band Day" one week from tomorrow are capped at 20 members per band, there will be tryouts next Tuesday to see who will be honored to represent the Hartland High School Marching Band at my alma mater."

I had forgotten all about the "Central Michigan University Band Day" thing. This doesn't sound like a fun way to spend a Saturday at all. This means that I'll have to get together with Jim Koop and have him come up with some type of master plan to get the two of us out of attending this event in Mount Pleasant, Michigan. Where ever that is.

Before my fifth hour "Michigan History Class", a course that I am actually enjoying and learning lot got started, some of my peers were talking about whether the football team would actually win the game tonight. The general consensus was a resounding, "No way!!"

Despite Tom Moran's pre-season prediction of the Hartland Eagles going 5-4 this year, which was the equivalent of my idol, Joe "Broadway Joe" Namath, quarterback for the New York Jets, guaranteeing that even as an 18-point underdog that they would defeat a far superior team in the Baltimore Colts for the Super Bowl Championship last January, I fully agreed with my "Michigan History" classmates' decision on whether this was going to be thumbs up or thumbs down night for the Hartland gridders.

"White Lake Road"

I rarely ever say a word in this class but took the opportunity to pipe in and say, "Well, don't worry everyone, because tonight you're going to have a winning band!!" The silence and the shrugging of shoulders of my contemporaries gave me a pretty good clue as to the importance of how my award-winning proclamation was taken.

Tonight, at "White Lake Road" was the traditional Beardslee halftime show supper; grilled cheese sandwiches and tomato soup. Add 30 pounds of Ritz crackers to mix in with the broth and that will hold Katie and I until we arrive home and dig into our traditional Beardslee post game snack of graham crackers squished in between gobs of peanut butter. Add a cold glass of milk to dunk these bad boys in and we're talking the type of eats that are worthy enough of Olympic Gods.

This evening's ride back to Hartland High School did not carry the same type of enthusiasm that was shown some 11 or so hours earlier. No, this time the four of us were actually very silent as we each individually prepared for tonight's half time show.

Separately the occupants of the jeep were getting psyched up and organized in a different manner. Katie was moving her hands in a motion that was mimicking her drum cadences. Terry Rodenbo was moving his feet and shoulders as he was mentally rehearsing his individual marching routines. Jim Koop was staring out the window of the jeep, but you could see the fingers on his right hand moving in the same exact manner as if he were pushing the valves down on his trumpet.

How do I prepare for a high school football halftime show? I do a combination of what my three compadres are doing. However, there are a couple of other concerns that I personally have before hitting the football field for our pre-game show.

Concern number one, and a huge one for me, are trumpet charges. These puppies are usually played when a football team makes a big play or a first down. After this short one measure is belted out it is followed by the home crowd yelling, "Charge!!"

Jim Koop and I grew up watching and listening to past Fenton High School trumpet players like: Ray Sortman, Guy Thompson and Dick Wilcox play these trumpet charges. And us two glory hogs could not wait until it was our turn to have the crowd's eyes and ears on us when belted these awe-inspiring notes out.

Well, last year it was finally our chance to play these trumpet charges. We were just salivating at this opportunity. In fact, Jim Koop and I were a little too anxious for this big step in our marching band careers.

During the game, typically, the cheerleaders would yell out to us something like, "Can we get a trumpet charge??" And voila!! A trumpet charge would be played. That was not the case with Jim Koop and I. If there was an incomplete pass thrown, a shanked punt that went three yards, or even a box of popcorn being sold, it didn't matter to Jim Koop and Mike Beardslee. We were going to play a trumpet charge!!

Between the two of us during the first-half of that football game, we must have set a world record for trumpet charges played by two trumpeters. I betcha we must have belted out at least 100 of those puppies. You would have thought that Jim Koop and I were riding along the side of General George A. Custer and the Seventh Calvary as we rode into the valley of the Little Big Horn.

The fact that Jim Koop and Mike Beardslee were graciously playing all of these trumpet charges was all well and good. The problem was that by the time we hit the football field for the first half time show of the "Whose Band is Better" era, we had nothing left. Our chops had pretty much all been played out. Shall we say that our contribution of trumpet blasting was very minimal that night. Bordering on nonexistent in fact.

After our little stunt, the two of us were the recipients of a stern lecture by Miss Franklin, which included the phrase, "That if we ever became smart enough to learn how to part our hair then would we be even more dangerous", allowed for an agreement of trumpet charges to be kept to a minimum as the half time show was more important than Jim Koop and I showing off for the whole town of Fenton. If you say so, Miss Franklin.

Jim Koop and I agreed that for 1969-70 marching band season I would play any and all trumpet charges for the first quarter and he would have them all to himself for the second quarter. Add to the fact that the Hartland varsity football team has only averaged one touchdown per game so far this season, I'll take my chances with the number of trumpet charges that I'll have to play tonight or for that matter, the remainder of the football season.

By now you have probably figured out that playing trumpet charges is not at the top of my list when it comes to a football marching night. I do have one regret, though, and that is before I had come down with my teeth issues and my trumpet range became restricted, Jim Koop and I had been working on a world-famous trumpeter, Harry James, type of charge that we were going to spring on everyone this season. Great stuff!!

But until I can hit a high "C", which comes at the end of our trumpet charge, that we named "Battling Trumpets", the two of us decided to hold off with our debut. Our last half-time show of this marching band season will be October 31st, just six weeks away. But the time line for me being able to hit that allusive high "C" is still a little shaky.

I get my permanent capped teeth placed in by Dr. Alfred two weeks from tomorrow. The question now becomes whether I have to go back to the drawing board so that I can develop and expand my trumpet range in four weeks so that Jim Koop and I can perform our "Battling Trumpets" charge at least once this marching band season. I mean this is the kind of event that all of Livingston County has been waiting for!! Maybe even parts of Genesee and Washtenaw Counties as well.

My second concern for tonight is that I need to show better leadership skills than I did when I was a first-year president of the Fenton Senior High Band. At that time, I was more worried about myself rather than how my bandmates were performing. I. E., Would the people in both

the home and visiting stands take notice and comment, "Hey!! That one Fenton trumpet player was really hot stuff out on that marching band field last night."

In my misguided opinion, leadership should be coming from the drum major, not myself, as I was too busy with getting people to notice my trumpet playing ability. I'd like to change that mentality for this marching band season.

We're now only a couple of blocks away from the Hartland High School parking lot but my mental preparation is to make sure that not only is Mike Beardslee ready for tonight's half-time show, but the rest of my bandmates as well. A 360-degree mental turnaround from my preparation for "MY" 1968 marching band season.

Items I want to drop on people will include; "Hey, let's have a good half-time show tonight. We're representing Hartland High School." "Make sure that you lift your knees and point your toes. That will make us look real sharp while doing our marching routines" Don't worry about making a mistake when you're out there on the football field. Just make it a loud one." That is what I should and will be saying as I make the rounds of us band kids tonight.

And that's the kind of guidance I should have been displaying last marching band season. But I just couldn't bring myself to do it. I was far more worried about whether my-half of the marching band was better than Jim Koop's half of the marching band.

As my mother would say, "Michael Kevin Beardslee, you're starting to grow up." We'll see about that.

We had finally reached our destination of the Hartland High School parking lot. I turned off the ignition and put the jeep in gear. The four of us just sat there very quietly for a few seconds. We finally opened and closed the jeep doors and it was then off to the Band Room where Mike Beardslee, Katie Beardslee, Jim Koop and Terry Rodenbo were going to officially make their first public appearance as members of the Hartland High School Marching Band.

"White Lake Road"

Chapter #66 – "Tunnel Formation"

September 19th – As the four of us walked through the front doors of Hartland High School, the first thing that you heard were the sounds of instruments coming from the Band Room. All sorts of squeaking and squawking!! It just never ceases to amaze me how marching band kids on the evening of a performance, seem to play louder during a pre-game rehearsal while in the safe confines of a band room, then when they actually get out on the marching band field.

The funny thing is that I rarely do much playing of my trumpet before I go out on to the marching field for a half-time show. I do some lip slurs exercises and that is about it. No blasting. I certainly don't play a favorite trumpet player's game of "let's see how many high "C's" we can hit in a row." And guaranteed, I do not practice any trumpet charges at all. As Jim Koop and I learned the hard way, "Save it for the field, man!!"

I did make my rounds and say a few words of encouragement to all of the various instrumental sections. The only person who looked down her nose at me for these efforts was Teri Andrews. It was then that I knew that I had made my first presidential mistake of the school year; I should have included the two-other senior band executive board members, Teri Andrews and Katie, on these inspiration walks as well.

Mr. Anderson blew a whistle blast and then started to walk us through what he refers to as our "pre-rehearsal." Mr. Anderson would say, "Okay. We march out onto the field playing the fight song, "Varsity". Then as a band he would have us play a few measures of same. We did this for both of the pre-game and half-time shows. Just a nice little review of what our entire program consisted of tonight.

Mr. Anderson then announced to us, "We're already to go for our first half-time show of the year. Let's have a good performance. Also, don't forget that tonight I will have my eye on all of you as I will be selecting the best marcher and best marching section based upon your efforts. So, do your best."

Mr. Anderson's final words before show time were, "Okay. Let's head out to the football field. We'll do this in single file with drummers leading the way making lots of noise on those drums. Katie Beardslee. As percussion section leader, you will lead the way and it is your responsibility to get us to the end zone for the start of our pre-game show."

With those marching orders, no pun intended, all of us band members lined up behind Katie and the percussion section and it was off to the football field. Jim Koop and I were the final two to exit the band room. And as soon we hit the parking lot pavement we did the equivalent of a "strut", our signature spin to the right turn move, and off we proceeded for the first marching band show of what is to be the final "Whose half of the Band is better" marching band season that the two of us will ever spend together.

Once reaching the Hartland end zone, I noticed that there something was different about this moment. This was the first time since 1965 that I wasn't seeing the Orange & Black of the

Fenton Tigers. There were no past Fenton football greats like Don Madden, Bob Niles or Steve Barker going through their warmup drills.

And I had to force myself to stop searching around for my former Fenton Tiger football buddies like; Bruce Gold, Dan Barkman, Denny Olson, Mike Terry and Jim Vincent. Where were these guys?? Strange.

I looked down the other side of the field where the Hartland opponent for the evening, the Stockbridge Panthers, were preparing for tonight's contest. I knew nothing about how good of football team Stockbridge was. But I did know a little something about the Stockbridge High School Basketball team.

These guys were the two-time defending Class "C" state basketball champions with a lofty 54 game winning streak on their resume. Pretty impressive stuff. It also made me wonder since Hartland is playing these guys in football, and if I am fortunate enough to make the "Eagles" varsity basketball team this winter, whether the two of us might not face off in a pre-conference basketball game in a little over two months from now.

I have a theory that high school basketball players are the best athletes in their respective high school. By that I mean they have the mental and physical capability to handle pressure situations as well as the necessary coordination and reflexes to participate and excel in any other sport. I have found this to be especially true when it came to sports such as golf, track, baseball and tennis. If my belief has any merit to it, then the Hartland Eagles football team is going to be in for a rough evening.

A shrilling sound of a whistle brought me back to my attention and the sole purpose of being in the Hartland end zone. And off we were!! We marched down the football at an eight step per five yards' clip playing the Hartland High School fight song of, "Varsity!!" From there we went into our pre-game routine of "Mr. Touchdown!!". Love that song!!

Then we form into a concert block formation for the third of four songs that we perform in our pre-game show, the "Star Spangled Banner". There is one part of our national anthem where the words sung are, "O'er the land of the free". This is where every trumpet player in the United States tries to hit a high "B Flat" in a semi- trumpet charge fashion. And surprisingly, probably at least 50% of them make fools of themselves when attempting to hit this climatic note by missing on a couple of attempts and settling to play this "dramatic note" at one octave lower.

For the past few weeks due to my teeth issues I have been one of those "50% ers". I was very inconsistent in reaching the high "B Flat." But not tonight. Both Jim Koop and I nailed this puppy!! One more song to perform and we will have our first pre-game show down with four more to go!!

From concert-formation the band ranks headed to the end of the football field where we would form a human type tunnel so that the Hartland Eagles' football team could run through to the cheers of the Hartland crowd. From a marching band standpoint, this was not easy task. We

have to mark time, which means marching in place, while awaiting the gridders. Once the football players are spotted we receive the command to play "Varsity", while still marking time. And let me tell you this, marching in place for any period of time makes for a lot of huffing and puffing as well as an accelerated racing of the heart.

"Mark Time" is probably the least favorite phrase for any high school band member. Right up there with, "Okay!! Back to the end zone!! Let's try it again."

We did the same tunnel maneuver during my Fenton Band days. But instead of playing "Stand Up and Cheer", the Fenton High School fight song, we played a little ditty by the name of "Tiger Rag", possibly with the exception of Mike Beardslee.

The sheet music I was given as an eighth grader to "Tiger Rag" was so light in ink color it was impossible to read the music notes printed on it. So, I could not make heads or tails what to play during "Tunnel Formation." Oh, I blurted out a note every few measures and marched in place like there was no tomorrow so as to at least look I was doing something, but I rarely ever played much of this song.

At the beginning of every marching band season at Fenton High School, I asked, no, make that begged, for a new piece of sheet music of "Tiger Rag". Never got one. I came up with the brilliant idea of borrowing Guy Thompson's or Jim Koop's copy of this tune with the intent of memorizing "Tiger Rag." Their sheet music was even less decipherable than mine. Which looking back on it, now makes me wonder what those two were playing during "Tunnel Formation."

To this day I have never played two full measures in a row of the "Let's welcome the Fenton Tigers football team!!" type of music in the four years as a "Marching Tiger." So, nobody in the high school marching band world is happier to never play "Tiger Rag" again as long as I live than myself. And I strongly suspect that one year from now when I am a member of some type of United States Air Force Military Band, they ain't going to be playing "Tiger Rag", either.

The Hartland gridders, led by Pete Mason and Tom Moran, finally ran through the human tunnel. I spotted Coach "Crabby" Appleton walking past us band members as well and made a mental note that if the opportunity ever arose, to stick out a leg and with my new white, vinyl, buckle up spats, trip him.

It was now a step-turn to the right and off the Hartland High School Senior Band marched to our seats in the bleachers with only two quarters of high school football separating us from the first half-time show of the school year. And make no doubt about it, we ready for it!!

"White Lake Road"

Chapter #67 – "Scramble!!"

September 19th – Once us Band kids were settled into the home side bleachers, life got pretty good for old Beardslee. Trumpet Charges!! Schumpert Charges!! The Stockbridge Panthers jumped off to a 21-0 lead in the first quarter. Thanks to my newest, favorite high school football team in the state of Michigan, I did not have to play one trumpet charge during my designated quarter.

So, what is it that I do in between pre-game and half-time shows, besides hoping not to play many trumpet charges? Not much. I watch very little of the football game itself, even though, out of sheer curiosity, I do take a peek at the action on the field to see if the Hartland Eagle offense can generate a first down. None so far.

I pretty much just sit there and watch the score clock wind down before it's again time to head back down to the end zone for the start of our half-time show. But tonight, I did a little crowd watching. The first group that I noticed was the 880 Relay team all seated together, wearing either their blue jean Demin or smooth nylon type jackets. I must admit that I did fight back the urge to mosey on over and ask this group if they needed directions to the "All Sports" store this weekend to place a future order for their varsity jackets.

A few places up and over from the 880 Relay guys I spotted an assemblage of the "UCLA of Junior High Basketball" team consisting of; Ric Adams, Tom Beaver; Al Dowty; Alex Felton; and Max Perry. It was not a surprise that they were sitting together but how they were dressed as compared to the 880 Relay team was what caught my eye. Their clothing style was different in an upscale sort of way.

This quintet was wearing their Hartland High School varsity jackets; bell bottom pants, and the style of hats that singer/actor Mr. Frank Sinatra would wear while gracing the record cover of one of his many LP record albums. In addition, each of these five guys would take turns shaping their hands and putting them over their eyes so that it looked like they were wearing aviator style glasses while watching the football game. Okay.

I'm not real super hip to the wearing of bell bottom trousers, and according to Jim Koop, "You're the only person within listening distance of "America Free Europe" who isn't, Beardslee." And just staring at the hand placement of these five for their imitation of what appears to be of a pilot who used to spend their time buzzing over the Pacific Ocean during World War II, made my thumbs start to ache really bad.

But man-o-man!! I gotta get me one of those Frank Sinatra stylish hats!! If those babies look good on what hopefully will be my future basketball teammates' skulls, then you just know how one would look on Mike Beardslee. Yeah, you got it!! Move over and make room for me on your next record album cover, Frankie, baby!!

Mr. Anderson stood up, which was our first clue that it was show time. Us Band kids headed down to the Hartland end zone for the second time this evening. And here we go!!

"White Lake Road"

After marching down the field playing "Varsity", it was in to the marching routine for "Going Out of My Head". I didn't see anybody tripping over their feet and falling to the ground right in front of me while we were doing our "pin wheels", so I take that as a good sign that things are going okay so far.

While I personally think that "Going Out of My Head" should have been played in concert formation, I must admit that I like this tune. However, "Up Up and Away" is just a great song to play. This melody is a candidate to make the Mike Beardslee "Marching Band Selection All-Time Hit List" along with such great songs as "Joshua", "Georgy Girl" and "Batman." "Tiger Rag", you ask? Not even worthy of a place on the ballot.

"Up Up and Away" is a good selection for this specific marching unit. It has a nice melodic line and not a "blasting" type of song. Again, taking a quick peek to see how the rest of the marchers were doing and the best I could tell was that no one had forgotten to turn around at their designated spot on the marching field when doing our step-two marching style routine for this song.

A band director's best friend is something called "Scramble!!" This term from a marching band standpoint means that once a marching band routine is completed, marching band personnel will literally then "scramble" to their next position on the field. Specific to us tonight, we would "scramble" back into block or concert formation to ready ourselves for the playing of the Hartland High School "Alma Mater".

A marching band scramble is a polite way to say "organized chaos." You can run, walk, crawl, hop on one leg, etc. It does not matter how you get to your next designated spot, but you better be there in time for the start of the next song.

"Scrambling" became part of my repertoire for during last years' marching season at Fenton High School. Us "Marching Tigers" got all excited about this new maneuver and would make jokes like, "I'm going to do back flips to get to my spot." Yeah right, I would love to see a tenor saxophone player doing back flips with their instrument strapped on to them. Or another comment was, "I'm going to run to my car, drive it onto the field and be back in plenty of time for what song we're going to play next."

Besides the obvious time constraints involved for a person to run from the marching band field, get in their car and then drive back to this same location was logistically impossible; my recommendation that day for my marching band colleague foolish enough to even consider doing his "car thing" was, "Once you get to your car, moron, just drive straight home. Do not pass "Go" and do not collect $200.00."

I mean come on, there are certain times that motor vehicles are probably allowed on a high school football field. Scrambling to the next song being performed on a marching band field is not one of them. Hello!! Hello!!

“White Lake Road”

Jim Koop and I of course had our plan for how we were going to make our debut at scrambling. Once the tune was completed, I believe it was “Joshua”, we had to move a total distance of maybe one inch to be established in concert formation.

As soon as “Joshua” was completed, the two of us just took off like a pair of running fools. Just imagine two trumpet players, in full marching garb, making a victory lap around the entire football field. This scramble method was all well and good except for one problem. By the time we had reached our designated marching band station we had missed playing the entire first measure of the next song. That went over really well with Miss Franklin and drum major, Mike Hicks.

Did that stunt get Jim Koop and Mike Beardslee enough votes to be elected into the “Scrambling Hall of Fame??” I’m sure it did. We just haven’t received our official notice yet from the “Scrambling HOF Committee.”

Shall we say that tonight as members of the Hartland High School Marching Band that Jim Koop and I took a more conservative route when it came time to “Scramble.”

We had the playing of the “Alma Mater” completed and then it was straight off the football field to the strains of “Varsity”, through the Hartland football team bench area and the first halftime show of the season for the Hartland High School Marching Band was done and done!! Now it was time to discover what grade Mr. Anderson was assigning to us, plus who the best marcher and best marching section were based upon tonight’s performance. With free ice cream on the line this is important stuff!!

"White Lake Road"

Chapter #68 – "Butterscotch Ice Cream Cones on the House!!"

September 19th – As the Hartland High School Marching Band members were walking back to the band room, floating on air I might add, you could feel the euphoria just bursting from all of us. The drummers were making all sorts of a racket!! Kids were screaming out loud!! Smiles as wide as the Flint River were on our faces!!

This is my fifth high school marching band season and I have vivid memories of far, far, far more silent walks across a high school parking lot, then entering into a hushed band room while us band kids quietly put our horns back into our instrument cases, than I do of the whooping and hollering we were doing tonight. Oh, and let us not forget that depressing three-mile ride home after a sad sack of a half-time show performance, either.

With the exception of the time that the Fenton High School Marching Band played the theme song from the TV show "Batman" and another half-time show where the drum majorettes did a fire baton twirling routine, I have been involved in more than my share of non-descript half-time shows. Tonight's, September 19th, 1969, half-time performance did not fall into the category. We done good this evening!!

Once all of us kids were actually in the Band Room, Mr. Anderson was making all sorts of attempts in trying to settle us down and hide a giant smile on his face at the same time. He stated, "I thought that you did a really good job tonight. The pre-game show was nice and crisp. The half-time show was very good, but during the marching routine of "Going Out of My Head", there were some marchers that were half a step behind the other members in their four-person squads when doing their pin-wheels. That looked sloppy".

"I also thought that the two-steps marching routine and the playing of "Up Up and Away" was the best performance that I have ever seen in my 10 years here as band director of the marching band of Hartland High School. Very nice job. Lastly, make sure that when you are marching from concert formation in the direction of the home stands, to lift your feet higher and play "Varsity" with great pride as that is the last thing that the crowd will hear, see and remember from your evening's performance."

Great feedback, but all of us teenage band students were still sitting on the edge of our seats and waiting in baited breath for our final rating. Mr. Anderson ceased keeping us in suspense and finally advised us of our performance grade. "Your efforts rated a B+."

Mr. Anderson continued talking but his words were drowned out by loud cheers, the pounding of snare, tenor, bass drums and the crashing of cymbals!! I'm no expert at lip reading but I think Mr. Anderson's final words were something to the effect, "This is the highest grade I have ever given for the first half-time show of a marching season."

Us marching band types will never know what Mr. Anderson's concluding statement was, but each and every one of this knows this; things went pretty darn good tonight!!

Now came time for the second part of Mr. Anderson's announcement in reference to the best individual marcher and section for tonight. I was hoping to get this prestigious award but deep down inside of me, I suspected that this was not going to go my way this time around.

If I had even the slightest notion that I thought that I would be the chosen one for this evening's award, I could have just see myself pretending that I was an actor from some old "B" type western movie, like either a Jack Elam or Lee Van Cleef, walk into the band room, pull out a six shooter to fire a couple of bullets up in the air and yell, "I'm buying!! Butterscotch ice cream cones on the house!!" Yeah. That's exactly what I would do.

I actually have won the best marcher of the game once before when Miss Franklin initially introduced this honor during my sophomore year of high school. Much like tonight I didn't think that I was going to be tapped on the shoulder and given a life time supply of free ice cream from "Patterson's Ice Cream."

Everyone in the Fenton High School Marching Band knew that Guy Thompson was the most likely winner and recipient of free ice cream for his efforts that night. But there was a surprise that evening when it came time for Miss Franklin to announce the winner by stating, "I have co-winners tonight. Guy Thompson and Mike Beardslee!!"

It was a well-deserved honor for Guy Thompson and stroke of luck, sneaking in the back-door type victory for me. Miss Franklin added, "I was watching Guy Thompson and then also noticed the marcher next to him lifting his feet as high and playing his trumpet just as loud as Guy Thompson. And that is why we have two winners."

Add to the fact that the trumpet section was awarded the best instrumental section of the night and I had ice cream coming out of my ears. The only kicker was the flavor that evening was vanilla and not my all-time favorite choice of ice cream, butterscotch.

The funny thing was, however, taking a ride on the Mike Beardslee time-machine, if I remember correctly, that was the only half-time show that a best marcher and best section award was ever presented. Not only for the 1967 marching band season but the 1968 one as well. And Miss Franklin never, never, never gave an explanation as to why she pulled the plug on this accolade. A mystery that is right up there with whatever happened to aviatrix, Amelia Earhart.

Finally, the big revelation finally came down from Mr. Anderson. Jim Koop was officially announced as the winner of the best marcher award and, the trumpet section was considered the best instrumental group that had graced the Hartland High School football field this evening. I was happy for Jim Koop as he is so far having a great marching band season. And I was really glad that the trumpet section was the winner of the best section as it at least showed that I made some type of positive contribution to our half-time show.

The only downer with Jim Koop winning best marcher of the game, at least for me personally and hopefully temporarily, it answers the question of "Whose half of the band is better??" With four half time shows remaining for the Hartland High School Senior Band, will I ever win this prestigious honor? Good question. I'll know better in 15 days when I get my permanent caps set in my mouth. So, check back with me then.

After gulping down a couple small plastic cartons of vanilla ice cream, Jim Koop asked Mr. Anderson, in a very innocent tone of voice, "Hey, Mr. Anderson. Do you want me to take the remaining ice cream cartons back to the cafeteria for you?" (Now don't sit there and tell me you don't know what is going to happen later!!)

I had no interest in watching the remainder of the football game and it was a joyous ride back to "White Lake Road." The four of us knew that we had done a good job tonight and we could hardly wait till this upcoming Monday when we start to prepare for next week's half-time show. Based on what took place tonight, the start of next weeks' show cannot come fast enough.

The traditional post game snack in the Beardslee household was put on hold tonight. Including my mother, it was ice cream for everybody, compliments of the Hartland Consolidated Schools!! We gobbled down this dessert while Katie gave my mother a blow by blow description of our award-winning efforts this evening.

The end of a long and happy day was finally upon me. As I was getting ready to pack it in, I turned to the radio station of WGMZ-FM, "107.9 on your dial," to catch some of the local high school scores. Stockbridge added seven more points to make the final tally: Stockbridge 28- Hartland 0, making the Hartland Eagles 0-3 on the season.

I thought to myself, Tom Moran's prediction of a five- win season is quickly going down the toilet. There is no way that the Hartland gridders go 5-1 for the remainder of their season. Not with the "big boys" like: Brighton, Fenton and Swartz Creek smacking their lips with the thought of keeping the Eagles on track for a perfect season of zero victories for the third football season in a row.

As my head hit the pillow I fell asleep feeling happy. That doesn't happen to me very often. I thought to myself, this is what "The greatest of year of my life" should be like every day. But that feeling of glee will be short lived as tomorrow brings an early wakeup call to a day that I am not looking forward to in any way shape or form.

"White Lake Road"

Chapter #69 – "Three Concerns"

September 20th – A day that I am not anticipating with great delight began as I would have expected with an early "up and at em" 6:00 AM wake up-call that was triggered by my mother turning on the lights in my room instead of waiting for my alarm clock to go off. Once I finally got my site back in my right eye, I thought to myself that this is one lousy way to start a Saturday morning.

Today, my friends, is Band Day. It's off to Ann Arbor, Michigan with about 10,000 other high school band kids to participate in a Band Day half-time show at the University of Michigan football stadium. And I want it officially placed on the record, not my favorite way to spend a September Saturday afternoon.

This is my fourth trip to this event. I got lucky that during my sophomore year that for whatever reason, the Fenton High School Band did not attend the University of Michigan Band Day. Let's put it this way, not making that trek didn't exactly break my little heart.

My first two Band Days were not much fun at all. Couldn't stand them in fact. I made my initial trip as an eighth grader and this was the first time that I had actually gotten to wear my Fenton High School band uniform, good old "# 40."

It was a difficult piece of clothing to struggle getting in to. I had never worn suspenders before; and the uniform was way too large for me. Add to the fact that as I was heading back to the Fenton school buses at the end of this tortuous day, a passerby pulled the orange plume off of the top of my band hat, dropped it on the ground and stepped on it a couple times before disappearing off into the crowd of people. Welcome to Band Day, Mike Beardslee. I hope you enjoyed your stay.

Next year's trip to Ann Arbor, Michigan wasn't a whole lot better. It was just flat out boring sitting there in the University of Michigan Stadium hours before the game even started and the game clock didn't go much faster once the football contest started, either.

I've mentioned previously that I do not like watching high school football games in person and based upon my first two Band Days, I liked watching college football games in person even less. I do not follow the Michigan Wolverines football program at all as I'm a professional football type of fan. I love watching the Detroit Lions; New York Jets and during their glory years, the Green Bay Packers.

With the graduation of All-American running back, Ron Johnson, now a member of the Cleveland Browns, and unless past Heisman trophy winner, Tom Harmon, is still a current member of this years' Michigan Wolverine football squad, then I am hard pressed to name one other player on the roster.

Whereas, once a Detroit Lion roster is officially set, I can name every player, the position that they play; their uniform number and what college they attended. On a good day and my brains

cells are hitting on all cylinders, I might even be able to tell you what round of the National Football League draft a Detroit Lion player was selected.

In addition to being totally bored to tears, there is another reason why I am not looking forward to attending Band Day. You could probably put this rationalization under the category of plain old fear. The seating arrangement for the high school bands attending Band Day are in an alphabetical style. Which means, the Hartland Band will be seated in the same vicinity of the Fenton Band. That's what is making my stomach a bit queasy this morning.

My high level of anxiety is resulting from whether or not I will receive the same treatment from my former Fenton band mates that Steve West got when he left Fenton High School after his junior year to attend the Interlochen Arts Academy. I still remember some of the adjectives that Steve West was thrown his way: "Traitor!!" "Turncoat!!" "Deserter!!" And for those who had taken "American History Class", they would even throw an occasional, "Benedict Arnold!!" in Steve West's direction. And this doesn't include the other phrases where the Lord's name was taken in vain to describe Steve West's departure.

When you get right down to the nitty-gritty, what Mike Beardslee, Katie Beardslee, Jim Koop and Terry Rodenbo have done this school year is really no different than what Steve West did. We simply all chose to attend another high school for the 1969-70 school year, same as Steve West. At least Terry Walker when he left Fenton was smart enough to move 200 miles to Gaylord, Michigan. And he had a legitimate reason to leave Fenton High School, as did Steve West. Whereas, the four of us are attending an out-of-town high school, a public school one at that, but still sleep nighty-night in our Fenton, Michigan beds.

Oh, there will be some Fenton Band kids that will be glad to see me. Pat "The Flying Dutchman" Goode; his girlfriend, Jan Sears; Larry Anderson and Paul Romska. But what about the John Perkins' and Tom Douglas' of the world and any other followers that they have? Classify this a big concern.

Even to a lesser extent is how will Miss Franklin act towards me and Jim Koop if we cross paths? Even with all of the harebrained stunts that Jim Koop and I pulled during our two years under her leadership as band director of Fenton High School, you don't simply replace two trumpet players like us who could blast our horns as well as we did, in addition to the spirit and personality that we brought to a marching band.

Counting Steve West, that's a total of five quality musicians whose names do not presently appear on the band roster for Fenton High School. I'm sure there are some high schools in the state of Michigan that could overcome that type of attrition. Flint Northwestern High School immediately comes to mind. Probably Chelsea High School as well. But Fenton High School, ah, no. So, meeting up with Miss Franklin today might cause some worry, but overall it is a minor concern.

But the biggest fear I have today, by far, even above the seeing of my former Fenton High School band mates that think I am the second coming of Steve West, is the absolute terror that

"White Lake Road"

I have in the possibility of seeing Jane Roberts. There's a very good likely hood that she'll be there sitting in the University of Michigan football stadium not far from me.

I haven't seen Jane Roberts in over three-and-a-half months, specifically since the end of the 1968-69 school year. And nary a word has passed between us since last November when she asked to borrow a dime from me to make a telephone call. Her obvious avoidance and dodging of me continued as she paraded the school halls of Fenton High School with new boy-friend after new boy-friend. None of whom even came close to being as charming, witty, ruggedly handsome, reflexes of a cheetah, and the owner of two trumpets just like you know who.

There was only one way that I would make an effort to seek out Jane Roberts this third Saturday in the month of September. And that's if screen actress, Stephanie Powers, flew in from wherever she woke up this morning, scurries out to the University of Michigan campus while dressed in her best April Dancer outfit, of course, and the two of us walk over to the Fenton Band, arm in arm, and I introduce my "Band Day" date to Jane Roberts. And, then casually mention in an Errol Flynnish suave tone of voice, "Tell the "Pillsbury Dough Boy" that Stephanie Powers and "sissy cross country boy" say, hi. He'll know who we are."

Major, no make that a colossus concern is if Jane Roberts and I cross paths today. However, if Stephanie Powers scenario plays out, there is no concern at all. None.

It was a slow drive into Hartland High School this morning, probably due to my tiredness, and I thought to myself, "Geez. We were here just less than 12 hours ago, and here we are back already. That's a lot of 28-mile round trip drives to make in such a short time."

Upon entering the Band Room, it was interesting to see the reaction that the four of are now starting to get from the rest of our band mates. Gone, or at least less of, are the distrustful looks of, "Who are these strangers from Fenton and what are they doing around us??"

With the exception of the Andrews' family, the four of us are becoming more and more accepted as friends rather than just members of the same organization. Even Jim Koop and I, who had an unspoken pact that neither one of us had any desire to make new friends or acquaintances with the Hartland students, are getting smiles and waves in our direction. That pre-school year agreement between the two of us is slowly disintegrating into tiny particles of dust.

Before us "band heads" started to load up on the two buses that were awaiting in front of the high school, Mr. Anderson went over the schedule for this long, excruciating day that we we're facing:

8:00 AM– Depart for Ann Abor, Michigan;

9:00 AM – Arrive at parking location and head to stadium seating area;

9:30– 11:30 AM– Rehearsal for Band Day Half-time show;

1:00 PM- Start of Vanderbilt-Michigan football game;

1:45 PM – (Estimated) – Band Day Half-Time show;

4: 00 PM – (Estimated) – Depart for Hartland High School;

5:00 PM – (Estimated) – Arrive at Hartland High School.

I must have looked, no, make that intensely studied the timetable that was written on the white board a couple of 100 times and thought to myself, thank goodness this is the last time I will ever have to attend a University of Michigan Band Day. With that dreary notion in my mind, it was off to the buses.

Chapter #70 – "A continuous vertical brick or stone structure that encloses or divides an area of land:"

September 20th – As I was sitting on the Hartland School bus that was maneuvering its way through the "metropolis" of Hartland, Michigan to U.S. 23, I noticed the excitement of my fellow Hartland Bandmates. It was more than obvious how much they were looking forward to attending Band Day.

This made me wonder what was so wrong with me that I could not even scrounge up one-tenth of the enthusiasm that these fellow bus riders had. Were my past Band Day experiences so negative that there was not at least one moment where a smile actually crossed my grumpy looking face?

Yeah, I must admit, and I really do not want to, but there was one single event where I thought to myself, "Hey, this wasn't such a terrible ordeal after all." At last year's Band Day, 1968 style, my feelings about this yearly occurrence had not changed one bit. I could not wait to get back home to "White Lake Road" and my "Sporting News" magazine. This is Saturday, right? While Jim Koop and I were walking back to our bus, some sleazy looking guy came up to us and asked if we wanted to purchase some kazoos for the price of $1.00.

The kazoos were brass in color and shaped like a trumpet. I mean, how could the two of us turn down owning a prized possession like that? I mean we are talking the equivalent of buying the "Super Ball" that I bought at the Michigan State Fair just a few weeks back. The decision to purchase a couple of kazoos was an easy one. In fact, we would have probably paid more than the one American dollar for these babies that this guy was charging us.

Once the we were back on the Fenton High School bus, Jim Koop and I started to mess around with our new trophies and discovered that if you hummed through the mouth piece you could create a sound that was the equivalent of a poor imitation of a harmonica. From there, the "Whose half-of-the band is better" partnership then turned this great find into a contest amongst our fellow passengers. We would play a TV theme song and whoever guessed the correct name of the TV series then got to use the kazoo to play their TV theme show selection. You kept possession of the kazoo until the next participant made an accurate choice.

Surprisingly this contest amused our little minds to no end and made the 35-mile bus ride back to Fenton High School a fast and entertaining one.

Who won the competition, you ask?? Yours truly, of course, and try to prove otherwise. I dare ya!! It's not my fault that none of the participants didn't recognize the theme song from a long ago cancelled TV series by the name of "Honey West", starring Anne Francis. Only the cool kids would remember that theme song. At least that is what I have been telling myself for the past four years.

So yeah, you got it out of me. A concession on my part that there was at least one moment when my University of Michigan Band Day trips were not as bad as I make them out to be. But that was the only one.

"White Lake Road"

The trip to Ann Arbor this morning was fairly quick and before you knew it the Hartland Consolidated School buses were parked amongst what was probably at least another 100 school buses. It's always fun getting off of the bus, half-asleep, wondering whether you remembered your instrument or not, then gazing out over the parking area and seeing all of the different band kids in all sorts of various marching band uniforms.

The color schemes ran from Hartland's blue and gold to your basic maroon and purple; red and white; orange and black; to an interesting combination of lime green and banana yellow styled band uniform. After seeing the latter decorated attire, maybe our Hartland Band outfits are not so bad after all. Maybe.

From the bus field, it's now time for the long journey to the football stadium itself. I must admit that when going to Detroit Tigers baseball games at Tiger Stadium, that once inside the stadium it's always a big thrill to walk up a ramp and the first view you see inside Tiger Stadium is the plush green infield grass. Just a beautiful site, especially on a sunny day.

But when you look into the University of Michigan football stadium at 9:00 AM in the morning on Band Day, where the facility is still pretty much empty, it's vastness just smacks you right in the face. To just think that you are looking at a facility that seats 101,000 plus people of all shapes and sizes. You can get more people in this stadium at one time than all but a handful of cities population wise in the state of Michigan. I readily admit that this is quite a scene.

There is one thing that is different about the University of Michigan football field from seasons past. It is now covered in something called, astro-turf, rather than your traditional grass field. As Jim Koop put it, "What you have right in front of us, Beardslee, is the world's biggest pool table." He just might be right.

Before I got into full panic mode about seeing certain members of the Fenton High School Marching Band, I saw that things were starting to get going down on the field. Students in casual attire carrying their instruments, probably members of the University of the University of Michigan Band, were starting to meander about. This observation was then followed shortly by some instructional blasts over a PA system. It was officially time for Band Day rehearsal!!

The instructions would go something like this. At the appropriate command, all of high school band kids were to head down to the football field, follow the leader style, and get into block formation. Once there, this mass band ensemble would proceed to play two tunes, "St. Louis Blues" and "The Victors." Once both songs were completed, it was an about face and back to the stands. Piece of cake, right?? In theory, yes.

Maybe I am the only one of us band kids that thinks this is a problem, but when entering onto the field itself, the 10,000 of us Band Day participants have to climb over and down a three-foot brick wall that encircles the entire stadium. Then when returning to your designated area in the stands, you have to climb up over this same wall carrying your instrument while also behind or being followed real close by your fellow mass band members. You do the math.

I personally think this wall is a hazard and I can guarantee you that some marchers and their instruments are going to get injured and damaged. Clambering over that brick barrier for Jim Koop, Aisha Tredeau, Randi Lynch and myself should not be too big of a problem. Our instruments are of the size that we can cradle them against our bodies to protect them.

However, this is the reverse for Terry Rodenbo, Jason Shattuck and Katie. The size of their musical instruments is not the issue when stepping up and down the three-foot obstacle, but could still cause some potential clumsiness. I just wonder how many brass instruments leave Ann Arbor, Michigan with dents in them as a result of their Band Day experience.

Once down on the marching field, the mass bands played through the two-musical selections despite the fact that as a participant, once you are playing these songs you have no clue as to whether you're playing in tempo with the other Band Day partakers. Dr. William Revelli, the renowned director of the University of Michigan Marching Band, is somewhere standing on a ladder conducting the mass ensemble. Then on the actual floor of the field you have the Mr. Anderson's and Miss Franklin's of the world trying to stay in sync with Dr. Revelli while directing us bandsters.

Starting a song together for us 10,000 bands people is usually not a problem, even when there are other bands that always yell" Up!!" to raise their instruments before they play the first note of a tune.

However, finishing one of these two musical selections together as an ensemble rarely happens. I know that the bands around us Hartland musicians, and by the way, a big fourth University of Michigan Band Day hello to the Fruitport High School Marching Band, it's good to see you guys again, completed "St. Louis Blues" at least a couple of full measures before some of the other bands that were on the opposite side of the marching formation as us. I guess that is the one of the misfortunes of war when it comes to Band Day.

These two melodies were followed by the previously noted command of an "about face" and it was back to our seats in the stadium for further instructions. Getting back to our designation over that brick divider was harder as now you had to make a step up from the ground to get over this obstacle. I saw some other band kids struggling when I heard that terrible sound of brass against brick and was glad that it wasn't my trumpet that was becoming warm and friendly with this enemy of a brick wall.

Once back to our seats, you just had to know what was coming up next. Us kids sat down for what felt like one second and the voice on the PA then had us go down to the field again. Only this time there was more of a sense of urgency coming from the mysterious voice, of which, I could swear was the same hidden voice from the movie, "The Wizard of Oz", to get us kids moving faster to get into our positions. And this second time down to the field I saw one kid from another band take a header but got up in time to avoid receiving the honor of "being the band person having the most footprints on the back of their marching band uniform" annual award.

All 10,000 of the state of Michigan's high school musicians again rehearsed through our two songs and it was back over the brick blockade again. Now when we attempted to exit the field from our second rehearsal, the PA voice was pressing us in a very aggressive tone of voice to get off of the field and back into the stands as quickly as possible. A sort of "Go, Go, Go, Go, Go" type of urgency.

Just before I got ready to make my assault on the three-foot brick wall, I saw another poor musician really struggling to get over the brick partition and was virtually pushed off of the cement siding by other band kids who were "getting off of the field as quickly as possible." And it dawned on me that when it comes time to enter onto the field for the actual half-time show, the adrenalin will really be a pumping, and there will be a handful of overzealous marcher(s), no doubt trumpet players, who will take no prisoners when trying to be the first ones to get into their field position.

I realize that the purpose of Band Day is to show off the University of Michigan, their marching band, and to create interest in their music department. But come on guys, even I could figure out that for safety purposes, everything would be better for us band kid's protection if you left us in the stands and let us play from there.

Finally, out of the zone of danger, I did a once over and it appears that all of us Hartland Band kids and their instruments made it back to our seats all in one piece. As I was sitting down getting ready to watch the University of Michigan Marching Band go through a pre-game show rehearsal, I saw a very recognizable face walking directly towards me.

"White Lake Road"

Chapter #71 – "Yellow Belts"

September 20th – Let me change what I just said. I actually heard a flamboyant type voice heading in my direction before I really saw who the owner of these vocal sounds belonged to. "CABIN FIVE!! COME ALIVE!! CABIN #5!! WE AIN'T NO JIVE!! DOC SAVAGE!! DOC SAVAGE!!" MY MAIN MAN!!

Who else could this person be? You're right. The eighth wonder of the world and my cabin mate of Cabin Five from All-State Boys Division, himself, Allen "Bad Hombre" Rothstein!!

Bad Hombre looked just the same since the day I first met him at Interlochen last Summer. His hair still parted right in the middle and hanging down to his ears; black horn-rimmed glasses and a hippie style headband with peace signs circling around his head. Like that type of headband is going to make a guy who wears the same style of glasses that I wear make him look cool. I don't think so.

The first words out Bad Hombre's mouth was not a typical greeting of, "How ya doing there, Doc Savage??" Or, "How's my basketball playing buddy??" No, Bad Hombre's official start of our conversation was, "Hey, Doc Savage!! Show me all of the girls in your band that I can compare embouchures with!!" I'm glad to see you too, Band Hombre.

Upon Bad Hombre's arrival, I made a point to look around at the faces of my Hartland bandmates. Their expressions could be classified into two categories. Based upon impression #1, I was pretty sure that none of them had ever seen anything like Bad Hombre before in their life. Let's just put it this way, Bad Hombre makes Jim Koop look like he is the poster boy for a publication of "Altar Boy Weekly."

The second look of confused facial appearances was accompanied by the unasked questions of, "Who and what is a Doc Savage?? And how did Mike Beardslee get a nickname like that??"

It was great to sit and talk with Bad Hombre again. He mentioned that there were a bunch of kids from Interlochen walking around here at Band Day and it was like old home week again, without the Allstate Division uniform of the day; light blue short-sleeved shirt; dark blue pants; and a yellow belt.

Bad Hombre advised that he had been accepted into Wayne State University and was going to be a business major with the long-term goal of getting into law school. He then asked, "How about you, Doc Savage. Where are you going to be attending school one year from now??"

I became amazingly quiet and changed the subject rather fast by answering Bad Hombre's question with a question. Over the past few years, I have actually gotten quite good at this answering a question with a question thing. It's a real art. Take my word for it.

I then blurted out, "Where's Howard "I was shafted" Feldman these days??" Bad Hombre replied, "Oh, Howie, he has an audition for Oberlin College's Conservatory of Music. Howie still thinks he's the best clarinet player in the United States. Maybe even Europe."

After about a 10-minute visit, Bad Hombre was getting ready to leave and you have to realize that Bad Hombre never does anything in a small type of way. He turned to the Hartland Band kids, who just kept looking at him in astonishment and said, "Good bye all of Doc Savages' friends!!"

Bad Hombre then gestured in a fond farewell fashion and headed back to wherever the Oak Park High School Band was located. He then stopped for a second, turned around in an extremely slow manner, and with a Bad Hombre type smile on his face, which means one of two things, and hopefully, not both; he is either going to say something amusing, or moon you. Bad Hombre yelled out, "HEY, DOC SAVAGE!! Al HIRT SENDS OUT A BIG HELLO!!" Yes, Bad Hombre, I'm sure Mr. Hirt does. Ha, Ha.

Bad Hombre!! The greatest nickname ever!! Even better than the self-proclaimed one that Bad Hombre wanted to hang on himself when it came time for the selection of our "Cabin Five identities", of "Kid Dynamite!!" Allen Rothstein, and take my word for it, is no "Kid Dynamite!!"

I was then bombarded by the Hartland Band kids with questions of "Who was that??" And, "Who stuck me with a dumb nickname like "Doc Savage??". My response to the latter question was easy, "The Flying Dutchman". That shut em up.

I now headed out with Jim Koop, Terry Rodenbo and Jason Shattuck to get the Hartland Bands' complimentary lunch, courtesy of the University of Michigan Marching Band, which consisted of a soft drink and one hot dog. The soft drink isn't too bad but the hot dogs are strictly United States Army surplus that were probably left over from the Korean War. They're terrible tasting. How bad are these hot dogs, you ask? They're so unhealthy that I would only feed three or four of them to Coach "Crabby" Appleton.

While walking back to the Hartland Band seating area, Bad Hombre's statement that there were a bunch of Interlochen types all over the place proved to be accurate. Sitting there all by his lonesome was Bill Zeigler. The pride of the Grosse Point High School Band and a guy who as a sophomore could high jump a height of 5'8" during track season.

To say the least, the majority of the guys who made up Cabin Five, didn't have "both oars in the water" and were never, ever going to be able to run for public office if and when any of us ever grow up. Bill Zeigler was the opposite of this. Very quiet. Very reflective. And an excellent clarinet player.

Last June after being dropped off by Mr. Goode, the father of "The Flying Dutchman" at the National Music Camp, "The Flying Dutchman" and I walked into Cabin Five for the first time ever. I sauntered over to a bunk bed and took the upper berth. It just so happened that Bill Zeigler took the bottom berth. Bill Zeigler's mother was helping him make up his bed and when she saw how helpless I was in trying to perform the same task, Mrs. Zeigler stepped in and ended up assisting me in the making up of top bunk as well. Thank you, Mrs. Zeigler.

I went up to Bill Zeigler this morning and he looked at me like he had never seen me before. Then it dawned on him that standing in front of him was none other than the infamous, "Doc Savage!!" Bill Zeigler's first words out of his mouth were, "I didn't recognize you with hair on your head!!"

When I first set foot on the campus of the Interlochen National Music Camp three short months ago, I looked like I was right out of Paris Island, where the United States Marines go through their boot camp training. Just a couple of weeks earlier, I had had my head totally shaved. Don't even ask. Ron, the barber at Leo's Barbershop, enjoyed performing this this restyling of my hair so much, he didn't even charge me the customary $2.00 for what truly had to meet the Webster Dictionary definition of "haircut."

So, I got me some strange looks when walking through Cabin Five for the first time, as well as every other place that I placed both of my size 11 shoes on the Interlochen campus. My hair started to grow back by the time I had completed my Student Conservation Association stint a couple of months later, at least to the point that I could actually start combing my hair again, rather than just running a comb through my "locks."

Bill Zeigler and I talked for a while and the big news with him is that he is applying to Interlochen to be a part of their "Nationals" program during the summer of 1970. This is where an individual will spend eight weeks at the National Music Camp verses the 14 days I spent as part of the Allstate Boy's Division. We're talking some serious time away from home and money for this type of session. I'm just guessing, but the freight to send a student there has got to be at least a minimum of $600.00 for tuition. That would be a lot of money for my parents to fork out so that I could spend my summer playing basketball and volleyball instead of practicing the trumpet.

In addition to the difference in time frames, another variance between being a National and an Allstate person is that the Nationals dressed differently than we did. They wore the same light blue shirt, but instead wore a red sweater and blue corduroys as their uniform of the day, less the yellow belt requirement.

Also, Nationals as a whole, were less than polite to us Allstate people. In fact, they were flat out mean at times. I always thought it was because of the yellow belt that us Allstate kids got to wear and the Nationals didn't. But as it was explained to me by Howard Feldman, it was because the Nationals were there for the whole summer and us Allstaters could go home after two weeks.

I hope that Bill Zeigler gets accepted into the Nationals program. A person has to be one serious musician to want to give up pretty much your whole summer vacation, or at least 56 days of it. And the cost of that place translates into a whole lot of clarinet reeds.

I said my good byes to Bill Zeigler and headed back to the Hartland Band contingency. As I got closer, a slight chill went down my back when I noticed that there were a couple of orange and black band uniforms with their backs to me talking with Katie.

"White Lake Road"

Chapter #72- "Honor's Cabin"

September 20th – As I got closer to the Hartland Band area, the two orange and black band uniforms of the people talking to Katie started to look familiar. It was "The Flying Dutchman" and his girlfriend since seventh grade, Jan Sears. And the two of them were getting the blow by blow details of the just recently completed visit from Bad Hombre as relayed to them by my younger sister.

The Flying Dutchman turned around to me and the first words out of his mouth were, "Good morning, Mr. President." I repeated this same phrase back to The Flying Dutchman. See, Bad Hombre!! This is how you receive royalty!!

This greeting between The Flying Dutchman and myself meant that the two of us had reached the honor of being president of a high school band. Granted, I had to leave Fenton High School for each us to reach this objective, but nevertheless, we both could now write "Band President" on our future resumes.

The funny thing about The Flying Dutchman and I when it came to the presidency of the Fenton High School Band, was that we were both qualified to hold this prestigious position. I might have been the more dedicated of the two of us Band wise, but I readily admit and concede that The Flying Dutchman was smarter than me and had the better leadership skills of the two of us. Correction. Make that much smarter.

The Flying Dutchman never came out and admitted it, but he had "bigger fish to fry" than becoming president of the Fenton High School Band. That's why he turned his efforts to being elected as student counsel president of Fenton High School for his senior year. That is also why he was selected to attend "Government Week" in Lansing, Michigan. Basically, a one-week equivalent of his Interlochen experience and the kind of stuff that The Flying Dutchman just ate up.

The funny thing was at the end of my junior year of high school, Miss Franklin approached me and said, "I know that you, Pat Goode, and Jan Sears will probably spend some time plotting out next years' band election campaign over the Summer. If I may, I would like to make a suggestion. Just to mix things up a little bit, how about if we have Pat Goode run for band president and you, vice-president." Miss Franklin quickly added, "And if you're the person who nominates him, Pat Goode will win pretty easily." Ah, no. I'll pass, thank you.

I never did bring this proposal of Miss Franklin's to either Pat Goode or Jan Sears. In all honesty, The Flying Dutchman was a standup guy who knew how much the Band world meant to me and probably would not have gone along with this suggestion any way.

I always suspected that Miss Franklin would have preferred Mike Hicks as Band president over me, but it wasn't until she came up to me last June that she tipped her hand that for the second consecutive Band election that she would have preferred someone else other than Mike Beardslee as Senior Band president.

"White Lake Road"

So, yeah, this "Good morning, Mr. President" greeting from The Flying Dutchman was great to receive and even better to reciprocate.

The Flying Dutchman after our exchange of greetings said, "Let's take a spin around the stadium concourse area. There is something that I want to run past you."

After we had separated ourselves from the Hartland Band, The Flying Dutchman finally brought up what he needed to discuss with me. "You remember Rod Romano, our counselor from Cabin Five last summer?" It was easy to remember Rod Romano. He was a nice guy and a first-time counselor whose very initial cabin assignment consisted of guys with nicknames like: "Louie"; "The Professor"; "Zeke"; "Wild Bill"; "Doc Savage"; "Bad Hombre"; "The Flying Dutchman"; "JC"; "Lover Boy"; "Ski Man"; and "Paul Bunyan."

Shall we say, that we were an interesting group. Especially when you compared us to the cabin situated next to us that I swear consisted of a group of guys who said their prayers at 8:00 PM and were asleep by 8:01 PM every night.

Poor Rod Romano, he just never really had any control over us. I suspect that if the All-State Boys Division counselors had anything that resembled staff meetings, the population of Cabin Five and our shenanigans would have been an hourly topic.

The daily routine of cabin life at Interlochen was to awake in the morning and clean out the cabin for the daily inspections, which consisted of making your bed, get the cabin swept out, put all trash outside in a dumpster, that kind of stuff. After breakfast, it was off to a private lesson or sectional rehearsal. The winner of the cleanest cabin, "AKA Honor's Cabin," would then get an award of ice cream, pizza, etc. To the staff counselors, this ritual was a big deal.

Some cabins took this tidying up procedure quite serious. Their goal was to win this Honors Cabin award every day. Cabin Five? Our combined housekeeping skills, unless Bill Zeigler's mother was there, were very minimal, at best. We did just enough upkeep for us to get by.

Well, one morning, our self-proclaimed cabin leader, Howard Feldman, came up with the brain storm that as a group we would not make our beds or do any of the other daily chores. In fact, we even went so far as to bring in sand/dirt from the outside and put it on the cabin floor. Oh, yes, we were quite proud of ourselves!!

When we got back to Cabin Five later that morning, there was a note written by Rod Romano and posted to the entrance door with blistering words that read; "IF YOU DO NOT WIN THE HOUSEKEEPING AWARD TOMORROW MORNING, YOU WILL HAVE TO RUN 10 LAPS AROUND THE RECREATIONAL FIELD TOMORROW AT MIDNIGHT!!"

Now that recreational field was quite large, at least the equivalent of a 440-yard track. Since Bill Ziegler and I were both track men, we knew that running around this field 10 times was not going to be easy even for us, let alone for some of our cabin mates, of whom, I'm not even sure that had ever worn any other type of footwear than wing tip shoes in their whole life.

Us Cabin Five guys felt bad about what we had done and made an outstanding human effort to get our cabin not only clean, but super-clean, so that we could win the Honors Cabin award of the day.

Luckily, we got it together and had the cleanest cabin for that specific inspection in the Allstate Boys Division history, at least in our minds, and at the same time allowing us to fall back into the good graces of one Mr. Rod Romano.

The Flying Dutchman continued by saying, "Well, Rod Romano and I have kept in touch over the Summer and he advised me that he was not going to be coming back to Interlochen as a counselor for the 1970 session. He just felt that he was not cut out for this type of a summer job."

"So, in his last letter to me, he recommended that I send in an application and apply for his old job. I mention this to you because I think you should apply as well. The Flying Dutchman and Doc Savage could then take the Allstate Boys Division by storm!!"

This recommendation by the Flying Dutchman caught me off guard and my response, a very weak, "Let me think about it" certainly did not match the same level of enthusiasm that The Flying Dutchman and Bill Ziegler had when they were talking about their plans for getting back to Interlochen as fast as they could. And I don't doubt that for one second that The Flying Dutchman would be an excellent Allstate Division Boys Counselor.

But I don't know if I could say the same thing about myself. Yeah, Mike Beardslee enjoyed the two weeks stay at Interlochen, no, make that the last 10 days, because I was homesick like you wouldn't believe for the first four days. But I was certainly not in love or infatuated with Interlochen like every other student that had over the course of the past 41 years attended the National Music Camp.

I realize the magic of the Interlochen name carries a fairy-tale like feeling with it, especially in the Beardslee household where my mother was broken hearted when I was not accepted there at the end of my sophomore year of high school. She always wanted her son to go to Interlochen, more so than I did. And the excitement will be stirred up again in my mother when Katie will get her chance, either this summer or next, to go to the All-State equivalent for piano students.

Two of Mary Beardslee's children having attended and anticipated to go to Interlochen will be the cause of some serious bragging rights in the teacher's lounge of State Road Elementary School for my mother.

But just like issue of attending college, Interlochen is not that big of deal to me. I know that is sacra religious to feel that way and may I recommend to you readers, for your own safety, that you should be standing at least four feet away from me when that lightning bolt comes down from the heavens and strikes me for thinking these thoughts.

"White Lake Road"

So, while the Flying Dutchman's', and Bill Ziegler's" of the world have their hearts set on being back on Interlochen in the next nine months, I also have my plans for the Summer of 1970 etched in stone as well. And they do not include worrying about when I have to attend some college orientation or, will I have to stock up on enough light blue short sleeved shirts and a couple of new yellow belts to last me for at least eight weeks.

The Flying Dutchman and I had been leaning on the top of a cement slab while overlooking the parking lot while discussing our futures. As the two of us got ready to turn around and head back to our individual band locations, the both of us could see and feel the sun being blocked out on our bodies as well as the immediate area that we were standing. I could have also sworn that the temperature had immediately just dropped by some 20 degrees.

There was only one person in the entire world that we each knew that could cause this type of eclipse of the Sun and I'm not talking about Bubba Smith, defensive end of the Baltimore Colts, either.

"White Lake Road"

Chapter #73 "Real Civilian Food and Jules Verne"

September 20th – Both "The Flying Dutchman" and I had a pretty good idea of whom the person standing behind us was. And we were correct. It was Randy Lape, another Cabin Five roommate who was born and raised in Hillsdale, Michigan. Wherever that is.

Now just imagine folklore hero, Paul Bunyan, dressed in a short-sleeved, light blue shirt, dark blue pants, a yellow belt and playing a sousaphone. You got it. Meet Mr. Randy Lape.

The difference between Randy Lape and the rest of us Cabin Five guys was that he looked like he could start right this very second on the defensive line for the Texas University Longhorns football team as a senior in high school. Randy Lape was a man!!

One of the rules at Interlochen was that all male employees or students could not have any facial hair at all. No beards, goatees, mustaches, Fu man chu, etc. None. Only the hair on the top of your head was permissible. I always wondered if Randy Lape ever got any flak about these Interlochen guidelines, because even as a 17-year upcoming high school senior, Randy Lape had a substantial five o'clock shadow. In fact, Randy Lape could shave first thing in the morning and then need to shave again immediately after breakfast.

Randy Lape when talking with The Flying Dutchman and myself brought up an Interlochen moment that was near and dear to my heart when he said, "Hey, Doc Savage. I have been walking around this place for the past 30 minutes, and this is no lie, I have had about a dozen or so kids that were in the Allstate Division this past summer come up to me and thank me for winning them free pizza." Ah, yes. Everyone in their life should be famous for something. And Randy Lape and I accomplished this feat last June.

There is a tradition in the Allstate Division where the Allstate men counselors play a volleyball match, the best two out of three, against a team that consists of two kids from each cabin in the Boys Division. According to a couple of kids in Cabin Five who were on their second tour of duty at Interlochen, mentioned that this was a gigantic deal to the counselors. The highlight of the Summer kind of thing.

"Profession Hinkle" advised, "The men's staff brags every year how they have never lost a game let alone a match against Allstate kids. In fact, last year I don't even think that the Allstate Boys team even scored a point against them. I still haven't figured out whether the men's staff team is that good or us musicians are that bad of volleyball players."

Part of the daily schedule at Interlochen was that there was a recreational hour. When I wasn't playing basketball with Bad Hombre, the game of volleyball had been adopted as the "team Sport" for Cabin Five. So, when it came time for two representatives to be selected from Cabin Five for this big game, Randy Lape and I were the designated spikers from Cabin Five.

Our life as elected delegates of the volleyball team and lifetime fame for Paul Bunyan and Doc Savage almost didn't take place. The two of us received the good news about getting our chances at the staff counselors from Rod Romano one evening. A couple of hours later this

newsflash was followed up by Howard Feldman convincing the rest of us Cabin Five types to not do any of the cleanup duties for the next morning.

In addition to being threatened to have to run around the recreational field "10 times at midnight", Randy Lape and I were not going to be allowed to play in the camp volleyball contest. As Rod Romano put it, "There will be no representatives from Cabin Five at the counselor-student volleyball game this Saturday." Man, that hurt.

Luckily, after us Cabin Five guys won "Honors Cabin", Rod Romano was so giddy that he let Randy Lape and I back in as participants of this athletic event without even having the two of us to do any begging or be the recipients of a stern lecture that would begin with, "This is against my better judgment, but…."

The day of the big game arrived and I was surprised by what a big deal this contest was. The girls from the Allstate Division all traveled over to our area to watch this match making the attendance close to 200 people. Plus, the Allstate Boy's counselors were really talking pretty big and playing it up to the crowd.

There were two counselors with the first name of Mike. One was a pretty good guy that everyone liked, and the other, shall we say, was born without a personality. The latter stood up in front of the multitudes and announced, "This is the annual volleyball match between the men counselors and the students. The counselors have never once lost a match to our competition. However, if the counselors ever lose a best two out of three matches to an all-star team of Allstate Boys, we will purchase pizza and pop for both the Boys and Girls Allstate Division."

His highness' statement caused a twitter among us Allstate types. Free pizza and pop!! Real life civilian food!! I could tell now that the weight of the world was upon us Allstate volleyball participants. And by looking at the faces of our opposition, they didn't seem to concerned about scrambling around to place any food and beverage orders for that evening.

The first game of the match started when the ball was served right to me. I set up a pass to Randy Lape who spiked that ball so hard into the ground that I'm sure that a character from a Jules Verne novel is still looking for it.

And that's how it was for the first two games. Us Allstate kids won 15-8 and 15-7. It was basically no contest. Not only did this mean free eats and drinks courtesy of the Allstate counselors, it also made every member of the Allstate volleyball squad a hero for the last Saturday of our two-week stint at Fort Interlochen.

You know what else made those slices of double cheese and ground beef pizza taste so good that night? It was just knowing that Randy Lape and I were the members of the first Allstate Boys Division volleyball team that had ever beaten the counselors. If and when the National Music Camp opens up its Allstate Boy's Division Athletic Hall of Fame, Randy Lape and I will be in the class of the initial inductees. In fact, I might even grow a beard for this big occasion.

But looking back on this historical event, I think Randy Lape summed it up best when he said, "Ya know, Doc Savage. Those guys on the counselor's volleyball team were not that good of players. Most of the time they looked like the Keystone Cops running around out there. Do you realize how bad some of the previous student teams must have been to lose to those guys??"

Yes. Yes, I do, Randy Lape. Now quit thinking about that and go back to the city of Hillsdale and start working on our Hall of Fame acceptance speeches.

Randy Lape and The Flying Dutchman also took the time to discuss future colleges that they were hoping to attend. The Flying Dutchman's final two selections are: Michigan Tech University and, Louisiana Tech University, located in Ruston, Louisiana. Wherever that is.

Randy Lape wants to attend Hillsdale College, but wasn't sure that he could afford the tuition. Randy Lape thought that ultimately Western Michigan University would be his future education destination.

Doc Savage??? I remained deathly silent on this topic and will continue to do so for a long, long, long time.

As Randy Lape, The Flying Dutchman and I started to part ways, The Flying Dutchman mentioned to Randy Lape about Bill Zeigler's plans to be a National next summer at Interlochen and that Rod Romano was not coming back as an Allstate counselor. Randy Lape's response to this news was, "The two of you should apply for that position. You, Flying Dutchman, for the actual counseling duties; and you, Doc Savage, to play on the counselor's volleyball team." Now I have two reasons to grow a beard when I officially become a part of the National Music Camp establishment.

The time had gone fast since the end of our final rehearsal from this morning and I noticed that the Michigan-Vanderbilt football game was now well into the second quarter. It was time to get ready for the Band Day half-time show in addition to getting two more shots at taking on that in dominatable brick wall.

"White Lake Road"

Chapter #74 – "Hey, Archie!! Hey, Jughead!!"

September 20th – I made it back to the Hartland Band area just in time as my bandmates were starting to gather up their instruments to head down to the football field. Mr. Anderson did something really smart and let the surrounding bands in our area get the first shot at the brick wall before us. This turned out to be a shrewd move on his part because by the time us Hartland kids were done scrambling over the brick wall, I noticed a musician from another high school band crying quite loudly, holding her nose with her right hand and her broken glasses with her left hand.

Once we were down on the football field amongst the masses, the two songs that we were to perform seemed to come off pretty good. Oh, there were still high school bands that were finishing a couple of measures behind everyone else, but hey, no harm, no foul.

The highlight of the half-time show performance was when one kid from the band of lime green and banana yellow style band uniforms, took a piece of gum out of his mouth, dropped it to the floor of the astro turf and grounded his chewed-up stick of gum with his foot into this pool table type covering. And, yes, he was a trumpet player. What did you expect??

In past University of Michigan Band Day trips, as soon as the halftime show was over, Miss Franklin had us band kids high tail it back to the buses and Fenton High School. That was not the case with Mr. Anderson. Despite numerous pleadings, no, make that naggings, from Jim Koop and Terry Rodenbo, these appeals for an early departure home were falling on deaf ears as Mr. Anderson's response to these requests was a terse, "I want to watch the rest of the football game. When the contest is over, only then will we head back to Hartland High School." Yes, sir!!

There was now something taking place at this Band Day that I had not seen on my previous three trips. Rolls of toilet paper were being thrown from unknown parties that were sitting above us. One came within a few feet of me hitting the cement area of where I was sitting and made quite a loud impact type noise. I have never been hit by incoming roll of toilet paper before in my life and didn't want to stick around to see what kind of black and blue marks it would cause to my body.

So, I then made the executive decision to walk around the stadium to kill some time before "when the contest is over" and I am finally allowed to get back on the Hartland Consolidated School "chariot "to go home, when I saw a familiar face walking towards me. It was another Cabin Five buddy, Jerry "Louie" Levine. Louie Levine was from Kalamazoo, Michigan. Where ever that is. And he was one smooth operator. Even more silver-tongued than Jim Koop. Those two could talk themselves out of any situation.

Louie Levine was back to Interlochen for his second tour of duty when I met him and he had the Interlochen routine down to a science. I still remember my favorite Louie Levine story as clear as day. The way that Allstate Division Boys' participants are awaken every morning is that you hear radio music come on over some type of PA system. I still remember my first night at Interlochen not being able to get to sleep because I was too worried about not being

able to hear the radio music so that I would not have a late start for my first full day at the National Music Camp.

Well, hearing that morning radio blast was not a concern. I could have been asleep back at "White Lake Road" and still heard that music jarring me out of a sound sleep.

Well, after Louie Levine's first excursion of the National Music Camp, he went back home to Kalamazoo, Michigan. Mr. Levine, Jerry Levine, Sr., had spent 28 years in the United States Marines, and ran his house like the former drill sergeant that he was.

Apparently, the first morning back from Interlochen Louie Levine's father turned on the kitchen radio quite loud, loud enough to wake Louie Levine up from a sound slumber, who then yelled down from his bed room, 'TURN THAT BLANKETY BLANK RADIO OFF!!!"

Louie Levine added, "My father put his Drill Instructor hat back on and promptly yelled, "LEVINE!! GET DOWN AND GIVE ME 50!!" I had to go down stairs, still half asleep, and give my father 50 push-ups. Not your typical high school gym class type push-ups. No, United States Marine style push-ups. My arms are still killing me from that morning." A great story.

Louie Levine and I discussed the potential futures of Bill Zeigler and The Flying Dutchman, Interlochen style, and Louie Levine added, "I have two visits to Interlochen under my belt. The first time as part of the Allstate Division, the time just dragged by. Last Summer when I got matched up with misfits like you and Bad Hombre, I had a blast and the time just flew by."

"Time either goes really fast or it goes super slow at the National Music Camp. If the Flying Dutchman gets Rod Romano's old job, he'll have new faces coming in every two weeks, so his summer has the potential to move pretty fast. For Bill Zeigler, being a National with the same routine day after day, that could become a real drag for 56 days in a row."

Louie Levine and I continued to talk some more and I never cease to be amazed of how much more marching activities that other high school bands do, performance wise, than either of the two similar organizations that I have belonged to ever did. He added, "Today, other than having to travel 100 miles to Ann Arbor from Kalamazoo, this is an easy day. We just show up and stumble through two songs. Piece of cake."

"Our band director typically has us involved in high school band competitions, usually down in St, Joseph, Michigan or South Bend, Indiana. Those are long days!! You go out there and do your marching routines and you are judged not only how you sound and march but you have to stand at attention for what seems forever. Then you get some jerk of a judge who tries to make you turn your head and look at them so they can take points off because, 'YOU'RE AT ATTENTION!!"

"So, give me this type of weekend band function all day long. There's no pressure here other than trying not to break your neck when attempting to get over that lousy brick wall."

"White Lake Road"

I was in serious thought as to what Louie Levine had mentioned about the marching band competitions. Such was the intensity of my thoughts about how come we never did this kind of stuff at Fenton High School, and from what I could gather, there was nothing like this scheduled here for the Hartland Senior High Marching Band this school year either, that I did not initially hear two different voices behind me yelling, "HEY, ARCHIE!!" HEY, JUGHEAD!! YEAH, YOU TWO!!"

I sort of recognized these voices, and was not so sure that it was safe to turn around, but like fools, both Louie Levine and I did. Standing behind us were two University of Michigan Marching Band members, Mike Hebert and Steve, "Chicken Little" Smith. Both of them were counselors during Louie Levine's and my Allstate Division fortnight stay.

I assumed that these two gentlemen were going to advise me of my selection, along with Randy Lape, into the National Music Camp Hall of Fame Athletic Division, and that the both of us should go out and rent tuxedos for this upcoming ceremony. From what was stated to us next, my thoughts were vastly miscalculated.

Just as Cabin Five was getting ready to depart to our homes at the completion of our stay last Summer, Louie Levine took out a magic marker and started to draw a little picture, similar to a "Kilroy was here" type art work. Except his words were drawn on a wooden window shutter and they read, "Doc Savage slept here." All of us Cabin Five types got a big kick out of it, then we stepped out of the Cabin Five front door and went on with our lives.

Well, Louie Levine and I were to discover that the two Allstate Boys Counselors dressed as University of Michigan marching band members standing smack dab in front of us, while also being surrounded by other miscellaneous high school band members, didn't have the same sense of humor that us Cabin Five guys did.

Mike Hebert proceeded to speak to the two of us in an oratory type voice, "It took the two of us, plus Rod Romano, an hour-and-a-half to sand down the picture that one of you two clowns drew on that window shutter board. And since we had another two-week Allstate section starting in 16 hours, we didn't want them to see your art work and think that this was some type of Allstate Boys Division tradition."

"All three of us had better things to do on a Sunday afternoon and the only reason why we didn't bill your schools or parents for our labor and materials was because Rod Romano did some fast talking to stop us from pursuing this. So, get one thing straight, Archie and Jughead; no one on the Allstate Boys Division counseling staff wants to see either one of you within 100 miles of Interlochen as long as myself and Steve Smith are affiliated with the National Music Camp!!"

Louie Levine responded by saying, "Aw, you guys are just upset because you lost your precious little volley ball match to us last Summer." After that remark, I thought to myself, does Louie Levine tape the telephone conversations between Jim Koop and myself?? Because, word for word, if Jim Koop was standing right next to me, that's exactly what he would have

said to Mike Hebert and Steve "Chicken Little" Smith. I mean, we're talking "The Twilight Zone" kind of stuff here.

The four of us parted ways and despite the stern lecture that Louie Levine and I received, it was interesting to see the looks that we got from other participating Band Day groups that had witnessed two high school students conversing with "real live" University of Michigan Band members.

These stares were of the, "You actually know someone that is a member of the University of Michigan Band??" "I can't believe that those guys were actually talking to the both of you!! Wow!! Far out!!" Yeah, real far out!!

And just for the record, readers, I'm "Archie" and Louie Levine is "Jughead." Take my word for it.

It was still in the third quarter of this college gridiron game and while the majority of the high school bands that had been in the University of Michigan stadium seated near the Hartland Band since 9:00 AM had been smart enough to immediately leave after the halftime show festivities were completed, there were still a handful of remaining high school bands around us, including, shockingly, the Fenton High School Band.

I took a peek over at my former Band and I saw Jane Roberts sitting there all by her lonesome. The question now for me was whether or not I could scrounge up enough guts to go over there and give her a "How ya doing" or not?

Chapter # 75 – "Coronet Blue"

September 20th – I walked over to where Jim Koop and Terry Rodenbo were sitting to see if they could help me get my nerve up to go and speak with Jane Roberts. That plan was short-lived as I felt something whistle by my left ear and then saw some other type of missile fly past Terry Rodenbo's right shoulder.

Both of these unidentified flying objects turned out to be hurled rolls of toilet paper. While both of these projectiles missed Terry Rodenbo and I, they did find the right shoulder and upper back of Mr. Anderson. And from the way that Mr. Anderson cringed, you could tell that he was in severe pain and down for the eight count after being struck by these projectiles. I mean the man looked like he was in real agony!!

Mr. Anderson then forced himself up, and with great physical effort, turned himself around very gingerly and announced to us Hartland kids, "Let's go home." Whereas, Jim Koop responded, "No Way!! Me, Beardslee and Rodenbo want to watch the rest of the football game!!" As the Spanish population of the world would say, "Touché', Mr. Anderson."

Well, Mr. Anderson's declaration that it was time to get back to the school buses and head home pretty much answered the question as to whether I was going to go over and visit with Jane Roberts. Deep down inside, I suspect Mr. Anderson unknowingly did me a big favor.

While back on the buses and all seated, I opened up my trumpet case and saw that the kazoo that I purchased at last years' University of Michigan Band Day was still there. I waved the kazoo in the direction of Jim Koop and he looked in his trumpet case and he still had his kazoo as well. This meant that it was time to play the award winning "The TV Theme Show Name Game!!"

Terry Rodenbo and Katie explained the rules of this contest. A TV theme show was to be played on the kazoo and who ever guessed the correct name of the TV theme song now had control of the kazoo and could play their selection.

The winner of the game was the person who correctly guessed the most TV tunes. Also, since this was the last University of Michigan Band Day I was ever going to attend in my life, whomever the winner was, especially if they were an underclass person, I would let them keep the kazoo under the guise that it was only on loan from the "Mike Beardslee Museum and Archives."

I was hoping to be a repeat winner from last year when Jim Koop and I did this same event with the Fenton Band crowd. So, I knew that I could not reuse the "Honey West" theme song that allowed me to become victorious when this game made its debut. However, I did have another TV theme song up my sleeve that was going to guarantee me a victory.

The game started and I quickly discovered that these Hartland Band kids knew their TV theme songs. I was tied with Aisha Tredeau and Katie. I got Aisha Tredeau out on an old TV show that starred veteran actor, Pat O'Brien, with the theme song from "Harrigan and Son."

"White Lake Road"

It was now time to go into the archives of my brain and nail down this much-wanted triumph. I knew that movie star, Steve McQueen, would not fail me and decided to go with his old TV series, "Wanted Dead or Alive." An old time western TV show. "Wanted Dead or Alive" has been off the air for the last eight years. This TV show also had two different theme songs. One tune for the first season, and a second musical piece for seasons two and three. Dirty pool, you say? You betcha.

So, let's get this straight. I'm using a TV Show that has been off the air since at least March or April of 1961 and had two different TV theme songs. One, of which, sounded more like it was suited for a TV show like "The Untouchables" or any other TV show featuring cops and robbers, rather than a TV western.

Success is close and it is mine!! After I win this contest I will change my middle name from "Kevin" to "Kazoo". No, make that "King Kazoo!!"

Katie then immediately proceeded to get the correct name of the theme song from "Wanted Dead or Alive." I about died when she nailed that. And I figured out real fast that "King Kazoo" was in big trouble. It was now Katie's turn with the kazoo. If no one guessed Katie's selection, then she is the winner of the "TV Theme Show Game", 1969 style.

Katie started to play her choice and I must admit that it sounded familiar, but I just couldn't come up with an immediate answer. Some of the guesses tossed out included theme songs from such TV shows as: "Family Affair", "A Man Called Shenandoah", a TV series that for one season starred Robert "Flint McCullough", love that name, Horton of "Wagon Train" fame and "Run for Your Life. "All excellent picks but they did not hit the bullseye.

I was desperate to keep my winning streak intact and thought I came up with the winner based upon a show that I did not particularly care for, but my mother and Katie enjoyed watching, by the name of "Going My Way." A mediocre TV show at best, that had the following actors starring in it: Leo J. Carroll; Gene Kelly; and Dick York."

And I was wrong!! Katie's winning music number was almost worse than me winning last year with "Honey West." At least that TV show was on for a whole season. Katie won by using a TV show that if it even ran for 13 weeks I would be shocked, by the name of "Coronet Blue".

The show starred an actor by the name of Frank Converse and had a plot line about a man that gets drugged, is tossed into a river, suffers from amnesia and has a bunch of killers who have targeted him to be assassinated. Actually, it wasn't a half bad TV show and I enjoyed watching it immensely. But for whatever reason Coronet Blue never had a regular run as a TV series.

Well, at least Katie's victory kept the kazoo in the Beardslee household and more specifically, my trumpet case. And I can just see her leading a group of band kids in this game next year on this annual trip home from the University of Michigan Band Day. It will be interesting, though, to see what school district bus that Katie will be riding on during her Junior year of high school.

"White Lake Road"

After "The TV Theme Show Name Game!!" was over, Jim Koop was just playing and humming along on his kazoo, the same tune over and over and over again. Mr. Anderson finally turned around and in an exasperated manner, said to Jim Koop, "Don't you know the name of any other songs that you can play on that thing??"

Jim Koop stopped his performance, set the kazoo down very slowly and with a patented Jim Koop smile on his face, responded to Mr. Anderson, "I don't even know the name of this one." That cracked up the entire occupants of this school bus and Jim Koop's words of wisdom lasted us until we pulled into the Hartland High School parking lot.

Later that evening after poring through my "Sporting News", I thought back to the days' events. While I am certainly relieved to be done with ever having to attend any more University of Michigan Band Days and attempting to scramble over that brick wall, I must admit that it was great seeing my old Cabin Five buddies again. I had missed them more than I even imagined.

But do I have any desire to go back to Interlochen as a student or a counselor? The answer to that $64,000 magic question is easy; none. There are no aspirations at all on my part. I'll leave the life style of light blue-shirts, dark blue pants/corduroys, red sweaters and yellow belts to The Flying Dutchman's' and Bill Ziegler's' of the world.

Nor when todays conversations switched to the selection of colleges, which included: Oberlin; Wayne State; Michigan Tech; Western Michigan; Hillsdale or Louisiana Tech, got me revved up enough so that on this upcoming Monday morning I was going to sprint down to a Hartland High School counselor's office, grab a bunch of college entry applications and start filling them out. No, my plans to enlist into the United States Air Force are still all systems go. Just nobody else knows yet of these intentions.

It was a good day today. The second one in a row for me in fact. Plans for tomorrow include getting a good workout run in the morning and then watching the first regular season Detroit Lions football game as they go on the road to face the Pittsburgh Steelers.

I finally went to sleep but it was good to know that some things in life remain the same. Bad Hombre was still Bad Hombre.

"White Lake Road"

Chapter #76 – "The Curse of Bobby Layne"

September 21st – Big day today!! The start of the Detroit Lions football season is finally upon us!! It also marks the end of an era where my mother and I have constantly battled over the starting time of Sunday afternoon dinner in the Beardslee household during the National Football League season.

A Detroit Lion football game typically starts at 1:00 PM. That is also the same time that our Sunday dinner is served. And I must admit, it is a feast with even the good silverware of the household being broken out on this day. I mean we're talking; swiss steak; mashed potatoes; corn that I put on top of my gravy and mashed potatoes; red flavored Jell-O; German chocolate cake with a piece of vanilla ice cream on the side. And maybe if life is really good, on that rare occasion, there might even be a bottle of soda pop in the refrigerator that Katie and I can split or use to make ice cream floats!!

The only problem with this excellent meal is that it usually means I miss at least the first 30 minutes of a Detroit Lion football contest. Hey!! Don't sit there and give me this "boo hoo" stuff. Detroit Lions football is important to me!!

Nothing has ever seemed to work out for me so that I could actually have the opportunity to see the kickoff of the Detroit Lions game. I have tried eating fast. I mean I was just a shoveling those mashed potatoes down my throat. I suggested the use of a TV tray and letting me eat my meal in the family room where our TV set was located. Yeah, like that idea went over real big.

My next suggestion was how about since we are eating in the dining room of "White Lake Road" that we simply turn on the radio in the adjacent kitchen and I can listen to the Detroit Lions play while I eat? Brilliant!! Maybe not Mike Beardslee brilliant, but it should at least rate an honorable mention.

But before the words even left my mouth on this proposal, I knew what I had just said wasn't going to fly. During the week when it's supper time, the first thing I do is go to the "kitchen radio", tune to the "Bob Reynolds Sports Show", that runs from 6:15 PM to 6:30 PM on WJR AM, so that I can catch up on the latest sports news while I chowed down. But like clockwork, the last thing my mother does before she sets food down on the supper table is to turn the kitchen radio off.

Once my mother forgot to do this without even thinking kind of step in life, and mind you, this only happened once, to not only forget to turn off the radio during this time slot, she also overlooked turning down the volume. I was never so happy in my life to listen to commercials for ALCOA and hear the race results from Hazel Race Parkway. I could have died that night and my life would have been completely satisfying.

You got it. The radio idea is out, too. Maybe even faster than the TV tray brainstorm.

"White Lake Road"

Katie recommended a compromise with my mother that Sunday dinner could start at 12:30 PM instead of 1:00 PM during football season. A mere 30-minute difference. That proposal had been, no pun intended, on the table for the past six Detroit Lions football seasons, and for whatever unknown reason, this year, my mother finally agreed to this time change. I have no clue as to why.

I still remember the very first Detroit Lion game that I ever watched on TV. It was on Thanksgiving Day in 1962. We were at my Aunt Betty's house in Saginaw. This Aunt Betty is not to be mixed up with my other Aunt Betty of, "Tomorrow morning I have to go into Fenton High School and straighten out old man Walker" fame.

My Uncle Ed, whom I have never, ever seen him without a big fat cigar in his right hand and shot glass of whisky in his left hand, turned me on to becoming a huge fan of the Detroit Lions. The first game that I ever saw of the "Honolulu and Blue" play was against the famed Vince Lombardi Green Bay Packers. That turkey day the Detroit Lions' defense just ate up the Green Bay Packers offense and seemed to be sacking Green Bay quarterback, Bart Starr, like every other play.

The Detroit Lions in an impressive performance handed the eventual National Football League champions their only loss of the season. A great Detroit Lion victory that to this day is always the topic of conversation, football wise, come Thanksgiving.

Uncle Ed was a huge fan of former Detroit Lion legend, quarterback Bobby Layne. Bobby Layne was the leader of the great 1950's Detroit Lions championship teams. He was the kind of guy who played hard on and off the field. And whenever my family went up to Saginaw to visit my cousins, Elizabeth and Eddie, Uncle Ed would always tell me a Bobby Layne story between puffs on his cigar and sips from his shot glass of whisky.

One Sunday afternoon he said to me, "Kid. I still do not forgive the Detroit Lions for trading Bobby Layne. He was injured at the end of the 1957 season. The Lions front office decided that old Bobby was all washed up and traded him to the Pittsburgh Steelers for probably a bottle of warm, flat bottle of beer."

"That's when Bobby Layne placed on the Detroit Lions organization what is today known as "The Curse of Bobby Layne." When he was leaving for the Pittsburgh Steelers, Bobby Layne said, "That the Detroit Lions would not win for 50 years." And he was right. The Detroit Lions have not won a league championship since 1957.

Uncle Ed added, "A few years later, another Bobby Layne quote, intended as a shot at the Detroit Lions franchise went something like this; "I'd like to win a championship for the Steelers and for myself to shove down Detroit's throat!" So, there was no love lost between Bobby Layne and the Detroit Lions.

One day when I was trading football cards with Ricky Loveland, I was able to make a trade for a Bobby Layne football card when he was a member of the Pittsburgh Steelers. I was going to show off this prized possession the next time I saw Uncle Ed.

"White Lake Road"

Finally, the Beardslee family made it up to the city of Saginaw to visit my cousins, whereas, I proudly showed my Bobby Layne football card to Uncle Ed. Once I handed him my prized belonging, Uncle Ed took an unusually long drag on his cigar, and an even slower sip on his glass of whisky. After barely given the card a glance, Uncle Ed handed the Bobby Layne football card back to me and said, "That's great, kid."

Based upon all of the stories that I had heard from Uncle Ed about Bobby Layne's Detroit Lion years, Bobby Layne quickly became my favorite Detroit Lions' player of all time, despite the fact that by the time I became introduced to the world of the Detroit Lions' and became a diehard fan of them, Bobby Layne had long been traded away to the Pittsburgh Steelers.

I only ever saw Bobby Layne play once. That was during something called the "Playoff Bowl", officially christened the "Bert Bell Benefit Bowl." This was where the two runner-up teams to the division champions would play for the official third place finish in the National Football League.

By sheer coincidence on that January 1963 Sunday afternoon, the Detroit Lions were facing off against Bobby Layne's Pittsburgh Steelers. The Detroit Lions won a close game, 17-10, when Milt Plum, quarterback for the Detroit Lions, decided to play the only good game of his six seasons stay with the Honolulu and Blue.

Bobby Layne played a little bit in that game, and I finally got to see my favorite Detroit Lion player, albeit, in a Pittsburgh Steeler uniform, a few pounds heavier and a step or so slower from his glory days as quarterback of the Detroit Lions. This game was considered nothing more than an exhibition contest by the NFL. The outcome of it and any statistics accumulated did not formally make it into any official NFL record books. Therefore, "The Curse of Bobby Layne" was considered by many football minds to still be in effect and in good standing.

After eating my Sunday dinner, I sprinted from the dining room to the family room for the official start of the 1969 National Football League season. On the first play from scrimmage, Mel Farr, the great running back of the Detroit Lions, gained eight yards. I immediately thought to myself, "Man, life is going to be good today in the family room of "White Lake Road!!" I can just feel it."

Well, guess what. "The Curse of Bobby Layne" was still alive and healthy on this September, Sunday afternoon, as the current Detroit Lions with some actual half way decent young talent, lost to the Pittsburgh Steelers football squad, 16-13. Just an overall poorly played game by the Detroit Lions.

Now, would someone please explain this to me. How do the Detroit Lions lose to a NFL franchise, the Pittsburgh Steelers, that based upon their won-loss record over the past some 40 years, has been the laughing stock of professional football???

Do not even bother trying to answer that question. I will tell you how. The Lions should have put Greg Landry in at quarterback in place of Bill Munson, who had a few too many offensive

turnovers for my liking today, so that the Detroit Lions offense could not even come close throughout the majority of the game of putting the football in the end zone. That's how!!

After seeing the Detroit Lions in action today, maybe my mother's idea of starting Sunday dinner at 1:00 PM for these past years, a curse in itself, is not such a bad idea after all.

The only thing that made this Sunday even tolerable for me was when I opened up the "Flint Journal" and found an extremely interesting article to amuse my little mind.

Chapter #77 – "Fifth Place?? Fifth Place?? Gimme a Break!!"

September 21st – With the Detroit Lions off to a losing start to the NFL season and the "proud" owners of an 0-1 won-loss record, I forced myself to get in a workout run. Nothing fancy, just a run to the end of the paved portion of White Lake Road, turn around at Ben Eisley's driveway and come back home. An out and back run totaling a distance of two miles.

I badly needed this training run to get into shape for basketball tryouts. I should have pounded these two miles out and worked me up a good sweat. But it was instead a plodding type of workout. Nothing more than one foot in front of the other with the intent of solely getting home, plopping myself down on the couch in the family room and hoping that there is a piece of German chocolate cake left with my name on it to be washed down with a cold glass of milk.

What do I attribute to this lack of motivation on my part? Believe it or not, I think the cause of this less than desirable physical effort was because I was emotionally drained from the events of the last two days. And you can add one woeful effort on the Detroit Lions part to the mix as well.

The first halftime show of the season and how well it went really pumped me up last Friday night. I was so pleased with how the Hartland Marching Band performed that evening and the free ice cream treats compliments of Jim Koop and the trumpet section, that I could hardly get any solid sleep at all. An early wake up call for a Saturday morning did not help the cause any, either.

And yesterday with the seeing and walking down memory lane with my Cabin Five buddies from Interlochen at the University of Michigan Band Day, just brought me to an extreme high of being with them again.

In fact, I was so ecstatic from seeing my former partners in crime, that when I woke up this morning, I was in some sort of funk. I just couldn't get in in gear, even knowing that the start of the Detroit Lions season, of which, I have only been waiting anxiously for the past nine months, was now only hours away. I felt like a was a cast member of the zombie movie, "The Night of the Living Dead."

I suspect when you put all of these events together, plus with Jim Koop and I breaking out of the kazoos on the school bus yesterday for possibly the last time in our lives, probably contributed as well to this emotional letdown from the past couple of super great days in the life of Mike Beardslee.

Also, you could add into the lack of get up and go equation was the fact that anytime the Detroit Lions lose a game, especially to the sad sack Pittsburgh Steelers, I mentally convince myself that the upcoming week is going to be one lousy seven days. How pathetic is that??

I later opened up the "Flint Journal" to the sports section, and a headline caught my eye:

"Genesee-Livingston County Conference 1969 Football Prognostications".

"White Lake Road"

This well written article did a nice job of analyzing and predicting who was going to end up where league standings wise for the upcoming football season. And I must admit that there was a surprise or two in this commentary.

#1 – Swartz Creek Dragons	***By far the best offense in the conference, maybe even all of Genesee County. Could have as many as six first team all-conference players on the offense side of the ball, led by pre-season, offensive player selection of the year, Rick Pertler.***
#2 – Brighton Bulldogs	***Easily the best defensive unit in the GL. Maybe even better than some past dominating Fenton defenses. The Brighton defense, led by the best athlete in the conference, Dave Austin, will be so controlling, that the only other defense that could rival them talent wise, are the NFL Minnesota Vikings, AKA "The Purple People Eaters".***
#3 – Lake Fenton Blue Devils	***The Blue Devils make a leap in the league standings this season as they have the best returning offensive line in the entire GL.***
#4 -Howell Highlanders	***Rarified air this season for the Highlanders. This first division selection is based upon them having the most returning varsity lettermen of all GL teams. Despite that, they will still have to overcome some serious inexperience at quarterback.***
#5 – Fenton Tigers	***Despite being overrated as a power house team last year, the Tigers still won their ninth straight league conference championship on the back of Marv Pushman. However, Marv Pushman is gone and so are the chances of Fenton winning their 10th straight league crown. The Tigers will also field one of the worst defenses in GL history. And there have been some pretty bad ones along the way. Right, Hartland?? Right, Fowlerville??***
#6 – Ainsworth Spartans	***Sustained the most loss of talent of any other conference team from the 1968 season. The Spartans will be helped by an infusion of talent from some Flint Southwestern transfers, but not enough for them to get into the first division.***
#7 – Linden Eagles	***Linden has the most talented group of sophomores ever assembled in GL history. Check back with them for the 1971 season***
#8 – Pinckney Pirates	***The Pirates have the Fowlerville and Hartland football squads to thank for not being rated any lower in these standings.***
#9 – Fowlerville Gladiators	***The Gladiators have the best baseball players in the entire GL conference. Oh, that's right. This is football season.***
#10 – Hartland Eagles	***Poorest offensive and defensive lines in the league. Add a QB that is a walking turnover and this spells doom for the soar less Eagles.***

I must admit that after reading this commentary that the mention of a fifth-place predicted finish for the Fenton Tigers was somewhat of a shock. Fenton High School athletic programs never took fifth place in any sport, that is, with the exception of the men's tennis team.

The Fenton gridders have won the GL conference championship for nine consecutive seasons. And with serious talk about the GL conference ending its affiliation after the 1969-70 school year, I knew how important it was for my old high school to be crowned conference champs in football this season so that the history books will show that Fenton High School was the only team to be conference football champions during the 10-year existence of the GL conference.

Volume I - Bad Hombre

“White Lake Road”

The newspaper article mentioning of Marv Pushman not being around for the 1969 Fenton squad is worth being noted. There have been a tremendous number of great athletes in Fenton High School history. Bruce McClenna; Bill Hajec; Bob Bruder; Jim Czmerek; Terry Walker; Don Madden; Bobby Niles; Ben Lewis; and the list goes on and on and on. When you think of great athletes that wore the orange and black colors of Fenton High School, Marv Pushman’s name should appear on that list.

I knew Marv Pushman, not very well, when he was a year ahead of me at State Road Elementary School. I looked up to him but was always too scared to ever talk to him. Even when the two of us spent three years together on the track team at Fenton High School, I would always shrink away from his presence whenever I was near Marv Pushman.

Marv Pushman was a great athlete and leader even in his elementary school years. People in Fenton spoke about him in the same tone of reverence that the people here in the town of Hartland talk about Steve Gilmore being the greatest athlete ever in the history of Hartland athletics when he finally walks out the doors of the Hartland High School.

The Fenton Tigers won the football GL conference in 1968, but just barely. And they won it only because of Marv Pushman. If there was a first down needed by the Fenton offense, you gave the ball to Marv Pushman. If a clutch tackle or turnover was to be made on defense, Marv Pushman made that key play.

I still remember a cheer from a “Fenton Football Friday Pep Rally”:

“Pushman, Pushman, he’s our man,

If he can’t do it, nobody can!!”

Corny?? All day long. But for that 1968 Fenton Tiger football season, no truer words were ever spoken.

One day while eating lunch with my Fenton High School buddies, Bruce Gold and Dan Barkman, near the end of the 1968-69 school year, the two of them had mentioned to me that they weren’t sure that there was any player on the Fenton football team that could step up and replace Marv Pushman, who is now a student at the University of Michigan where he is on the Wolverine wrestling team, from a leadership or talent standpoint. Marv Pushman was not only an excellent high school football player, but he made the players around him better.

In addition to that concern, Bruce Gold said, “You didn’t hear this from me, but next season we just might have the worst defense in whole conference. Even worse than Fowlerville and Hartland. On offense, we’ll score points against anybody. But there are junior high football teams in the area that will be able to move the chains on our defense all game long.”

So, I had a hint that the Fenton footballers might be in for some rough times this season. But a fifth-place finish?? Seriously?? Come on, gimme me a break. That’s unheard of and will

never happen. I guarantee it. The individual who authored this article must be the same person who invented buttermilk!!

The funny thing is, while I think that I am making a better transition to the fact that I am no longer a Fenton Area Schools student, but a Hartland Consolidated Schools enrollee instead, and I readily admit that I am light years behind where Katie, Jim Koop and Terry Rodenbo are in this category. In fact, Katie already is more of a Hartland Eagle after only three weeks of school than some students who have been enrolled in the Hartland Consolidated Schools their whole educational life.

But I still find myself rooting for the Fenton Tigers football team. When I pull out the sports section of the "Flint Journal" or try to locate the final score of a football game or radio station scoreboard shows of "WJR" and "WGMZ-FM", it's not to see whether Hartland won their contest, or if my old, old school, Swartz Creek, put a couple of thousand points on the scoreboard. No, it's to see how the Fenton Tigers did that evening and if they are getting closer and closer to their goal of winning a 10th straight league GL football championship.

At times, I seriously wonder if my allegiances will ever totally switch from being a Fenton High Tiger to a Hartland Eagle.

Tomorrow morning starts the fourth week of the "greatest year of my life." And as Mike Beardslee's head hit the pillow tonight, the big question for the next seven days in my mind will be what type of halftime show that the Hartland High School Band is going to be putting on for this upcoming Friday night's contest against the Brighton Bulldogs.

September 22nd – The jeep ride into school for this Monday morning was a happy one. This is where the four of us play the infamous game of "What are the titles of the songs that we are going to perform at this upcoming Friday nights halftime show?" Just a great pastime!! And if Katie mentions, or even thinks of saying the theme song from "Coronet Blue", I will slam on the brakes, stop the jeep and make her walk the rest of the distance to Hartland High School!! I'm not kidding, either!!

Jim Koop, as reigning "Marcher of the week", started us off. First, though, he said, "Hey, Beardslee. I'm going to mention a name of a song and the group that performs it. You just nod your head in the affirmative like you have actually ever heard of the piece and the band." Okay, I can do that.

"My choice for one of the melodies this week," Jim Koop continued, "is from the group by the name of, "The Doors". And I vote we play one of their biggest hits, "Light my Fire." It's got a good beat to it and would be very easy to march to. Old man Anderson can go crazy with his grape vine and pin wheel marching routines with that tune."

Jim Koop added, "This is where you start nodding your head, Beardslee. Beatnik style." Okeydokey, one Maynard G. Krebs nodding of the head style coming up. That drew what was to be the second biggest laugh of this AM drive.

While I was nodding my head in a groovy style type of way, at least I think I was, the remaining occupants of the jeep were humming or singing Jim Koop's selection of "Light my Fire." I must admit that it does sound like it could be a pretty decent candidate for a halftime song.

Katie was up next and went with an oldie but a goodie, "I've Got Rhythm." Katie's explanation was this, "It's a snappy song and you could very easily do a drum feature with this song." She has an excellent point there and "I've Got Rhythm" is a tune that every kid in the Hartland Marching Band has probably heard before at least once before in their life. Never under estimate that point when it comes to the selecting of and performing halftime show music.

I must admit that I could see us playing Katie's recommendation as part of a Hartland High School Marching Band halftime show. But I am still not sold on the drum feature thing, however. The talent in that percussion section is just not there. I do hope those guys prove me wrong, though.

All of us held our breath as we a waited for Terry Rodenbo to say his traditional halftime song selection of "Spinning Wheel." But he caught us off guard when he stated, "How about a song by the "Beach Boys." Even you, Beardslee, have probably heard of them." Eh, don't bet your lunch money on that, Mr. Rodenbo.

Now just imagine in your mind actor, Bob Denver, nodding his head towards Dwayne Hickman during an episode of the former TV show, "The Many Loves of Dobie Gillis." Now

imagine me driving south bound on U.S.23 and using that nodding motion at the same time. You got it.

Terry Rodenbo continued by saying, "We could do "Good Vibrations." It's an easy tune to listen to. And if Mr. Anderson uses his imagination and comes up with a swinging marching band routine, it would be the best halftime show that we would do this whole season!!"

What Terry Rodenbo had just said about "the best halftime show of the whole season" is an interesting point. This is my fifth season of high school marching band. And one of the consistencies during this time frame is that I have never been a member of a marching band unit that has ever performed two worthy of bragging about halftime shows in a row. Never. Not even close in fact.

There are various reasons for that. And confronting us this week is probably the main issue. We are facing a marching band's worst nightmare of back to back halftime shows. We had three weeks to prepare for our first halftime show from this past Friday. With that much practice time, a marching band has no excuse to not perform well.

But are we the type of marching ensemble that can come off one tremendous effort and sustain that energy with only five rehearsals to work with? Which includes, playing music selections for the first time today plus learning anywhere from two-three new marching routines. And then hope that Mother Nature cooperates this week as well. Well, we're going to find out.

I know how this group does with three weeks to prepare for a halftime show. Geez, Louise, that's a life time to prepare for a halftime show. But I silently admit this to only myself, it will be interesting to see how we do with one weeks' prep time.

Which led to my turn to mention a recommendation of a musical selection for this Friday night. "On one of my "Baja Marimba Band" record albums, they play a great arrangement of "Windy" … I don't know if was the fact that I said the name of the group "Baja Marimba Band" or of the fact that I mentioned that I owned some of their albums, but that drew the biggest laugh of the drive in this morning. We're talking belly laughs here. Well, at least I can finally stop nodding my head.

Band Class could not get here fast enough for me this morning. I just knew in my bones that we were going to be performing some type of musical arrangement from the Baja Marimba Band. I could visualize the sheet music just sitting on a music stand calling out to me in the language of Spanish.

Well, I was half right. When I entered the Band Room, there was indeed some half-size pieces of sheet music placed on a music stand. But when I hurriedly reached out to grab the sheet music to see the titles of same, I was extremely disappointed.

The two songs that Mr. Anderson had selected for the upcoming halftime show were titled, "What a Wonderful Life", a song that world-famous trumpet player, Louis Armstrong, was known for, and the latter tune was from a hit song by crooner extraordinaire, Mr. Frank Sinatra, "It Was a Very Good Year."

Now, I admit that these are nice songs to listen on the radio. But there ain't no way that these are songs that any high school band should use for a halftime show. One, maybe, but certainly not both in the same night.

I have a personal theory for the picking out of marching band songs for performances at a halftime show. And that was to match the musical selection up with what is the strength of your marching unit. Right this very second in Hartland, Michigan, that honor belongs to the trumpet section. We should not be playing melodic songs that appear on a Frank Sinatra bestselling LP record album. No!! We should be playing "Joshua", or some other similar type songs that allows people like Jim Koop and I to blast our little brains out!! And these simply are not the jingles to do that.

I looked around the rest of the Band Room to see if it was just me that was discouraged with these music choices. I saw no other member of the Hartland High School Marching Band jumping up and down in excitement with a thrilled expression on their faces that these music selections had all of the elements of another great halftime show. Nothing.

What I saw instead was Terry Rodenbo with a disgusted look on his face, then proceeding to throw the pieces of sheet music up in the air and letting them fall to the floor of the Band Room. My sentiments exactly.

Could things get worse for this morning's Band class, you ask?? Yeah, they could and did. Mr. Anderson announced to us Band kids when we were gathered around him on the marching band field, "This Saturday, my alma mater, Central Michigan University, will be hosting their annual "CMU Band Day." Because the date of this event has conflicted with the University of Michigan Band Day for the past few years, Hartland has not been able to attend. Well, good news. This year we will be there."

I again made a visual survey of my bandmates and they were about as enthused as traveling to Mount Pleasant, Michigan, where ever that it, as I was. In fact, there was more excitement generated by the discovery this morning of our halftime show music, than knowing that there was an event by the name of "CMU Band Day."

There was no way that anything further that Mr. Anderson could do or say to make this class session be any worse than it was already. You got it. Keep on reading.

Mr. Anderson added, "Now, the CMU Band Day format is different than how the University of Michigan Band Day works. An attending band for this Saturday is only allowed to bring 20 bands people. I know all of you want to attend this big event and I apologize that I cannot bring all of you."

"White Lake Road"

"So, tomorrow after school, Tuesday, we will have tryouts and from those results I will select the 20 lucky persons to represent Hartland High School as our CMU Band Day Honors Band members at my alma mater." Yippee, skippee!!

Tryouts?? Tryouts?? Now let me get this straight, Mr. Anderson. You're asking us Band kids for the second weekend in a row to give up a Saturday, to travel what, 250 miles round trip in a school bus and on top of that, have to audition for this glorious honor?

Just for the record, Mr. Anderson, I was born at night, but not last night. I have a date with a "Sporting News" magazine and a Lazy-Boy chair this Saturday morning. So, no thanks, Mr. Anderson, but I will pass on the opportunity to set foot on the sacred and hallowed grounds of your alma mater.

And to make sure that this one lousy Monday was not solely restricted to Band Class, Mr. Collins gave us kids in "Economics Class", our first "30 Seconds" of the year for being a little to vociferous when class started.

It was finally off to jeep and back home to the safety of "White Lake Road." I couldn't get out of Hartland High School fast enough. And I didn't.

Mr. Anderson caught me before I could make my escape. As he approached me the first thing that came to my mind was that I hoped he was not going to ask me about the music he had selected for this weeks' halftime show. After our conversation was completed, however, I wished that was what we had talked about.

Mr. Anderson specifically wanted to talk to me and get my thoughts about how tomorrow nights' auditions for CMU Band Day should be run. I made a simple recommendation that the tryouts should consist of playing the Hartland school fight song, "Varsity", marching around the Band Room while in front of all of the other auditionees.

Mr. Anderson seemed to like that idea. In my mind, I was just one second from pushing in the clutch of the jeep when Mr. Anderson asked me, "Are you looking forward to being on the campus of my alma mater this Saturday?" Oh, man, you're killing me, Mr. Anderson!!

I looked him in the eyes and said, "I think that I will sit this trip out. You should be able to easily get the 20 kids that you need. In fact, I probably won't even be missed."

Mr. Anderson looked at me with a facial expression that I had not seen him display in the nearly six years that I had known him. He then stated to me in a short, cold, biting type of speech, "You are the president of the Hartland High School Senior Band, Beardslee. I hold you as well as the other two officers in this Band to a higher standard. If the three of you don't show any interest in the CMU Band Day trip, then the rest of the Band members will not either!!"

At the end of this discussion, Mr. Anderson performed a text book "To the Rear March" marching step and off he went with smoke coming out of his ears with every footstep he took while striding down the school hallway. Well, that conversation was fun.

Later that evening I gave some serious thought about what took place between Mr. Anderson and myself some six hours earlier. Believe me, I do not want to attend the CMU Band Day. I don't care whose alma mater is. Even if it's Stephanie Powers'.

The problem is that I don't have a built-in excuse like Jason Shattuck does. He will be off with the cross-country team this Saturday in Albion, Michigan, where ever that is, for the "Albion Relays." Hey, Coach Campbell, is it too late for me to join the cross country team?

But what really perturbed me about today was the way that Mr. Anderson verbally lit into me. I have been reamed out by more than my share of coaches and teachers at Fenton High School. But I didn't respect them enough that it made me want to go into "Beardslee's Barn" and cry my eyes out.

I thought that Mr. Anderson and I had a different relationship than that of the normal teacher-student type. In my mind, we were friends. Sort of a big brother-little brother kind of rapport thing. I guess I was wrong.

I talked to Katie about my after-school chat with Mr. Anderson and specially emphasized what Mr. Anderson had stated with his line of, "I hold you as well as the other two officers of this Band to a higher standard." Katie agreed with me that the message of Mr. Anderson could have been delivered in a more mature manner, but that he did have a valid point in what he said.

Katie added, "I mean let's face it. The two of us, as well as Jim Koop and Terry Rodenbo, are the primary leaders of this Band. Whether we like it or not, we are going to have to attend tomorrow night's tryouts, give it our best and set an example for the rest of the Band kids."

As usual, Katie was right. So, guess who is going to be auditioning for the opportunity to attend CMU Band Day tomorrow night after school?? You got it. The kid with the ruggedly handsome looks and spiked teeth.

With today finally behind me, I tried to get to sleep but a variation on an old nursery rhyme kept running through my mind before I finally dozed off:

"The nodding of the head;

The nodding of the head;

Hi ho the Dario;

The nodding of the head."

"White Lake Road"

Chapter #79 – "Wrath Mode!!"

September 23rd – Today was the second strange consecutive Band practice day for the Hartland High School Marching Band. The marching band rehearsal had some good news and bad news to it today. The good news was that Mother Nature cooperated and we were able to get a full rehearsal completed.

The bad news was that the marching routines for these songs are just to slow, no make that methodically slow, similar to the music we're playing. There is no sharpness or crispness to the steps. We're doing routines that are sluggish and lethargic. This Friday night's halftime show is going to be a rough one to pull off.

But the you know what was hitting the fan before marching band practice even started. Katie and I met with Mr. Anderson this morning and agreed with him that Senior Band officers should be held to a higher standard and that the three of us, including, Teri Andrews, as vice-president, should be setting an example for the remainder of the Band membership. Therefore, we will be there with "bells on" for the CMU Band Day Honors Band tryouts after school tonight.

Mr. Anderson stated, "Before I forget, Beardslee, I need to talk to you about something important after tryouts tonight." Then he added in a tone of voice that had a touch of snippiness in it, "I'm glad that the two of you have come to realize your obligations to this unit as Band officers and will be attending this evening's auditions. Having two officers there tonight will guarantee a good turn out."

I didn't give to much thought as to what Mr. Anderson had just said to us. I was actually more intrigued by what was so important that he wanted to wait to talk to me about after tryouts and not in front of Katie. However, the "wrath of Katie" was about to surface. She had listened to every word that Mr. Anderson had said and immediately responded, "What do you mean only two officers being there tonight?? What about "her highness", Teri Andrews? She's going to be there, right??? Right??"

Mr. Anderson's face immediately got red. Santa Clause garb type red. The medicine that he was dishing out to me yesterday, was now being forced down his throat with a filthy and grimy spoon. He had been caught with his "Having two officers there tonight" line. He then proceeded to stammer out a very weak, "Teri Andrews mentioned that she had no desire to attend the CMU Band Day event this Saturday." Finally, Teri Andrews and I have something in common!!

I suspected that there was more to this story then Mr. Anderson was letting on. In his never-ending battles with Mrs. Andrews, I'm sure that this was one more skirmish that he could do without. However, Katie, being very protective of her older brother, said to Mr. Anderson, "You're using a double standard, Mr. Anderson!! And the first time is free. The next time…well, there should not be a next time."

"White Lake Road"

Aaahh. The "Wrath of Katie." There is nothing better in life when I am not on the end of that fury.

Mr. Anderson knew that he had messed up in a big-time way and murmured something to the effect the he would discuss this with Teri Andrews and see if he could get her to change her mind about attending the CMU Band Day. Katie kept the foot to the pedal and said, "Make sure that when you talk to her that you thoroughly explain the standard that you hold ALL of us Senior Band officers to"

Do I smell a possible boycott, led by Katie, of the CMU Band Day by the members of the Hartland High School Marching Band??? I suspect it wouldn't take much to get this type of movement in gear.

After Mr. Anderson swallowed his pride from the "lecture" that he was on the receiving end of from Katie, he immediately went over to Teri Andrews, pulled her off to the side off to the side where he must have been giving her the "higher standard" speech that I received yesterday. I could tell by Teri Andrews' body language, the quick up turn of her head in a defiant look, fists placed on her hips of the black, flower print dress that she was wearing, that the message had been delivered and she was not taking it well.

I thought to myself, Mr. Anderson will be hearing from Mrs. Andrews about that conversation. And real soon.

At the end of the school day, it was time for the after-school tryouts and when I walked into the Band Room, I did a head count and there were exactly 20 people here. I thought great. Wave a magic wand over our heads, Mr. Anderson, and make it official that we are the CMU Band Day Honor Band students that will be representing the Hartland Consolidated Schools and call it a day.

My course of bad luck continued, however, and Mr. Anderson went through the ritual of auditions. I was called on first and gave it a good effort. My trumpet tone was good and my penny loafers were just a marching up a storm on the floor of the Band Room!! Despite still having no urge to go to Mount Pleasant, Michigan this Saturday, aside, it felt good to have, at least in my mind, a good tryout in front of my peers.

Not to out done, Jim Koop went next and after his excellent efforts of blasting, Varsity", said to Mr. Anderson, "Hey, Mr. Anderson!! I can add a sharp or a flat in front of every note and do my tryout over again if you want!!"

Despite this generous offer of display of musicianship on Jim Koop's part, Mr. Anderson passed. And Jim Koop should be happy that Mr. Anderson didn't take him up this suggestion.

I know the difficulty of what Jim Koop was proposing to do. By adding a flat or a sharp in front of every note, it not only changes the musical key of a song, it also makes the trumpet player have to use a whole new set of fingerings. To march and do that at the same time would

be no easy feat. Jim Koop, however, I must thank you, you just may have stumbled onto something new for me to try during my trumpet practice sessions at "White Lake Road."

Since Mr. Anderson wanted to speak with me about some "important" topic, I had to stick around to see the rest of the tryouts. Katie, Terry Rodenbo, Aisha Trudeau and Randi Lynch, all had exceptional auditions and in my humble opinion, would have easily made this honor's band no matter how many other Band kids would have tried out.

It was interesting, however, to see Teri Andrews' efforts tonight at the tryout. She was on the opposite end of the scale. First of all, she was just standing there watching the rest of us go through the paces. Her clarinet case was unopened and, in fact, still located in the band instrument storage bins area.

Mr. Anderson then said to her, "Teri Andrews you're are up next." Teri's response was, "I would think that since I am a Band officer that I am automatically a member of this Honors Band and should not have to audition."

Wow!! I about died when I heard the words come out of her mouth for two reasons. First of all, I was just positive that Mr. Anderson was going to light into her like he did to me yesterday.

The second reason for my almost premature death was that I wish I had been smart enough to first mention to Mr. Anderson the phrase of, "I would think that since I am a Band officer that I am automatically a member of this Honors Band and should not have to audition." That's a great line. I'm kicking myself for not thinking faster on my penny loafers.

However, Mr. Anderson didn't even get to say one word before Katie piped in saying directly to Teri Andrews, "Hey, little queenie!! Yeah, you!! My brother and I were out there auditioning in front of everyone else in this room and we're Band officers. What makes you so special??"

Aaahh, the wrath of Katie in action for the second time today!! She should charge admission when she goes into "wrath of Katie" mode.

Teri Andrews, despite some pleading looks with her emerald green eyes towards Mr. Anderson and the rest of the occupants of the Band Room, shuffled over to get her clarinet case; took an agonizingly long time to put her clarinet together; and an even more excruciating amount of time to put the reed on her clarinet. I mean this whole saga must have taken at least 10 minutes.

Finally, a "Come on, Andrews!! Supper is getting cold!!", comment from Jim Koop, ultimately got her out in front of the rest of the Band. And shall we say, her performance was mediocre at best. She didn't pick up her feet when marching. And put even less of an effort when it came to the playing of "Varsity." It was not played in a marching band style and the ending musical notes of the school song coming out of her clarinet were badly out of tune.

It was like Teri Andrews was deliberately trying to flunk her audition. Man, I should be taking notes from her!!

Jim Koop leaned over to Terry Rodenbo and said, "Maybe we can get away with only having 19 members of this Honors Band." Despite the fact that that comment was probably only intended for the ears of Terry Rodenbo, it drew a lot of snickers from all parties sitting in the rows of bleachers in the Band Room.

You could tell that Mr. Anderson was non-to happy with the tryout efforts of one Teri Andrews. However, when he stood up in front of us auditionees and read off the names of the people who would be leaving Hartland High School at 6:00 AM this Saturday morning to travel to Mount Pleasant, Michigan, yes, I said 6:00 AM, Teri Andrews' name was on that list.

With the crowd starting to thin out, Mr. Anderson then motioned me into his office and shut the door behind us. I was fully expecting an apology from him for being so sharp with me yesterday afternoon.

Instead he turned towards me and asked, "Starting next Monday, how would you like to be the drum major of the Hartland High School Marching Band? Give it some thought, but I will need an answer by Thursday at the latest."

"White Lake Road"

Chapter #80 – "A Strutting Peacock"

September 23rd – Mr. Anderson's question about whether I wanted to become drum major came out of left field and truly shocked the fizzies out of me. During one of my trumpet private lessons with him a few years ago, he mentioned that the high school band that he marched in only had a total of 15 kids in it. So, his band director made the decision that actual marchers were more important than having a drum major. In essence the band director was the drum major. He would blow the whistle for all commands of halftime shows, parades, in addition to doing the conducting of all songs.

Mr. Anderson added that when he took his first band director's position at Beaverton High School, where ever that is, his band's total number of students were a little bit larger than his old high school band, but not by much. So, he also went without a drum major in order to get another music producing player on the marching band field as well.

This was a totally different set up of what I had seen during my marching days at Fenton High School. There was always a drum major and holding that title was a big deal. And according to "The Flying Dutchman," Miss Franklin is going with two drum majors during marching band season for this current school year.

That's a lot of drum majors. I guess the need for two drum majors is that if one gets lost during a parade, the marching band will still have the remaining drum major to lead them back to the high school.

I had never really had any grandiose desire to ever become a drum major, with the exception of one time, and that was for all of the wrong reasons. There is something called the "Arion Award". This honor is presented to the "most valuable senior" in Band. I became aware of the Arion Award during my sophomore year when Miss Franklin initially introduced it to us Fenton Band kids. I have salivated over winning that award ever since.

So, at the end of my junior year, I made up my mind that if I added the title of drum major to my Band resume, which already included Band officer, Band Council member, solo and ensemble appearances, All-Star Band selectee and attending Interlochen later that summer, that might be enough to get me this badly desired prestigious honor.

When I met with Miss Franklin to discuss this brilliant idea on my part, she didn't hesitate one second. She shot my notion down faster than 1964 Olympic gold medal winner, Bob Hayes, running the 100-yard dash. Her response was, "You're too important to the marching band as a trumpet player. I simply need you more as a trumpet player than a drum major." End of discussion.

I didn't particularly like Miss Franklin's message and immediately went to "Beardslee's Barn" and sulked over it for a couple of days as I had fully made up my mind that her denial to me for becoming the next drum major of the Fenton High School Marching Band had done severe damage to my chances of ever winning the Arion Award.

"White Lake Road"

It took a while, but looking back on it, I can now understand her decision. Guy Thompson and Dick Wilcox, both excellent trumpet players and "Blaster's Extraordinaire", had just graduated from Fenton High School.

The next generation of trumpet players were myself, Jim Koop, Greg Risner and Vaughn Bollinger. Entering into the 1968 marching band season, none of us had really established that we were worthy replacements of Messrs. Thompson and Wilcox. Two of that foursome eventually did reach this lofty goal and maintained the tradition of "Trumpet Blasters, Extraordinaire."

So, this request from Mr. Anderson was truly a shocker for me and one that I had to look at seriously. Two immediate thoughts came to my mind based upon this invite.

Question #1 was easy. Why?? The drum major position was all mine. No questions asked. No tryouts. Nothing. I could take the never been worn before, or rarely been dressed in drum major uniform home tonight, see how it looked on me and "parade" around in it in front Katie and my mother.

The only reason I can think of is that in 12 days, I go back to Dr. Alfred's office for the final stage of the putting on of my permanent caps for my front teeth. Does Mr. Anderson think that my new teeth will impair my trumpet playing like it did for a brief moment at the end of August?

At that same time when I had advised Mr. Anderson of "the end of my trumpet playing career", I had also been pretty vocal with him that I had no interest in switching over to the playing of any other instruments. Knowing that, plus the concern about my future as a trumpet player, is this Mr. Anderson's way of keeping me actively involved with the marching band instead of hanging out with Greg "Pretty Boy" Sanders during fourth hour study hall? It's possible.

The second issue that gave me some serious reservations about this offer, was; would I even be any good as a drum major? I readily admit that I would rather be a trumpet player than the person leading a marching band down the football field or on the main street of a city during a parade.

During my four years as a member of the Fenton High School Marching Band, I had witnessed two drum majors up close and in action. The first was, Brian "Beany" Bretzke. Now he was a showman!! While he didn't twirl a baton at all, he knew how to get a crowd to notice every physical movement that he made when leading the band during a pre-game and halftime show.

Beany Bretzke was an equally impressive performer off the football field as well. While the Fenton Tigers varsity football teams were in the process of winning their umpteenth consecutive football game and on their way to another GL Conference championship, Beany Bretzke, while in the stands with the rest of us Band kids, would stand up and yell out his favorite cheer:

"RAH RAH REE!!

KICK HIM IN THE KNEE!!

RAH RAH RASS!!

KICK HIM IN THE OTHER KNEE!!"

Us Band kids always knew what Beany Bretzke's punch line was going to be, but we always held our breath and squealed with delight when he finished with, "KICK HIM IN THE OTHER KNEE!!" Great stuff.

The drum major that followed the Beany Bretzke era, was Mike Hicks. He was of a different style than Beany Bretzke. Less flair. Not as much personality. More disciplined with very, very mechanical movements. Mike Hicks was also more demanding of us Band kids than Beany Bretzke ever was.

The primary difference between the two drum majors was that all of us lowly marchers wanted to please Beany Bretzke and that was how he got that extra effort out of us. The feelings toward Mike Hicks were pretty much the opposite of Beany Bretzke. I never had any problem with Mike Hicks. I liked the guy and considered him along with Guy Thompson to be mentors for Mike Beardslee early on in my Senior Band career.

But that wasn't always the case for a certain portion of the Fenton High School Marching Band members. Right, Jim Koop and Bill Wilhoit????

If life was perfect, you would combine the strengths of Beany Bretzke and Mike Hicks. You do that, now you have yourself one halfway decent high school drum major. If I would have had a choice of whom I would have patterned my drum major career after, I would have preferred to have been a Beany Bretzke type drum major. Always having the crowd watching your every step and turn. Never being able to take their eyes of off you because the multitudes in the stands not once would know what marching maneuver I was going to perform next. But that opportunity never arose for me.

While Terry Rodenbo and I were waiting at the jeep for Jim Koop and Katie to meet us for the trip home, I mentioned to Terry Rodenbo the offer that was on the table for me from Mr. Anderson. He looked at me for a second and proclaimed, "You're a trumpet player!! Not a strutting peacock!! Why would you even consider such a foolish idea of becoming a drum major??"

I was silent upon hearing Terry Rodenbo's response. But he was right. I am a trumpet player, not a drum major. Or, to put it in Terry Rodenbo lingo, "not a strutting peacock." I have my answer for Mr. Anderson and I won't even need till this Thursday to reach my monumental decision.

Terry Rodenbo then said, "I can tell by the look on your face that you are going to remain a trumpet player. Good for you. But let me give you some advice. Old man Anderson is probably not going to be happy with your verdict. So, this is what you do. Tonight, the both of us will give some serious thought about who you can recommend instead as drum major. Give him a couple of names and your reasoning. That will get you back in Anderson's good graces."

An excellent plan. In fact, it was so superb that let the official record show this was my idea and not Terry Rodenbo's.

While I was practicing my trumpet this evening and playing out of one of the few million trumpet etude books that I am the proud owner, I was thinking about two things. One. I was putting a sharp and flat in front of every note being played. Man!! That's harder to do than I realized!!

Secondly, I came up with the names of nine other people to consider for the position of drum major, finally narrowing them down to two first-rate candidates that I would recommend to be the "strutting peacock" of the Hartland Senior High School Marching Band starting next Monday. I mean we are talking about two, "KICK THEM IN THE OTHER KNEE!!", quality candidates.

I turned off the lamp in my bed room and turned on the radio to the WGMZ-FM, to fall asleep to. Before my eye lids officially put the close on this September day, I thought to myself, "Good evening, Beany "RAH RAH RASS" Bretzke, where ever you are."

"White Lake Road"

Blog #81 – "10-8=2"

September 24th – Last night I had given a lot of thought as to my meeting with Terry Rodenbo concerning the issue of who was going to be the new drum major of the Hartland High School Marching Band. I ran 10 names, including mine, through my mind, and ultimately came up with two recommendations that I will compare with Terry Rodenbo's endorsements. Here we go:

Mike Beardslee – I gave this offer of the drum major position from Mr. Anderson even more thought during breakfast this morning. I have not changed my viewpoint at all. Bottom line is that I have no desire to be a drum major. I'm a trumpet player. At least at this point in my marching band career. If the permanent caps prove to be the end of my trumpet playing days, then I'll change my thinking on switching over to another instrument, just grab me a baritone and hang out in the low brass section with Terry Rodenbo and Jason Shattuck. At least that experience will be good for a few cheap laughs.

Jim Koop – I would never wish the position of drum major on him. Much like myself, Jim Koop is a trumpet player. But he's the type of performer who needs a trumpet, snare drum sticks or a microphone in his hand when out doing his thing in front of a crowd. Not a drum major's baton. I seriously doubt that Jim Koop would ever consider being a drum major. Besides, with me still not being back at full strength trumpet playing wise, his "half of the band" still is better than my "half of the band."

Katie Beardslee – Now this is interesting selection to look at. I doubt that Katie would ever show any serious interest in becoming a drum major at this point in her high school career. Despite the fact that she does have more than her share of, "Look at me!! Look at me!!, in her. This is her first shot at being a section leader of the percussion section. And contrary to her opinion that this section is ready for a drum feature at a future halftime show, of which I am not fully convinced is ever going to take place during my life time, the improvement in this mostly freshmen laden percussion section is starting to come on. Primarily because of Katie's leadership. As Jim Koop always says to Katie when she brings up the topic of a drum feature, "Katie Beardslee. Your percussion section is only two drummers away from being ready to put on a real super drum feature. Ringo Starr and Buddy Rich." Whenever I hear that Jim Koop line I have to bite my lip not to laugh out loud and also avoid drawing blood at the same time. Now next year, or the year after that, if Katie is still a student of the Hartland Consolidated Schools, and that's not a gimme, I could see her taking on this challenge very easily, especially if it meant that she was a trail blazer opening up the doors for other female members of high school bands in the state of Michigan to become future high school marching band drum majors. I don't doubt for one second that in the not so far upcoming months when I come home on leave from a United States Air Force base, that when I walk through the front door of "White Lake Road", that one of the things I will see laying on the dining room table will be a bunch of brochures for Drum Major Camps that Katie will be asking my mother to send her to. No doubt.

Terry Rodenbo – I know where Terry Rodenbo stands on this issue. Much like Jim Koop and myself, he has no interest in the drum major position. He likes taking his baritone out on the marching band field and just a blasting away. Would Terry Rodenbo be a good drum major? Yeah, I think so. Would he enjoy being one? Now that's the magic question. I suspect not. So, put me down for a certified no vote. I do wonder, however, if Terry Rodenbo would look at this drum major position a little bit closer if he was going to be back at Hartland High School for his senior year? Which, by the way, based upon the most recent update from the Rodenbo household, has him still going to be back at Fenton High School come September 1970.

Teri Andrews – She is the only reason why I would even somewhat consider taking on the duties of the drum major position, but again, for all of the wrong motives. I would take this role only to prevent Teri Andrews from getting it. Could she do the job?? Maybe. From what I have heard about her is that she is a pitcher/first baseman on the Hartland High School Softball team, so she probably has the physical coordination that goes with the territory of being a drum major. But that little show that she put on at CMU Band Day Honors Band tryouts yesterday was a total turnoff to a good many of us who witnessed that behavior. Is this someone, who definitely displays an attitude of entitlement, the individual that you want to be the face of your high school band?? I'm not so sure. And make no ifs, ands, buts, about it, Teri Andrews, will fully expect the drum major position to be handed to her by Mr. Anderson, just like he did with me. Another reason why you cannot under estimate Teri Andrews' reasoning for wanting this prestigious position is based upon some recent rumors floating around Hartland High School. The Hartland High School Homecoming night festivities are just a little over two weeks away. And Teri Andrews has let it be known that she wants the title of Homecoming Queen on her future resume. And being named as drum major, the first one that the Hartland High School Senior Band has had in quite some time, might be a nice calling card when the Hartland faculty looks at a person's eligibility to have their name placed on an official Homecoming Queen ballot. There are probably better, and I am not saying that I am one of them, drum major candidates than Teri Andrews. But, man, I would never count her out, especially if Mama Andrews gets involved. I have no doubt that Mama Andrews is still smarting over the fact that Mr. Anderson never went along with her demand of, 1) A flag corp; and 2), that her oldest daughter be the captain of the flag corp. Don't go to sleep on Teri Andrews and the drum major position just yet.

Randi Lynch – I place Randi Lynch in a similar category as Katie, except that Randi Lynch probably does not get the credit that she deserves as the result of being in the shadow of Teri Andrews. Teri Andrews is the section leader for the clarinets during marching band season. But, very much like Katie, Randi Lynch is the driving force behind making the clarinet section picking up their feet in marching routines, trying to be the first group to restart a pregame or halftime show drill when Mr. Anderson pulls up the megaphone and yells at us, "Okay!! Back to the end zone!!", and to have the clarinet section out blast the trumpet section. (Don't bet your hot lunch money on the latter taking place, Randi Lynch. It ain't going to happen.) Both the clarinet and percussion sections, especially from a marching standpoint, have made great strides since our first marching band practice of the year. Much like Katie, I can see Randi Lynch as a future drum major, if she wanted to go that route. Where I really think that Randi Lynch would be a tremendous benefit to future Hartland High School Marching Bands, however, is if the flag corp idea ever gets off of the ground. And I could see Mr. Anderson

implementing this idea, oh, say, 15 seconds after Teri Andrews receives her high school diploma in early June of 1970. Randi Lynch would be the perfect Band member to be the first captain of that unit to get them up and running.

Mark Nevers – When Terry Rodenbo and I will meet later and discuss who we are going to recommend to Mr. Anderson for the drum major position, I can just hear him say, "ARE YOU CRAZY?? JUST BECAUSE YOUR MOTHER LOVES MARK NEVERS AND HE'S THE SON SHE NEVER HAD, DOESN'T MEAN THAT ANDERSON WANTS ANYTHING TO DO WITH HIM!!" And Terry Rodenbo would be absolutely right in his thinking. However, in my humble opinion, Mark Nevers would be a very good compromise candidate for drum major if; 1) I take a pass on the position and, 2) if Mr. Anderson does not bow down to the pressure of Mama Andrews and hand the reins of the marching band to Teri Andrews. The funny thing is, and I have no idea why I even remember this conversation, it must be some type of instant recall thing, but after leaving Mark Nevers' house that one evening over five years ago, when I was too embarrassed to play the trumpet in front of him, I specifically recalled Mark Nevers telling my mother that one day he was going to become the drum major for the Hartland High School Marching Band. I also recollect the proud look on my mother's face when he told her of this goal. Will the Mark Nevers recommendation to be the next "strutting peacock" here at Hartland High School go very far with Mr. Anderson? Just as about as far as Mike Beardslee's chat with Miss Franklin when I approached her with the idea of me trying out for this same position just a short five months ago. We're talking "Nowheresville". And the express way ramp for that mythical town is closed down for construction repairs.

Greg Sanders – Stop right there. You think that I am stupid, right?? I know when it comes right down to it me recommending this guy to Mr. Anderson is not going to happen. I would suggest Mark Nevers one million more times for the drum major position than Greg "Pretty Boy" Sanders. Other than Teri and Trecha Andrews, I suspect that no else in the Hartland Senior Band even likes or has any use for him at all. So, I am going to be very careful when bringing the name of Greg Sanders up to Terry Rodenbo, let alone, Mr. Anderson. But I gotta admit, flashy dresser that "Pretty Boy" is, you know that if he was selected to the drum major position, that he would dash out and purchase a tailor-made drum major outfit that would probably cost him about $5,000.00. It would be interesting to see what type of uniform that he would conjure up, because you can bet your bottom dollar that when you open up that dictionary that is collecting dust down in your parent's basement and look up the definition of "strutting peacock", Greg "Pretty Boy" Sanders' face will leap right out at you.

Jason Shattuck – When I came up with Jason Shattuck's name, I immediately think of Beany Bretzke and the show man qualities that he displayed in his role as drum major. I can see Jason Shattuck doing the exact same marching moves that Beany Bretzke would have used for the people attending a football game or parade. The crowd would never be able to take their eyes off of every step or motion that he made. However, Jason Shattuck is going to be facing a similar choice that I had to make when I was a sophomore in high school. Do I make Band or athletics my number one priority? Once I got my varsity letter for Track, I made Band the most important thing in my life when I walked each and every day through the front doors of Fenton High School. Jason Shattuck will undoubtedly receive his first ever varsity letter this fall in cross country. From that day forward, which direction does he go? Future questions

that Jason Shattuck might have to ask himself include: does he take a marching band practice off on the same day that he has a cross country meet? Does he attend a cross country invitational or a Band Day when there is a scheduling conflict, as is the case this upcoming Saturday. Jason Shattuck has a lot of varsity letters coming his way over the remaining three years of his high school athletic career. I do not see him turning these opportunities down. But he still remains an excellent candidate for the drum major position. This name will have to be seriously discussed with Terry Rodenbo when the two of us meet and go over our lists.

Aisha Tredeau – Her name is the only member of the Hartland High School graduating class of 1973 that made the Mike Beardslee drum major candidates list. And despite being a freshman, she has some positive things going for her. Instead of playing the flute in marching band, Aisha Tredeau asked Mr. Anderson if she could play the piccolo so that it could help provide more sound to a marching band with almost two halftime performances in the books, still lacks the volume of an even average sounding marching unit. In fact, one day recently Aisha Tredeau and Katie were talking and Aisha Tredeau mentioned that she was even thinking about experimenting with playing the E Flat Alto Saxophone in the pep band for basketball season, again with the notion of providing more "sock" to that music ensemble. I have noticed Aisha Tredeau on the marching field when a marching formation allows a close proximity between us. She is very disciplined, precise, but not mechanical or stiff, in her marching band steps. Aisha Tredeau is not the vocal leader like a Randi Lynch or Katie, but does lead by example. And I must admit that the Flute section here at Hartland, while not generating any significant noise to the sound of the marching band, they do make an effort to march with a certain exactness. Will being a ninth grader and one of the younger students in the marching band be a detriment to Aisha Tredeau as a candidate for the drum major position? Possibly. But it will be interesting to see if Terry Rodenbo gave Aisha Tredeau any serious consideration on his list of candidates.

Terry Rodenbo and I met up at lunch time today to compare our individual rosters of contenders. And despite the fact that Mike Beardslee was on the receiving end of a "ARE YOU CRAZY, STUPID, OR BOTH??", from Terry Rodenbo when I had tossed out the names of Mark Nevers and Greg "Pretty Boy" Sanders for drum major applicants, we finally did arrive at an agreement of two names to present for Mr. Anderson's review tomorrow just before the start of marching band practice.

"White Lake Road"

Chapter #82 – "Even as a personal favor to me …."

September 25th – Terry Rodenbo and I met first thing this morning and did another brief comparing of notes. He had only one name on his list to go along with my two recommendations. We both had Jason Shattuck on our listings with Aisha Tredeau being the other name to make the final cut. But before we parted ways for our next class, I asked Terry Rodenbo, "On the count of three, let's each say out loud the name of the person that we think will ultimately be named as the drum major by Mr. Anderson."

After I counted out the three consecutive numbers, the both of us simultaneously said the name of, "Teri Andrews", and that is in despite of the fact that she was not on either one of our final lists. I just have a sneaky feeling that when it's all said and done, Teri Andrews will be the "strutting peacock" of the Hartland High School Marching Band starting next week. Sad. And what is even more depressing, I don't have enough interest in the drum major position to even attempt thwarting Teri Andrews from getting that honor.

A couple of hours later while I was in Mr. Anderson's office when I advised him that the drum major position did not appeal to me. I think Mr. Anderson sort of understood my line of reasoning, "that I am a trumpet player". Kind a sort of. And while I did refrain from using the Terry Rodenbo created phrase, "strutting peacock", from the look on Mr. Anderson's face, he was not too thrilled with my decision.

To save further questioning from Mr. Anderson, I hurriedly brought in Terry Rodenbo to join us and we then started to explain to Mr. Anderson that even though I was not interested in this privileged position, both Terry Rodenbo and I had compiled of list of candidates to present to him of whom we thought would be excellent candidates. The names on that roster were, Jason Shattuck and Aisha Tredeau.

Mr. Anderson reviewed over the two names and advised, "I have had one other person who has shown interest in this position, possibly giving me a total of three candidates for tryouts next week." Mr. Anderson never mentioned the name of the third contender, but I would be shocked if it was anyone other than, Teri Andrews.

I then did some fast thinking on my feet, solely with the purpose of trying to get back into Mr. Anderson's good graces, and added, "If you decide to go with some type of open tryouts for this position, then I would be happy to be there and play the fight song so that there will be some music to accompany any marching steps that you want to take them through." Mr. Anderson liked that idea and added, "Also, bring your sister along. She can provide some type of drum cadence as well for them to march to." Just like that, I was back in the good graces of Mr. Anderson!! Smoooooooooooooooooooooth.

Marching Band practice this morning was just so-so. Maybe that's okay if this is a Monday rehearsal, but today is Thursday. And if a marching band unit has not warmed up to either the songs or the routines that they're going to be putting on for the next night's performance, and the Hartland High School Marching Band has not, then that's going to make for one long evening.

And the shame of it is, the Brighton Bulldogs are coming to town as the Hartland Eagles opponents in just a little over 36 some hours. The Brighton High School fans always travel well to see their teams play. Especially for varsity football and basketball contests. This translates into a big crowd. Maybe that will get us Hartland marching types excited about this halftime show. Something has to.

Also, strangely enough, there has not been one word mentioned about the fast approaching CMU Band Day trip for this Saturday, either. Not even by Mr. Anderson.

The school day was over and as I entered the band room to grab my trumpet case and head out to "White Lake Road", Mr. Anderson gestured for me to come into his office. After closing the door, he asked, "Are you definitely positive that you have no desire to become the drum major of your high school band, even as a personal favor to me?" I advised him that I had not changed my mind since this morning.

Mr. Anderson then said, "Well, I talked to the three candidates that were either recommended or had come to me and shown interest in the position. And I have reached a decision as to who I am going to select as our new drum major."

"Much like yourself, Jason Shattuck did not show any fascination with the drum major position at all. He's too much into the athletic scene. Teri Andrews seemed interested until I advised her of the tryouts that would be necessary to be completed to help me in making my final selection. Therefore, and under the threat of death, Beardslee, yours, not mine, do not repeat or say one word of what I am now going to advise you to anyone else. After tomorrow night's halftime show, I am going to announce to the Band that Aisha Tredeau will be the drum major starting next Monday."

I must admit that I was somewhat surprised by Mr. Anderson's choice, enough so that I asked, "This is none of my business, but aren't you going to get some serious grief from Mrs. Andrews about your decision??" Mr. Anderson responded, "Yes, I will. And in a big-time way."

Mr. Anderson then added, "But when talking to Teri Andrews about this leadership role, she again used the reasoning, and I quote, "That since I am a senior, I should not have to try out for any position with this Band that I have faithfully served for the past three years." When I talked to Aisha Tredeau and started to mention the open tryouts for drum major, she interrupted me and asked, "Could you please provide me with some pointers as to what I should do to prepare for this tryout?" I made my mind up right then and there. Aisha Tredeau was my selection as drum major."

Mr. Anderson seemed very happy with his choice and was also very receptive to my second piece of advice today that I was throwing his way. "After tomorrow evening, we have three more halftime performances, plus one parade before marching season is completed. Why don't you break Aisha Tredeau in really easy? Prepare her over the next two weeks to be totally in charge of the Homecoming Parade; then pregame show only for the Fenton game;

and halftime show only for the Pinckney game? Then turn her loose for the Memorial Day Parade and next year's marching band season."

Mr. Anderson gave my suggestion some thought before responding and added, "You're right, Beardslee. That's a good way to get her started in her new role. I have to remember that Aisha Tredeau is still relatively young when it comes to marching band experience. I mean, after all, she does only have one completed halftime show performance in her career."

Later that evening while practicing my trumpet and forcing myself to play through our halftime show selections for tomorrow night's performance, I mentally asked myself if I was disappointed about not jumping at the opportunity to become a drum major? And the answer is still no, I am not.

The obvious reason was that I enjoy playing the trumpet too much to exchange it for a drum major baton. But my biggest fear about being in that role was that I don't know if I had it in me to bark out the necessary commands to get the show on the road, or get on an entire Band's case when they were not picking up their feet when marching; not focusing on the necessary execution needed for a marching drill once out on the practice field; or not following along when I was conducting a song once every one was in concert formation.

I mean, seriously, can you see me shouting out marching commands to Jim Koop for him to pick up his feet; Katie to have her drummers keep a straight line when marching down the field, or Terry Rodenbo to put more spin in his spin move? Come on!! You think I'm crazy!! Please count to a million by ones before you answer that.

I must admit, however, that at the end of the day, there is a teeny, weeny bit of me where I almost crumbled and accepted the drum major position. When Mr. Anderson said the phrase, "Are you definitely positive that you have no desire to become the drum major of your high school band, even as a personal favor to me?"; it was almost if I was personally letting him down. And while I do not want to do that to Mr. Anderson, I suspect that I have.

Tomorrow night brings the second halftime show of the football season for the Hartland High School Marching Band. Man, I just wish I could get fired up for it.

Chapter # 83 – "The UCLA of Senior High Basketball"

September 26th – It's game day and that means the second halftime show of the marching band season for the Hartland High School Marching Band. But before that event took place, a couple of other things made news today in my world.

During second hour Study Hall, an announcement came over the PA system stating that all senior class members needed to head for the gymnasium. I was unsure of what this command was for until I walked into the location where I hoped to be playing varsity basketball rather than being a member of the basketball pep band in a little over two months.

As soon as I arrived, however, it dawned on me what the deal was. It's the fourth Friday of the school year, which means today is "Fourth Count Friday!!" If that is not a great name for a title of a "Chip Hilton" novel authored by Clair Bee, then one does not exist on the face of this earth.

Fourth Count Friday has a different importance to school personnel than it does to me. My mother during a slow, slow drive home from Flint one Saturday afternoon explained the real purpose and the importance of this function to Katie and I.

This is the day of the year that a school district determines the actual population of their students. That information is sent to the state of Michigan, where upon any necessary verification completed by the state, a school district will then receive school financial aid in "x number of dollars per student." The larger the school district is, the more state dollars they are eligible for.

My mother added that this has a huge impact financially to all the school districts in the state of Michigan. Which means, that when the four of us former Fenton High School students transferred to Hartland High School for the 1969-70 school year, that in theory, there was four less" x number of dollars per student" for the Fenton Area Schools and some more drachmas in the treasure chest of the Hartland Consolidated Schools.

For me, however, Fourth Count Friday means something entirely different and in my viewpoint, an issue that is far, far, more important than how much money an individual school district receives. Well, at least in my little mind it does.

When the state of Michigan officially tallies up the head count for all their statewide schools, it uses that approved number to put these institutes in a classification. I.E.; Class A; Class B; Class C; and Class D; with the largest categorization of schools being "A" and descending in size by alphabetical division order.

This is also the determining factor as to how a high school's basketball team is slotted to play in a certain grouping when it comes time for the Michigan High School Athletic Association Basketball Tournament. Only the greatest time of the year in state of Michigan athletics!! One and done!! When a team loses, they are out of the tournament which now allows those

basketball players whose basketball season has come to an abrupt end, more time to get ready to gorge themselves silly of Easter candy.

In the Genesee-Livingston County Conference, it's always interesting to see come tournament time where our league teams are classified. Some schools participate in the Class A tournament and believe it or not, there are a couple of schools in the GL that are on the bubble every year to see whether they participate in the Class B or Class C tournament. It varies every year. For example:

Ainsworth High School – They always border between being a Class A or Class B classification. Last year Ainsworth played in the Class A tournament and I hope that they stay there again for this year, too.

Fenton High School – My former high school has always been a solid Class B school. I see no change in that, despite losing us four former "Fentonites" to the Hartland Consolidated Schools within this past month.

Hartland High School – They fluctuate between a Class B and Class C classification. While they were a Class B school last year when it came basketball tournament time, they have a long history of being a Class C school. Strictly speaking for basketball tournament purposes, I hope that the Hartland Eagles play at the Class C level this winter.

Howell High School – The same thing with the Ainsworth Spartans, Howell High School borders on Class A and Class B classification with the last few years showing the Highlanders playing in the Class B portion of the basketball tournament. This always surprises me because Livingston County is such a large county. In fact, the actual physical location of "White Lake Road" and it's 51 acres are in Livingston County. To break it down even further, the Beardslee family resides in Tyrone Township. Which means, that for any county issues or payment of taxes, my folks have to call or travel all the way to the city of Howell, rather than Fenton, to get any matters of this type settled. Strange.

Swartz Creek – Last year for the first time in their school athletic history, the Dragons had to play in the Class A tournament. When you have high level high school athletic programs like: Flint Northern, Flint Central, Flint Northwestern and Flint Southwestern, just a stone's throw from the Swartz Creek school boundary lines; that makes for a short basketball tournament run. I hope that Swartz Creek remains at the Class A level for the 1969-70 school year because they're going to have a varsity basketball team that will border on being a powerhouse come this winter.

While the basketball players who are seniors here at Hartland High School and played in what is known as the two years of "The UCLA of Junior High Basketball" era, there is another school here in the state of Michigan that can rightfully call themselves, "The UCLA of Senior High Basketball." And that would be the River Rouge Panthers.

Over say, the past 15 years, they have won, oh, off of the top of my head, at least seven or eight Class B State basketball championships. They are just an impressive basketball program. In

fact, there was a story that one season River Rouge had such a talented team, that their second and third string players were just as good as the starters. So, the River Rouge basketball coach, Mr. Lofton Greene, would simply substitute a whole new unit instead of just one individual player into the game.

I still remember the excitement that this caused in the town of Fenton when the Fenton High School varsity basketball team faced "Rouge" in the Class B quarter-finals on a cold Wednesday night in March of 1965. Even with Terry Walker leading the way, which sadly, turned out to be the last game that he would ever play as a Fenton Tiger, because that night the panther species proved to be superior to a group of subspecies tigers.

I mention the River Rouge High School varsity basketball team only because today is Fourth Count Friday. In the state of Michigan High School basketball world of gossip, you would traditionally hear how River Rough High School would always "ship a few kids out of their school system" just before the official student count was scheduled. And that is how "Rouge" was always able to stay as a Class B High School and continue to win as many of these classification's championships that they have. I mean this "River Rouge must be shipping out a few students today" story comes up every year just before the start of the high school basketball tournaments. Guaranteed, you could set your calendar by that story.

Whether those rumors/stories were true or not, I don't know. What I do know is this, that during their championship winning seasons, the Mr. Lofton Greene coached River Rouge Panthers were probably the best high school squad, regardless of classification in the state of Michigan. But like every other Class B high school in the Wolverine State, I hope and pray that this is the year that River Rouge High School forgets to "ship out some students" and participates in the basketball tournament as a Class A High School.

As the Hartland High School Senior Class contingency was making way out of the gymnasium for the class of 1971's turn to be counted, I was on the end of a, "Hey, Beardslee. Come here." I looked around and I saw Ric Adams motioning for me to come over his way. As I was walking towards him, I thought to myself, "Please, please don't bring up the topic of why I didn't make a serious effort for the drum major position to me."

Well, thank goodness, the subject to be discussed was an entirely different issue. Ric Adams stated, "I saw Coach Decker earlier this morning and he made a good suggestion about the upcoming basketball season that I wanted to share with you."

"With Coach Decker being the varsity basketball coach this season and not affiliated with the varsity football team at all, he came up with the idea that after all of the Homecoming events are out of the way, that starting the week of October 13th, any Hartland High School male student that is interested in trying out for the men's varsity basketball team, meet on Tuesday, Wednesday and Thursday nights right after school for about an hour. During that time, we could shoot baskets, free throws, play some one-on-one games, etc. As Coach Decker pointed out, it would allow us to start to get into basketball shape, mentally and physically."

Ric Adams further went on to explain, "This is for the guys who aren't involved in football or cross country, so there will not be a huge crowd. Dan Brown, a sophomore, who is 6'5", but with very, very limited basketball experience, wants to be a part of these sessions as well."

"Coach Decker outlined a time frame as to how all of this would take place. Football season for the varsity team will be completed on October 31st. He will give guys like Tom Moran, Pete Mason and Steve Gilmore and other interested football players the following week off before official basketball tryouts are to take place on November 10th and November 11th."

"The cross-country season will be over on November 1st. Max Perry, Al Dowty, Tom Beaver and Jason Shattuck, plus any other cross-country guys interested in trying out for the varsity basketball squad will also be given one week off to rest up and hit the books."

"So, Coach Decker will want the pre-season basketball skills practices to run for the weeks of October 13th, October 20th and October 27th. And then everyone shows up for the actual tryouts with our first game of the season scheduled for November 29th against Whitmore Lake High School.

"So, what do you think? Is this something that you would be interested in signing up for?"

I liked that idea. I liked it a lot in fact. I need something to get me motivated to get into basketball shape. And this would do it. It would allow me to get head-start basketball skills wise on other players that also want to make the varsity squad. And I will need every edge that I can get. So, my response to Ric Adams was a simple, "Sign me up."

"White Lake Road"

Chapter #84 – "The Three E's"

September 26th – The rest of the school day was uneventful. No "30 seconds" from Mr. Collins or any further discussion on the topic of drum major, well, at least until this evening.

The ride back to Hartland High School tonight showed a stark difference as compared to this same time exactly one week ago. The four occupants of the jeep were quiet. Oh, we were still doing our individual pre-game rituals, but they were not being done with the same intensity or anxiety that we had for the Stockbridge game halftime show.

I noticed the same effect after parking the jeep while the four of us walked to the entrance of Hartland High School to find our way to the Band Room. The noise level coming from our destination was a lot lower than last week. In fact, the sound level coming out of the Band Room was the equivalent of a music group warming up for a band concert rather than getting all charged up for a high school football game halftime show.

There are certain things in my life that I get nervous about. Marching in a high school football game halftime show is not one of them. So, for me personally, walking into a Band Room the night of a performance during football season will not cause my adrenalin to flow in such a super electric manner that it will cause me to start bouncing off of the Band Room walls. In fact, of the four of us former Fenton High School kids, Katie, is the one who gets the most outwardly fired up for a halftime show. I know this because on the night of a halftime show the closer and closer she gets to the door of the Band Room, the faster and faster she talks. Take my word for it.

Mr. Anderson walked us through the pre-game show like we did last week by playing a few measures of every song scheduled to be played later this evening, but again something is missing. Even Mr. Anderson, who had a huge look of concern on his face last Friday, seemed to have something else on his mind and was miles and miles away emotionally. He said something about our performance being graded and that again, there would be a section of the week and best individual marcher selected, but even those words were spoken in a monotone type of voice.

I made myself, and I mean I had to literally had to force myself to perform my presidential duties and try to get the rest of my Band mates to show some type of excitement for a pre-game show that was now no more than 10 minutes away. And I generated very little of the three "E's" that you want to see a marching band have as they get ready for a performance: "enthusiasm, eagerness, and energy." There was a dash of the "Three E's" in various instrumental sections, but only a smattering. Nothing compared to last weeks' pre-game emotions that were running sky high.

I was disappointed in my efforts to generate the "three e's". I suspect that there was a reason for this lack of pizzazz. But you can only place so much blame on the mediocre selection of music and marching band routines before some type of school or self-pride has to kick in.

"White Lake Road"

I wonder if an outfit like the Flint Northwestern High School Marching Band ever faces these same issues that we're having tonight when they head out to get their pre-game shown under way? I suspect not. Those guys have too much pride, spirit and tradition ingrained in them. Something that the marching band units that I have ever been a member of, rarely showed. Maybe for halftime or pregame show here or there. But certainly, not for an entire marching band season.

It was time to have Katie lead the Hartland High School Marching Band out to the football field for our pre-game show and off we went. Despite not being the most motivated Band members tonight, Jim Koop and I still remembered to do our traditional to the right spin turn move once we hit the Hartland High School parking lot. Only three more of these to do together in our lives, Jim Koop.

While waiting for the football teams to finish up with their pre-game drills, I had my eyes on the Brighton Bulldog gridders. I recognized some of these guys from basketball and track seasons. These fellas look physically imposing when they have their basketball and track uniforms on which consists of shirts and shorts. But when you put shoulder pads and a football helmet on them, now they look twice as large and daunting.

I spotted Dave Austin who plays tight end and defensive end for the Bulldogs. He will be a top-notch candidate for the GL male athlete of the year that is to be announced in the month of May. Then there was Reed Williams, a two-way player at tackle. Reed Williams only has to be the dirtiest basketball player ever in the nine-year history of the GL conference. In addition to being the filthiest athlete in the GL, he is also easily by far the most hated hoops player.

The last Brighton Bulldog that caught my attention was Frank Walters. He is just such a smooth looking running back. That kid just glides when he is running with the football. He also makes playing point guard for Brighton High School basketball team look effortless. A great athlete who is always in the large shadows that Dave Austin and Reed Williams cast.

Hopefully my path will be crossing theirs come this basketball season. However, having been on the receiving end of some bruising basketball screens set by Dave Austin and Reed Williams, maybe I should be careful in what I wish for.

A quick blast of a whistle by Mr. Anderson, brought me back to the reason why I was standing in the end zone in the first place. Four more consecutive discharges of the whistle and it was the start of the pre-game show!!

This part of the marching band performance always moves fast. Before you know it, we were in tunnel formation watching the Hartland Eagle football players dash past us. From what I could gather, the initial part of our marching band duties went pretty well. Hopefully that momentum will carry us over to our halftime show performance.

Jim Koop and I for the second, first half of a Hartland High School football game caught a break when it came to playing any trumpet charges. Before the first quarter came to a close,

the Brighton Bulldogs defensive squad was living up to their press clippings by scoring two touchdowns on pass interceptions and the Bulldogs led Hartland 14-0.

When it came time for us Band kids to start heading for the end zone to get our halftime show underway, the score was now 35-0. Not that I actually pay any attention to what is happening down on the football field when I am in the stands, but I sure don't remember the Pete Mason led offensive ever getting a first down. Not a touchdown, mind you. But a first down. That also helped contribute to a no trumpet charge night for Jim Koop and I.

Despite the fact that I felt that our pre-game show went well, and we have no excuse for it not to, my fear of how the halftime show was going to turn out came true. Was it a disastrous performance? No, I wouldn't say that. But it was not the type of presentation where we should have been building on from last week's effort.

I hope that we as a marching band are not an ensemble that has one early season halftime show that is something special and then digress for the rest of the marching band season. Just like a sports team, you want to improve more and more as the season goes on. In my humble opinion, the Hartland Consolidated Band, as a whole, has not improved from week one to week two, when the largest type of improvement should be occurring.

Last week when our halftime show was over, it was almost like the marching band was so stimulated that we could not get back to the high school fast enough to hear what our overall grade was going to be from Mr. Anderson. It was the total opposite tonight. As a group, we sort of poked along, heads down, dragging our feet type of thing, trying to avoid this week's evaluation.

Once in the Band Room all forty plus of us Band members awaited the pearls of wisdom from Mr. Anderson and our final grade. I had us pegged for a "C- ". I was basing that on the fact that our feet were not being lifted as high as they should; and that we didn't show the flashiness that we displayed last week. By the latter, I mean, a to the rear spin movement was made cautiously and not with a quick precise movement of confidence.

Now, part of this you could attribute to the selection of songs and marching routines that this show consisted of. These were not songs that allowed for the blasting of a trumpet section. Nothing music wise to get the crowd fired up so that they would not leave for the concessions stands and rest rooms because they didn't want to miss the Hartland High School marching band perform. Where is the theme song from "Batman" when we need it??

I think Mr. Anderson cut us a break when he gave us our final grade, stating, "I thought that the pre-game show went very well tonight. Not as good as last week but still a quality effort. We do need to pick up our feet more when marching down the field while playing, "Mr. Touchdown", because this is the first time of the night that the crowd will see us in action and we want to keep their attention focused on our marching efforts."

"I thought our halftime show performance was not as inspired as it should have been. At times, I thought we were going through the motions. More so, to get the show over so that we

could go home rather than to get to the next song and give it our best effort." Ouch. That statement hurts.

"My final grade is a "C+. This is based upon a solid pre-game showing and a so-so halftime show. I realize that it is difficult to put on back to back halftime shows. So, we have two weeks to prepare for our next performance. That should give us the time to get the type of grade back that I handed out last week."

"There were some positives that came out of tonight, however. Section of the week goes to the percussion section. This is based upon the fact that they were the most improved section from last week. Marcher of the week goes to Aisha Tredeau, as tonight her piccolo playing could have been heard all of the way to the city of Ann Arbor, Michigan."

Jim Koop leaned over to me and whispered, "How embarrassing is that, Beardslee. A piccolo player beats the two of us trumpet players out for marcher of the week. And I don't even know whose half of the she's even in, yours or mine."

For a trumpet player losing out to any woodwind player for marcher of the week is truly distressing. No, make that very, very humiliating.

Mr. Anderson added, "And for the big announcement of the evening, is that starting next Monday, Aisha Tredeau, will be our drum major for the rest of the school year. Now her piccolo will be replaced by a drum major's baton."

Us marching band kids gave Aisha Tredeau a big round of music applause and it was a great night for her and Katie. They were the victors and the recipients of free ice cream!!

The night wasn't a complete total waste, however. Mr. Anderson again asked Jim Koop to go down to the cafeteria and get the rewards for the marcher and section of the week champions. Yeah, you got it. Despite not being honorees like last week, don't worry, Mike Beardslee, Jim Koop and Terry Rodenbo were still able to get their daily federal government required quota of dairy products inside our tummies by evenings' end.

Just before us Band kids were heading out the door, Mr. Anderson said, "Now don't forget. Tomorrow is the day that the members of the CMU Band Day Honors Band will be going to Mount Pleasant, Michigan. Due to the distance involved and rehearsal start time of 9:00 AM for all mass bands, we will need to be on the school bus and ready to leave by 6:00 AM tomorrow morning." Now that, my friends, is how you officially ruin an evening.

Thirty minutes later, the four of us were sitting around the family room of "White Lake Road" eating our little cartons of ice cream, with less enthusiasm than last week, with the exception being Katie, as she got to brag to my mother that the instrumental group that she is section leader of was voted as the best marching band section of the week. And, that in no time at all, "my drummers" will be doing a drum feature for a halftime show.

"White Lake Road"

While I was waiting for Jim Koop to pipe in with his "Ringo Starr and Buddy Rich" line, which he did not as he was working on his third or fourth carton of ice cream, I must admit that I was proud of the improvement of the percussion section. The strides that they made from the first halftime show of the season to this evening was impressive. Good for them.

But I have to admit, the sting of losing as best marcher of the night to a piccolo player still does smart a little bit. This is the second straight performance of the marching band season where "Mr. President" has not been named marcher of the week. So, make that a double ouch.

However, the biggest concern for Mike Beardslee this evening, is that in eight days I go back to Dr. Alfred's office for the final setting of my permanent caps. Depending on how that goes, the $64,000 question now becomes, was tonight the last halftime appearance ever for me as a trumpet player while a member of a high school band?? I hope not, but it is a definite possibility.

I eventually fell asleep listening to the WGMZ-FM local football scoreboard show. The final score of the Hartland-Brighton game was 49-0. That's gotta hurt for the Hartland Eagle varsity football players. Not as much as losing marcher of the week to a piccolo player type of hurt. But that's still gotta sting.

I also caught the final score of the Fenton Tigers game. They're off to a good start in the defense of their GL League Championship by beating Linden High School, 42-21, even without Marv Pushman. Good for them.

Tomorrow I'm facing an early wake-up call and a long, long round-trip bus ride. And I am not looking forward to either one of them.

"White Lake Road"

Chapter #85 "The Chaperone"

September 27th – I woke up this morning without the use of my mother's "alarm clock" system of turning on my bed room lights while I was still in a comatose state. I looked outside my bed room window and noticed how dark it was at 5:00 AM. I MEAN IT'S DARK OUTSIDE!!

Despite the fact that there were four "Gloomy Guses" gathered around the dinner table in the breakfast room of "White Lake Road" this morning, my mother had fixed up what I would classify as a "Sunday morning type breakfast" for this hungry quartet to gobble down. I suspect that we have Terry Rodenbo's presence to thank for this excellent meal. It was then back to Hartland High School for the start of one loooooooooooong day.

I pulled the jeep into the Hartland High School parking lot and headed to the awaiting school bus to grab a seat to myself near the emergency exit. I still cannot believe that the four of us were back here again at Hartland High School just some nine hours later since we left here last night. As soon as I set foot in the bus and prepared to make a left turn to locate the seat I was going to immediately fall asleep in, I received my first of three surprises for this day.

Sitting in the very front seat of this Hartland Consolidated School bus was none other than Greg Sanders and Teri Andrews. While it was somewhat of a surprise that Teri Andrews had not come up with some flimsy excuse to get herself out of today's activities, it was an absolute shock to see Greg Sanders on this mode of transportation.

And there he was, in all of his glory, perfectly dressed in fancy sweater and a brand-new pair of corduroys, just sitting there with that goofy smile of his on face and his right arm tightly secured around Teri Andrews' neck and shoulders. I made the assumption that once it was time for us "Honors Band Members" to hit the road, Greg Sanders would simply get off of the bus, go home, then proceed to select and iron the ties that he was going to wear to school next week.

Jim Koop was one step behind me when he saw Greg Sanders and promptly yelled, "WHAT ARE YOU DOING HERE, "PRETTY BOY"!! YOU DIDN'T AUDITION FOR THIS TRIP. WHAT'S THE DEAL?? SPIT IT OUT, PRETTY BOY!!" COME ON, DAYLIGHT'S BURNING!!"

Now this whole incident could have been easily smoothed over if Greg Sanders would have simply said, "Hey guys, I'm just here to see my girl-friend off. I'll be out of your hair in a couple of minutes."

Life should be so easy at 5:55 AM on the last September, Saturday morning of the month. The day of the week, I might add, where I should be laying in his bed mentally counting the seconds away until my "Sporting News" is delivered by the United States Post Office. After that, the rest of the day is strictly, "Lazy Boy City."

Instead the response from Greg Sanders to Jim Koop was, "I'm here as a chaperone and you have to do everything I say. You understand, "punk."

This was probably not the retort that Greg Sanders should have made. Now it was Jim Koop's turn to verbally respond. But instead answering directly to Greg Sanders, Jim Koop turned to Mr. Anderson and stated, quite emphatically I might add, "Hey!! Anderson!! If "Pretty Boy" is a chaperone and has the right to tell me what to do, then I am not making this trip!! I've got better things to do on a Saturday!!".

With that, Jim Koop promptly headed to the front of the bus to make his grand exit. The funny thing was, you could feel a ground swell of people agreeing with the Jim Koop phrase of, "I've got better things to do on a Saturday!!" Because the other 18 of us Band kids, less Teri Andrews, of course, now started to stagger out of our seats, walking down the aisle way so that we could head back to the cemented ground of the parking lot and then back to the safety of our homes.

Mr. Anderson quickly put two and two together. If he had not quite realized that none of the CMU Band Day Honors Band members had any desire to travel to his alma mater on this or any other Saturday morning, it was starting to hit home right this moment.

Mr. Anderson stood in front of the school bus exit area and asked very politely for us potential mutineers to stop where we were. Mr. Anderson then said to Greg Sanders in a surprisingly calm voice, "Now, Greg. I cannot physically force you off the bus by myself. And I will not allow anyone else to forcibly throw you off the bus, either." Darn!!

"However," as Mr. Anderson continued, "If you do not exit off of this bus on you own volition, I will go back into the school, call the police and have them escort you off of the bus, which may then ultimately cause me to press charges against you. Is that what you really want??" Whoa!! This is getting serious.

Mr. Anderson continued, "In addition, there is a monetary cost issue here as well. Hartland High School has had to pay the following charges out of their budget: registration fee for the CMU Band Day; transportation cost for the bus such as gas, and overtime wages for the bus driver. I don't have an exact figure, but I am very certain that the total amount of these expenses will be well into the hundreds of dollars range."

"And I do not want the school to request reimbursement from you or your parents, of which, could very easily happen if the police get involved. So, for what is best for you and your family, I am asking you very politely, to exit from the bus and go home so that this incident doesn't become any uglier."

Even "Pretty Boy" realized that this day was not going the way he had planned. There was not going to be any free trip for him to Mount Pleasant, Michigan so that he could spend time with his girlfriend. So, with that simple request from Mr. Anderson, Greg Sanders reluctantly stood up and alighted from the Hartland Consolidated School bus, bringing to an end his young, fledging career as a chaperone of high school band students.

I must admit, I was impressed how Mr. Anderson handled this situation. Despite all that, though, it nevertheless meant that I was still out of a morning and afternoon of reading the

"Sporting News", but I was still amazed how flawlessly Mr. Anderson had gotten Greg Sanders' cooperation.

The bus driver finally shifted the bus into first gear and started to inch the members of the CMU Band Day Honors Band out of the school parking lot. But just for good measure, Jim Koop, who had spotted Greg Sanders still standing just outside of his car, rolled down the bus window and yelled a farewell greeting over to him, "YOU HAVE A NICE DAY, PRETTY BOY!! YA HEAR!!"

If that wasn't bad enough, I now heard the slamming down of some more bus windows as more of my Bandmates joined in the chorus of, "YOU HAVE A NICE DAY, PRETTY BOY!!" YA HEAR!!" Followed immediately by piggish sounding type squeals of laughter.

Did yours truly join in on this childish behavior of good bye serenading that was being directed to Greg Sanders? No, I did not. And that was only because I lacked the motor skills to get my window opened in time before the school bus made a turn that was starting to block my vision of the lone figure of Greg Sanders and his 1970 Mustang being there all by their lonesome in the Hartland High School parking lot.

But while all of this was stuff was taking place, one thought did cross my mind. This group of Band kids had just displayed a perfect example of the "three e's", and at 6:05 AM in the morning no less, that certainly was not on exhibit for last night's halftime show. That disappointed and bothered me. We have the "three e's" in us. All we have to do now is learn how to use them for good instead of evil.

I was now able to get one final good look out the school bus window. I gazed over in Greg Sanders' direction and saw his response to the choral type of good byes that he was being showered with from the participants of us bus riders. Now, it should be noted that in life, there are certain internationally known hand signals for an individual to show their displeasure, and that was the send-off that Greg Sanders was displaying to the school bus that had just made a left-hand turn onto Hibner Road to officially get us on our way to Mount Pleasant, Michigan and onto surprise number two.

"White Lake Road"

Chapter #86 – "I kid you not, she was flat out dead serious"

September 27th – How was the two-and-a-half-hour ride from Hartland, Michigan to Mount Pleasant, Michigan, you ask? Not a clue. I just shut my eyes and it was sleepy time land for Mike Beardslee at least for 99% of the drive. So, if you really need to know about this excursion, then please ask either Katie, Jim Koop or Terry Rodenbo.

As soon as the Hartland Consolidated School bus pulled into the designated parking area, I could immediately see the differences between the CMU Band Day and the University of Michigan Band Day. Today, there was less of everything. Less school buses; less high school bands, which meant less high school band personnel.

The reverse of this showed that there was also more space to move around in without the chance of running into a bunch of other high school musicians or be situated only two feet away from another school bus. Add to the fact that this was a very pleasant state of Michigan, September morning, with enough coolness in the air to wake you up but not make you shiver and wish for a jacket and gloves. The only thing missing from this moment was the start of the fall color change. Only the best time of year on Planet Beardslee!!

After stretching and trying to get the kinks out of a 150-minute bus ride, the "Hartland 20", gathered up our instruments where it was then an easy stroll over to where the rehearsal field was. We found ourselves meeting in a bleacher section that was assigned to all of the participating honor bands.

This now allowed me to notice another variance between the first and second Band Days of this year that I had attended. All of us honors bands were sitting extremely close to the football field. There was no wall to scramble over like there was in the University of Michigan stadium. All we had to do today was simply stand up and walk to the area that we eventually were to march onto the football field. Piece of cake!!

We got our instructions over the PA system and all of the honors bands were going to come in from four different locations out on the football field. Once the Central Michigan University Marching Band started to play our entrance music, the selected 20 from each high school marching unit would simply march out to our designated positions on the field, play the Central Michigan fight song with the CMU Marching Band, do an about face and then head back to the stands.

For this AM rehearsal, there were no multiple attempts of risking injury or damage to an instrument by hurriedly scrambling over a three foot in height brick wall simultaneously along with hundreds of other high school musicians. Today was a low keyed and well-organized approach to get us Band kids safely on and off the field. I think I'm liking this format.

All of us CMU Band Day Honor Bands attendees did this this rehearsal a couple of times through and that was it. Now we had some serious free time to walk around the Central Michigan University campus or, as 90-95% of us high school bands people were thinking, go back to our respective buses and get us some serious shut-eye.

"White Lake Road"

Much like last week in Ann Arbor, Michigan, I spent my down time looking for people that I knew or some of my Cabin #5 Interlochen buddies. So far, no luck. I did see a trombone player in the CMU Marching Band that was part of the Allstate Boys Division last summer. He was the first chair trombone player and was from Durand, Michigan. But that was it as far as any Interlochen connection. Again, far different from just seven days ago.

A few minutes later that all changed as the second Mike Beardslee surprise of the day popped up when I heard a voice from behind me say, "Doctor Savage, I presume." I knew that voice and when I turned around it was not only a member of the Cabin #5 fraternity, it was an old buddy of mine from my days at the Fenton Area Schools, Eric Douglas. Man, it was great to see him again!

Eric Douglas, was probably the smartest kid that I knew during his five year stay as a Fenton Tiger. He was brilliant. Even more so than the Flying Dutchman. And that's saying something. Between Eric Douglas and the Flying Dutchman, their combined IQ's are probably in the low thousands.

One day at the beginning of my fifth-grade school year, I was just sitting in the back of Mrs. Weigandt's class room thinking about my baseball card collection, when this one new classmate sat down in the empty school desk next to me. He shook my hand and said, "Hi. I'm Eric Douglas. Glad to meet you." Okay.

From that day forward at State Road Elementary School, Eric Douglas, myself, along with Tom Rhodes, and Chuck Miller, the four us became the best of friends. We played touch football every day at recess. Wrote stories where we were secret service agents and how we were always protecting, President Lyndon Johnson, from any type of danger.

When we weren't protecting the President of the United States as secret service agents, we became governmental special assignment agents going on top secret missions to the planet Mars or the country of South Viet Nam. Sometimes both places in the same day if one mission was easily taken care of. Typical elementary school stuff, but it was great fun.

Despite hanging around with a low life like, Mike Beardslee, Eric Douglas was designated for greatness. Class valedictorian. Student Council President. And he wasn't a half bad baritone player, either.

When it came time for the first ever election of officers for the Fenton Junior High Band, Eric Douglas, who was far more qualified for this position then I was, nominated me for president and he gave a speech that even Guy Thompson would have been proud of, as to why I was the worthiest candidate of all nominees. Eric Douglas did not need to do that for me, but he did.

During the summer of 1967, the city of Detroit, much like other metropolitan cities across the United States, had a riot that led to thousands of injured people, millions of dollars in damaged property and the start of people actually moving or seriously looking to get out of the city of Detroit.

"White Lake Road"

By sheer coincidence the day that riot had started, my folks and Katie, were in Detroit at Cobo Hall, attending a show featuring the world-famous horses known as the "White Lipizzaner Stallions." While my parents admitted to spotting clouds of dark smoke coming from another part of Detroit while driving back to "White Lake Road" that afternoon, they simply assumed that it was an out of control building fire. They later heard on WJR radio that they were only blocks away from where a full out race riot was taking place.

While the city of Fenton is some 60 miles away from down town Detroit, there were concerns of riots starting up in Flint, Michigan and extending to nearby communities such as Swartz Creek, Grand Blanc, and Fenton. Even my father, who had never misses a day of work while employed at General Motors, had some doubt about how safe it was going to be in the Plant, "Old Buick", for the start of his shift that next afternoon.

While the riots of Detroit never extended to the metropolis of Flint or the surrounding areas, according to Eric Douglas, his father was quite shaken by this event. As Eric put it, "My father, a retired military man, woke up the following Monday morning after the Detroit riots, got in his car, and then very late that night after arriving home advised my mother, my brother, sister, and I, that as soon as all the details were to be worked out, we were moving to Gaylord, Michigan."

Now I still remember this specific morning like it was yesterday. I got a telephone call from Eric Douglas, just before the start of my sophomore year of high school. He said that he wanted to meet with me and the Flying Dutchman to discuss something. I just assumed Eric Douglas wanted to get together with the two of us to advise that because of a heavy class schedule for this school year that Eric Douglas had to carry, that he was going to drop out of Band or something important like that.

Then while in the family room of "White Lake Road", he dropped the bombshell on us two that he and his family were moving up to Gaylord, Michigan. At first, the Dutchman and I both thought that he was just pulling our leg. Certain students of Fenton High School just do not move away from Fenton, Michigan. Not Don Madden; not Bob Niles; not Ben Lewis; not Marv Pushman. It just doesn't happen. Terry Walker being the exception. And I would put Eric Douglas in that same category as the first four names listed.

After getting over our shock of Eric Douglas' news bulletin, The Dutchman and I started to kid him that the only reason why he was going to Gaylord High School was so that he could be with Robert C. Walker again. But, Eric Douglas went on to explain the fear that his father had for his wife and children. Mr. Douglas just simply did not feel safe in raising his kids in the southeastern part of the state of Michigan any longer.

It was sad to say good-bye to Eric Douglas that day. There was the occasional letter back and forth to each other, and he did come down for Homecoming at Fenton during the fall of 1967. But that was about it communications wise between the two of us.

That changed the day that the Flying Dutchman and I walked through the doors of Cabin #5 at the National Music Camp. Lo and behold, sitting on a lower bunk was Eric Douglas. So, fate made it a great two-week reunion for the three of us.

Eric Douglas said to me, "Come on, Doc Savage, let's go over to the student union on campus and get caught up on life, starting with, what in the heck are you doing wearing a Hartland High School band uniform? And, let me guess, the number of that uniform is, oh, don't tell me, number 40." Ha Ha.

Katie joined Eric Douglas and I and it was off to the student union for a lunch that consisted of a cup of hot chocolate and the greasiest hamburger in I have eaten in my life. I gave Eric Douglas the low down of how it became that Katie, along with Jim Koop and Terry Rodenbo and I were now official members of the Hartland Consolidated Schools.

Eric Douglas then shared with Katie and I that he had been recently accepted to Alma College and he was all fired up about getting started with classes. Of course, that now meant that the conversation was going to shift to what my college selection was going to be. I just mumbled something, and I mean mumbled like I had a mouthful of marbles, that I had a couple of schools that I was looking at but had not narrowed it down to any one favorite. Katie, just less than three years from graduating from high school, then had to pipe in and advise Eric Douglas that she was going to attend Colorado University when it came time for her to go to college. Showoff.

Eric Douglas gave us some Robert C. Walker stories; that "RC" still carried himself like the former member of the United States Marine Corp that he was. Robert C. Walker also bought a beautiful house for next to nothing that was built as part of the Industrial Arts Class project by Gaylord High School students.

Eric Douglas then added, "I remember the first day of school as a sophomore at Gaylord High School. Now you have to remember that this was the start of Robert C. Walker's third year as principal of Gaylord High School, so he is now pretty well established in the school and the area. He saw me as I took my first step into Gaylord High School for the start of a new school year, and shockingly, he remembered my name. I was expecting a greeting from him like, "Welcome to your new school; or, Good to see you again, Eric. Something like that."

"Instead, he looked at me with those steely, Clint Eastwood type eyes he has and said to me, "I wondered when those townspeople of Fenton were going to send someone up here to spy on me." That was my official Robert C. Walker welcome to Gaylord High School."

"The thing is, I have been heavily involved with student council as president, so over the last couple of years I have had to meet with "RC" on various topics. One time I got brave enough to ask him if he missed being the high school principal of Fenton High School. He just said that he liked it here more at Gaylord High School then at Fenton for one specific reason. The reason being, and I quote, "There are more snow days here, Douglas."

As the three of us were laughing at this Robert C. Walker story, when I looked up and as chance would have it, I could not believe who I saw standing a few feet away from me grabbing a soft drink out of the pop dispenser. No, it wasn't Al Hirt!! It was Terry Walker, himself, looking taller than I remembered him, and sporting a Central Michigan University varsity jacket.

Eric Douglas offered to introduce us to Terry Walker, but I declined. Mainly because he would have no clue as to who I was. Also, I did not want him to mix me up with my cousin, Davey, the son of the parent whose idea of a productive day in life was "Straightening out old man, Walker."

It was time to start thinking about heading back to the bus area, when I heard a voice yelling out, "KATIE BEARDSLEE!! KATIE BEARDSLEE!!" Now, a lot of kids that had graduated from Fenton High School, currently attend Central Michigan University. I also knew that a lot of the senior class members of 1970 from Fenton High School that were going to go the college route, had CMU at or near the top of their college destinations. So, it was no big surprise that Katie would know a currently enrolled college student here in Mount Pleasant.

I looked up half expecting to see a familiar face but took one look at the girl hugging Katie and had no idea of whom she was. Katie then made the introductions and I officially met Angie Powers, who I discovered was doing her student teaching at State Road Elementary School as a physical education teacher. She and Katie had met through my mother.

Angie Powers took one look at me, and said, "I didn't know that Mary Beardslee had a son." I honestly thought that she was joking and expected Eric Douglas, Angie Powers and Katie to all burst out laughing followed by a loud, "Gotcha!!"

But when I looked at the quizzical expression on the face of Angie Powers, it was rather obvious that she was serious with the statement that she had just made to me. I mean, I kid you not, she was flat out dead serious of what she had just said to me.

Now I know how Greg "Pretty Boy" Sanders was feeling emotionally when he "waved" good-bye to all of us departing bus riders some nearly five hours ago.

"White Lake Road"

Chapter #87 – "We Want a Chip Flip!! We Want a Chip Flip!!"

September 27th – After that unintentional, but still somewhat hurtful statement from Angie Powers, Eric Douglas, Katie and I then headed back to the bus area where as soon Mr. Anderson spotted me, he started to wave to me in an inpatient type of manner for yours truly to hurry up and come over to where he was standing. "Come here, Beardslee. There are a couple of people that I want you to meet." I had no clue who he was talking about, but surprise number three was about 60 feet away.

Mr. Anderson and I walked towards where the Central Michigan University Marching Band was seated. There were two gentlemen standing about 20 yards away from the rest of the conglomeration when the introductions were made.

Mr. Anderson started the amenities and said to me, "Mike Beardslee, I want to meet the director of the Central Michigan University Marching Band, Professor Norman Dietz. I also want you introduce to you one of my former students at Beaverton High School, John Cummings, who is currently the low brass instructor here at CMU." I remembered that latter name for some reason, but could not immediately place it.

Professor Norman Dietz said to me, "Mike, I am pleased to meet you. Mr. Anderson has advised me that you are a pretty special type of trumpet player. Now, I do not know if you have yet finalized your college future, but when you do, I want you to remember that there is always a need for outstanding trumpet players here at Central Michigan University. I hope you give us your consideration."

Hands were shaken all around again in a goodbye manner and I must admit that I was taken aback by what had just taken place. There are apparently three people on the face of the Earth who think that I was worthy of being a college trumpet player. Four, counting my mother. Surprise number three had just officially come out of left field.

When Mr. Anderson and I had rejoined the Hartland Marching Band contingency, the Central Michigan University Marching Band had taken the field for their pre-game show and they were indeed something to watch. As a college marching unit, they do not have to take a back seat to any of their peers. You put those guys in a big enclosed area like the University of Michigan football stadium instead of the miles of vacant land surrounding the CMU campus, and their instrumental sound would be really something special.

I did not pay much attention to the football game itself. In fact, I do not even know who the CMU Chippewas' opponent was this day. All I remember was hearing over the PA system that some CMU running back was having a great first half.

Probably the most exciting event during the first two quarters of this college football game was the chanting that was coming from the surrounding honors bands. I had never heard of some of these high schools before but they must have been local institutes of learning because all of them seemed to be reciting the same phrase over and over again: "WE WANT A CHIP FLIP!! WE WANT A CHIP FLIP !!" Okay.

Well, what happened next was that the CMU cheerleaders all huddled up together and proceeded to throw one of their troops in what seemed like a couple of hundred feet up in the air. While sky bound, this cheerleader would then do some type of acrobatic flip midcourse up in the atmosphere and then land in the arms of her fellow squad members, all to the mighty applause of all the CMU Band Day Honors Band attendees. I mean these guys were going crazy with joy!!

I must admit that I was impressed with what I had just seen. The honors band people that were closest to us Hartland kids, were not satisfied, though. They wanted more action, which led to further screams of, "WE WANT ANOTHER CHIP FLIP!! WE WANT ANOTHER CHIP FLIP !!"

The halftime show was just as easy as the morning rehearsals. Another difference between this Band Day and the one on September 20th, was that this grouping was small enough, that all involved bands were even able to end a song at the same time. And no brick wall!! I just cannot get over that!!

Despite the concern that Mr. Anderson had that if the Hartland Eagles twenty participants would be seen departing before the football game was completed, that there would now be a case for his name to be mysteriously entered into a secret black book in the Central Michigan Music Department with a demerit marked next to it; once we got back to the bleachers and saw all of the other bands were heading out, there was no question of whether us Hartland musicians were going to stay for the second half or not. It was bee line straight back to the Hartland School bus and time to beat feet home.

Even the bus ride home today was different than the quick trip last week from Ann Arbor to Hartland. For whatever reason, and I have no idea why, Jim Koop and I did not even break out the kazoos.

The only real item of hilarity on the trek back to Livingston County was when Jim Koop said to me, "Hey, Beardslee. I heard one of the kids from the Farwell High School Band say that your trumpet playing stunk. But don't you worry, Beardslee, my good friend. I defended you. When that same Farwell Band kid said to me again that your trumpet playing stunk; I said, "Like crap it does." Get it!!"

Yeah, I "get it." I mean, come on, based upon the witticisms that have been tossed at me today, I had to ask myself if Jim Koop and Angie Powers related to each other?? I sure hope not.

Later that evening while back in the confines of "White Lake Road", while contentedly sitting in a recliner and leafing through my "Sporting News", I must admit, that considering the fact that I had no desire to attend the CMU Band Day today, and I mean zippo, it wasn't a half bad day.

When you factor in the serenading of Greg "Pretty Boy" Sanders; the seeing and catching up with Eric Douglas for an hour or so; meeting Professors Dietz and Cummings; almost getting introduced to Terry Walker and, most of all, the discovery of what a "CHIP FLIP" is, it was an enjoyable 12 hours. Very pleasing in fact.

Now, an agreeable enough time that on this upcoming Monday morning Mike Beardslee will immediately sprint down to the counselor's office in Hartland High School, grab a college application and start filling it out so that I can start the steps to becoming a trumpet player in the Central Michigan University Music Department? Yeah, right. Just as soon as I starting belting out the application for a counselor's position at the Interlochen National Music Camp this summer along with the Flying Dutchman.

So, don't hold your breath to see whether either of these two applications ever see the inside of an envelope with the address of "White Lake Road" on the outside of its covering.

Out of nowhere, I finally remembered where I had heard the name of John Cummings before. He was the former student of Mr. Anderson's who also had a bad set of front teeth and eventually had to switch from playing the trumpet to the baritone. One week from today, I will learn whether I will have to make that same decision about playing another type of brass instrument with a larger mouthpiece.

Today started with an early wakeup call and so will tomorrow. I have a busy day on tap, starting with a trip to Swartz Creek, a Detroit Lions game to listen to on the radio as the New York Giants come to town; and finally, most importantly, the preparation of an upcoming meeting on Monday that even at this very moment my stomach is getting a little queasy about.

After this long day, I was whipped. I barely even made it to the opening theme song for the start of its third season of the TV series, "Mannix" tonight. The last sound that I had running through my mind before dozing off, though, were the screams of, ""WE WANT A CHIP FLIP!! WE WANT A CHIP FLIP !!"

"White Lake Road"

Chapter #88 – "The Boarder"

September 28th – A busy day for this last Sunday in the month of September. For my birthday, which is tomorrow, Katie has decided to get me a present of a birthday cake. Now, mind you, not just your everyday birthday cake that you could purchase at a grocery store like a Comber & Fox or Hamady Brothers. Nor even at the Fenton Bakery, which by the way, has fantastic cream filled long johns, with powdered sugar sprinkled on the top.

Nope!! This morning we are traveling to Mrs. Jones' house to get a "Mrs. Jones made birthday cake!!"

Mrs. Jones is my Godmother and lived just down the road from the Beardslee family when we used to reside at 4227 S. Linden Road, Flint, Michigan, Zone #7. Mrs. Jones teaches third grade at Holy Redeemer and probably is the nicest and funniest third grade teacher that ever-set foot in a classroom. If you were a second-grade student at Holy Redeemer, Mrs. Jones is the person that you spent time over the summer wishing for her to become your third-grade teacher.

My personal favorite story about Mrs. Jones was the time that the Jones and Beardslee clans were having a picnic at Byron Lake. Mrs. Jones made some hamburgers that upon me biting into one of them, I made the mistake of saying in front of Mrs. Jones and my mother, especially my mother, "This is the best hamburger that I have ever eaten in my life!!"

I was eight years old at that time when I made that foolish comment and from the immediate look that I received from my mother, the odds of me reaching the age of nine, were not in my favor. Just for the record, three years later, I was finally allowed by my mother to officially reach the age of nine.

Mrs. Jones has a sideline business of where she would bake cakes for all types of occasions; birthdays, weddings, reunions, you name it. And let me tell you this, these babies were the greatest tasting cakes within the listening range of Radio Free Europe!! I kid you not, the frosting on a Mrs. Jones made birthday cake was so thick, that if any of it got on your driveway, it would cause your car to get stuck and you would be in need of a tow truck. Gotta love those dairy products!!

Last summer, Mrs. Jones' typical busy season, asked Katie if she wanted to earn some extra spending money by helping out with the cake business. Katie jumped on the opportunity and for three days a week my mother hauled Katie to the Jones' residence for her part time job.

Katie worked with Mrs. Jones' oldest daughter, Phyliss and for lack of a better word, a boarder, by the name of Dani Ward. The latter becoming great friends with Katie. While my presence was somewhat sparse from the "White Lake Road" residence last summer, what few times I was ever around Katie, every other word that came out of her mouth was, "Dani Ward and I did this. Dani Ward and I are going to going to such and such event."

"White Lake Road"

So, on the way to Mrs. Jones' residence this morning I took a back way so that I could get the full story on who Dani Ward is and how she ended up living with my Godmother. The non-expressway travel included heading west down White Lake Road; a quick turn onto Bennett Lake Road; then head north on Linden Road.

This route was also a trip down memory lane. We would travel past Byron Lake, my favorite place to go swimming in this area; through the town of Linden, Michigan; past 4228 S. Linden Road, a house that my father built all by himself and the first family home for Katie and I. Then it was a left-hand turn into Mrs. Jones driveway just before you drove under the viaduct that crosses above Linden Road.

I always loved to come to the Jones' house when we lived just a short walk down Linden Road from them. The Jones family had a different life style than us Beardslee's did. I was always amazed when I would go into their garage and see cases of bottled pop just stacked up against a wall there. When you opened up the Beardslee family refrigerator, if you saw more than one bottle of M&S bottle of soda in there at the same time, it was either some one's birthday or the Detroit Tigers had just won the World Series. The Beardslee's were a bottled milk family, not a bottled soda family.

And when you initially entered the side door of Jones' house, the first area that you walked into was the kitchen; AKA: "Command Central for the Baking of Cakes." Guaranteed, there were always baking contents all over the kitchen, but it smelled great. If Katie and I timed our visits just right, Mrs. Jones would always hand us a couple of spoons and let us clean the bowl that had the remains of cake batter. And if we were really lucky, we could also lick the cake beaters that were just dripping with cake batter.

On the way to our destination this morning, while I was mainly concerned about whether Fran Tarkenton, quarterback of the New Your Giants, was going to pass and scramble, his specialty, all over the Detroit Lions defense this afternoon, I heard the story of Katie's latest and bestest friend, Dani Ward.

What I gathered from Katie was the following; the Ward and Jones' families were very close friends. Dani Ward was currently a senior at Holy Redeemer High School, a cheerleader for basketball and football seasons, the shortstop on the softball team, flute player in the Band, senior class treasurer and a former third grade student of Mrs. Jones. Not in that order.

Mr. Ward, had just retired from General Motors. He had a brother, Dani Ward's uncle, who resided in Marquette, Michigan, and who owned and operated some extremely successful restaurants and bars in that area. The uncle wanted to expand into the snowmobile and motorcycle business and had asked Dani Ward's father to become his partner in this venture.

This now meant that the Flint, Michigan, Wards' would have to pack up and move to the upper peninsula. When Dani Ward heard about the possibility of moving away for her senior year of high school, she was none too happy and stated, "This is unfair. No high school senior should ever have to move to another school district and spend their 12th grade year with a bunch of teachers and students they don't know at all."

"White Lake Road"

Hello!! Hello!! Mike Beardslee and Jim Koop here!!

Mrs. Jones stepped in and said that since her son Ron, who was in the United States Air Force and currently stationed in the state of Texas, there was a spare bedroom that Dani Ward could use so that she could stay in the Flint area and spend her senior year at Holy Redeemer High School. A Typical Mrs. Jones gesture and problem solved.

As Katie and I entered into the Jones' kitchen, the first thing that I saw was a birthday cake decorated with vanilla frosting that had to be, at least in my sweet toothed mind, a good three inches thick. Add some blue and gold trim around the sides of the cake, a "Happy Birthday, Mike" on top of it and you now have a first-rate kind of birthday cake that is fit for the "King of Planet Beardslee."

The only problem with this cake was that I knew Terry Rodenbo was going to have his "birthday cake radar on" and at some point, today, under the guise of "I want to share my recipe for toast with your mother, Beardslee," would be finding his way to "White Lake Road" for a piece of my birthday cake. The difference being is that my mother will cut me a slice of my birthday cake. She will then cut Terry Rodenbo a slab of my birthday cake. My birthday cake!!

After being given a spoon by Mrs. Jones to slurp up the remains of a cake batter bowl, I saw someone in a distance coming from the living room into the kitchen. I about dropped the spoon in the bowl when I initially noticed of whom I deducted, all on my own I might add, was one Dani Ward.

My initial impression of her was that she was the spitting image of Jane Roberts. Or at least an older sister. As Dani Ward entered the kitchen, my thoughts now were that while there was indeed some similarity to the looks of Jane Roberts and Dani Ward, especially facially, the two could have passed for first cousins rather than siblings. Or was it the fact that any girl I meet is automatically compared and held up to the Jane Roberts' standard?? Either way, Dani Ward had my attention.

And that was about all she had. Introductions were made by Katie and after that she and Dani Ward totally disappeared from my site, while I got stuck carrying bags of flour up from the basement, three trips in all, for Mrs. Jones.

Even my favorite Godmother didn't say one word to me about Dani Ward!! There was no, "She's not dating anybody right now." Or, "You ought to give her a call some time." All I got out of Mrs. Jones was, "Be sure to turn off the light in the basement, Mike." Hey!! Gimme me a break!! I'm company!!

This silent and less than hearty welcome from Dani Ward must mean one of two things; Mrs. Jones and Katie have a conspiracy against me; or, Dani Ward is going steady with another guy. You are right. It just has to be the former, correct?? I mean, come on. We are talking about Mike Beardslee here. The guy with the ruggedly handsome looks!! And, the real

clincher of all, a subscriber to the "Sporting News" magazine. Seriously, what girl could turn down any male with those qualities??

Let's just put it this way, the line forms to the left, and it's one long, long, long procession. So, girls, be sure to pack a lunch.

We finally made our farewells to Mrs. Jones and when she said goodbye to Katie and I, Dani Ward was with her. Dani Ward's waves and adios', however, were directed to Katie and not me. No, "Hey, I am glad to meet you." Or, "I hope you enjoy your birthday cake." Nothing like that at all. She's just gotta be related to Jane Roberts.

I tried to pump some information from Katie about Dani Ward but with no luck. It's not like this hasn't happened before between the two of us. This was Katie's way of being overly protective of her big brother. In essence, what she was communicating to me about Dani Ward translated to, "Don't go there."

Once home, the birthday cake tasted absolutely fantastic. And I have gotten a little smarter since I was allowed to reach the age of nine years old, as I made a point of saying out loud at the Beardslee dinner table, that the birthday cake could have used some more frosting on it. Very much to my mother's delight I might add.

From there it was to my bedroom to catch the start of the Detroit Lions-New York Giants game. I am not a huge fan of the Detroit Lions' radio announcers, Van Patrick and Bob Reynolds. In my opinion, they could take a few lessons from the Detroit Tigers' radio broadcasting team of Ernie Harwell and Ray Lane. The latter two are just excellent at their craft.

But there is the one phrase that Van Patrick uses that I love to hear whenever the Detroit Lions scored six points. "Touchdown, Detroit!!" That radio saying is almost as good as when an opposing major league baseball player is struck out by a Detroit Tiger pitcher. That's when Ernie Harwell coins one of his greatest sayings, ""He stood there like the house by the side of the road …"

I heard the magical phrase of "Touchdown, Detroit" a total of three times today by Van Patrick, as the Detroit Lions scored three TD" s and beat the New York Giants 24-0. This is a nice win for the good guys that wear the Honolulu and Blue football uniforms. The Detroit Lions travel to Cleveland next week to face the Cleveland Browns. A football squad, I might add, that is getting a few votes to make it to Super Bowl IV this upcoming January.

A few moments after the conclusion of the Lions-Giants game, I got a shout downstairs from my mother saying, "There is someone here to see you." My heart almost leaped out of my mouth. You just know that it's Dani Ward coming out to "White Lake Road" to apologize to me for not being a better host from this morning or, at the very least, ask me to assist her in her Latin Class homework.

All of Gall is divided into three parts, here I come!!

"White Lake Road"

Chapter #89 – "The Big Kids"

September 28th – Was Dani Ward the mystery person that was sitting in the breakfast room of "White Lake Road?" Or just maybe instead, Stephanie Powers?? All of you are correct. It was Terry Rodenbo, sitting where my father normally sits at the breakfast room table, chomping down a huge piece of birthday cake, my birthday cake I might add, and washing it down with a cold glass of buttermilk.

Despite the fact that Terry Rodenbo had just asked my mother if he could take a piece of my birthday cake home with him for a snack later tonight, I was actually quite glad that he was here, as this week starts the building of the Band Float for the Hartland High School Homecoming Parade.

As president of the Hartland High School Senior Band, it is my responsibility to make sure that the Band Float is constructed and all ready to go for the Homecoming Parade that takes place on October 10th in downtown Hartland, Michigan.

I don't exactly have a great history of working on, or being in charge of Band Floats. In fact, after some of the events that took place about one year ago from this time, I wanted nothing to do with a Band Float ever again as long as I am a member of the human race.

As mentioned in an earlier writing, I was in the Fenton High School Senior Band as an eighth grader. I was very aware that there was the existence of a Band Float and also knew that it was being built at Doug Walker's house. But I had no interest in giving up a night of good television watching to travel three miles into downtown Fenton just to work on the Band Float.

My mother got wind of the Band Float being built, and to this day I have no clue how, ordered me to get in car and off it was to Doug Walker's house. Katie, who was in sixth grade at this time and a member of the State Road Elementary School Band, tagged along. Once she saw the Band Float being constructed by "the big kids", she asked my mother if it was okay to stay and help "the big kids."

Permission was granted much to my dismay. I knew exactly what was going to happen next. Katie was going to have the time of her life, plus be an excellent worker, while I would sort of hang around being even more worthless that what I already was in life, just killing some time waiting for my mother to order me back in the car and then head back home.

When my mother finally did arrive, "the big kids" praised Katie to no end. "She was no trouble at all. What a great worker" kind of stuff. Nothing was said to my mother about me but there was a sense in the air of, "Mrs. Beardslee. Next time bring Katie by herself to work on the Band Float. And be sure to leave your useless son at home." Fine by me.

My freshman year come Band Float season I caught a huge break. As much as I did not particularly enjoy being a member of the Fenton High School cross country team, it got me out of working on the Band Float. After a two-hour practice and being dead tired when I got

home, my mother knew that there was the practicing of the trumpet to be done, television to be watched and maybe some Algebra I homework to be totally ignored.

Thus, I was not required by my mother to work on the Band Float during the fall of 1966. It broke Katie's heart, but not mine.

My sophomore year I was again a member of the cross-country team, and despite the fact that I had improved as a runner, I still did not care for the sport that much. But, for the second consecutive year, this was my ticket out of working on the Band Float!! At least I thought that would be the case.

One day just before Band class started, Guy Thompson came up to me with an excited, wild type look in his eyes and blurted out, "We will not be able to have the Band Float built where we planned to for this years' Homecoming Parade. Can we use your barn to have the Band Float constructed??"

This was not what I exactly wanted to hear, so I stalled and said, "If you get my mother's permission, then yeah, go ahead." As soon as Guy Thompson left me I thought to myself, "Stupid!! Stupid!! Stupid!!" I knew that Guy Thompson would easily be able to talk my mother into having the Band Float built in Beardslee's Barn. It was as good as a done deal while I stood there, trumpet and trumpet case in hand, thinking to myself of what the cartoon character, "Snidely Whiplash", always says in a similar type moment. Oh, yeah, "Curses, foiled again!!"

As I was soon to discover when I got home from cross country practice that evening, the Band Float trailer was in the barn and there were kids working their little fingers away on it. I showed very little interest in the proceedings. My life style stayed the same. I ate. I practiced the trumpet and spent long hours going through the pages of the TV Guide hoping to find reruns of "The Girl from U.N.C.L.E.". With no luck, I might add.

I knew that the Band Float was in good hands under the leadership of: Guy Thompson, Jean Vosburgh, Gayla Woolford; Beth Rhodes, Mark Swade and Mike Hicks. Plus, Katie, now an eighth-grader and a member of the junior high band, was constantly up there in the barn working away on the Band Float and having the time of her life with the "big kids." In my line of thinking, I was home free. I was surely not needed.

While nothing at first was ever directly said to me, I could tell by the looks and body language of my fellow Band members, that I was slowly becoming a not to popular person. Finally, Jim Koop pulled me aside and said, "Beardslee, my friend. It's probably not to bad an idea if you took the time to come up to work on the Band Float. People are starting to make comments like, "The Band Float is in his own barn. Would it kill him to come up and work on it for a couple of minutes every night??"

Or, "He's less than 50 feet from his house front door to his barn. I have to travel six miles' round trip to come out here. He's got no excuse to not be working on this Band Float!!"

Katie started to urge me as well to get out and, "At least show my face". But it was Guy Thompson, as usual, and only as he could, who got the point across to me. He came at me with two very direct questions, "Do you want to be Band President some day?? Do you want to be vice-president of this Band one year from now?? Then if you do, I strongly suggest that you get yourself out there and start assisting in the building of this Band Float!!" Duly noted.

Guess who was out there right after supper every night to work on the Band Float? You're right. Guess who also discovered that it did not kill him to walk from the back door of "White Lake Road" to the front door of Beardslee's Barn to work on the Band Float?? Congratulations, you are now two for two.

Overall, it turned out to be a great experience. Excellent enough that I could hardly wait for the Band Float to be built at Beardslee's Barn during my junior year of high school, especially now that I was Band President and I was to be in charge of this project.

As positive of a time that I had working on the Band Float under the leadership of Guy Thompson and some other very dedicated senior class Band members, I learned one thing really quick during my regime of building the Band Float. I was no Guy Thompson. And that group of dedicated seniors were no longer available to keep everything going smooth. The total opposite took place under the Beardslee administration when it came time for constructing the Band Float. You name it, it went wrong.

The first major issue was that the Homecoming week for Fenton High School in October of 1968 happened to take place at the same time the World Series was being played between the Detroit Tigers and St. Louis Cardinals. I have lived through three events in my young life that if I live for another 100 years, that with no hesitation I would be able to specifically tell you where I was at that very moment and what I was doing.

That second such monumental moment was when Detroit Tiger catcher, Bill Freehan, caught the foul ball pop-up off of Tim McCarver's bat for the final out of game seven of this fall classic, allowing the Detroit Tigers to become world champions. I was working on the Band Float and jumping up and down like crazy.

Truth be known, however, I spent more time listening to the World Series on the radio in the barn or coming up with some flimsy excuse that would allow me to go into the family room of "White Lake Road" to catch some of the action on TV, rather than working on the Band Float. So, sue me.

The biggest problem, however, when it came to working on the Band Float was getting kids to come out to Beardslee's Barn to work on the lousy thing. When I completed Driver's Education training in August of 1968, I had a driver's permit that allowed me to drive a motor vehicle as long as there was a licensed driver accompanying me. This constraint was in effect until my 16th birthday.

I made the huge mistake of bragging in front of my mother that once I got my driver's license, I would be able to haul kids back and forth from down town Fenton to work on the Band

Float while using her car. Well guess who didn't get his driver's license until way after Band Float season was officially a part of world history. Shall we say, it wasn't Katie.

That is where my Band Float mentors like Guy Thompson, Mike Hicks, Jean Vosburgh and Mark Swade had it all over me. The four of them had access to cars. And when they came out to work on the Band Float, they always brought a bunch of Band kids along with them.

I did not have that luxury under my watch. There were nights when the only people working on the Band Float were myself, Katie, Terry Rodenbo, and Jim Koop. And I have no idea how the latter two arranged transportation to get to Beardslee's Barn and back to their homes. I suspect that they walked both ways or hitch hiked. Probably the latter.

Things took a temporary turn for the better, when my State Road Elementary School buddy, Mike Ogilvie, got his driver's license and said, "Don't you worry my good friend. I'll haul some Band kids out to your barn to get that Band Float completed in time!!"

Well, Mike Ogilvie, while only very briefly, was good to his word until one day he showed up and there were no kids with him. I asked, "Where is everyone, Oge??" He just shrugged his shoulders and went to talk to my mother about who knows what.

I finally got the real story about Mike Ogilvie from two different sources, Miss Franklin and Jim Koop. One day at school, Miss Franklin pulled me aside and in a demanding voice asked, "What is going on with this Band Float. I am getting all sorts of complaint calls from parents!!"

"I am being threatened to be sued personally by parents because when Mike Ogilvie picks up their kids to take them out to your home, he is swerving his car all over the road; running red lights, driving through stop signs and always traveling speeds that are in excess of the speed limit. These students are too scared to get in a motor vehicle with him!!"

"For my part, I do not want to be sued and I can guarantee you that the school district doesn't want to be taken to court over this matter, either!! So, what are you going to do about this, Mr. President??"

Luckily, the problem solved itself as Mike Ogilvie simply quit showing up to work on the Band Float. Later in talking with Jim Koop, I told him of the tongue lashing that I had received from Miss Franklin. His response was, "She's right about Ogilvie's driving skills. I rode with him once out to your place and he was doing every one of the things old lady Franklin said he was doing."

"Part of it was just showing off to the kids in the car. The other cause for his reckless driving is that he wears those eye glasses of his that might as well be the bottom of Coca-Cola bottles. Once he's behind the wheel of his car he probably can't even see where he is going half the time. I know me and Rodenbo won't ride with him again."

So, that explained why no one would come out to work on the Band Float. Which, in turn caused us to make all sorts of short cuts construction wise. Our physical labor efforts, as well as the spirit that goes into a project like this paled miserably to what took place the year before.

Bottom line is that I will now get to go down in history as the Band president who broke the six-year winning streak of first place finishes in the Float Competition by the Fenton High School Band. It was embarrassing then and some 50 weeks later I still have the occasional nightmare when I hear in my sleep the announcement during halftime that we took sixth place, instead of our customary first place, out of eight competing floats. Man, those seventh and eighth place finishing floats must have been flat out hideous looking for us to rate higher than them.

But the thing that still stings me the most about my debut of being in charge of the Band Float was the one night a bunch of Band kids, including my arch enemies, John Perkins and Mary Morrison, actually did come out to do what I thought would be to toil away on the Band Float. The Calvary had arrived and the Band Float was going to rescued!!

This group stuck around for a few minutes and then totally disappeared. I looked throughout the rest of the barn and could not locate them. I then looked out of the second-floor barn window and I saw lights on in "White Lake Road." My mother was in Ypsilanti, Michigan for a graduate class at Eastern Michigan University, so I knew that she was not home.

I went down to the house and when I entered it, the first thing I saw was that the refrigerator door was wide open in the kitchen, followed by the noise of kids banging on our piano; playing pool on our pool table in the basement; and the television set was blaring away. But what really made me mad was when a couple of my fellow Band mates saw me and yelled, "Hey, Beardslee!! Don't mind us, we're just taking a tour of your house. By the way, that's a real cute pink telephone that your folks have in their bed room!!"

I screamed in a voice that was so loud, that for the next two days, my vocal chords seemed like they were still on fire, 'GET OUT OF MY HOUSE RIGHT NOW!! RIGHT THIS VERY MINUTE!! I MEAN IT!!"

I didn't know what hurt worse, my vocal chords, or that it took at least a good minute or two before it dawned on these members of the Fenton High School Band that I was not joking around and that I wanted each and every single one of them out of my house. They eventually left, but man-o-man, the smiles and laughter they had on their faces and coming out of their mouths while going out the door of "White Lake Road" made me even more upset.

How upset?? Thank you for asking. I was enraged enough that I opened up a cupboard door in the kitchen, grabbed a book of matches, headed out to the barn with only one thought in mind: "Burn down the Band Float!! "Burn down the Band Float!!"

Katie finally calmed me down and after doing a walk through the house with my Band Float partners to make sure that nothing was broken or stolen, especially any back issues of my

"Sporting News'", Jim Koop came up with the remark that ultimately brought my blood pressure down and made my heart stop from beating at the rate of a couple of hundred miles an hour, "Ya know, Beardslee, he stated, "Those guys are correct. That is a cute pink telephone up in your parent's bed room."

That same evening, I had given a lot of thought of what I was going to say to the Band kids before rehearsal the next day as I am sure word would have had gotten out of what had taken place last night at the Beardslee residence. I had given some consideration about just shutting the Band Float project down entirely, but the finish line for this venture was only two days away. We had come this far, so that idea was out.

Instead I took the recommendation of Terry Rodenbo who said, "Why don't you cancel the Band Float clean up party? The four of us can do that by ourselves. And it will also mean more of the home-made rolls, pizza and oat meal cookies that your mother is making for us."

An excellent idea and that is exactly what I did. I cancelled the above stated festivity and made more than a few Fenton High School Marching Band members very unhappy with that decision. Especially the ones that had not worked one second on the Band Float but who had planned on showing up for the cleanup party anyway.

I did get more than my share of flak about that executive decision. But, hey. Boo is the first word. Hoo is the second word. When you put them together what do they spell? You got it. Boo-Hoo!!

After tonight's session with Terry Rodenbo and Katie concerning the Hartland Senior Band Executive Board meeting scheduled for tomorrow morning with an agenda strictly concerning the Band Float and all its particulars, plus another piece of birthday cake, I felt prepared for this planning conference with all of the key points I wanted to bring up. But I must admit, there are still plenty of bad memories in my brain cells that remind me of what took place one year ago when I was in charge of the Band Float.

"White Lake Road"

Chapter #90 – "Presidential Pants"

September 29th – Despite the fact that there is no half-time show this week as the Hartland High School gridders travel to Fowlerville High School for their next contest, this week marks the start of Band Float season. And as you have probably gathered, I am in charge of this project for a second consecutive season. Simply put, this is God's way of punishing me.

I hope that things will go better Band Float wise for me then it did some 350 days ago. Already I am ahead of the ball game, no pun intended, as sadly, there is no post season play for the Detroit Tigers this major-league baseball season. Secondly, let's hope that I learned from the numerous mistakes I made during last Band Float season.

As I entered the breakfast room of "White Lake Road' this morning, I was greeted by my three traveling partners with various comments of, "He's got his presidential pants on!! Beardslee is wearing his presidential pants!!"

Last spring, I purchased what I thought were a nice-looking pair of gray, charcoal dress pants. And, of course, it never dawned on me to try them on while I was at the Smith-Bridgman's store in downtown Flint. When I got home the slacks were way to big and baggy on me. They wore poorly and looked even worse.

However, it still didn't stop me from wearing these trousers to school where on that particular day I had to be in charge of a Band Council meeting. A meeting that went surprisingly well and I attributed my good fortune to the wearing of my "presidential pants." So, any time there was something formal going on with a Band Meeting or a concert at a school assembly, I automatically break out the presidential pants.

With the Band Float meeting on the agenda for today, the presidential pants will make their debut, Hartland High School Senior Band style.

There were five participants in this mornings' conference; Mr. Anderson, myself, Teri Andrews, Katie, and by special invite, Terry Rodenbo. When Teri Andrews saw Terry Rodenbo, she had that look on her face that clearly read, "What's he doing here?? He's not on the Band Executive Board!!" Luckily, Teri Andrews bit her tongue and the summit went startling well.

There were many questions that I automatically had answers to when I was in charge of the Fenton High School Band Float. Such as:

- ***Where was the Band Float going to be built?***
- ***Whose trailer could we use to build the float on?***
- ***Who would drive the Band Float in the Homecoming Parade?***
- ***What was the theme of our float going to be?***
- ***How much money did we need to go beg from the Band Boosters' Club for supplies?***
- ***And when we ran out of the money from the Band Booster's, which one of us kids would run to my mother and solicit her kind heartedness for a financial contribution***

towards the first of many, many more boxes of Kleenex necessary to complete building the Band Float?

- *And most importantly of all, will there be a problem getting Band kids to actually come out and work on the Band Float?*

The good part of this gathering this morning was that almost all of the questions, and I readily admit unexpectedly, were addressed by Teri Andrews:

1. *The Band Float was going to be built at the Andrews' residence. Apparently, there is a pole barn on their property and this is where the Band Float has been constructed for the past two years.*
2. *Teri Andrews had also arranged for a trailer from Jason Shattucks' folks for the Band Float to be constructed upon.*
3. *Mr. Andrews, father of Teri and Trecha Andrews, will drive the Band Float with their family owned car in the Homecoming Parade.*
4. *I, presidential pants and all, finally got a chance to have some input in this meeting, specifically in reference to what the theme of the Band Float would be. My suggestion was that we use the quote that Astronaut Neil Armstrong made when he first set foot on the Moon just less than three months ago, "That's one small step for man, one giant leap for mankind." The executive board liked that idea so much that Katie immediately hurried down to the high school office to get it officially registered as the title theme of the Band Float.*
5. *Mr. Anderson weighed in on the money request from the Band Boosters Club by saying, "They're really good about contributing to this activity. I will hit them up for $25.00. But, I should add, that is all that they will be willing to give us. So, spend that money wisely."*

I guarantee you this, for sure we will run out of these funds so generously given to us by the Band Boosters. What that means is that either Katie or Jim Koop will have to turn on their charming personality to get my mother to underwrite the cost of another Band Float. Even one that is not being built this year on her property. Believe me, those two will get the money out of my mother.

6. *The last issue was my biggest concern. Worker!! Workers!! Workers!! Will we be able to get a sufficient amount of Band kids to work on the Band Float? Not just for one night, but every night through October 9th? Because this is not just Mike and Katie Beardslee simply walking out to their barn to gain access to the Band Float or Jim Koop and Terry Rodenbo hitch hiking out to Beardslee's Barn just to stuff Kleenex in wire mesh. No, this project will include the driving of at least 28 miles' round trip in the jeep. And that's potentially on top of one round trip already made that day. That's a lot of time and gas money.*

I realize that these Hartland Band kids are very dedicated to the Band. But just how devoted are they when they will have to contribute time outside of school hours on a nightly basis? I know for a fact that Randi Lynch and Aisha Tredeau will be there every breathing second that they have in their bodies. But will others? Mr. Anderson and Teri Andrews both stated that this was not a problem since it had never been an issue in the past.

Teri Andrews stated, "The first year that we had the Band Float built at our place there were kids coming and going at all hours of the day. So, my parents laid down the law and set scheduled hours for when the Band Float was to be worked on. So, from 7:00-9:00 PM on Tuesday, Wednesday and Thursday nights, we can work on the Band Float. On the weekend, we can work from 2:00-4:00 PM, but only on Saturday afternoons. Also, my parents will only allow a total of 10 kids at a time to be in the Pole Barn."

I about choked when Teri Andrews said they could only cap it at 10 workers per session. Last year at Beardslee's Barn, I'd be shocked if we got more than 10 kids total the whole time spent working on the Band Float. And that's counting returning workers.

Mr. Anderson said, "Like we did last year, there will be sign-up sheets for the kids to pick a night(s) that they're going to work on the Band Float. Now, since this is a Band related project, it is your duty as student leaders of the Band, that if a person signs up for a date to work, and does not appear, then please let me know, as that lack of responsibility will be reflected in their grade for Band." Man, these guys take this Band Float stuff serious!!

All systems are go and tomorrow night starts the beginning of Band Float building season!! I cannot wait, and Guy Thompson, I hope to make you proud this time around.

I mentioned to Jim Koop before the start of Band class as to how well the Band Floating meeting went, especially how knowledgeable and cooperative Terri Andrews had been. Jim Koop's response was, "Oh, Beardslee. She's just buttering you guys up to get votes so that she can be elected Homecoming Queen."

The truth hurts and I have no doubt that Jim Koop's statement hit the nail on the head. That would indeed be Teri Andrews' style.

Overall, from a marching band standpoint, today was an "inside" day. Mr. Anderson passed out the two pieces of music that we will be performing for our next halftime show. Now the one thing that you have to take into consideration is that a Homecoming halftime show is a little different that your typical game performance. There is a lot of standing in place for the Band while the various floats are paraded around the field; introductions of the Queen's Court and their escorts are made; and the big moment of the evening, the announcing of the Homecoming Queen.

Basically, the Hartland High School Marching Band will be standing in concert formation playing background music while all of the above is taking place. This week, Mr. Anderson has selected the song, "I Enjoy Being a Girl" for that portion of the program. It's not a half bad tune. It has a nice beat with a little snap to it and would be a good song for a marching band routine. But certainly, not a tune to be played over and over again while in concert formation.

"White Lake Road"

The main song for our halftime show marching band routine will be a number by the name of "Fever." I believe that I have heard vocalist, Peggy Lee, sing this song many a time on the radio.

Now, this is my fifth marching band season, and I can usually tell within the first measure of playing a song for the first time whether or not I think that this is going to be a tune that will trigger a "WOW" halftime show. I immediately knew this was the case when we started rehearsing the songs, "Up Up and Away" and "Goin Out of My Head" for our first halftime show of the year. Those babies were an instant, "WOW".

And for the second consecutive halftime show of this marching band season I just do not get that "WOW" feeling. I looked around the rest of the Band and saw the facial expressions of the; clarinet section; flute section; saxophone section; trumpet section; percussion section; and French horn section. Those groupings, along with myself and Jim Koop, had grimacing looks on their faces after a once through of playing "Fever."

However, I then looked over to the baritone, trombone and sousaphone sections, the low brass guys and home of Terry Rodenbo and Jason Shattuck. Those two were just going crazy!! They were ecstatic with the selection of "Fever"!! And after the playing through this halftime music selection again, I could see why the duo liked this musical choice so much. If there was ever a halftime show song written for low brass players, it was "Fever."

I don't know which it was that I got more tired of hearing about during Fourth Hour today; the song "Fever", or Terry Rodenbo and Jason Shattuck constantly crowing about how Mr. Anderson should right this very moment automatically name the low brass group as winners of the section of the week. Then, Mr. Anderson should arrange for a delivery truck full of ice cream cartons ASAP, to be sent in care of the, "Low Brass Section. Hartland High School Band Room, Hartland, Michigan, USA."

Why do I think that for the third consecutive half-time show of the season I am going to get shut out again in my quest to be named, "Marcher of the Week"?

"White Lake Road"

Chapter #91 – "A Trip to Pellett's'"

September 29th – I was so worked up about the Band Float meeting that for a second or two I almost forgotten that today was my 17th birthday. Now is my birthday a special day for me, you ask? Yes and no.

While I enjoy the fact that this is "my day" and I came into the world by-way-of McLaren Hospital in Flint, Michigan just a few weeks before former United States President, Dwight D. Eisenhower, won the 1952 presidential election, any birthday celebration for me is very low key. Certainly, nothing compared to Katie's birthday. Now that is a major production in the Beardslee household!! But by now you have probably figured that out on your own.

There are definite things that I do enjoy about my birthday and a memory or two that makes me dread this annual day of the year. The most favorite moment of my birthday history is the birthday cake that my mother would bake for me. Nothing like the Mrs. Jones made birthday cake that Terry Rodenbo had three slices of as compared to only my two yesterday.

No, this was an angel food cake that has thick pink stripes of frosting on the side. But what made this birthday cake so great was that my mother would take pennies; nickels; dimes; quarters and a couple of Ben Franklin half-dollar pieces, wrap them up in wax paper and then bake them as part of the cake.

So, when you got a slice of this delicious, tasting angel food cake set on your plate, there would be a piece of wax paper, or two if you were really lucky, in the piece covering up a certain coin that was compliments of the United States Mint. Whatever amount of money that your piece of cake contained, that lucky person got to keep all to themselves.

For all the years that this tradition took place, I never once got the piece of angel food cake that contained a fifty-cent piece. I mean you get that baby at one time that was enough money to purchase two issues of the "Sporting News." Now, you can only obtain one of these treasured periodicals for $.50.

Who was getting all of my "Ben Franklins"??? Jim Koop over the course of the last three years has pulled in five of these babies. Katie got the other fifty- center, where upon she immediately used that money to purchase me a bottle of "M&S Soda." Orange, my favorite flavor.

What did Jim Koop do with the financial haul that he was getting as the result of my birthday cake?? I believe the exact quote, with a big smile on his face, went something like this, "Happy birthday, Beardslee. Now I gotta go and get me some smokes." You're welcome.

Surprisingly, my least favorite part of my birthday is when it comes to receiving presents. The yearly question from my mother of, "What do you want for your birthday, Michael Kevin Beardslee?", always seemed to bring a grimace to my mother's face when I would respond, "Could you please renew my "Sporting News" magazine for another year." Reluctantly, and make that extremely reluctantly on my mother's part, this favorite weekly publication of mine will somehow remain friends with me for the next 52 weeks.

And, of course, then there is the federally mandated birthday gift from your parents that I have no use for at all. Then it's time to sit back and see if I can get a reservation for Katie's birthday festivities next March.

Katie has reached the point in her life where she cannot get enough new clothes. When she worked for Mrs. Jones last summer, I would think it was safe to say that is where the majority of her cash, "bread" as Katie refers to it, went for, mainly new blue jeans and tops.

Other than for the start of the new school year, I never asked for new clothes. Not for my birthday, especially my birthday, and not even Christmas, either. I learned the hard way to get down on my knees the night before my birthday and pray that I do not get new threads on my one special day of the year. Let me fill you in as to why that is.

When I was in seventh grade, September 29th came around and on that day, it was time for me to open my gifts. One present was from my mother and it was a short sleeve shirt, that for a lack of better description was a prism colored shirt. It had some green, dark pink and some blue in it. Not a half bad shirt to parade around in the hallways of Fenton Junior High School.

After holding up my brand new short-sleeved, prism colored shirt, my mother said to the me and the rest of the Beardslee family, "Now, Mike, when you get in trouble with the police, any witnesses that the police talk to will not be able to accurately describe what clothes that you were wearing. One witness will say he had a pink shirt on. Another witness will say it was green in color. And the last witness will say it was a blue sweater. So, the police will not be able to identify you."

The dining room became very quiet after my mother's pronouncement that her oldest son was going to grow up to be exactly like Scott Berns, lead a life of crime and have my picture hanging in every Post Office in the United States. I swore that very moment on a stack of "Sporting News" that I would never wear that shirt in my life. Not even to Confession at St. John's Church.

Luckily, I was not the only resident of "White Lake Road" that got into trouble over this birthday shirt. Katie knew that I was upset about what was said to me by my mother. Katie was also smart enough to know at an early age that at some point in her life, she was going to have to either "look over" or "take care" of her older brother when he reached his elderly stage of life. And that birthday shirt might have been the start of this curse for her.

The next day after getting home from another rock-em, sock-em day at State Road Elementary School, Katie went to my room, grabbed my new prism colored shirt, got on her bicycle and pedaled her little fifth grade legs to Pellett's, a clothing store in down town, Fenton. Katie proceeded to exchange this shirt for a bright yellow long-sleeved shirt.

"White Lake Road"

Upon arriving back to "White Lake Road", Katie was on the end of a stern lecture from my mother for a whole bunch of criminal acts, but mainly for:

Riding her bike into town without my mother's permission; and,

Not telling my mother where she had disappeared to.

But the worst and the severest portion of this scolding was reserved for the taking of her older brother's shirt without his permission and exchanging it for a lesser quality styled shirt.

Did I ever wear this yellow long-sleeved shirt from Pellett's Clothing store? You betcha. Once a week all of the way through the end of my freshmen year of high school. This shirt then went on to a higher purpose in life and became a dust rag for my mother's annual Sunday morning ritual, thee dusting of furniture.

Readying myself for bed tonight, I must admit, that I was getting excited about the start of a new Band Float season. I must also confess that it is a little strange not to have this project being built in Beardslee's Barn as it has been for the past two years. I suspect that I will eventually get over that feeling of sorrow.

What also came to my mind, however, before my head officially hit the pillow, was how much my life had changed since my seventh birthday that took place in the year of 1959. I was living at 4228 S. Linden Road; in the second grade; head over in heels in love with Janice Simonson; and proud to be a Swartz Creek Dragon. I even knew most of the words to the Swartz Creek High School fight song. And Mike "Beardsley" was only a few months away from learning how to correctly spell my last name.

The Beardslee's were a one income family at that time in life, so there was not a lot of money to splurge on a bottle of soda or even a bottle of chocolate milk rather than the traditional bottle of white milk. But I was happy. I enjoyed life, which is not always the case in the current world I reside.

Now the $64,000 question is how will the world be treating me in the year 1979 when I am at the grand old age of 27? Will I be playing the trumpet in the United States Air Force Band as I fully anticipate? Or, will I be working on the assembly line at General Motors next to my former Fenton High School Band buddies, Terry Goff and Mike Ogilvie.

I suspect, regretfully I might add, that the days of residing at "White Lake Road" will be reduced to fading thoughts of the past and I will instead be living in an apartment somewhere on Miller Road in the Swartz Creek, Michigan area, next door to some loser that plays his stereo way to loud.

I can just envision myself spending an evening catching up on a "Sporting News" magazine that is at least six months old and hoping beyond all hope, that if and when the telephone rings, that it will be Stephanie Powers on the other end of the line wishing me a happy birthday.

"White Lake Road"

Chapter #92 – "To the Rear March"

September 30th – When I walked into Study Hall this morning, I noticed that Max Perry had a big smile on his face and was surrounded by a bunch of his classmates. Max Perry also had an envelope in his left hand and what appeared to be a business type of letter in his opposite hand.

Max Perry then announced to the small crowd of his friends that he had been accepted by Washington University of St. Louis, Missouri. My first reaction was that when he said Washington University he must have meant the one located in Seattle, Washington, and that someday, I would come and visit him on my way to Port Angeles, Washington. Nope, he meant the Washington University that was in the state of Missouri. Okay, if you say so, Max Perry.

Later I spent a few minutes with Max Perry and learned that his family was originally from the state of Kansas and had moved to Hartland, Michigan for the start of his seventh-grade year. Apparently, it was always the Perry family's household plan to eventually move back to Emporia, Kansas; where ever that is, thus, the purpose of applying to the Washington University not located in the great northwest portion of the United States but instead in the state of Missouri.

Max Perry advised me that he was going to major in Biochemistry. Somehow hearing the words Bio and chemistry in the same sentence is very scary to me.

I asked Max Perry if he was going to participate in any athletics while out in Missouri. He responded, "For sure, track, where I will high jump. They asked me about cross-country as well, but unlike Al Dowty, I'm not so sure that I want to go from running a two-mile high school course to a five-mile college course."

"I might try to walk-on to the basketball team, but being only 6'3", I would have to transition from a center position to a guard spot. I have played with my back to the basket for so long that I have never developed the ball handling skills of a Ric Adams or an outside shot like Tom Moran. And making the freshmen basketball team might be a tall order for a non-scholarship converted guard to pull off."

I was happy for a one Max Perry. But I certainly will not be talking about his good fortune around the dinner table at "White Lake Road" any time soon.

The topic of college has never been broached by myself and all systems are go that in 364 days that I still plan on enlisting in the United Stated Air Force. I just wish that Katie would keep her yap shut about looking forward to going to Colorado University in three years. When she does that, my mother then looks at me with an upturned eye brow that is silently asking me, "And, pray tell, my oldest son, where are you going to be attending college?" Not a conversation that shall we say is for the weak of heart. Mine, not my mothers.

"White Lake Road"

It will be interesting to see which of the next few Hartland High School students that I know breaks the news of their future college destination. My money is on Pete Mason. Maybe, Tom Beaver as well.

As I pulled into the Band Room the first thing that I did was look at the sign-up sheets for the Band Float project. Todays' list had all 10 slots filled up. Wednesday's list had six names on it, but nothing on Thursday's sheet, with the exception of Randi Lynch and Aisha Tredeau. Jason Shattuck was signed up for the Saturday afternoon session.

Since Katie, myself, Terry Rodenbo, as well as Jim Koop, whether he wants to or not, are going to be at all of the work dates any way, none of us put our names on the sign-up sheets. I did find it interesting, however, that neither of the Andrews' sisters had put their names on any of the volunteers list. The big question for those two is, were they using the same executive privilege as us four, or were they simply not going to work on this project? It's one of those two reasons and I have a gut hunch which one it is.

Marching Band practice had a different twist to it today. The Hartland High School Marching Band hit the streets for the rehearsal of our homecoming parade route. So, us marching band types staggered out to the front of Hartland High School where we lined up on Hibner Road: marched west till we hit Hartland Road; turned right, or north, on that road and marched through what would be considered down town Hartland, Michigan.

We then marched past Cromine Library and Cromine Elementary School. Now this is where it gets interesting. We trooped down a hill, an actual hill mind you that has some serious steepness to it, then we come to a baseball park where we march around a circled driveway allowing us to again tackle that sharply inclined hill.

Now the parade route has us heading south back through the down town area. However, instead of turning left, or east on Hibner Road, we now go straight a couple of more blocks to Crouse Road, where some interesting marching skills were soon to be implemented.

Once at the intersection of Crouse Road, the Band has two options. We can turn left and circle back to the high school through a back street residential type area, or we perform a marching maneuver that is called a "To the Rear March" that takes place within the marching ranks.

By that I mean there is a designated place where Aisha Tredeau, as drum major, plants herself. At that point, the front rank will then make two consecutives To the Left step turns and funnel back down within the marching band itself on Hartland Road where we eventually make our way back to the high school parking lot. I must admit that it's a little scary at first to see all of those instruments marching towards you, especially the trombone players. Once in close ranks those guys usually don't take any prisoners.

Arriving back to the high school parking lot we did another practice run or two of the To the Rear March maneuver before calling it a rehearsal. I think that we are getting better at this To the Rear March stuff. I think.

"White Lake Road"

The parade route was much longer than what I had anticipated. My guess is that it's about two miles long.

In comparing the Fenton Homecoming Parade route to the Hartland one; Fenton's was probably a little bit longer and did have some type of slight upgrade on certain streets. But there was nothing like the hill we marched up this morning on the Fenton parade course. Today we took on a cross-country course type hill. Also, the streets in Fenton were in far better condition than Hartland's'.

Aisha Tredeau made her debut today as drum major and did a real nice job. She gave good voice commands; blew the whistle loud enough and not at a rushed pace. More importantly, her timing for when to send a command to the drummers for the drum roll off, the indicator that it's time to play the school fight song, was timed where the biggest crowd of people would be settled in for this Friday afternoon's parade.

But probably what Aisha Tredeau did best was the command of her drum major staff. She was exact in her movements of where we needed to turn right or left on such and such street. This was really important to me as I had no clue whatsoever as to where this parade route even went.

Not only was it good to get outside and become use to the parade route, it was even better not to play the song, "Fever" for this rehearsal. We will start practicing the marching routine that goes with that tune in 24 hours. Maybe that will get me starting to like this song. But don't bet the money you got out of a piece of my angel food birthday cake on it though.

With the start of the Band Float project tonight, my personal schedule is way out of whack. I will practice the trumpet from 4:00 PM to 5:30 PM. Any mileage or physical workout for the pre-basketball workouts or actual tryouts are out the window. And that bothers me plenty. Those varsity basketball trials will be here in two seconds.

After trumpet practice is completed it's time to throw some supper down my throat and then it's back to Hartland, Michigan for the allotted two hours of Band Float work time. And then home by about 9:30 PM. That's a tight schedule when you throw a full day of school and travel time on top of it.

During supper, I was thinking about the many mistakes that I made while in charge of the Fenton Band Float last year. I readily admit to making my share of blunders in life. However, I also pride myself on not making the same mistake twice. Exception: when it comes to Jane Roberts.

This Band Float season I am going to do something different. The actual construction and working on the Band Float itself, doesn't really excite me. So, this year I am going to put Terry Rodenbo and Katie in charge of the real construction of the Band Float from a supervision standpoint. They're both more creative than I am and have a far better idea than I do of how the Band Float should look. They are perfect for this role.

"White Lake Road"

What will I be doing while my two cohorts are giving out orders? That's a good question, especially since the Detroit Tigers season will end at some point tomorrow. I think my role will be more of a person who has to answer any questions that Terry Rodenbo and Katie have, then I make any final decision.

I'll also fill in where needed. But putting Kleenex into a wire mesh opening is not one of my most favorite things to do in life. And as to any items or materials that have to be attached or built onto to the Band Float, I am equally worthless there as well. Man!! I wish the Detroit Tigers had qualified for post season play this baseball season so that I could at least listen to them on WJR Radio while trying to properly spread open one single Kleenex that will be giving its life to the Hartland High School Band Float cause.

It was finally off to the Andrews' residence and pole barn for the first night of Band Float season. Was there excitement in the jeep? Yeah, there was. I think the four of us have a feeling that things are going to go a whole lot better than last year Band Float wise. I mean, come on, there is no way that they could go any worse. Right??

We found our evening destination fairly easily. My initial fear was that, just like last year, we would be the only four to start the work on the Band Float. But when I saw the pole barn for the first time I saw that there were lights on inside and when alighting out of the jeep I could hear voices coming from within "Band Float Command Central." My biggest worry has just been eliminated.

As the four of us traipsed to the entrance way of the pole barn, my first impression of this structure was that while it lacked the charm and uniqueness of Beardslee's Barn, it was long enough and had sufficient height that it would do construction wise. It was also only a couple of miles away from Hartland High School. A straight, flat shot. No hills like Denton Hill Road in Fenton that was so steep that coming down that grade could damage a float big time before it ever arrived to the Homecoming parade destination.

As we got closer to the pole barn, I took a peek inside and it looked like to me there were 10 human bodies in there already. However, it was the eleventh person standing at the entrance way of the pole barn that was causing me the biggest reason why I was now feeling an oncoming tense feeling in my stomach.

It was Mrs. Andrews, herself. And the look on her face gave me a definite impression that she was not going to be greeting us four kids with a big hug and kiss. Why did I think that I was facing a different type of "To the Rear March", Mrs. Andrews' style?

And Mrs. Andrews didn't pull any punches. The first words out of her mouth were, "Unless you're a student that is officially enrolled in the Hartland Consolidated Schools, you are not allowed to come onto my property and work on the Band Float."

I must admit that this alcohol laced breath statement caught me by surprise. And I did not appreciate this last second bombshell taking place in front of a bunch of Band kids that I was the president, either. I looked at Mrs. Andrews for a second or two and then responded,

"White Lake Road"

"Really!! Really!! You're going to try and pull that stunt again on us? Mr. Thompson and Mr. Anderson already explained to you three weeks ago when you tried to get the Band election for officers overturned, that the four of us were full time students of the Hartland Consolidated Schools. And still are I might add!!"

Did my bold statement phase Mrs. Andrews one bit? Nope. The old bag didn't even flinch. She again repeated her line about it being her property and that only registered Hartland High School students were allowed in her pole barn.

There wasn't much that the Katie, Jim Koop, Terry Rodenbo or I could really do. Mrs. Andrews had us on just the fact that it was her property and she could let or prevent anyone from setting foot on it that her evil heart desired.

Mrs. Andrews then said to me, "How about this, big shot. If you immediately resign as Band president and put it in writing for all of us here to witness your stepping down, then, and only then, will I let the four of you into my pole barn to work on your precious little Band Float."

Before I could even react to this ridiculous statement, Katie interjected and said to the 10 Band Float workers, who had by now crowded around the front entrance of the pole barn, and said, "Everybody out and go home!! If the four of us are not allowed to work on the Band Float by Mrs. Andrews, then you should not have to give up your evenings and personal time, either. So just go home!!"

My Band mates did not have to be told this twice. Like rats deserting a ship that had no more cheese supplies in its hold, those guys and gals were out of there in two seconds!! It was flat out funny how fast they scattered out of the pole barn. Almost as speedy as some of them getting off of the school bus on CMU Honors Band Day when there was one brief moment where all of us thought that we could get out of going to Mount Pleasant, Michigan for an entire Saturday.

This was not what Mrs. Andrews had anticipated to take place. She had no problem throwing the four of us off of her property. But I am sure that she did not anticipate everyone else leaving as well. That was at least some type of victory for the good guys over the malicious Mrs. Andrews.

Well, it was back into the jeep and heading out to "White Lake Road" with the thought in my mind that my streak of bad luck and Band Floats continued. No matter where the location of this project.

That was not the only concern on my mind. When Teri Andrews had mentioned yesterday that the hours that we could work on the Band Float were capped at two hours and certain days of the week only, my initial thought was could we even get this project done by October 10th?? As the crow flies, that ain't that far away.

With the first portion of tonight's two hours budgeted to be spent explaining the roles of Terry Rodenbo and Katie, plus the theme and design of the Band Float to be done before even one

box of Kleenex was to be popped open, we were going to be reduced to just maybe 60-90 minutes of actual work time. But now we have already lost an entire work night. It's day one and we are behind schedule right this very moment. This is not good.

So, while tonight's work efforts, production wise would have been somewhat lessened, no work time at all really hurts. I was hoping to avoid the last-minute scrambling that we had to do a year ago. But it might again come to that type of desperate feeling to get everything completed this time around as well.

The consensus of the four great minds in the jeep as to what our next step was this; simply advise Mr. Anderson of what took place tonight and hope he or Mr. Thompson can get things straightened out with Mrs. Andrews. My feeling is this, and I am keeping it to myself for now, that if we cannot get started on the Band Float tomorrow night, then I will recommend to Mr. Anderson that we scrap the whole Band Float thing and not let Mrs. Andrews think that she can call the shots as to who can and cannot work on the Band Float. And for sure, she will certainly not be allowed to dictate who is going to be the President of the Hartland High School Senior Band.

Will it break my heart to not get that final crack at a first-place float finish? Yeah, at the end of the day, I have to admit that it will.

"White Lake Road"

Made in the USA
Coppell, TX
03 July 2021